St. Cu̇...   . 1979

We walked in sile...   ...ged track, which eventually became a steep uph...   ... Only the sound of our footsteps crunching the dry bracken disturbed the stillness of the Summer Solstice. Although the midsummer night was balmy, a soft breeze whispered through the trees, rustling the leaves and cooling the air. A lone owl's cry rudely punctured the quiet, raging against the coming dawn.

In the distance, flaming torches lit the way and three blazing beacons heralded our arrival. As we drew closer, a faint chanting and steady drumbeat could be heard. Many others had come earlier to prepare for the occasion. Everything had to be in its exact position. It was essential that the details of the ceremony should be observed precisely. I gripped the sacred cloth tightly. Within the deep pocket of be attached to the arrow.   *muddled.*

Verbius my green cloak, I checked that the precious phial was safe and ready to was walking by my side and I noted that fittingly, our steps were synchronised. Each footprint exactly placed, marking our journey to its sublime culmination. This was to be our exquisite moment. An occasion for us that could never possibly be repeated or forgotten and I was fully aware of the consequences of any perversion of the ritual.

Our breathing became more laboured as the route became steeper. Turning to look at his pale face and dark hair in the moonlight, I felt overwhelmed by the magnitude of the impending ritual, our selection and its significance. He reassuringly grasped my hand, imagining I was anxious - which I was - but not for the reasons he imagined. Thankfully, naïve, trusting Verbius was blissfully ignorant of my intentions.

Now I could I could see Scire, standing alone on top of the huge rocks forming the roof the cave. He was silhouetted against the skyline, in front of columns of almost beatific pine trees fittingly assembled into a secular cathedral of worship. Facing the east, where the darkness was becoming more anaemic, he leaned against his huge bow, waiting patiently for the mystical moment when his arrow would launch into the dawn sky.

Thirty figures, wearing identical robes to ours, flanked the entrance to the cave. Deep hoods shadowed the faces and concealed their identities, bodies completely hidden by the long, green cloaks. Even so, I could just recognise the tall, willowy outline of Dafo standing beside the more solid profile of Llyriad and was relieved that they couldn't read my thoughts. The cloaks appeared to become collectively aware of our approach. Shuffling quietly and mechanically, like precisely programmed robots, they repositioned themselves into dual, ceremonial columns. Thirty green sleeves held their blazing torches high to form a walkway of salutation for our arrival.

I straightened myself, checking that my robe was falling appropriately and my belt fastened securely. It was a prerequisite that I conducted myself with the utmost dignity. Looking straight ahead, I walked slowly between the rows of flaming torches, my face emotionless as a death mask. Sweat streamed down my neck. Smoke wafted around us. Verbius began coughing and our watery eyes met briefly as we made our way closer to the entrance of the cave. The chanting stopped and we were being thoroughly scrutinised. We moved past the assembled figures, accompanied only by the steady beat of a single drum to our left.

We stood perfectly still, glorying in the moment, in front of the sumptuous, green velvet curtains attached to the natural, proscenium arch of the rocks. The curtains were exquisitely embroidered in silver and gold threads fashioned with designs of athame, wands, pentangles, chalices and other magic symbols. Although, I had seen these hangings before, their magnificence had not been so obvious. The sequins and jewels shimmered and dazzled, spotlighted by the thousands of stars in the clear, black sky.

The green cloaks slowly and deliberately moved closer to form a glowing, semi-circular auditorium, an arc of light all around the front curtains. I noted Dafo, his torch illuminating his dramatic expression and sharp, aquiline nose. I shivered. I took the small bottle from my pocket. The sacred cloth felt warm to the touch. What mystical properties was this piece of material supposed to have? Certainly, it was very old and decorated with intricate patterns of what appeared to be curious fruits. Verbius took his cue from me and carefully removed the bottle from the pocket of his cloak. We turned, raised them to our audience and theatrically showed the cloth. Two robed figures parted the curtains for us. We disappeared into the cave and the curtains were closed behind us.

Inside the cavern dozens of tall candles sparkled like jewel encrusted sceptres and the air was heavy with the smell of incense. Realising I was holding my breath, I exhaled slowly and took a few more steps deeper into the cave. I spread the cloth out on to a flat rock and then placed the coloured, glass bottle on top of it. I watched Verbius, wondering how he was going to react when he realised what was going to happen next. Verbius caught my gaze and looked puzzled at my expression but then quickly placed his bottle next to mine. Although it was ancient, the threads of the sacred cloth still held their vibrant colours and the strange symbols glistened mystically, befitting the occasion.

"So…what happens now…," Verbius ran his fingers across the ancient cloth looking at the unusual designs of grapes, pomegranates and figs. "Do we just pour the two liquids together?"

"You could say that," I answered, very matter of fact. "Yes … that would be a good way of putting it."

Verbius looked at me sharply, uncomprehending. "Okay…I'll take the corks out. We need to hurry …I'm not sure … I don't even know what this stuff is…we need to be careful…got to work quickly …wish I knew what…."

He was babbling nervously.

"Just wait a while." I managed to get in before he continued. I spoke slowly and deliberately and looked about, soaking up the scene. "I want to enjoy the moment. All of this…" I raised both arms and brought them across my chest, embracing myself. The moment had arrived when the two forces were to be united together to create the all-consuming power. Male and female, high priestess and lord of the night. The event needed to be given its correct culmination.

"Aradnia, are you crazy? Everyone's outside waiting for us … dawn's nearly here…" Verbius began pacing the floor.

"Hush, my Lord, they and the dawn can wait a short while…"

Verbius was incredulous. "What are you talking about? We have to hurry. It's important we do this as soon as possible."

Nevertheless, as usual, he felt unable to do anything but dance to my tune.

I unfastened my cloak slowly. His face was a picture of at first, bewilderment, then astonishment, as he realised I was naked.

"Shhh - don't say anything." I stepped closer to him, peering into his eyes. "Do what you're supposed to do. Do what you're destined to do".

"Are you mad…this isn't supposed to happen? This, this is crazy." He snapped back, his head swaying from side to side, trying to avoid looking at me

"It absolutely is supposed to happen."

"We can't."

"Why not?"

"I don't know…it's not right…it's not meant to be like this."

"*It is meant to be exactly like this*"

"How do *you* know?"

"Because I decide." I toyed with him like an inquisitor with a heretic.

"Someone might come in."

"No-one will come in. We're completely alone …for a few minutes at least."

"I don't know…I didn't think anything like this would happen…I'm not sure about this…"

"This is what was always meant to be. Stop wasting time. This is of the utmost importance. This opportunity will never happen again. This is our ceremony – not theirs." I rested my hands on his shoulders pulling him closer to me. I knew he couldn't resist.

"Aradnia, no!" But, by then it was already too late for him and we both knew it. His green cloak was pulled open. We locked eyes, mine, firm and steady, his, shocked and excited. Green Man and Mother Earth united on Litha. This had been meant to happen all along. This was a fertility festival and this act of ours was honouring the Mother Goddess in the most fitting manner. When I had finished with him, I gave him a long, triumphant smile and moved him away. Unnerved, he stumbled backwards and fell against the flat rock, knocking over the two phials. Down, down the rock and all across the sacred cloth the dark liquid seeped, before dripping onto the floor of the cave, like the blood of a slaughtered offering.

Verbius pulled himself up and shuddered at the sight. His voice took on a high-pitched screech. "Oh no…. Oh no…oh my God! What'll we do? We've failed …what…whatever are we gonna' do now? We shouldn't have done it. I told you!" He had a crazed look in his eyes and he shivered again, violently, from side to side, like a dog drying itself.

"Stop shouting Verbius!" I shot the words at him. "Just stop shouting first of all. They'll hear you outside and wonder what's going on. Get a grip."

He lowered his voice to a deep, thick rasp. "But what are we going to do – they'll kill us!"

I punched him hard in the chest to bring him to his senses. He staggered a step back and his face crumbled in obedience.

"Don't be stupid – nobody's going to get killed." I kept my voice level and calm. "Just be quiet and follow me. Scire isn't going to look is he? He's got other things to worry about." I gathered up one of the bottles, corked it and made for the curtain.

Verbius followed me outside the cave, I could almost taste his anxiety. The audience of cloaks, practised and ceremonial, bowed their heads in respect and subservience to the new king and queen of the Litha. I held high the empty bottle, exalting in the moment. One small slip was not going to spoil my moment. I was the goddess. We were the Litha.

We walked around the entrance to the cave with slow, measured steps and stepped up the smooth rocks until we reached the roof platform forty feet above. I handed the phial to Scire just as planned. The tip of the sun was just beginning to appear on the horizon as he started to attach the small vessel to the arrow. The arrow should be in the air now.

Scire looked nervous. "Long time." He muttered. "Why the hesitation?" His fingers fumbled awkwardly with the twine, hurrying to fasten the small bottle to the arrow.

Inexplicably, something made him look inside the phial. He took the cork off, frowned, and then his head shot up and he scowled at us.

"The phial's empty," said Scire. "What's going on? What kind of deceit is this? This profanity has never happened before. Why are you deliberately defiling the sacred ritual? Where is the product of the divine harmony?" Scire's confusion was turning into rage. He growled. "How can you have tainted this? We'll have to postpone the ceremony – we can't carry on. I have to inform Dafo and the others. *This is not a game.* The ceremony's ruined - and someone will have to pay for it."

This was starting to get out of hand. "Be quiet!" I snarled, catching a glimpse of the green cloaks down below turning to each other in their agitation at the delay.

I tugged at Scire's arm. "Just attach the bloody phial and fire the damn arrow. Everyone's waiting and this will all have been for nothing."

He shrugged me off. "Exactly. This has all been for nothing. They've got to be warned about you."

Scire turned to take the rocky path leading to the others below. Momentarily he was lost from their sight as he took the first step from the ledge.

"No – don't go. Don't do that!" There was panic in Verbius' voice. "Give me the bow – I'll shoot the arrow."

Scire's hand went to his belt and in an instant a short, curved blade flashed in front of Verbius' face.

"Don't be stupid! Don't be stupid!" I shouted – to both of them. The words came rushing up over the knot in my stomach.

Scire fired me a look of contempt, and in that instant of distraction Verbius made a grab for the bow. Scire lashed out with the knife aiming for Verbius' face but the sudden swing caught him off balance. He clawed at Verbius' cloak to stop himself falling. There was a brief, desperate struggle as the two both fought to regain their footing. Then, abruptly they parted. There was a short gasp as Scire tottered backwards. He looked at us with despairing eyes as he plunged over the ledge, arms flailing. We could hear the sickening smacks as he crashed down, arcing from rock to rock.

The hoods were flung back as a figure came into sight, tumbling down. It came to a shuddering halt, legs and arms contorted unnaturally. They could now see that it was Scire.

We leaned over the ledge and stared at the crumpled, ragdoll below. Even in the dim light we could make out the motionless eyes staring up at us and the dark patch slowly radiating from beneath his head. Every single face below was now turned upwards. I could see half of the figures below beginning to run to Scire's body, cloaks flapping. The other half were starting to scramble up the rocks by the side of the cave.

Verbius was transfixed, still gaping at the body. I grabbed him by his hood, yanked him back and spun him around. "RUN!" I screamed into his face. "RUN! THEY'LL BLOODY KILL US! RUN! "

Chapter 1

Tynemouth - October 2009

Stepping at last from the empty carriage, Rebecca pulled her heavy travel bag onto flimsy wheels where it wobbled across the uneven floor. Surely it couldn't be too far to walk from here? In contrast to the busy hubbub when she had transferred from the mainline train, the large Victorian station with the sturdy, green, iron columns and white framed, windowed ceiling appeared almost deserted. She could see only two people, an elderly man, coughing loudly as he shuffled along with a small, subdued terrier, and an intensely hooded youth demonstrating his flair on a skateboard and spitting every few yards. Rebecca locked eyes with the teenager as he rolled by and noted the defiant face. She gave a small shake of her head when he had passed and then set off, trundling towards the exit.

She negotiated the cobbled street and was confronted by a forbidding red door leading to what appeared to be an expensive private school. This looked very different to the places she was used to. She read the Latin inscription of "Moribus Civilus" beneath the keys, crowns, crosses and ship on the coat of arms. She briefly wondered how effective the school would be in delivering its motto of instilling civility to the skateboarder.

Turning the corner on to the main street, she was impressed by the houses. Large properties in a variety of styles mixed pleasingly with the porches, turrets and ivy clad walls. It was as if money was oozing from the bricks and gold-coloured letter boxes. She smiled, tightened the belt on her coat and rearranged herself into a more upright posture. 'This looks most positive,' she thought to herself

However, as she strode along, appraising optimistically each side of the road, almost immediately everything began to look less substantial and slightly threadbare. More commonplace houses were now mixed with shops and pubs. She could hear laughter and babbling from the Cumberland Arms. Animated dark shapes jostled together in the brightly-lit, pub window, like an Indian shadow-puppet show, and a solitary smoker stood outside, studying the pavement and sucking hard on his cigarette.

She was cold and tired. She had expected that she would have arrived long ago. The delicious, unmistakable smell of fish and chips sliced through the air and fuelled her senses. It had been hours since she had eaten.

Although it was only late afternoon, the sky was already turning a deeply speckled amethyst colour. On the pavement, leaves were glued to the concrete, making it greasy underfoot. A bell from a nearby church, chimed five, chilling notes.

Raucous shrieks from seagulls told how close she was to the sea. The biting wind was testament to that, but even more so was the sharp saltiness that infused the coastal air. She was twenty-nine years of age and she had visited seaside towns on countless occasions before but she had never felt any desire to live in such places. Since adulthood, with her prejudices firmly in place, she had avoided them, with their gaudy amusement arcades and garish, impertinent shops. Yet, as she walked down this street which seemed far removed as could be from her preconceptions, she began to experience an uncomfortable feeling of familiarity.

She remembered her mother telling her that she had been here before, as a very small child. She had thought that her mother had confused her with her elder sister. She was sure that she knew nothing of this place but at this moment she didn't seem quite so certain. There was something about the arrangement of the buildings that seemed strangely familiar from long, long ago

Concentrating on the task in hand, she took out the map which she had printed off. She stood under a streetlight to see more clearly and calculated that she ought to be very close. It had appeared only a short distance from the Metro station when she had studied the route.

A few feet away she was surprised to see a light still on in a small book shop. (unusual for so late on a Sunday afternoon). She was glad there was a bookshop. A middle-aged man in the shop was counting what appeared to be coins and stacking them neatly into uniform columns. This meticulous order seemed incompatible with the books that appeared to be haphazardly arranged and strewn about the place like the remnants of a flash flood.

She walked on, at last saw the sign for Silver Street, and knew she wasn't far away. This was a sorry, inconsequential type of street with nothing whatsoever shiny about it. As she had feared might be the case for the past few moments, the balloon that begun to deflate earlier was now totally squashed. For there, at the bottom, running perpendicular to this ill-named road was Huntington Place, a row of what appeared to be medium sized, neglected terraced houses. No fancy structural designs here.

Taking a deep breath, she turned into the street and set about looking for number 10. She spotted a faded green door, guttering hanging loose, and on the wall, a small, metal number one with a zero just to the side and below it, hanging on determinedly from one screw. She exhaled loudly before rummaging in her bag and taking a key from a crumpled, brown envelope.

As the door swung open, she felt the wall to her left and found the light switch. Thankfully, the electricity had not been turned off, and soon the passageway with its heavily-patterned wallpaper was flooded with the harsh light from a naked bulb. There was a peculiar, musty smell to the place, which she found strange as it had only been unoccupied for a short period of time. An unwelcoming, steep flight of stairs loomed directly in front of her and two apologetic doors to the left.

Opening the first door, she found a small sitting room with two, sagging, mismatched sofas and an ancient television. The walls were a soulless beige, and the thick, rust-coloured curtains looked in need of cleaning, or better still, replacing. A confused, antique clock suggested that it was midday and a yellow leafed plant sat wilting on a table. Through the wall adjoining the house next door she could hear muffled, unfamiliar music. She sneezed suddenly and loudly, and then twice more.

Over the mantelpiece, in a large, heavily embossed mirror, she saw a pale, drained face with lifeless, long, dark hair. The journey had been longer and more tiring than she had anticipated. She flopped down on one of the sofas for a moment. This wasn't what she had been expecting.

Rubbing her eyes, she looked around more carefully. Her gaze settled on the tiled fireplace and she noticed a cheap, plastic frame with a photo inside. She dragged herself up, walked across and picked the picture frame up, tilting it to the light to get a better view. It captured a happy moment shared by a young couple. They were laughing and smiling and looking very much in love. Was this her Aunt? The photo was old and the clothes from long ago, maybe thirty or forty years ago. It was difficult to date the women's clothes, with her tassels, scarves, bangles and beads, which must have been considered over the top in any fashion era. Surely, her aunt hadn't been old enough to be part of the Hippy craze, nevertheless her outfit screamed of the 1967 'Summer of Love'. Even through the faded photograph, the woman's vitality was obvious and infectious. It made Rebecca smile, she seemed to be the type of person who would have been excellent company and fun to be with.

And who could the man be? In fact, he looked little more than a boy with his floppy, fair hair, strange tunic and eyes that crinkled attractively as he smiled at her from the photo. They made a handsome couple, but her mother had never mentioned Sylvia having any long-term partner.

Her mother, Cynthia, had always spoken disapprovingly and given her the impression that her sister flittered from man to man. This photograph, if it was of her aunt, was testament to the fact that she had had at least one, meaningful relationship. Rebecca gave a small clucking noise and placed the photo back where she had found it.

Yet, if this was her Aunt, what dreadful events could have happened in her life? Admittedly, over the past few months she had been very ill, and home improvements would have been the last thing on her mind. But this was such a cheerless house that muttered only of the lacklustre and monotonous existence of its owner. Surely, the flamboyant, young woman in the picture would never live in such a bleak place.

She knew so little of her aunt and on receiving this unexpected legacy she wished she had been better acquainted with her. Why had she never been in contact with her all these long years, when she may have so badly needed some family? In fact, up until a few days ago she had almost completely forgotten she had an aunt at all. She had so many questions that needed answering.

Rebecca decided she might as well go and explore the rest of her increasingly, unprepossessing inheritance. With low expectations she ventured into the back room to find a small kitchen area and dining space. On the rectangular wooden table was a packet of expensive looking biscuits and next to them a note.

Dear Rebecca,

Hope your journey wasn't too unpleasant. I have left you with a few items that you will hopefully find useful. Sorry the house is in such a mess, but I have just returned from visiting some friends. The heating is straightforward, just a switch next to the sink. There is an immersion heater upstairs in the cupboard next to the bathroom ,as I expect you will want to heat some water. In the bottom drawer of the front bedroom there are plenty of towels and clean sheets. Inside the box are details of electricity accounts etc,that you will need to transfer to your name.

Hope you find everything you need and have a pleasant first evening in your new house. Will pop round tomorrow and give you a hand clearing up if you like. Look forward to meeting you.

Yours,

Caroline Eastern

(I was a good friend of your aunt).

If she kept company with her dour Aunt, thought Rebecca, this Caroline Eastern was no doubt of a similar ilk. Nevertheless, she had been kind enough to leave the note and the offer of help. Although she didn't feel too happy about an unknown person having a key to her house and if she had been the 'good friend' that she claimed to be, then she surely could have tidied up the house a little. However, she was curious to meet this woman and she would be a good starting point to find some information about her mysterious Aunt Sylvia.

She opened the fridge door to see what Caroline Eastern had left her. There was some bread, butter, milk, a casserole dish and a most welcome bottle of white wine. Finding a glass in the cupboard over the sink, she felt comforted hearing the familiar glug of the glass being filled. Then she inspected the casserole dish, filled with a homemade chicken meal which would prove to be very welcome.

****

After carefully arranging the last of the coins into neat columns, Robert made a quick calculation, wrote the amount on a small notebook, pushed the coins once more into an untidy pile and scooped them resignedly into a drawer. Taking a sip from his long-cold cup of coffee he looked with irritation at the random stacks of books occupying almost every flat surface in the shop. Why didn't people have the graciousness to return them to their original places? Still, it would have to be another job for tomorrow, he thought to himself, he certainly couldn't be bothered with any tidying tonight.

Business hadn't been too bad that day, as was often the case on a Sunday when visitors to the town often stumbled unwittingly upon his modest establishment and had the time to browse his wide-ranging collection over a coffee and cake. If the confectionary that he offered wasn't the most exciting, at least his prices were reasonable. His no-frills shop had a small band of regular clients who stopped by to pass a short period reading, taking refreshments and even sometimes making small purchases. Unfortunately, most people bought their reading materials on-line these days but thanks to some loyal customers combined with the fact he operated a café, he was able to just about break even.

Robert was a tall, rangy man who, due to his fondness for taking an excessive number of long walks had managed to prevent himself from gaining weight during his middle-age. This wasn't a self-conscious decision on his part, he just loved to move about in the open, listening to the birds and the crash of the waves. Now that he lived in this place, so close to the sea with its inviting array of coastal walks, he was in his element. If he was not in his bookshop or flat, he was either to be found striding along the promenade or in the 'Turk's Head' pub. Robert had lived in this area for a few years now, running his small business, but was cagey about where he had come from beforehand. Many people were intrigued about his whereabouts because his accent wasn't local. He was often asked but evaded the questions and kept his cards close to his chest.

Usually, he closed the shop earlier, especially in the winter when he had so few customers but today, he had a special reason for staying longer on the premises. He had been curious to observe any strangers in the vicinity and his inquisitiveness had been amply rewarded by the sight of a young woman, first hesitating, then, after consulting a piece of paper, turn into Silver Street. There was something about the way she held herself and her defiant gait that seemed familiar. In fact, just watching her had made him smile. Wondering what she was doing now, and how she was finding the place, he guessed she was bound to have been quite disappointed. Without a shadow of doubt, he knew the house desperately needed serious work done but then again not many young women of her age were lucky enough to inherit any property, no matter what the condition.

Despite Caroline assuring that she was going to leave a note and some food for Rebecca, this would be a sorry welcoming because of the neglected state of the house and, he also imagined, because the young woman would be feeling very alone. With his curiosity, partly at least, satisfied, Robert began locking up his shop for the night. He stopped short as he stepped out into the chill air, his mind flicking back to the dreadful events all those years ago, as it often did, but understandably, after seeing the young woman, the memories came back with increased vividness and clarity.

Chapter 2

North Shields - October 2009

Caroline paced the floor, drinking her third coffee. She had been up early, unable to sleep, feeling anxious about how this first meeting with Rebecca would go and unsure about the rules of the game. She looked through her bookshelf as a means of distraction and came upon a book she'd had for almost four decades. A book that had had a profound influence on her life.

Caroline flicked through the pages and clearly remembered the first time she had read the book, just before she had left home to study. It was entitled 'The Early Christian Church in the North'. It wasn't that she had been particularly interested in Northumbrian saints, it was more the fact that the Celtic Christianity of that time had been entrenched in its earlier pagan roots, that grabbed her attention. There was an appeal about this former type of Christianity that had immediate attraction. The Christianity of Saint Cuthbert and Saint Aidan worked much more closely with nature, following the rhythm of the seasons, its rites of passage and ancient traditions.

She slumped into an armchair and read one of the early pages.

'During the times of the Celts, the spirits of the natural landscape were worshipped as deites: Latobius, god of mountains; Cernunnos, horned god of the forest and trees; Danu, goddess of fertility and motherhood and Brigantia, goddess of rivers. After Christianity was introduced to the Celts, round about the second century during the time of the Roman occupation, there were attempts made by some to demonise the pre-Christian gods.'

'In the seventh century, two branches of Christianity flourished, existing hand-in-hand. While King Oswi of Northumbria ruled his kingdom observing the customs of Rome, celebrating their calculation of the date of Easter, their monastic tonsures and baptismal practices others, including St. Cuthbert and his followers favoured those customs practised by the Irish monks on Iona. It has been suggested that 'Celtic' Christianity as it was known, was more spiritual and connected to nature, friendlier to women and not answerable to the Pope. Most importantly, it was more able to incorporate aspects of Celtic polytheism and mysticism within its beliefs.'

'The Roman and Celtic churches clashed in 597 AD. Pope Gregory dispatched Augustine to convene a synod at Chester to call on the Celtic church to help with the conversion of the Anglo Saxons. Augustine asked the Celtic bishops to fall in line with Rome. They rejected all of his demands and his authority over them. A 7th century passage, attributed (some say wrongly) to Gildas (a 6th century British monk and historian) reads: "Britons are contrary to the whole world, enemies of Roman customs, not only in the mass but also in regard to the tonsure."'

'The converted, pagan Celts worshipped Christ, but through their own culture, thus combining both sets of belief. The sacred places where pagans had interacted with their gods remained the same, but additionally the Trinity was fused into their worship. This Celtic form of Christianity showed a far greater acceptance of the feminine, as the worship of Mary became synonymous with the ancient Mother Goddess. Likewise, the male dominance that pervaded the Roman church was absent here, with women like Brigid, Ebba and Hilda leading large, mixed monasteries, where women and men worked in cooperation with each other.'

Caroline had often wistfully imagined an idyllic, Ancient Britain with its pantheon of mysterious gods and goddesses. And it seemed to her, with her dour, religious upbringing, and being forced to the Anglican Church each Sunday, that this modern Christianity had a lot to answer for. If Christianity could still have been practised in this earlier form, then the original beliefs could once more be incorporated. The stone circles that still dominate the landscape in mystical places like Stonehenge and Avebury would have their true significance restored. Celtic Christians, similar to the pagan Britons, knew these to be 'Thin Places' where the gap between heaven and earth was closer. Here, the two worlds of the living and dead could communicate and these places were sacred. She remembered thinking that to be present for a solstice celebration in a 'Thin Place' would have been marvellous. And who was to say that it couldn't still be? Who would want to relinquish a magical pagan lifestyle, being at one with nature, to follow the gloomy regime of a modern-day church?

She skimmed to the next chapter.

'St. Cuthbert and Celtic Christianity had embraced the old ways and the two religions had dovetailed together with ease. The rebirth of Christ or Spring each Easter- or Eostre to give it the correct pagan name- was deeply engraved into the collective 5th century psyche. So, the most important Christian festival was already being celebrated along with Yuletide or Christmas, long before the name of Jesus Christ had ever been heard. The Celtic Christianity practiced by Cuthbert,

Aidan and the monks of Iona was greatly different to the politically motivated Roman Church.'

'The consequences of the decision made at the Synod at Whitby in 664AD meant that the British had to suppress their heritage and beliefs and conform to the patriarchal domination of the Roman Church and Pope. No longer could monks wear their tonsures as they chose, no longer could Eostre be celebrated as of old, and most importantly, no doubt to the chagrin of Hilda (who had actually organized the Synod at her own monastery) no longer were women allowed to consider themselves equal to men.'

'St. Cuthbert accepted the Synod's decision, adopted Roman practices and was sent to the priory of Lindisfarne. He had a reputation for sanctity and devotion, and the fact that he had been raised in the Celtic tradition and now supported Roman rule made his calm leadership ideal for the role of converting Celtic Christians to Roman rule. However, because of that deep Celtic tradition from which he came we can only guess at the enormity of the dilemma which faced St. Cuthbert.'

What sort of existence was that? Surely, the only true form of religion had to be that which celebrated life and our need to connect to the wild. What type of lacklustre God would advocate a life of deprivation.? Worship, through joy in the very exuberance of life had to be a prerequisite of any sane religion, not the self-righteous glorification of temperance and piety. She thought of the jaundiced, colourless religion followed by her parents and shuddered.

Caroline still remembered, all those years ago, feeling as if a light had been switched on. If the only God she could make any sense of was embedded in nature, then surely Spring had to be Jesus Christ with his resurrection embodying the rebirth of the world after the long death of winter. This was the only interpretation that could make any sense to her.

Everything had seemed to fall into place. A Damascus moment that would redefine the rest of her life. Uncanny, that after almost forty years she could still recall this incident and that almost immediately she had felt the need to make contact with likeminded souls. Those revelations couldn't have arrived at a better time because a few weeks later she had gone to Lancaster University.

It all seemed like yesterday. She shook her head, freeing the memories, and returned to the present.

Caroline glanced at the clock and saw it was nearing ten. Rebecca would have had plenty of time to sleep. Being her Aunt's old friend of many years, she was expecting awkward questions from Rebecca, but she didn't know what plausible answers she could give. She placed the book back on the bookshelf, reached for her coat and fumbled in the pocket for her car keys. She would be there in under ten minutes.

***

Rebecca awoke with a jolt, to find thin sunlight streaming through the pale, green curtains and felt immediately confused as to her whereabouts. She squeezed her eyes shut and began rewinding to the events of the previous night. Arriving in Tynemouth, leaving the station, the smells and sounds of her new surroundings, finding the house and being disappointed as to its gloominess and poor state of repair. She remembered choosing the smaller of the two rooms. Not being sure as to where her Aunt had actually passed away, she thought this bedroom cum study to be the least likely place. She had found the clean sheets mentioned in the letter and she had managed to get the water to heat, as a relaxing bath was a necessity after her long journey.

She was surrounded by plain, cream-coloured walls, at least where they weren't covered with crammed bookcases. Sitting up in the bed, she looked across at a collection of the mysteries and romance stories that she imagined a woman in late middle age would like to read: 'The Skull in the Box', 'The Unwelcome Guests' and 'The Chance Encounter'. *Well, no surprises there*, this was exactly the type of book she would have expected – not too dissimilar to her mother's taste, but then again, they had been sisters. On the opposite wall she could see cookery, gardening and craft titles. Rebecca's choice of reading material was something, she liked to imagine, a little edgier.

Turning on her phone, she was shocked to see that it was nearly ten o'clock and that she had slept so long. Although Caroline Eastern had not specified at what time she would be coming to call, she guessed that she had better put some clothes on quickly, as it could be any time. She pulled on the hastily discarded sweater and jeans from the floor before hurrying to the bathroom. As she returned to sit on the bed and to pull on her boots, some unexpected book titles caught her eye: "Paganism and Celtic Christianity", "Thin Places where you Wouldn't Expect", and "Long Forgotten Myths and their Meanings". She started to pull out the last book from the case but was interrupted by a knock on the door, gentle at first but a second, louder and more assertive, shortly followed.

"Rebecca, are you there?" *The woman was shouting at her through the letter box.*

Rebecca quickly straightened her hair in the mirror and ran downstairs. "I'm coming …won't be a moment." She gingerly opened the door to see a vivacious, strikingly dressed woman in her fifties standing on the doorstep. She was swathed in a bright, red coat, shiny black boots and lipstick of such a vivid shade, it was neither suitable for her age or the hour of the day. Rebecca could feel the giggle swirling from the pit of her stomach, but swiftly clamped her mouth shut, only allowing her lips to curl up at the corners.

"*Hello*, I'm *so* pleased to meet you." The apparition beamed broadly, showing glistening white teeth. "I'm Caroline. I assume you're Rebecca. I've been really looking forward to meeting you."

She gave Rebecca a searching, unabashed up and down look, starting at her face, then moving down to her neck, chest, legs and feet, taking all the time in the world, before retracing her scan upwards for a second scrutiny.

"Erm…yes, yes, I'm Rebecca … hello. Pleased to meet you too … and thanks for the things…in the fridge."

"Well. I was sure you would be hungry after your long journey. I know I get ravenous after travelling and it's much better to have something just ready to heat up, don't you think?" Caroline looked at Rebecca expectantly, waiting for a compliment regarding the meal she left. When one didn't appear, she continued with wide-eyed, mock puzzlement. "Aren't you going to invite me in then?"

"Of course, of course ... I'm so sorry. how rude of me, keeping you standing there... please, please come in."

Caroline breezed into the hallway like a ship in full sail. She removed her scarlet coat and flung it over the bannister rail at the bottom of the stairs, to reveal black trousers untidily tucked into the boots and an alarmingly busy, floral shirt.

"Right, shall we put the kettle on?" said Caroline. "I don't know about you but I'm definitely ready for a cuppa." Oblivious at first to the younger woman's surprise at her directness, she suddenly paused and cleared her throat. "Oh, I'm so sorry. I can see what you're thinking Rebecca. It's just that I'm so used to coming into this house and treating it like my own. We were such good friends you know. But it's not your aunt's house now. It's yours isn't it? Although," she said, a liquid, molten-red smile oozing about her face. "I'm sure it's only a matter of time until *we* become friends".

"It's okay, Caroline." Rebecca nodded and gave a hesitant smile, not knowing quite what to make of her, but marvelling at her audacity. "And thanks for the information in the letter. Please, come through to the kitchen and we can have some tea." She gestured for Caroline to take a seat at the table before switching on the kettle.

"Well it was the least I could do," said Caroline. "I can see that at least you managed to get the heating working, which is good, very good, because it's absolutely freezing cold outside." She rubbed her hands together vigorously. "Important to be cosy, don't you think? Can't be doing with feeling chilly. What about the water? Did you manage that? Nice bath sorts you out after a long day. Did you sleep well? It isn't too noisy is it? Can be noisy on the main road. I'm sorry I didn't tidy the place up more but I've been away visiting some friends, you know."

As Caroline prattled, Rebecca was aware that, although the woman was talking, seemingly for the sake of it, she continued staring straight at her. It made her feel uncomfortable.

"If you need anything," continued Caroline, "anything at all, you only have to ask. I live just around the corner. Well, maybe a little further than that, but not far away. There are quite a few shops nearby that are…."

"Caroline," said Rebecca quickly. "Why did my aunt leave the house to me? It's not like we were close. In fact, I can't really remember anything about her at all?"

"Sylvia…" Caroline paused, floored by the bluntness of the question, "… always spoke about you very fondly … yes, very fondly…and of course she never had any children of her own …I think she just wanted to help… but I don't really know … she never discussed it with me …not really." She looked down at the table, hoping it could provide her with some credible explanation. She knew the question would be asked but all the same she was disappointed in herself in giving such a weak response. She should have prepared better for this meeting.

"But she could have left it to my mother." Rebecca seemed to be pleading for an answer and Caroline thought she sounded far younger than her almost thirty years. "They were sisters after all … and what about my elder sister Jessica? She isn't very happy that I've been left the house and she's been left nothing, you know. I can see things from her point of view and I don't understand it. I don't really understand at all."

"Rebecca, I realise that you must be confused, but I'm not the person to help you with this. As I say she didn't really discuss the matter with me. I'm sorry." Caroline looked at Rebecca's face but couldn't quite meet her eyes. "I do know however, that there was some disagreement years ago between your Mother and Sylvia."

Caroline threw the comment in as an offering, a consolation – not a hand grenade.

Rebecca looked up sharply.

"Disagreement?"

"Yes, some sort of disagreement. I don't know what it was about but maybe it's connected with that."

Rebecca's brow puckered, desperately trying to re-align itself with the rest of her face

"But what could it possibly be? What can have been so bad?"

"I'm sorry. I don't know. I wish I did and could help - but I can't."

"I know. I know. I'm very lucky to have such a legacy. I *am* very grateful - but it seems so strange." Rebecca stared at the damp spot in the corner of the ceiling where the paint was cracking.

Caroline followed the younger woman's gaze and then gave what she considered her coy, bashful look. "I know there's an awful lot of work that needs to be done, but I'm sure that you'll have a lot of fun decorating the place, don't you think? I know you could get it looking beautiful, you know."

"I don't know about that," said Rebecca. "There's a lot of work here."

"I could help you." Caroline nodded eagerly, all she needed was a wet tongue hanging loosely from her mouth. "In fact, I've had lots of experience in interior design. It's what I do, choosing fabrics and furnishings for people who have no taste."

Rebecca blinked and looked at the almost animated, intensely bright, patterned blouse that Caroline was wearing. *This woman's mind is an inhospitable environment*, she thought to herself. *When would she realise, she would need years of therapy?*

"This is a lovely area you know, and Tynemouth's a great place to live," continued Caroline. "Have you seen the beautiful Priory on the front? Splendid. Don't you think?"

A distant glaze came across Rebecca's eyes as she imagined outrageously ornate rooms, courtesy of Caroline. The steam from the kettle brought her back from her reverie. She finished making the tea and placed two mugs on the table.

"No, I haven't had a chance to look around the area properly," said Rebecca as she took a sip of her drink. "It seems a nice enough sort of place, but of course I can't possibly stay here."

Can't possibly stay here.

A prickling sensation raced through Caroline. Her spine seemed to be immediately negatively charged.

Can't possibly stay here

The words fell with a damp, cold, thud in the space between them, like setting cement. Caroline focussed on her mug, eyes wide, unblinking, lips folding and unfolding. She felt as if someone was kneading her brain.

"It would take thousands to do this place up," Rebecca continued, unaware of the effect of her words. "And I just don't have that kind of money. I was just left this house you know - no other money. Also, I have a job. It's half term this weekend but I have to be back at school in Lancashire next week. It's totally impractical for me to live here."

Caroline couldn't disguise her feelings for long. She stared at Rebecca, aghast. This wasn't supposed to happen.

"But you can't sell the house," Caroline said, in a quick, small voice.

"What?"

"You can't sell the house. I do know that *isn't* what your aunt would have wished for." The words were passionate, overly eager, not meant to offend but …

"What do you mean? Why not?" Rebecca bristled and straightened her back. *What the hell was she talking about? Rude, overbearing woman. It was none of her damn business.*

"Your aunt would have wanted you to stay here – make this your home."

"I don't think that…"

"Also," Caroline cut in desperately, "you would only get a fraction of what the house is really worth while it's in this state."

Rebecca calmed her rising temper and measured her words. "I don't think that it's a good idea. Yes, it was lovely to have been left this house, but as I say, it's entirely unrealistic for me to live here – whatever the state of the house. I've obligations back in Lancashire, which, as you know, is about one hundred and fifty miles away!"

They were like two trapeze artists reaching for each other, nearly catching a hand but missing and swinging back again, losing momentum.

"I just think … I know … that it would be a bad decision – financially. And you would be better off if you … you know …" Caroline took a slow drink, trying to think of the right words, treading water.

"I'm not being funny Caroline, and I *am* very grateful for you taking an interest in my affairs but I need to have time. There's a lot to take in. I have to find out a lot more. I have to try and find out more of this disagreement." *Please just leave now and let me be alone to think.*

"Yes, I'm sorry Rebecca. I wish I could answer your questions about your aunt - I really do, but she was a very private person. I'll have a think about who might be able to help."

"That would be great, thank you." Rebecca pursed her lips, the muscles tightening at her jaw. She was about nine tenths of the way along her tether.

Caroline read the signs and placed her mug on the table. "Well, maybe I should be going now." She wished she could have started the conversation all over again and avoided the obvious tension between them which wouldn't help her plan at all. It was absolutely crucial that Rebecca kept the house and lived in it. "I'll try and find out more and see you shortly?"

"Of course, anything would be very welcome." Rebecca said curtly and tried her best to give a smile.

Chapter 3

Preston, Lancashire - October 2009

Bill tended the remaining flowers in his garden as the last glints of autumn sunlight covered the lawn in a gentle glow. The trees were already bare but a few sparse roses, along with some faded, orange chrysanthemums added at least a little, cheering colour. He was happiest of all places in his garden but soon it would be time for everything to close down for the winter. He would be forced to spend more time indoors, or at least shiver in his shed, sorting out little jobs, with nothing but his electric fan heater and radio for company. Bill noticed a robin sitting in the hawthorn hedge, eyeing a fat ball hanging nearby.

"Go on then, its waiting for you, lovely. It's all yours." He stood back and watched as the little bird pecked at the ball.

Bill took his spade and began to turn over the soil for the faraway spring daffodils and tulips. Then he went into the greenhouse to collect the last of the tomatoes and think about the events of that morning. He could quite clearly see things from both sides. It couldn't be easy for a young woman at the age of nearly thirty, still having to live at home with her parents, but these were difficult times. Despite the fact that Rebecca had a good job teaching, house prices were phenomenally expensive, especially round these parts, and although he knew that they could have helped her out financially, with a deposit, his wife's mind could not be shifted on this one – Cynthia was adamant.

When the letter for his daughter had arrived in the post a couple of weeks ago, he had initially feigned disinterest, but as she read the contents of the letter, he couldn't conceal his alarm at the deep creases furrowing across Rebecca's brow.

Rebecca re-read the letter, put one hand to her face and slowly shook her head. "I don't get this. I don't get this at all." she said. "I can hardly believe it. Who's Sylvia? Who on earth is Sylvia?"

Bill's wife, Cynthia had rushed in from the kitchen immediately, wringing a dishcloth through her hands like some textile worry beads. "What's that? What you talking about Rebecca? Why do you mention Sylvia? What's Sylvia got to do with anything?"

She sounded scared Bill thought, sensing instantly that the day was going to be difficult.

It wasn't that Cynthia begrudged her daughter her own home, it was just that she didn't like change. Yes, Rebecca's older sister Jessica now lived in her own house, but she had a husband to help her. It had been bad enough when Rebecca had to insist on leaving her parents to go to university. Despite being ill, Cynthia had done her utmost to prevent it but had failed. Bill knew that his wife had never forgiven him for his lack of intervention, but he had realised all along that Rebecca had been set on it. It was time for their daughter to spread her wings, experience new places and people, and why shouldn't she?

In fact, he had been decidedly saddened for her when Rebecca had no other option but to take a job locally and move back home. He had never seen his wife so happy. For a short time, her two children were both restored to the nest and life was as it should be.

Shortly after this, Jessica married and Cynthia resigned herself to losing her, but consoled herself with the fact that Rebecca was back where she belonged, with her parents. And even as her daughter became noticeably more irritable and dissatisfied as the years progressed, Cynthia was adamant that this was the way matters would stay.

Imagining her horror as the contents of the letter were revealed Bill couldn't help but allow himself a certain feeling of guilty pleasure. Cynthia couldn't always have her way and even from beyond the grave her sister Sylvia had been able to deliver a decisive blow.

***

Tynemouth - October 2009

Caroline marched down the street with a face full of fury, her coat unfastened and billowing behind her, flying red for danger. This had not gone well at all, she thought to herself, not at all well. The ungrateful girl should have been delighted to have been left any property to call her own. Yes, unfortunately the house had been allowed to fall into a bad state of repair. Yet, surely that would be part of the fun, redecorating and putting her own mark on the place. She had even offered to help herself, but maybe upon reflection that had been an ill-judged mistake. Was it normal behaviour for an aunt's close friend to be overfamiliar? Caroline bit her lip.

Rebecca hadn't seemed to mind at all that she had left some food for her when she arrived. She had noticed both the empty wine bottle and half-eaten packet of shortbread. No, the girl hadn't minded Caroline's gesture of friendship then had she? Actually, she didn't think she had been out of order, after all, the girl knew nobody else from round these parts, so she ought to be pleased that she was offering her friendship. She was almost sure she had seen the girl flash her a scornful look. Nevertheless, there was no way that she could be permitted to sell the house. No way. But what could she do to convince her of this?

Admittedly, Rebecca had a job in Lancashire, but teaching jobs were surely pretty easy to come by. From what she had read about the current educational climate, it seemed there were few people foolish enough to take on the role of teacher in the first place, let alone stay in the traumatic profession! Rebecca wasn't yet thirty. It wasn't like she was anywhere near the 'unwanted teachers of over forty-five' age, who weren't quite ready for retirement but were deemed superfluous or dinosaurs or both. She'd heard of teachers of a certain age being 'got rid of', so there must be an abundance of vacancies that she would be perfect for. There were plenty of schools around here. Yes, for goodness sake, she had a friend Karen who was a governor at that King's School. She could pull a few strings. For what other possible point could there be in actually being a governor in the first place unless there were perks to be had?

Instinctively, her feet were taking her to the only person that could help her make some sort of sense of the predicament, and presently she found herself outside the bookshop. Charging through the door she scanned round the mess of a room, looking for its owner. One small stack of books fell in her wake, but she didn't stop to pick them up, didn't even give them a second glance. There he was, she thought, Sebastian, Robert's feckless nephew, re-arranging some books in the section on 'walks and wildlife in Northumberland'. He was dressed in his usual torn jeans and a T-shirt that looked in need of a good wash and hanging loose on his tall, gangly frame. Caroline made a mental note to tell Robert that he needed to have a word with Sebastian, as his unkempt appearance must be putting customers off entering the shop, let alone buying anything.

"Where's Robert?" she demanded in an imperious voice as Sebastian swung round to face her.

Sebastian immediately deflated. "He's just out the back cataloguing some books. I'll give him a shout." Sebastian called for Robert and carried on shuffling the books about the floor avoiding eye contact as Caroline sat herself down at the small table that served as the coffee shop part of the establishment. Even this table had two piles of books sitting on it, one stack with a potted geranium perched precariously on top. Rapping her fingers in irritation, she called for a coffee to no-one in particular. Sebastian was forced to slowly unfurl himself and sidle between the shelves to obey her command.

Several minutes later, as Caroline took a sip from the unusually, pleasant drink, Robert emerged from the room at the back.

"Caroline. This is a pleasant surprise." He poured himself a drink from the coffee pot and sat down beside her at the table.

"Well Robert, I wish I had come with some more pleasing news." She stirred sugar angrily into her drink, grinding the spoon around the mug. She was in a dark place and had the face to prove it.

"What's Rebecca like then?" Robert said cheerily, used to Caroline's easily aroused state of irritation and ignoring her obviously black mood. "I saw her arrive last night. She looks lovely. In fact, she reminded me of you a little when you were her age …"

"Never mind all that. Robert, listen to me," she interrupted. "I just don't know what to do. Can you believe that the unappreciative girl only mentioned that she is intending to sell the house! We can't let that happen, can we? No doubt that spiteful mother of hers Cynthia has put this idea into her head. She's just peeved because her sister didn't leave her anything. As if Sylvia was going to do that," she snorted a contemptuous laugh. "But the bottom line is, Rebecca *must* stay in the house. She *can't* be allowed to sell up. It would ruin everything, don't you think?"

Sebastian, although pretending to organise the local section, was in fact, peering between the books and listening with interest. Of course, he was used to her eccentric outbursts but the intensity of Caroline on this occasion made him extremely curious as to what she and his uncle were discussing.

"Caroline, you must have realised this might happen. The girl has her own life. I'm sure she appreciates that she's been left the house, but you've seen the state of the place. What did you really expect her to do?" Robert glanced up towards the door as a customer entered.

"If I had had such an opportunity at her age, I would have welcomed the chance of breaking free from my family and having such independence. And, having the prospect of decorating a house just as I like it...."

"Yes Caroline, but Rebecca isn't you, is she?" Robert, stood up, glad of the opportunity to tend to the customer, leaving Caroline festering over her coffee.

Chapter 4

Preston, Lancashire - October 2009

. How dare Sylvia do this? What right had she after all these years? Cynthia seethed in her armchair and, looking at her watch, noted that her daughter's train, bound north for Carlisle would have just left the station at Preston. Bill had taken Rebecca to the town, as she felt no desire to have any part in this ridiculous charade. She hated railway stations at the best of times, but even more so for this purpose on a bitterly cold, Sunday afternoon. If Sylvia was indeed dead, which she found very difficult to believe, then that should be the end of the matter. The book should have been properly closed, and she could have been allowed to completely forget that her ridiculous sister had ever existed.

Pouring another cup from the pot, Cynthia reflected that perhaps she was being overly harsh, she was her sister after all. But there had never been much love lost between the two of them. Cynthia had always tried to do the right thing, whereas Sylvia just did as she pleased - always. She took another chocolate digestive from the packet and dipped it absent-mindedly into her tea, fully preoccupied with her thoughts.

Cynthia would never been allowed to get away with such behaviour but it seemed that somehow Sylvia always did. What was good for the goose should have been good for the gander. Even as a young child, it had seemed their parents had indulged Sylvia's wilful behaviour. When Sylvia had obviously been lying, faking illness because she was more than likely in trouble at school, she had been pampered and allowed to stay at home. All she had to do was open her eyes and toss her long brown curls, and it seemed she could get whatever she wanted. Whether it was a new dress, a bicycle or a kitten. It had never seemed fair, and it wasn't fair. Cynthia fastened her cardigan buttons and pursed her lips angrily until they looked like a knot in an overblown balloon.

After her 'O' levels, Cynthia had got herself a tedious clerical job, never even considering that further education was an option. In fact, she wouldn't have wanted to learn anything else as she knew what she needed to know and therefore saw little purpose in superfluous studying. However, Sylvia, typically, had gone off to university to waste her time doing some pointless 'arty' degree when she could have been gainfully employed earning money. At the age of twenty-one when her sister had been supposed to finish studying, Cynthia had already been working for five years. Of course, Sylvia's degree was never completed. So, it had been nothing but a great waste of money and time. Just like Sylvia herself in fact. And by that same age, goodness knows how many boyfriends Sylvia had had, while Bill had been her only one and she hadn't met him till she was twenty-six. Although her sister was only a few years younger than her, they seemed to belong to different worlds.

Through the window she could see her new neighbour Alison putting what appeared to be six wine bottles into the blue recycling bin. Tutting to herself, she imagined that this had been something that Sylvia had plenty of experience doing. However, it seemed that she wasn't around to do that anymore. Cynthia wondered what had killed her sister. Probably something self-inflicted, caused by her self-indulgent, dissolute lifestyle. Possibly some insidious cancer induced by smoking, drinking or laughing too much.

Cynthia picked up the remote control and flicked through the TV channels looking for something to distract her, but there was no escape.

If it hadn't been for her sister then she would have had only one daughter, not two. But Sylvia had given up any claim on Rebecca years ago. She remembered the day Sylvia had arrived on her doorstep with the baby, distraught and desperate. She had pleaded with Cynthia, showing real tears, real agony. Cynthia remembered the scornful way she had treated her sister, revelling in her own piety – cruel yes, but necessary.

What could Sylvia have been involved in that made it 'impossible' for her to keep 'Heaven' (a preposterous name which she soon changed). Couldn't be bothered was more like it, no doubt the child would have spoilt her hedonistic, shameful lifestyle. Cynthia never found out what the reason was. Cynthia didn't press her to find out what personal demons Sylvia was facing, it was probably best not to know the disgusting details. But Rebecca was her child now and her sister had no business meddling in her life. If she had felt the need to leave an inheritance, then it should have been left to her, not Rebecca. And they wouldn't be dragging up a part of the past which was best left alone and hidden away. After all, she was the one who had brought up Rebecca for the last thirty years. She would have made sure that the money was used properly and definitely not have required her daughter making ridiculous journeys to the North East. Anyway, Rebecca would soon be putting the house on the market and hopefully this annoying episode could soon be forgotten.

Cynthia frowned, nibbled on another biscuit, changed the channel once more and tried again to sink the memories as deep as possible. But her gaze soon lifted and settled on a space to the left of the screen, a still, vacant patch which allowed her mind to drift off again ...

***

Tynemouth - October 2009

Immediately after Caroline had left, Rebecca had just felt baffled. Not only had the woman's behaviour been most peculiar but she had actually been extremely rude. From the very onset she had seemed excessively familiar and she was sure that if she hadn't arrived at the door, the damn woman would have thought it totally acceptable to barge in with her own key. It was her house now and who did this Caroline Eastern think she was? She was after all, just a friend of her dead Aunt Sylvia. She clearly needed reminding of her place.

She decided she needed to go for a walk to clear her mind. There was so much that needed organizing in such a short period of time. The half term week only allowed her a few days away from school, then she would have to jump back on a train to face all her other problems. She was surprised that her Mother hadn't wanted to come up with her. In a way it was quite pleasant to have different worries to concern herself with. Actually, a great deal could be accomplished in a few days and she felt the time could only be empowering.

Through her Aunt's yellow, floral curtains the day appeared bright and the neglected houses on Silver Street seemed at least to have had had a good night's rest. The room in which she had slept had taken on a cheerier tone, as indeed had the whole house from the previous night, seeming far less dismal, and the shabbiness, with a decent leap of imagination almost becoming chic. Catching a welcome glimpse of her face smiling in the mirror, she added an extra sweater before tugging on her thick coat and scarf as it was bound to be cold on this autumn morning. Then, fortified against the elements she set off in the direction of the coast.

Surprisingly, she only had to walk to the end of the street and then a further twenty yards to find herself next to the sea. Not only did she have the pleasure of being able to watch the rolling waves crashing against the shore, but there to her right was the majestic outline of the ruins of Tynemouth Priory and castle, founded in the seventh century and jutting out on a rocky headland surrounded by a deep moat. It was a breathtaking sight and still maintained its dignity. Somehow, she thought paradoxically, that buildings in ruins seemed more poignant, more elegant than those left intact. Henry VIII, five hundred years later had done the building a great aesthetic favour by his brutal violation, as in her remnants, the monastery's skeleton radiated a beatified glory.

Seagulls, of monstrous proportions dominated the whole area, seeking sustenance from leftovers donated by the tourists. Rebecca watched a particularly vicious looking one perched on a tall railing like some massive golden eagle- fashioned lectern. It was too still, with its gigantic yellow beak, enormous white tipped grey wings and cruel orange eyes watching her. A smile formed on her lips as she wondered if maybe Caroline was a shape shifter. The bird gave a loud squawk before extending its wings to find some other subject to intimidate.

Rebecca sat down on a bench to consider the strange woman, with her wild, dyed, curly hair, flamboyant clothes and officious manner. What sort of person thought it was okay to flounce into somebody else's house and take over? Help her redecorate the house! Heaven knows what ideas the outlandish woman would come up with. If it was anything like her dress sense- all black and red, with ruffles and chandeliers everywhere... Rebecca grinned again, imaging some tasteless bordello.

Looking to her far right, Rebecca noticed a large white statue well defined against the azure blue of the sky. She walked across to read the inscription There, Admiral Cuthbert Collingwood was standing in sentinel, guarding the mouth of the River Tyne. The man, who had a reputation in life for being both compassionate and deeply human, was staring out to sea with his hand resting on a rope-wrapped bollard. He had watched for nearly two hundred years for any approaching dangers. Flanking the steps at the base of the column, were the four cannons from his ship the 'Royal Sovereign'. The ship that had bought him such glory at the Battle of Trafalgar when he had taken control of the British Fleet after the death of Nelson.

Rebecca wondered what life would have been like, here in Tynemouth all those years ago. Many of the mullion-windowed houses would have been largely unchanged since the days of Trafalgar. She thought about how long her Aunt had lived here and for how many years she had known that woman. Why was she so keen that Rebecca should stay here? Whatever concern could it be to her? And if she was so used to treating her Aunt's home as if it was hers, was did that say about her Aunt? From what she had gleaned from her Mother (albeit little and late), this didn't seem to connect with the picture of her Aunt Sylvia that her Mother had painted. It seemed as if Aunt Sylvia had always been some sort of black sheep whose deviant behaviour had meant that the rest of her family had shunned her. Yet, this was certainly not the impression the house gave of the person who had lived their life there.

Unhappily, the decoration of the house screamed of blatant indifference, as if some beige person had spent their tepid life there. Yet something didn't tally. If Sylvia was such a pathetic doormat how come Caroline hadn't bullied her into injecting some life into the place? And what about those books? Paganism, Celtic Christianity ... and whatever was a *thin place*? They seemed a complete anomaly with everything else in the house.

Rebecca's head was spinning and she needed to get the ball rolling. She had estate agents to contact and rubbish to clear out of the house. But before that, she wanted to have a good look round to see if there was anything else mysterious in number ten to be discovered. The thought was beginning to roll around her head that Caroline didn't want her to stay up here, and stay in the house because she was a good friend of her aunt's, and wanted to look after her – that was absurd. It was more like the *house* needed looking after, for some reason, and Caroline couldn't trust anyone else but her. Why on earth did the house need looking after?

Chapter 5

Whitley Bay, three miles from Tynemouth - October 2009

Lydia sat in front of a mirror decorated with spangling stars and resigned herself to the unkind reflection that greeted her. What else could she do? She ran a wide-toothed comb through her long, coarse, jet black hair, the roots of pure white cruelly betraying its deception. Surely another application couldn't really be needed already. More to the point why should she bother? But she understood it was all part of the necessary performance. It was what was expected from Madame Llyriad.. She slipped the large golden rings through her ears and hoped the candle light would disguise the greyness of her cheeks and the lines that ran down the sides of her mouth and etched her face.

She applied the cobalt blue shadow on her eyelids which couldn't hope to disguise the bitterness beneath. The same relentless thoughts crossed her mind. Even after all this time she couldn't help but dwell on the memory. It was all very well others saying 'make peace with your past'. It was to have been the moment she had waited so long for, their reign of glory, but then *she* had arrived to spoil everything. That sneak thief had stolen what was hers. What made it even more sickening was the fact that she herself had facilitated events, she had brought her into the group. She should never have had the chance. The rejection and humiliation had been difficult to cope with but the scheming bitch had taken much, much more.

She began painting her long, fingernails the deepest shade of jet. She knew she was covering well-worn ground but she could never forget - or forgive. It had been all so utterly unexpected, first the change to the plan then the horrific aftermath. As if they were on a loop, the events played through her mind endlessly, a perpetual reminder of the need for vengeance. So, she waited, knowing for sure that her moment for retribution would come.

He, unbelievably, had been quite happy, having being given a role of seemingly equal significance, although it wasn't. He had thought it was acceptable and that there would be other years, but she had known that there wouldn't. And it had all happened in a brief moment... so quickly... so dreadfully. But her revenge would happen too and she had a feeling, a hunch (and she was excellent at those, a trick of the trade so to speak) that it wouldn't be too long now. She knew what had to be done ... and it would be done ... even after all this time. It would be done, as slowly and vindictively as possible.

She painted on thick, red lipstick to complete her facade. For so many years the same routine. She was now a parody of her former self. Where was that striking young woman with the long raven black hair? She was still inside and waiting for her moment once more. But her client would be here soon and it was what was expected. Lydia heaved her bulky frame from the chair and pulled her blue cloak around her shoulders. She sat herself down behind the table. It was too warm in the cloak in the small room. She felt a bead of sweat trickle from her left armpit but she sat perfectly still, composing herself and waiting for the knock.

***

Tynemouth - October 2009

Robert was tired. He had left Sebastian to lock up the shop and he now stood in his kitchen making himself a much-needed cup of tea. These days it seemed as if Caroline always wearied him. She must have only been in the shop for twenty minutes but the amount of energy she expended remonstrating, shouting and strutting up and down, was exhausting, both for her and him. At her age he thought, she ought to be slowing down, but no - she just continued to breeze through life certain that her way was the best and only way.

He had tried to tell her repeatedly, but she never listened. She never had done and he…well he should have put his foot down and stood up to her, but that was her all over. Always had been. Caroline, who had blazed like a whirlwind into his life all those years ago. He remembered the crazy, preposterous predicaments she had landed them in, as well as the downright stupid and dangerous. As she sped through the waters like a motor boat, he merely followed obediently in her wake. And he couldn't help himself, that was just the way of it. What was it the stoic Seneca said? A dog is tethered to a cart by a long lead. The dog can happily run alongside the cart regardless of where it goes, or, it can resist and be dragged along all the same. The cart is fate, the dog is man, thought Robert. A smile started to break at the corner of his mouth and he knew he couldn't be angry with the incorrigible woman for long.

Robert took a long mouthful of tea. It was obvious to him that, the severity of this current dilemma was because of Caroline's thoughtless, reckless behaviour from decades before. Did she not realise that her poorly thought through plans could be leading to real danger for all of them? She couldn't force the girl to stay in the place. Why would Rebecca want to? Undoubtedly, the house would need thousands spending on it to make it half way decent. All of Rebecca's life was back in Lancashire. That was where her parents and friends lived, that was where her job was. For her sake, the best course of action would be for her to sell the house and get herself back to the place where she had grown up. However, Robert knew only too well why Caroline could not allow this to happen, because events from years ago could still have awful repercussions for them. There didn't seem to be an easy answer or indeed any answer to the situation.

***

Lancaster University - March 1979

"Come round to my room at eight o'clock," whispered the girl with the long, dark hair. Around her neck was an assortment of wooden beads, shiny stars and colourful feathers. Her flowing, peasant skirt, diaphanous top and assortment of trailing, chiffon scarves completed the nomadic, dreamcatcher look. "Some of the others will be there. It'll be a great opportunity for you to meet them."

"Will it be ok?" Sylvia had known there was to be a gathering tonight. She hadn't actually been invited as such, but now as a result of this seemingly chance meeting she would finally get her first foot in the door.

Actually, she had been walking about all morning, up and down the walkway leading to the main square hoping for some such encounter and she had already missed two lectures. She felt a fluttering of excitement. "I mean…they haven't met me before. They won't know who I am."

"It'll be cool. Don't worry, everyone's quite relaxed. Nobody's going to bite you! They're great and only the few of us that live here on campus will be there tonight." The wind picked up, the girl gave a slight shudder, grabbed hold of her scarves trying to tame them and rearrange them compliantly around her neck. As the university was situated on a hill, this walkway known as The Spine was perpetually exposed to the elements.

"And these meetings," Sylvia looked about conspiratorially, as figures battled by on either side of them, "How long do they usually last?"

"It depends really on what needs to be covered. I think there are quite a few interesting items on the agenda tonight, but I can't say too much here," Lydia looked over her shoulder warily, "We usually go to the bar for a drink or three afterwards, so it's important to look normal." She glared at some passerby who, almost to her annoyance, seemed have little interest in the important matters being discussed,

"Don't tell anyone else though. That's really important." She looked directly into Sylvia's eyes, "Do not repeat to anyone else, what we talk about either. Do you understand? Other people mustn't know. And once you are in, that's it - no turning back. You do understand, don't you?"

Sylvia nodded, "Of course, I won't breathe a word of this to anyone." Out of the corner of her eye she noticed a familiar figure striding down the walkway towards her.

"Good, I knew we could trust you." The girl seemed suddenly serious and older. Sylvia had assumed her to be a similar age to herself but as she looked more closely, she could see fine lines spidering round her eyes and a sprinkling of grey in her hair. The girl checked her watch, the bangles on her wrist jangled and Sylvia sensed the conversation was over.

"What number's your room again?" Sylvia knew already. She had been following the girl's movements for weeks but she didn't want her to know that and she needed to ask quickly before he caught up with them.

"Twenty- nine. Cark Block." The girl pulled at her hair blowing across her face and then strode across the square with the heels clacking on her pointed boots. Sylvia looked down at her own trainers and jeans, wondering what she could possibly wear this evening. She waited until the familiar figure was level with her and turned towards him.

"Hi Sylvia," Robert smiled and peered at her from beneath his floppy fringe. He was wearing a thick, chunky sweater and it suited his slight frame. "Who was that you were talking to?"

This was the last person she wanted to talk to. She could do without the interrogation.

"Nobody, just a girl from one of my tutorial groups," *What the hell's it got to do with you.* "We were just talking about when an essay needed to be handed in."

"Ah, okay, okay, I was just wondering..." he hesitated, sensing that she seemed in an odd mood, "if you'd fancy meeting up for a drink later."

"Well, no, sorry... I need to finish an essay, got to be in tomorrow." She focused on some people coming out of the bakers in the distance. An enormous gust of wind took hold of discarded paper bags and sent them whirling across the square. It started tugging at Sylvia's hair, whipping the long, dark curls across her cheeks. She folded her arms, rubbing herself to keep warm.

"Ok, No worries. I guess I should probably be doing some work as well." He pretended indifference but he was irritated by her response. He wondered what she was really doing. "If you get finished though, and fancy a drink ...?"

"Yep, yes, 'course.... I don't think I will though. I'll probably have to work through the night to get this finished for tomorrow." She could tell that he didn't believe her but there was no way she could share what she was doing. At least not yet. "I'd better be going, I'm running late for a lecture" Sylvia gave him a half smile and set off, but he knew she was going in completely the wrong direction.

Although Sylvia really was supposed to be going to be studying, she knew she wouldn't be able to concentrate. Sylvia wondered what

'*It's important to look normal*' meant. On the campus there weren't many places to choose from but there was a little gift shop that she knew sold some long, flowing skirts and patterned scarves. This wasn't after all an indulgence but a necessity.

***

Tynemouth - October 2009

Sebastian quite enjoyed working in his uncle's shop and that in itself was surprising. Despite the fact he had a decent degree in English from Durham University, no conventional career path had any particular appeal to him. Also, he knew his parents were very disappointed in their son who had shown so much early promise. What he could he do though? Teaching and lecturing were out of the question. He hated any form of public speaking.

Likewise, although he enjoyed writing, any career linked with journalism or anything of that nature he found equally abhorrent with their schedules and deadlines. He did like the idea of writing fiction, but he had quickly become disenchanted with the several, science-fiction attempts he had made so far. He enjoyed making music and he played the guitar quite competently, he just needed to find some kindred souls to be in his band. Sebastian knew that he had some excellent ideas for songs, it was just that Tynemouth didn't seem the place to do it. Why his Uncle hadn't opened his shop in the city he really didn't know, as he would do far better business there for sure.

He couldn't stand being answerable to anyone else. His uncle made very few demands on him and he knew that that's what he liked about working in his bookshop. On the small wage that his uncle paid him, with an additional subsidy from his parents, he could just about afford to rent his small flat and have some money left over for a few a few drinks. Materialism wasn't a concept that interested him. Looking at the overflowing ashtray and assortment of half drunken cups of coffee he was glad his mother wasn't watching him. He was also aware that she was furious with her brother for giving him the wherewithal to indulge this carefree, simple lifestyle, and the thought quite pleased him. Sebastian was very fond of his laid-back uncle who was about as far removed from his high-flying, accountant father and driven, medical consultant mother as it was possible to be. Uncle Robert just liked to drift through life surrounded by his beloved, old books. As long as he could eke out a meagre profit from his business, he was content. Through Sebastian's eye this was no bad way to be. However, Sebastian couldn't fail to notice that his uncle seemed oblivious to the arrival of the twenty-first century. If he were to incorporate the use of internet to promote his business then surely his profits would considerably improve. However, Robert had no interest whatsoever in this, much to Sebastian's puzzlement.

Rolling himself another cigarette, he realised that his uncle would already have expected him at work by now. Although it was nearly ten o'clock Sebastian hadn't long been out of bed and he needed a couple of coffees before he could entertain facing the world. He'd had a late night, so he knew that his uncle would understand. Uncle Robert was such a decent and sympathetic man. No, Sebastian smiled, Uncle

Robert was a gullible fool and he knew that he shouldn't take advantage of him as he was genuinely fond of the man. But really, why did he put up with that dragon woman, and what had that business all been about the other day, when she stormed into the shop?

There seemed to have been some mention of someone called Rebecca, and some house she had been left in a will. He wondered if this was connected with the old dear that had lived next door who had died a few weeks ago. Hadn't she, for her sins, been a pal of the demanding Caroline? He had often watched Caroline noisily letting herself in and stomping off down the street especially just before the old woman had died. Who on earth would want to be friends with her, was way beyond his comprehension? Especially as his neighbour, with her quiet, mild ways had been the opposite of his uncle's domineering friend. Sebastian had actually quite liked the old girl but hadn't been particularly sad when she died, as he thought she must have been in a lot of pain. In fact, she must not have judged him so harshly herself unlike some, because she had entrusted him with a spare key to her house, in case she locked herself out. He took a long drag on his cigarette.

However, whatever it had all been about earlier, Caroline certainly seemed to be upset by it. Well, he was glad, he was no fan of the woman and he suspected the feeling was mutual. Her coming into his uncle's shop like she owned the place, clattering about the floor in her high heeled boots and expecting him to jump to it on her command.

Sebastian added another cigarette butt to the mountain in the ashtray before grabbing his coat. As he stepped out onto the pavement, he noticed a slender, young woman entering the house next door. Now could this be the mysterious Rebecca he wondered, as he set off for the bookshop?

Chapter 6

Tynemouth – October 2009

Rebecca had been quick to appoint an estate agent but had been disappointed by the paltry valuation placed upon the property. She recognised immediately that the money from the sale would not buy her much of a place in her hometown. A career in undertaking would have been infinitely more suitable for the tall, middle-aged woman with sallow skin and hollowed cheeks, she had opened the door to. Ms. Hope, *mizz* as she proclaimed and insisted on being addressed as, (surely inappropriately named, thought Rebecca, as hopeless would be so much more apt) had dourly refused her offer of tea. She had carefully opened her large bag for the necessary equipment and placed each item fastidiously on a small side table. She then walked gloomily around the property scribbling on her clipboard, taking photos, measuring floors and tutting.

Loud music was blaring from next door. Ms. Hope winced and rolled her eyes. Rebecca had previously heard music from next door but never this loud. Ms. Hope regarded the cracks on the ceiling, dark stained patches, tiles hanging loose, and made meticulous notes. After inspecting both kitchen and bathroom, she condemned them as prehistoric and in urgent need of replacement. She thought the state of the electrics and heating should quite simply be omitted from any property description, as to suggest there were any would be a lie and to fail to comply with building regulations, not to mention health and safety guidelines.

It appeared that this woman, in her black, tailored suit, was regarding this as a largely futile chore, as she knew full well that nobody would entertain buying this decrepit building for any decent figure. However, she had said, if it was marketed at a suitably low price there might just be a few modest spoils for her own company.

Rebecca thought she might try and manoeuvre the woman to the mirror above the fireplace and see if there was any reflection.

When Ms. Hope sighed loudly, before suggesting that £100,000 was a suitable starting point with the expectation of achieving a true sale value of £90,000, Rebecca couldn't even attempt to conceal her disappointment. Surely, Tynemouth was considered a desirable place to live? Ms. Hope raised her eyebrows in a 'what did you expect' manner, then attempted a smile before saying that she hoped Rebecca would be in touch soon. With the papers back inside the bulging bag, she made for the doorway, allowing Rebecca to thankfully close the door behind her.

Sitting despondently in a faded armchair, Rebecca considered the unwelcome fact that this figure couldn't possibly buy her anything half decent. *'Never mind dear, you can come back, this is your home, this is where you belong'.* She could almost hear her mother bleating with relish, delighting at the news.

She had however, arranged some other estate agents to come and value the house, and maybe their estimations would be more promising, although it now seemed doubtful. Who would have thought the valuation would have been so low? It had seemed such a promising sign when the yellow card for Hope's Estate Agency had been pushed through the door, as if they were interested in the property as a prospective financial investment. Caroline had seemed enthusiastic enough about the possibilities of the house but maybe that was just through a sense of allegiance to her friend. She could hear music blaring from next door once again. Her disappointment turned to anger as she considered that her selfish neighbours had ruined any pleasant mood for the viewing. It was almost as if the horrible music had been played as loud as possible on purpose for pure spite. Perhaps she should have a curt word with whoever lived in the flat to turn off the music before the next estate agent came.

Next door, the house seemed to have been converted into flats so maybe if that was done here it would be of some financial advantage - not that she had any money for investing in such a project. But then again, she thought, this house wasn't very big to start with so if it was made into flats, they would be very cramped. The music suddenly stopped and she heard a door slam. Looking out of her window she could see the culprit, a thin, youngish man dashing across the road as if he was late for some meeting. She wondered where he was going and if he planned to upset any more people that day.

***

Caroline waited in the coffee shop trying to read her newspaper. She had long ago stopped silently rapping her fingers on the table. She knew her friend's appointment had been at ten o'clock, so by now, forty-three minutes later, she ought to be finished. A tinkling noise made her look up. She smiled, removed her reading glasses and waved for her friend to come over. Susan Hope unbuttoned her jacket to reveal a grey blouse buttoned severely to the collar. She pulled up a chair opposite, glad to be sitting down. Caroline noticed in passing that her friend looked weary.

"How did it go? What price did you offer?" Caroline's eyes met hers hungrily, eager for information.

"Hello, and nice to see you too,' Susan Hope bristled. 'Well I suggested that it should be marketed at first for £100,000…"

"That's too expensive," Caroline interrupted. "That's a lot of money to Rebecca. You could have said much less than that, then she would have been bound to see the importance of not selling at all!"

"Hang on Caroline, wait, you have to understand," Susan Hope gestured for the waitress to bring her a coffee over. "If I was to offer any less… the girl isn't stupid you know. She's bound to have done some research about house prices in this area. The coast, Tynemouth, it's a desirable place to live. More than likely she will ask for valuations from other Estate Agents. Any lower price would just have been ridiculous and she would have become suspicious."

Caroline took an irritated sip from her coffee. "I still think it's too high. What was Rebecca's reaction to it - the more than generous figure you mentioned?"

"She looked disappointed, understandably. I mean, come on, what properties sell for that price in this day and age Caroline? Don't forget I did this as a favour to you, but I can't say it was a very enjoyable experience for either of us." She noticed Caroline staring vacantly out of the window. It seemed to Susan as if she had failed to serve her purpose and was now of no further use. She was being held in a telephone queue. Wasn't that just typical of the woman? "Anyway, what's the big deal to you? What does it matter to you whether this Rebecca stays in the house or sells it? You hardly know the girl - I don't get it Caroline."

"There's nothing *to* get. It's for Sylvia … I'm doing it for her. She had a long-standing feud with her sister. You know Sylvia was ill for a long time … Cynthia never came to visit her even once."

"From what I can gather she didn't live close by and from my recollections, well … Sylvia was hardly the most scintillating company was she?" Susan's scathing eyes met Caroline's, baiting her.

They sat like two gunslingers at a rigged poker game, eyeing each other carefully. Trigger fingers twitching. Trying to work out who was cheating.

"As a matter of fact, Cynthia only lives in Lancashire," said Caroline, continuing to look at the passing cars. "It's only a couple of hours drive away. She never phoned either. Blood is supposed to be thicker than water and she did know her sister was ill. Coldhearted, judgemental … Rebecca was her only niece and she wanted her to inherit the house so she could move away from her miserable mother."

"Caroline something doesn't add up and tell me if it's none of my business, but what is really going on here?" Susan poked Caroline on her arm, forcing her to face her. "Rebecca gets the money if she sells or keeps the house, she has her Aunt's inheritance. Doesn't she have a job and family somewhere else? You know it seems to me that Sylvia's mind must have become fuddled with her medication and I think you're becoming too involved in something which is quite clearly none of your business. If someone gets that house for £90,000 that's one hell of a bargain. Next door has been converted into two flats perhaps it'd be a good investment opportunity. In fact, I might well buy it myself for that price…"

"What d'you mean? You can't do that. I mean, I thought you were my friend?" Caroline stared at Susan, horrified. Everything was backfiring on her.

"Yes, I am your friend Caroline, but sometimes I wonder why. I am also a business woman and I think that's something you sometimes forget," Susan looked at her watch and stood up. "And if you're not really going to tell me what's going on, I need to be on my way, as my time, unlike yours, is precious. Cancel the coffee for me please."

The doorbell jingled again as Susan left, leaving Caroline fuming, furiously rapping her fingers on the table and thinking very, very hard.

***

Lancaster University – March 1979

Sylvia had taken a long time getting ready and eventually she settled on her new long blue skirt with lots of interesting bead and thread decorations. She added a favourite, black blouse then threw a couple of scarves nonchalantly round her shoulders. The new skirt had been quite expensive. She probably could have got something far cheaper if she had caught the bus into town, but she just hadn't had the time. She swirled the skirt in front of the mirror. It sparkled as it caught in the light and she smiled at the effect. Round her neck she added some blue, glass beads. Despite the fact she rarely wore much make-up she thought on this occasion she ought to make the effort and she considered the way that Lydia presented herself. Carefully, she smudged the smoky blue powder round her eyes and the carmine red on her lips. Lydia was bohemian and she certainly wouldn't be seen dead wearing jeans and trainers. At last satisfied with her appearance, Sylvia set off across the campus.

Keeping her head down she continued walking, hoping that she wouldn't bump into anyone that she knew. Although she had only been here a few months she had made a few friends but she was conscious that her new look was quite different to the way that she had presented herself so far. But who was to say that had been the real her? Surely that was being a young student was all about. No-one one knew anything about her background here, it was like having a clean slate to start over again. She could be whoever she wanted and dress however she pleased.

After walking up two flights of stairs she found the right door and knocked nervously, wondering what she would find. Lydia's face appeared, nodded and gestured for Sylvia to enter. The room was small. Three figures were huddled on the bed, one was perched on a table, one on a chair and two were sitting cross- legged on the floor. The closeness of the figures made everything seem more intense.

"This is Sylvia everyone," Lydia announced. Sylvia looked around the room as an assortment of faces turned to scrutinize her. "I know there's not much room Sylvia, but have a seat if you can find one." The three bodies on the bed squashed together so she could sit down.

There was folk music playing that she didn't recognize. Candles were planted precariously on a bookshelf adding heat and a warm glow. There was also a pungent smell, perhaps of incense or maybe something earthier. On the wall was a selection of pictures of women, maidens, mothers and crones, hooded figures, swirling Celtic symbols and interlaced Celtic crosses.

"Well, Sylvia let me introduce everyone. I know you know me as Lydia but within the company I am known as Llyriad. Everyone here has their own special names. We don't use our original given, first names or Christian names, whatever you prefer to call them, because our interests lie in the ancient ways. So, we've all chosen our own more fitting craft names from pagan, Celtic times. She gestured to a blond-haired man with sculpted cheekbones and intense blue eyes sitting cross-legged on the floor. "This is Scire." Scire gave an obligatory smile with a slight bow of his head.

Llyriad continued the introductions and reeled off a list of impressive sounding names.

Dayonis, a slight blonde girl sitting on the chair. Loic, a round faced boy with a cheeky grin. Olwyn, a girl with short dark hair sitting next to Sylvia. Ancantha, a plumpish girl sitting on the desk, Adla, a slim boy with very long hair. Lastly, Cedonia, a boy she recognised as Neil from some history lectures. He concentrated on a square of carpet in front of him and pretended he didn't know her.

"Now," Llyriad continued, assuming control of the proceedings, "We have a new member here tonight who is no doubt somewhat mystified about what is about to happen."

"Oh well, in ten minutes time we all remove our clothes and have group sex," announced a voice from the floor followed by an assortment of sniggers and tuts.

"Loic, please," reprimanded Llyriad. "Although some people think we engage in that sort of thing at our meetings, I can assure you Sylvia, that is not what we are about at all."

"Pity," whispered Loic under his breath.

Llyriad chose to ignore the remark. "Now," she said, "the first item on the agenda is next week's Esbat. And for the benefit of our newcomer, an Esbat is a … special meeting … a ceremony … to welcome the new moon and give thanks to the moon goddess. It is a very significant part of why we are all here. We must never forget that. Also, our numbers will be much stronger, important people will be present and," she looked directly at Loic, "we must all acknowledge the sanctity of the Esbat and understand the consequences of imprudent behaviour."

Sylvia's curiosity was increasing by the second. The safety net had been taken away. This was going to be fascinating.

Chapter 7

Preston – October 2009

Bill and Cynthia were having their tea and Bill was enjoying his shepherd's pie. Although he was frequently irritated by his wife's pettiness and harsh judgmental attitudes, he still appreciated her cooking. While some would find her traditional fayre bland, it suited him fine he thought as he placed a forkful of creamy mashed potato into his mouth.

"I haven't heard anything from Rebecca you know Bill. I mean… she's been there more than two days now. You would have thought that she might have been in touch. That girl can be so thoughtless." Cynthia liberally added some more salt to her food.

"Why don't you give her a ring love? I expect she's feeling a bit lonely… I mean she won't know anyone there will she. It must be strange being up there all alone. In fact, I think I'll send her a text, just so she knows we're thinking about her."

"I wonder if she has had an estate agent round yet? I'm curious to know what sort of place it is. Anyway, I can't imagine that any home of Sylvia's will be much to write home about. She was always such a spendthrift and so wasteful with money…it's a marvel she actually owned any property. No doubt Rebecca will be disappointed by its value." Cynthia clattered her knife and fork down on her plate." "You really would have thought she might have had the decency to get in touch. That girl can be incredibly selfish you know. I mean, after all, we are her parents."

"Hang on, love," Bill was concentrating on sending a text to his daughter and was attacking the keys with his index finger, "There, I've just asked her how she's doing and said we're missing her."

"Ask her if she's got the house on the market yet … and when she's coming back home." Cynthia checked her own phone to see if she had received any messages. Unsurprisingly she hadn't. She never really bothered with her own mobile phone and most of the time it was switched off.

"You know, if she doesn't get much money for this house, we could help her out." Bill looked at his wife hopefully, laying a lifeline through the minefield. "I mean, you know she's desperate for a place of her own and that way she might buy somewhere close by."

"Bill, not that again. You know what I think about it. Did anyone help us out when we first got a house? She's got a good job. If she wants a house that badly she can just get a mortgage like everyone else, but I don't think we should really encourage that either." Cynthia switched off her phone and placed it back in her bag.

***

Lancaster University – April 1979

Sylvia was grateful for the warmth provided by the heavy cloak as she went out into the April night. Luckily, the night was clear and the new moon, luminous and lovely hung high above. She shivered, wondering what enchantments the night would bring. The very word 'Esbat', sounded mystical and intriguing.

On a small hill, hidden by a dense curtain of trees, shapes were congregating, poised deliberately in a large circle. Each figure holding a tall candle and moving obediently towards their allotted place. Sylvia noticed Llyriad standing to one side. Like everyone else she wore a simple, green cloak. Befitting the occasion her face looked sombre, as she stood behind a small table, dispensing candles.

As every individual received a candle, they made a small bow first towards Llyriad then a more grandiose one to the moon. Smiling benignly at Sylvia, when her turn arrived, Llyriad offered a lit, white candle. Sylvia imitated the bows and Llyriad gestured for her to take a place in the circle. Looking closely at the narrow white candle, she noticed in the flickering golden light from the flame, that it was decorated with intricate carvings of the moon in its various stages of waxing and waning. A silvery, white cloth, embroidered with fruits and vegetables, their silky threads glistened stunningly in the glowing candlelight, was spread on the table.

Eventually, as everyone took their places in the ring, she noted that there must have been around thirty people present. A ring of hooded cloaks waiting in anticipation for events to develop. Nobody spoke, but as she looked about the circle she saw plenty of familiar faces. Olwyn looked at her and they acknowledged each other with a slight nod. Loic was staring at a tall figure with a distinctive curved nose making his way into the centre and soon she noticed that other eyes were watching him too. A tall, distinctive man with an angular face, chiselled jaw, broad forehead and flat, smooth cheeks, making him seem, in this candlelight, like an animated cubist painting. Sylvia had not seen this person before but she sensed his importance and that he would orchestrate events.

He held his candle high, using both hands, and solemnly drew an imaginary circle by turning slowly, pausing for the briefest of moments to point the candle at each figure. He was a tall man, and he moved with a skilful grace. While everybody else wore similar dark, green cloaks, his was pure white, indicating the importance of his position.

Then, Llyriad, taking long deliberate strides, moved the table with the cloth into the centre of the circle.

"In the name of the Requisite, I bring the sacred cloth to you Dafo," said Llyriad with well-practised, expected words. "To you Dafo, our leader, our priest, our guide. May you be blessed with the words to enlighten us this night. May you keep us in your heart this night. May the Mother Goddess bring you wisdom."

Dafo bowed and placed his candle upon the cloth, transforming it into an altar. Llyriad brought a glinting, silver bowl containing a dark, glutinous liquid and placed it on the table. Dafo stood erect, facing the bowl. He stretched his arms wide and then, tilting his head dramatically towards the moon began to speak in a profound, resonant voice: *" Goddess of the moon, queen of the night,*

Keeper of women's mysteries, Mistress of the tides,

You who are ever changing and yet always constant,

I ask that you guide us with your wisdom,

Help us grow with your knowledge,

And hold us in your arms."

Dafo paused, lifted the bowl from the table and held it symbolically up to the sky. All eyes were fixed upon him as he drank deeply from it and then resumed his prayer.

> *"The moon is the mother,*
> *She watches over us day and night,*
> *She brings the changing tide,*
> *She brings the passion of the night,*
> *Her wisdom is great and all-knowing,*
> *We honour her this night,*
> *Keep your watchful eyes upon us, great mother."*

He placed the bowl on the table and lifted his arms once more to the sky. This formed as a signal for everyone in the circle to lift their gaze to the sky. Sylvia was only too willing to follow and replicate their actions, beginning to feel a deep and unfamiliar sense of belonging

Dafo's voice became increasingly intense and theatrical. Excited voices repeated his words.

> *"You are the Mother of all life,*
> *The one who watches over us,*
> *You are the wind in the sky,*
> *You are the spark in the fire,*
> *You are the seedling in the earth,*
> *You are the water in the rivers,*
> *We all welcome you,*
> *The requisite prayer is for you,*
> *We all praise you,*
> *The Requisite praises you."*

He picked up the candle once more and held it as an offering to the moon. The whole circle repeated the words, holding their candles to the sky.

Sylvia could feel the shared euphoria hypnotically swirling about the circle. The cloaked figures no longer still but swaying rhythmically, chanting the prayer.

"*Feel the power of the goddess*!" called Dafo.

Oh yes, thought Sylvia, she could definitely feel it. She knew that this was what she had been looking for and where she belonged.

***

Tynemouth - October 2009

Although Rebecca had been initially disappointed with the valuation of the property, given a little while to consider matters, she realised that it was churlish of her to feel anything other than gratitude to her aunt. Even if when she bought another property, knowing she would be forced to take out a small mortgage, she was still in an extremely fortunate position. After all, the loan would be comparatively small as the sale of the house would provide her with a fabulous deposit and she certainly wouldn't be saddled with the enormous monthly repayments that many of her friends were burdened with.

Rebecca sat in the kitchen looking at the faded yellow walls with the cracks running down from the ceiling. Having definitely seen better days, the cooker seemed almost apologetic for being such an unattractive shade of brown. The taps in the heavy, square, porcelain sink continued their constant, weary drip. Although shabby chic was in fashion, Rebecca smiled to herself thinking that what the room lacked in style it more than made up for in threadbare qualities. She tried to imagine her aunt sitting here in this tired kitchen. It was almost as if the house was trying to be as anonymous as possible and not draw any attention to itself. What did this say about the character of her Aunt? This was nothing like the impression that her mother had painted of her wayward sister in her younger days. People don't change that much with age. What had happened to the carefree, young woman with her unquenchable thirst for life?

She walked into the sitting room to look again at the photograph on the mantelpiece of the smiling young couple. She had a deepening sensation that something was greatly amiss. This surely couldn't be the same person that would have chosen to live in a house like this. Life and vitality exuded from the laughing face with the dancing curls and eyes glinting with fun. What could have happened to transform her so completely? And who was the young man with the kind face gazing at her? Maybe, for some reason, this was how she liked the house to be. Maybe she had no spare money to renovate the place, certainly no other savings had been mentioned. There were so many questions that needed answers to and regrettably Caroline seemed to be the only person she could ask.

Although Rebecca had no desire to see that wretched woman again, she knew that she had to, because of the questions spiralling out of control in her head.

Chapter 8

North Shields – October 2009

Caroline stood on her balcony, sipped from a large glass of wine and gazed out towards the river. On the other side of the water she could see the rooftops and spires of South Shields with the street lights just beginning to glow. To her right she could see the ghostly skeletons of the red and blue cranes that belonged to the region's shipbuilding past, standing proud, like frozen dinosaurs. Although it was only half past four, it was already a pink dusk and the burnished, orange sun was low in the sky. She shivered, pulling her fluffy, red cardigan around her shoulders and moved back into the warmth of her apartment. Comforting cooking smells filled the room from the chicken casserole in the oven. She had company coming to dinner later that night. If Rebecca had been a little less hostile to her, she would have invited her too *but the time will come*, she thought to herself, *it must come*.

If she could somehow find a way of inviting Rebecca round, she would be able see her elegant decorations, and be suitably impressed. Caroline knew that her home shouted her sophistication and good taste. Once Rebecca saw her beautiful apartment, she would be convinced of the sensibility of allowing her to help redecorate the house in Huntingdon Place. She was sure that Rebecca would favour a discreet, neutral décor especially when she considered the clothes that the girl wore. She was also sure she would be able to persuade her to inject a little colour. She thought back to her own taste in clothes when she was that age, and wondered if perhaps Rebecca needed some fashion advice too. It really was the most sensible option for the girl to live in Huntingdon Place. She just had to convince the girl of this.

Caroline relaxed on one of her sumptuous sofas and placed her glass on a large, wood-inlaid coffee table. She was glad to remove the bulky cardigan in the warmth of the room. Flickering, realistic flames from her top of the range, fire-effect fireplace, were reflected in the crystal beads of her sparkling, ornate chandeliers, making them, *like bubbles in a glass of champagne,* she thought to herself. Over the marble mantelpiece on the scarlet wall was a large, flattering portrait of herself painted some years ago. She was wearing a midnight-blue robe that draped seductively round her body, her long dark ringlets cascaded over her shoulders, and her eyes looked alive with mischief. Sometimes people had remarked that she looked a little like Nell Gwyn and that was a comparison she had no problem with. Actually, Caroline was secretly very pleased when others compared her to those with a slightly risqué reputation. She enjoyed the idea of being viewed in this light. She was extremely fond of this portrait and it was given prime position in the room.

"Well, Caroline," she said out loud to her younger self. "What are we going to do about matters? What do you suggest?" Shaking her head, Caroline sauntered across the room to her ultra-modern kitchen to refill her glass. Checking the oven to ensure all was well with the chicken chasseur, she began assembling the vegetables for her signature dish. She racked her brains as she neatly sliced potatoes, thinking how she could persuade Rebecca to stay. Maybe, if she were to offer to give the girl some money. A loan, for example that she could pay back as and when. Would that seem too weird? She had to devise some method of luring Rebecca to stay. Perhaps she could enlist the help of that useless Sebastian. Granted, she wouldn't see him as much of a catch but they were of a similar age and ... there was no accounting for tastes. Rebecca's mother wouldn't be happy about it, but then what had Cynthia ever been happy about?

Perhaps Rebecca's teaching job could afford some leverage. Surely, if she had a choice in the matter she wouldn't choose to work in a school. Caroline couldn't think of anything worse than having to deal with a class of bothersome children and couldn't see how it would appeal to any sane person. Especially as it was always in the news about how stressful, underpaid and downright awful, teaching had become. Apparently, droves of young people were leaving after just two or three years. Rebecca must be crazy to want to work in such a pressurised job. Caroline actually very much enjoyed her job as an interior designer, and she made quite a lot of money for very little effort. Maybe she needed an assistant?

This Autumn, half-term week was almost half way through, so she needed to act fast. She must convince Rebecca to quit her job and come to live here in Tynemouth. If she were to hand in her notice now then the school could release her at Christmas, and she could enjoy herself interior designing. They would have such fun together.

Caroline smiled as she continued her preparations. Of course, she could have got someone in to do it, but she liked to make the effort, which was always much appreciated by her dinner guests. She chopped some broccoli and took a large sip from the glass. Eventually, satisfied that everything was as it should be, she returned to the sitting room and put some Vaughan Williams into her state-of-the-art sound system. Listening to 'The English Folk Song Suite' amplified throughout the apartment, she waited for her visitor. She didn't have long to wait until the buzzer told her that her dinner guest had arrived.

***

Tynemouth - October 2009

Robert had told Sebastian to go home early as the shop had been particularly quiet. Unfortunately, only about a dozen customers had passed through the door all that day. In fact, if it wasn't for the weekends, he would have been forced out of business years ago but as things were, he was just able to keep afloat. He was a man of simple tastes, the flat above the shop was sparsely furnished but he had all he needed. Of course, he knew that Caroline would never entertain living in a place like his and that was just one of their many fundamental differences. But despite their apparently polar opposite points of view, there were ties that bound them together in the essentially solid relationship they had shared for many years.

Would things have worked out if they lived together? That he couldn't answer because it had always been impossible that they ever could do. It was far too risky. Upon many occasions throughout the years they had been forced to move home, just when they had started to get their lives into some sort of order. The danger was always there and they had to be constantly vigilant. He had learned his lesson now and was careful as to the products he stocked to avoid attracting certain types. His 'Early history of Britain' started in the eighth century. There was no section on paganism, wicca or early Christianity. Now of all times was not a moment for complacency. They had both lived here in Tynemouth for almost fifteen years and unquestionably they had Sylvia's discretion to thank for that. He reflected that he did indeed miss her quiet company.

Robert tried to push recent events to the back of his mind, for despite all their other complications it was perhaps it was for the best that they lived apart. Consequently, their differences failed to become a serious problem. They still enjoyed each other's company whenever they could. The same thing could not be said of many married couples who had been together for as long as they had. Robert was certainly looking forward to seeing Caroline that evening and more importantly he wondered what tasty meal she had cooked for them. Caroline had many flaws and imperfections but she was definitely an excellent cook.

As Robert opened the door of his battered old Peugeot, he couldn't stop thinking about the strange events of the day. More specifically the two customers who had visited the bookshop.

He had been surprised and delighted when Rebecca arrived that morning, giving him the opportunity to study her more closely, although of course he pretended that he had no idea of who she was. As his business was only a stone's throw away from her house, it wasn't unexpected that a school teacher would have an interest in reading and bookshops. Yet, as she wandered randomly amongst the shelves of books it had seemed as if her mind was elsewhere. He had asked if he could help her find anything in particular but she had replied that she was just browsing. He had nodded and smiled, glad to have been able to say a few words to her. She leafed through a selection of books about the local area while he concealed himself behind some shelves and continued studying her.

As he stopped at the traffic lights on the coast road out of Tynemouth, he thought about how he could mention this to Caroline. She would be bound to think it a positive sign that Rebecca was taking an interest in the neighbouring surroundings. It would certainly aid her determination to get Rebecca to stay in the house.

A sudden change had come over Rebecca in the shop. She had noticed Sebastian, sticking price tickets on some new historical biographies he had bought the previous day, and she almost seemed annoyed. Later that day, thinking about this, he remembered that his nephew lived in the flat next door to her, but he wondered what earth he could have done to upset her in such a short period of time. It was all most peculiar, he thought to himself, but then again, that was Sebastian for you.

The customer in the afternoon had been much more disturbing and cast a dark shadow over the whole day. A tall, elderly man with a familiar gait had come in and began looking through his shelf of antique, rare additions. Intuitively, Robert sensed danger, an instinct which had served him well in the past. He had scuttled into the room at the back of the shop where he couldn't be seen, leaving Sebastian to deal with the old man who appeared to not be in the best of health.

Recalling this customer, whose path he was fearful he had certainly crossed before, he heaved a large sigh. He pulled up outside Caroline's Union Square apartment, parking next to her shiny blue Beetle, wondering what he was going to say to her.

***

Lancaster University – April 1979

Robert really didn't know what to think about what he had seen last night, as he flipped through the pages of an uninspiring, history book. This essay on the significance of the early Northumbrian Saints in the spread of Christianity, needed to be completed immediately to be handed in today, but he just couldn't concentrate. Was it really so important when Easter was celebrated? Was it really of such great consequence, the manner in which monks wore their tonsures? It seemed to be of paramount importance to the Synod at Whitby in 664. Robert rubbed his eyes and ran his fingers through his hair.

He just couldn't get Sylvia out of his mind. They had been out together on only a few occasions and he had really enjoyed her company. Robert had had several girlfriends before coming to Lancaster but nothing really of any great consequence. Of course, he had liked them well enough, but the feelings he had for Sylvia were something he had never experienced before. But of course, he couldn't tell anyone this, certainly not his male friends, whose conversations were limited to the consumption of alcohol and football and especially not her.

It was the way she laughed as she expressed her mad ideas and thoughts on a wide range of crazy subjects with such conviction that completely fascinated him. She could be reciting nursery rhymes to him and still he would be enthralled. At this very moment he could imagine her, eyes sparkling as she gesticulated wildly, waving her hands about, laughing out loud and making some preposterous point seem charming.

To be honest, he considered most of her notions were downright ridiculous, but that, in his eyes only added to her appeal. He chewed on the pen and scribbled some zig zags in the margin of a page. In fact, most of the time, he wasn't sure what point she was making, but that didn't matter in the slightest. Yes of course it was important to look after the Earth and treat it with the respect it deserved. He had no problem with that. He could see the sense in pollution control or not over-fishing in particular waters where numbers were dwindling. Of course, resources needed to be conserved to protect the Earth for future generations. He couldn't really understand why she was so passionate about matters that were really just common sense. However, these were just her more sensible ideas. The actual worship of the earth, stones, trees and rivers as living beings or spirits seemed to require some kind of faith or comprehension that was way beyond him. Of course, he would never have said this to her. He didn't want to lose her. He just compliantly nodded and agreed.

The way she moved, spoke and grasped life with both hands only combined to enchant him. It was as if she had woven a spell upon him with those ever-gesturing hands. She was constantly in his thoughts and wherever he went, it was with one eye always looking out for her. But he knew he needed to get a grip on himself in order to finish the damn essay.

Yet something had changed. He had sensed that immediately when he had bumped into her by the square. She had been talking to a strange woman. He recognised her from somewhere because of her peculiar dress and excessive jewellery, but it wasn't someone he actually knew.

He had a bad feeling about the woman that he couldn't really explain. Maybe it was the way she always seemed to be lurking in the corners of bars and coffee shops whispering to her other shady friends. Although he had no idea what they were talking about, he could tell from the expressions on their faces that it was something dubious. There was just something about the woman with her jet-black hair, pale face and wild eyes that he didn't trust. But more disturbingly, why had Sylvia been talking to her?

It was obvious that Sylvia had felt uncomfortable when she saw him and why was that? She had made light of her discussion with the woman, claiming it to be someone from one of her tutorial groups but he wasn't fooled. Also, from what he knew of her already, Sylvia didn't seem to be one of those people who worked through the night to get an essay finished. She seemed more organised with her time than that. It was as if she was just fobbing him off. As she had stood there with her cheeks flushed from the biting wind looking lovely, he had felt embarrassed and dejected because she clearly wasn't interested in him any longer.

Later on, he thought he would walk past her room just to see if he could see her light on and the silhouette of her hunched over her table working. Looking at his watch he saw that it was 1'o clock in the morning. What was he doing, stalking her? But there was no light on in her room. She wasn't working at all. She was probably fast asleep, or with someone else. Whichever way, it was quite clearly the brush off for him and he cursed himself, embarrassed at his own stupidity.

He was suddenly brought back to reality. Through the still night air, he heard the sound of footsteps. Someone walking towards him. He darted behind a bush. As the person drew closer, he realised that it was Sylvia. She wearing a cloak, trailing to the ground and smiling in such a strange manner that he wondered if she had been taking drugs. She looked in such a weird world all of her own that she probably wouldn't have recognised him if he stepped out from behind his hiding place – which he most certainly wasn't going to do. On the other hand, he did feel worried as to where she had been at this time of night. An image of that woman Lydia, yes, that was her name he remembered finally, flashed through his mind. Something told him that she was in some sort of danger and that Lydia was somehow also involved. He realised he had to protect Sylvia.

***

North Shields - October 2009

"I'm not sure that's a very good idea Caroline," Robert said, putting a hand over his glass, as she attempted to pour him more wine.

"Yes, yes, I know, I know you said you were driving, but really... it's not necessary. You can always stop over here tonight, don't you think?" She pushed his hand away and refilled his drink.

"Caroline, you know I wasn't referring to that. I was talking about your fixation with making Rebecca stay up here and live in that house. Is it really for the best, all things considered?" Robert put the drink to one side and poured himself a glass of water. He glanced at his watch. Time was moving on and he was beginning to feel nervous. Despite Caroline making a delicious meal, he hadn't really been able to appreciate his food.

"But you know why the house can't be sold. Don't let's go over it again! You know it's imperative that she stays in the house." She furrowed her brow at him but then smiled. "Anyway, you said that she came into your shop today but seemed annoyed. More information please."

Robert displayed his palms, surrendering the point. "Yes, it was all a bit odd because, oh I don't know ... it was as if she caught sight of Sebastian and ... and then she was furious with him. I can't imagine what he could have done to offend her in such a short space of time. It was very puzzling, very strange."

"Well, she's obviously a good judge of character," snorted Caroline." Although, I had thought we might be able to use your useless nephew to our advantage. We must persuade her not to sell. We need to convince her that she must stay here … and I was hoping that her and Sebastian might become friends."

"What? But you despise Sebastian."

"I'm just grasping at straws. I thought if they became friends … well everyone needs a friend, don't they? A special *friend*. Know what I mean?" Caroline put her knife and fork down on the plate carefully, so as not to disturb her train of thought. She also had more important matters on her mind other than eating. "And … if they could become very *good* friends, then so much the better for our plan."

"*Our* plan?" Robert started, and flicked his head to one side, an involuntary objection to her use of the word, gave her a scathing look but decided to plough on with what was on his mind. "It's not safe, it's not safe for Rebecca or us. There's something else I need to tell you about today." Robert looked at her anxiously, not sure of how she was going to take his news.

"If I was to give her £10,000 as a gift", said Caroline, obsessed with her own thoughts and not picking up on the fact he had something of importance to share, "then she could use the money to improve the house and then…"

"Caroline, firstly she would just think that peculiar. Why would an old friend of her Aunt's give her that sort of money? No, she would be bound to smell a rat. Secondly, have you really got that amount of money to give her?" He looked around at the expensive furnishings in her flat knowing this answered his question. Still, he needed to get to the real point and quickly.

"Well, we'll see ... maybe you can..."

"For goodness sake. Please, please be quiet for a moment and listen..." Robert's voice rose, "You have to know what happened today. Something else happened. *Something very important.*"

Caroline raised her eyebrows and looked hard at him, longer than normal, weighing him up and giving him a disparaging stare. She gave him her full attention, surprised not only at this directness from Robert but also his emphasis on the words 'something very important'.

"Listen," continued Robert. "Someone else came into the shop today. I wasn't sure at first ... if my suspicions were correct ... but even after all this time, I would recognise that face anywhere. Also, it was his manner... despite all the years that have passed." Robert's stared at the floor, not wanting to see her reaction. "Anyway, I took myself off into the back. I certainly didn't want him seeing and recognising me. Sebastian dealt with him ... but you do know who I'm talking about, don't you?"

Caroline took a long drink from her glass. "Could you have been mistaken? Surely it couldn't have been him. Not after all this time. You must have been mistaken. I had rather hoped that by now he might have died. But now of all times ... it's surely too much of a coincidence." Caroline stood up and began to pace about the room.

"Well of course I'm not definitely certain," his eyes followed her warily as she moved about. "I couldn't risk taking a proper look but it left me with such an unsettled feeling. I don't think there's any doubt. And you know what this means don't you?"

"Yes Robert, I know exactly what this means. It means that there is no way the house can be sold now, is there?" She sat down at the table. "Don't you see there is even more at stake this time? It's not only us that's in danger now. Rebecca, well she's involved too, isn't she? You know what I mean?"

"Of course, I realise that. I can think of nothing else. Is this never going to end?" Robert gazed out of the window hopelessly, "I'm just so tired …and I really don't know what we should do for the best."

"We need to keep calm and think things through."

"I am calm and I am thinking things through. But I get no answers to all my questions. Just more questions."

"We can't keep running."

"Agreed." said Robert.

"If it's him, we need to find out what his plans are? Where's he staying? How long he's been here?"

"Agreed. And then what?"

"We need to seize the initiative. Be proactive."

Robert gave her a quick, sideways glance. *'This does not bode well'*, he thought to himself.

Chapter 9

Lancaster University – April 1979

When Sylvia awoke the next morning, the sunlight was streaming invitingly through the window, summoning her. Life was precious and should not be wasted in sleep. She yawned and stretched like a young bear cub, fresh from hibernation. She had been so tired the previous night that she had completely forgotten to close the curtains.

She looked outside over the almost empty car park and opened the window. The daffodils were a dazzling yellow under a clear, springtime sky. Birdsong was everywhere accompanied by the sweet aroma of freshly cut grass. This wonderful time of nature awakening. How fitting and appropriate she thought, considering her recent initiation into the Requisite. Recalling the significant events of the Esbat, she remembered the mesmerising voice of Dafo as he led the offering ceremony to the Moon Goddess. She felt the delicious ecstasy of the occasion again. How wonderful it now felt to belong to a company of kindred spirits, and she wondered where this exhilarating journey would take her next.

Her cloak and the rest of her discarded clothes lay on the floor where she had flung them before collapsing into her bed in such a delightful exhaustion. And now, after the most satisfying, dreamless sleep, she felt energised, ready to face whatever the day saw fit to present.

There was a knock at the door.

"Sylvia, are you okay?" It was Robert, bringing her back to reality with a jolt. *Oh no, no, no, no, why was he banging on her door so early in the morning?* She looked at her watch. It was eleven-thirty.

"Yes, of course I'm alright," she shouted. "Why shouldn't I be?" She quickly bundled up her cast-off clothing and threw them into the wardrobe. "Go and wait in the kitchen, I'll join you in a minute."

Sylvia pulled on jeans and a T-shirt. Why had he come to see her? He had never done this before. She certainly didn't want him to know she had only just got out of bed. Before brushing her teeth and splashing water on her face, she scattered open books and papers on her desk and bed, just in case.

Robert sat in the communal kitchen a little apart from Liz and Theresa, two girls who shared the same block as Sylvia. They were reading newspapers, eating a late breakfast of bacon and eggs and casting furtive glances at him. The greasy, cooking smells made him feel queasy and he wished Sylvia would hurry despite knowing she was going to be feeding him lies about her nocturnal activities. He looked out of the window and watched the students walking by, until Sylvia eventually arrived.

"You've got company Sylvia," smiled Theresa, nodding towards an awkward-looking Robert. "You'd better make him a coffee, he's looking all neglected."

"Sylvia," said Liz with mock scandal, noticing Sylvia's dishevelled hair. "Surely you haven't just got out of bed?" The two girls exchanged knowing looks.

Sylvia ignored the comment. "Robert, let's go to the coffee bar. I think I'm out of milk"

Theresa waved a half full bottle of milk at her.

"Thanks, but I could do with some fresh air." Sylvia jerked her head towards the door, gesturing for Robert to follow.

As they left the kitchen Sylvia could see Theresa and Liz whispering. It could be no great mystery as to what the subject of their gossip would be. Well, it was better they thought she'd spent the night with Robert, rather than knowing what she'd really been doing.

***

Tynemouth - October 2009

Rebecca couldn't believe it was Thursday already and that the half-term week was really beginning to fly by. She could say with all honesty that the job was becoming increasingly more difficult. Incredibly, she had now been teaching for almost five years. It was amazing how quickly the time had flown, but the truth had to be faced, that she definitely wasn't looking forward to returning to school. She had already done a lot of preparation for next half term, but had been forced to bring her laptop with her as there was plenty of *extra, essential* work that needed to be done. She really couldn't face taking the wretched piece of equipment out of her bag but she was forced to acknowledge that she had little choice in the matter.

If only this puzzling aunt had left her some money aside from the house, then Rebecca would willingly have given up her job. She was slowly coming around to Caroline's way of thinking. Renovating the house, with perhaps a little supply teaching thrown into the mix to keep her hand in. Giving this place a much needed make over would have been a brilliant way to spend her time and also help her escape from a job she was increasingly starting to loathe. But that just wasn't a viable option with no additional funds. She knew she shouldn't delude herself into imagining she had enough for the electrics, plumbing, plastering, tiling and goodness know what else that needed to be done.

She felt that familiar sick feeling in her stomach when she reluctantly switched on her laptop. To add to her gloom, she was sure that just after Christmas the school would have a delightful visit from Ofsted and she really couldn't abide the thought of going through another one of those. Although she wasn't involved in the management of the school, there were too many issues that needed to be addressed. Everyone knew what the outcome would be, and what that would mean for the staff – more work, more pressure, more stress. She wished there was someone else she could think of that she could trust to give her some unbiased advice.

Certainly not her parents. They didn't have a clue about how miserable her job was really making her.

She didn't feel able to discuss it with her mother. She would just urge her to sell the property as quickly and unprofitably as possible. Likewise her father, because although she loved him dearly and she knew the feeling was mutual, he would just side with his wife. He allowed himself to be ridiculously henpecked by her domineering mother. And could she really face contacting Caroline again? It seemed regrettable, but if she wanted answers to her questions, she would have to.

She slammed the lid down on her computer in frustration. She knew she needed to get out to clear her head.

As Rebecca left the house, the irritating neighbour from next door was also closing his front door and was obviously just about to walk up the street alongside her. She had been annoyed to see him in the bookshop and she certainly didn't have any desire to keep bumping into him. Diving back into her hallway to pretend she had forgotten something would just look ridiculous.

"Hi there, I guess you must be Rebecca,"

His voice was unexpectantly pleasant and his accent obviously not local. She also noticed that his shirt and jeans needed ironing. And how did he know her name?

"Have you settled in okay?"

"Yes thanks," this was not a conversation she could be bothered with, especially after his selfish behaviour with his loud music. She pretended to look for something in her bag, hoping this would bring the discussion to an end.

"So, how long are you here for? Have you decided what you are going to do with your aunt's house?"

She was actually starting to feel quite angry. How did he know all this information about her, and what business was it of his anyway?

"I haven't made any decisions yet but actually there was something that I had been wanting to mention to you." She thought she might as well use this unwanted encounter for some practical purpose.

"Oh dear, that sounds ominous," grinned Sebastian. "Surely even I can't have done anything to upset you in such a short space of time. I mean you've only been here since Sunday…"

"Well … it's the noise. When the estate agent came round the other day, the cacophony of noise coming from your flat made us both wince. The volume was way too high and it could hardly be defined as music."

"Cacophony."

"Yes, cacophony – look it up."

"And not music?"

"Hardly."

"I'm sorry, but how was I supposed to know you had an Estate Agent round?"

The tone of his voice didn't imply any regret and she could no longer bite her tongue.

"I'm surprised you didn't because you seem to know everything else about me and my movements since I arrived here!" Rebecca's cheeks flushed angrily.

Sebastian burst out laughing. "My Uncle ... I work in his bookshop and I've heard him talking to Caroline about you. They're friends. You saw me there when you came into the shop the other day. In fact, I was a bit mystified. You looked so furious to see me. I could understand this if we'd met before but you had me well confused..."

"Just try to keep the volume down. That's all I'm asking from you,"

"The cacophony."

"Just keep the volume down – please."

It come as no great surprise to Rebecca that Caroline had been gossiping about her. In fact, she had probably told him to play music as loudly as possible so she couldn't get a good price for the house.

" Now, if you'll excuse me," said Rebecca. "I have things to do." She turned her back and smiled as she walked down the street, feeling quite pleased that she had confused him.

Having no particular plan as to where she was going, Rebecca wandered about the streets aimlessly. She walked for quite some distance, more than three miles, as Tynemouth turned into Cullercoats then further on to the faded seaside resort of Whitley Bay. The ghostly pavilion dome of the Spanish City was left in a badly neglected state surrounded by a tall wooden fence. At various points were posters showing artists' interpretation of what the dome would look like after restoration but there seemed little progress judging by the dates on the posters

She walked on past the dome and stopped in front of a small shop that caught her eye for some inexplicable reason- *'Madame Llyriad. True Clairvoyant. Step inside and have your future revealed.'* It was impossible to see inside as thick, black curtains covered in spangled stars and mysterious-looking symbols screened the windows. There were photographs of minor celebrities pictured alongside the acclaimed lady with her ample frame and long raven black hair. Rebecca had always been dismissive of claivoyants, but had never actually been as close to one as she now was. She felt strangely intrigued. After all, she thought, it was only some harmless fun, it couldn't do any damage and it might, just might, give her some idea of what to do next.

***

Tynemouth - October 2009

Sebastian arrived at the shop late as usual and found his Uncle sitting on a battered, leather armchair, staring into space, deep in thought. After two 'good mornings' had no reply, Sebastian went to make himself a coffee, thinking that it was perhaps best to leave him alone. For the past couple of days his Uncle had definitely been troubled by something but he didn't feel it was his place to ask. Sebastian was actually quite a sensitive soul but didn't like to reveal this to others. It hadn't escaped his attention what had happened yesterday, when the old man with the shuffling walk and shoulder-length, white hair had come into the shop. Robert had scurried off and hidden at the back like a frightened animal.

Sebastian had watched the man look at some expensive, old additions that his uncle kept: archaic Northumbrian maps and folklore of the local area. He hadn't been surprised, considering the prices of the books, when the man tottered out of the shop without buying anything. Certainly, the man didn't look like anyone to be frightened of, in fact he looked positively ill, but Sebastian had sensed the fear in his uncle. It was quite disturbing. He didn't know much about his Uncle Robert's life before he had come to own the bookshop but his mother, Robert's sister, had hinted at him having a nomadic and irregular lifestyle. There was clearly something alarming his uncle and he was sure that Caroline Eastern was somehow involved.

Sebastian began tidying shelves, dusting and placing books back in the correct order. He smiled, remembering his encounter with Rebecca, especially when she had reprimanded him as if he was one of her naughty pupils. At least he now knew why she had looked at him with daggers when she had come into the shop yesterday. He didn't even think he'd been playing his music particularly loudly. She had been even more furious that he had known information about her and it had really amused him immensely to wind her up.

He thought he should have been more elusive about his connection with her Aunt's friend, Caroline. Still it had been good fun. Sebastian enjoyed to tease people but not, he had convinced himself, in an unkind way. In fact, he might knock on her door later on to ask her if she would like to go out for a drink with him, even if it served no other purpose than to further antagonize her

Chapter 10
Lancaster University- April 1979

Robert took a long cold drink from his pint of cider, not feeling quite able to process accurately the events that had transpired in the last few hours. Feeling as if he were in some type of heady trance, he placed his straight glass upon the brown formica table top, stared at the dream-like figures from the jazz-age that were painted as a mural on the wall and listened to the haunting sound of 'Don't Fear the Reaper' by The Blue Oyster Cult. It was playing on the jukebox in the corner of the bar next to the flashing pinball machine. Were his feelings reciprocated or had it just been an outlet for the delirium the experiences of the previous night had induced in her? Well he guessed only time would tell as to her true feelings for him but Robert knew he was under her spell and he knew he would do whatever she asked, no matter how ridiculous and preposterous it seemed to him or anyone else. He wasn't humiliated by it. He knew it was just a fact. He couldn't do anything about it.

At first, as they had sat on the orange plastic chairs in the coffee shop, drinking their instant coffees from the glass cups and saucers, Sylvia had seemed disturbingly self-absorbed and cagey. However, there was also a strange glow about her, as if she were party to ancient riddles and untold mysteries. The enigmatic smile that played about her lips had a touch of the Mona Lisa. Robert was concerned. He was glad to see her happy but there was something alarming about her mood, something he couldn't quite read or place his finger upon. There was a disconcerting, manic quality, as if such elation was bound to have an unpleasant flipside. Sylvia took little sips from her cup then looked about the 'Greasepit', as the café was known. It seemed as if, even in here, of all places, she was taking a perverse pleasure from her unsavoury surroundings. The air was thick, as if an unpleasant cloud-like matter had enveloped the room with pungent smells of bacon, sausage and fat. Yet it didn't matter to him where they were. Robert was just happy to be with her. But he needed to keep focused, because importantly, he needed to find out what had been happening.

He couldn't think of where to start so opted for the direct approach, dived in and hoped for the best.

"So where were you last night Sylvia?" Robert began, avoiding her eyes, "I couldn't sleep… so I went for a walk past your room quite late… but there was no sign of you working. The lights were all off." He failed to deliver the all-important question with the casual nonchalance he was hoping for.

"Oh, I just finished my essay quicker than I thought I would, so I went to sleep."

Sylvia also seemed reluctant to make eye-contact. Robert was surprised that she didn't seem at all bothered that he had been spying on her. He had been expecting to be told to mind his own business in no uncertain terms, so he continued to dig deeper. He knew he was right in the middle of a minefield, tip-toeing about, wondering which way to go.

"Then, as I was about to return to my room, I saw you." He challenged her and Sylvia's face immediately looked startled.

"What?"

"I saw you when I was going back to my room."

"What d'you mean – saw me?"

He knew this all sounded very weird but he couldn't stop now.

"You were dressed in a strange cloak and you were behaving in a very peculiar manner."

"*I* was behaving in peculiar manner. It's a wonder you weren't arrested – snooping about in the girl's block."

"It wasn't like that."

"Wasn't it? I didn't see you – you must have been hiding. Were you?"

"Well I …"

"So, you were hiding."

"I don't think you would have noticed me anyway."

"Where were you hiding – in the bushes? This gets better and better."

"Look, I know it sounds strange but…"

"So, you admit you were being strange."

"I was just looking out for you."

"I don't need you to. I don't need someone lurking in the bushes and snooping on me."

"Don't you? Maybe you do?"

"God's sake Robert. What *are* you talking about?"

"I'm talking about you acting strangely, going about in the middle of the night, wearing a cloak and looking as if you're high. In fact, you're still acting strangely now. What's going on Sylvia?" Robert was surprised by his own tenacity and instantly wondered if he would regret it.

"I don't know what you mean Robert," snapped Sylvia. "What business is it of yours what I do? Since when did you become one of my parents?" She tossed her hair like the mane of a bad-tempered horse and her cheeks crimsoned angrily.

"Well, I'm just saying, y'know … you have to be careful."

"Have to? Have to? I don't have to do bloody anything. I can look after myself. I don't need anyone to tell me what to do."

Robert winced. He looked about the café searching for some words from anywhere. Someone was clumping about in his stomach with big, heavy boots. There was nothing else for it.

"Well, I'm saying this because…because I care Sylvia. Something bizarre seems to be happening in your life and I'm worried about you, that's all. You told me you had to finish an essay last night but quite clearly, well…you were out. Weren't you?" Despite finding her fury so annoyingly attractive, Robert took a deep breath and continued. "I'm saying this because I … I … y'know… we haven't known each other long but I … I just don't want anything bad happening to you. I … I really care about you Sylvia. I'm sorry if that offends you … but there it is. I really care about you." Robert looked awkwardly at Sylvia, knowing he had said more than he should have. It wasn't like him to wear his heart on his sleeve and as a result he was now waiting to be delivered a killer blow, either verbal or perhaps even physical.

Sylvia sat very quietly and thought. She arranged, then rearranged her eyebrows, trying to find a suitable place for them to settle. Her mouth contorted and twisted as if she was trying to spit. She was flattered by his words. She didn't want to torment him anymore. She also felt as if she would burst if she didn't divulge her secrets to someone else. Although she had been told not to breathe a word to anyone, Robert had just proved himself worthy of her trust.

"Okay Robert, okay. I'll tell you but you mustn't tell a single soul," she said flatly, trying to hide her excitement imagining his reaction to her revelations. Robert knew at last he was getting to somewhere near the truth.

Then Sylvia proceeding to launch into an account of such incredulous nonsense to Robert's ears, that it surpassed any of the previous notions he had ever heard from her before. Apparently, there was a Moon Goddess who needed to be worshipped alongside a horned Green Man god. Their happiness was paramount in order to maintain the stability of the Universe and the balance of nature. This was the main reason for global warming and climactic shifts apparently. Robert hadn't really paid attention to all the details, but it seemed that St. Cuthbert, although probably unbeknown to him, had somehow been dragged into the ridiculous equation.

So last night, she had been to some ceremony connected with this. Robert dutifully nodded, pretending that her secrets, ceremonies and preposterous subterfuge made some sense. But he didn't care, Sylvia was sharing this with him and to him that was all that was important. More significantly to him, was that there had been no mention of any other man in her life and this was what mostly had concerned him. At least she didn't seem to have fallen under the spell of some Lothario, and this pleased him greatly. The tumbling tirade of gibberish that he had been subjected to, was, in fact, music to his ears.

"Robert, I'm so pleased you know and you…you will be so grateful to me opening your eyes to all this, when you've experienced what I have. Don't you think?"

He was caught, completely ensnared. She was sharing her bizarre secrets with him and all Robert could do was nod his head in agreement.

"I knew I could trust you with… all this. And I know you won't breathe a word to anyone." She put a finger across her lips. "Other people wouldn't understand… but I knew you would because… well, you're just like me. Don't you think??"

"'Course I am," Robert answered quickly, not wishing to spoil this precious moment, "It sounds…amazing, wonderful."

Sylvia gazed at him, unblinking. A slow, warm smile flowed across her face, lighting the blue touch paper.

"Come with me," she said.

***

Whitley Bay- October 2009

Hearing the shop bell jingle, Madame Llyriad stubbed out her cigarette quickly in the ashtray, placed it behind a bookshelf and then gave the room a quick blast of jasmine air-freshener, before bidding her client to enter through the heavy, purple curtain. Her mouth came slightly ajar as she stared at her customer, overwhelmed at what seemed like a golden aura emanating from the girl. Forcing a smile, she introduced herself.

"Good morning, my name is Madame Llyriad. And how may I be of assistance?" Her voice rasped, largely due to the number of cigarettes she had smoked that day already.

"Morning," replied Rebecca, holding on to the curtain, letting the bright daylight help her adjust to the darkness. She could see the small room had no windows and was dimly lit by a small table lamp. Wisps of tobacco smoke floated upwards. Rebecca stifled a cough and wrinkled her nose. Before her she saw a large woman sitting at a circular table. Rebecca could make out an abundance of gold and silver bracelets, and the woman jangled at the slightest movement. Madame Llyriad remained silent for a few, drama-inducing moments longer.

"The fee for a basic reading is £10." Said Madame Llyriad eventually. "Which I think you must agree is very reasonable." She cleared her throat. "If it takes longer than half an hour then this will be reflected in the price."

"Of course, I am sure the basic will be ample." Rebecca nodded and considered Llyriad's predictably clairvoyant appearance of long black hair, dark rimmed spectacles, and big, round earrings. She wore a long, billowing, dark top, a flowing bright red, chiffon scarf, lots of thick make-up and jewellery. Her face was fleshy and the bright lipstick reminded her of Caroline's.

Madame Llyriad gestured for her to take a seat on a shabby armchair in front of a table covered in a variety of crystal balls, runestones and other intriguing fortune-telling paraphernalia. Rebecca edged forward, sat and winced, both from the stale tobacco smell in the room and the clichés all around her.

"And how in particular can I help you?" The fortune teller enquired, staring curiously at Rebecca.

"Well I'm …er…I'm not quite sure what to…you see I was … I was wondering if you could tell me what the future may bring me as…. as I have very importance decisions …very important decisions … that I need to make … as soon as possible."

Rebecca's jumbled, awkward words unsettled Llyriad even more. There was a certain familiarity about the accent. It was an educated version but through the long, flattened vowels, lilt, and nuances of speech she could almost pinpoint exactly from where it came. Many years ago, she had had experience of that part of the country.

Rebecca looked about the room uncomfortably, feeling the need to avoid eye contact with the older woman, yet becoming more and more fascinated by the strange fortune telling equipment displayed all around.

"And...I feel you are a spiritual person?" Madame Llyriad removed her glasses to rub her eyes and instantly looked less foreboding.

"Yes...yes...I suppose I might be. I have never really thought about it."

"Never thought about it?" Madame Llyriad repeated the words, slightly clicking her tongue, producing a peculiar sound, reminding Rebecca of a dripping tap.

"No – yes – sorry, I am. I am a spiritual person."

"Don't worry," said Madame Llyriad trying to sound comforting." There's nothing to be worried about. Tell me...have you looked for answers before...in this kind of place?"

"No...I haven't...I've often thought about it. But I am open to..." Rebecca's words trailed off. She was uncertain as to what she was open to and was beginning to think this was an extremely bad idea. The woman was obviously a fraud and she should lighten up and treat it as a bit of fun. But this was more easily said than done.

"Again- no need to worry or be nervous. It's completely painless." Madame Llyriad managed a low, grating chuckle and Rebecca took this as her cue to smile.

"Have you lived here long? I can sense from your speech that you are not local to this area." Llyriad attempted to ask the question in as unconcerned manner as possible, as she affected great interest in the bag of rune stones.

"No. I'm not from here. Just visiting …for a few days."

"And you say you have to make some very important decisions." She held a pebble in her fingers tracing her long fingernail meaningfully around its edge.

"Yes." That was all. Rebecca was determined not to give her anymore help.

"And you only have a few days to do this." There was something disturbingly familiar about this girl thought Llyriad.

"Yes"

"Well we must see if we can help you." Llyriad shuffled and jangled uncomfortably in her seat, aware she was making a faux pas. No reliable clairvoyant would ask such questions of a client. Llyriad was glad that the girl seemed a novice to this type of discussion so hopefully would be unaware of the usual protocol. There was something about this girl that had raised alarm bells, but she must make sure she didn't let this show …

"You are right to explore every available avenue to help you make your decisions." Madame Llyriad lowered her voice and spoke slowly and levelly, attempting to create the right atmosphere in the room. She replaced the runestones carefully back into their bag. "An educated guess is not good enough. We need to be sure. And I am sure I can help you. Let me consult these first of all," Llyriad began, as she removed some colourful tarot cards from a black, silken scarf. "Let's see what the ancient wisdom has to share with us."

She met the girl straight in the eye and immediately had the unsettling feeling that she was looking into a familiar face from long ago. There was something about this girl. She couldn't quite place it - but she would.

Llyriad's bracelets clanked again as she passed the cards to the young woman and asked her to shuffle them. Rebecca fumbled, spilling the cards onto the table before rearranging them clumsily in the pack.

"Make sure you shuffle them well, entirely to your satisfaction," said Madame Llyriad, watching Rebecca closely. "It is very important that you are entirely happy with the way the cards will fall. They will give you the answers you are looking for so it is vital to make sure they are gathered together to your complete satisfaction."

Rebecca nodded, took a few more moments to shuffle the cards and then handed them back. Madame Llyriad received the cards carefully, with overly dramatic caution, as if they were a tiny, delicate, damaged bird awaiting release, emphasising her, and their importance, and ensuring that Rebecca was suitably impressed.

The clairvoyant slowly placed the pack on the table to one side of her and let her hand gently caress the top card before purposefully clasping both hands together as if in prayer and regarding Rebecca with her practised, 'all knowing look' for several seconds. It was her favourite pose and she always enjoyed this part of her performance, establishing her power, gaining the trust of the client, relishing their reverence and ensuring control of what was to follow. Rebecca made a huge effort to remain still but then shifted uneasily in her seat, forcibly fixing her eyes on the cards, unwilling to show the old woman how nervous she had become.

Llyriad, without taking her eyes off Rebecca, slipped one card from the top of the pack and placed it face down in front of her. Slowly she took four others and placed them face down around the first card, one above, one below and one to either side. She looked thoughtfully at the cards, blinked behind her large glasses like a wise old owl, then set some further cards out on the table to align in the order of the Celtic Cross.

Sombrely turning over the cards, Madame Llyriad wiped some beads of sweat from her face, then began to describe, with suitable gravitas, what she saw before her in the arrangement of the cards.

"Firstly, in the centre, we have the unpredictable 'Juggler', who represents: willpower, initiative, cleverness and skill. Possibly this person represents you, showing that something new and important in your life has already started. Great changes are happening all around you but you must beware of swindling, cheating and trickery."

Llyriad took a sip from the glass of water beside her then looked hopefully at Rebecca for some response. Thankfully the girl was hanging on her every word so this was enough for her to continue with this difficult reading.

"Behind you in the recent past lies 'Temperance'. This represents an oppressive, controlled environment, where no doubt you were safe but all things were moderated and you felt stifled and repressed." Llyriad paused for a moment once more, to acknowledge any recognition in the girl's face before looking at the next card.

"Oh yes that's my childhood," blurted Rebecca, she couldn't contain the shrillness in her her voice as she clasped her hands together. "That so describes how I was brought up."

Llyriad nodded, pleased that her words seemed to be striking a chord.

"The Queen of Swords of Swords sits above," Llyriad looked woeful, rolling her eyes upwards as if in receipt of some divine heavenly intervention, "You should beware of this woman! This woman may appear charming, delightful and intelligent…but her childish petulance is the least of her evils. She is a capable of cruelty, malice and deceit. She appears to have your best interests at heart but beware of her. The woman has her own plan and is not to be trusted. "

"Oh, oh, yes, oh yes, I think I know who that is," Rebecca whispered, an image of a beaming Caroline filling her mind.

"Below we have The Moon." The fortune teller's voice became even more intense.

Rebecca was beginning to feel quite uneasy. The words were mesmerising and seemed to contain uncanny accuracy about her situation that the woman couldn't possible have known. Rebecca had expected a charlatan but now she wasn't so sure…

"This sorrowful card stands for darkness, fear and bewilderment." Madame Llyriad's face had taken on a strange look of elation, at odds with the terrible future she was predicting, "All around there are hidden things looking for retribution which maybe not obviously connected with you. They are related to wrongs committed years ago but need to be avenged."

Rebecca was becoming paler by the moment. She hung on every word. What she had spoken of earlier had made a lot of sense. This made no sense whatsoever and didn't sound at all good.

"Usually, swords are not favourable cards," Llyriad's eyes were now glazed and her voice high pitched as if she were no longer in control of the words, "but this shows a great power that can be used by you for good or evil."

She looked at Rebecca for some affirmation but Rebecca just stared back.

"You have stresses and strains caused by work," Madame Llyriad attempted to moderate the level of her voice, worried that she might have overstepped the mark. "But you are fortunate because you have the power to enable you to do something about this. There is a way to end this. Also, there is more…."

Llyriad froze and held her head in her hands. What was she saying? This was dangerous talk. She needed to take over and control her tongue. She was beginning to feel exhausted and baffled as to where the words were coming from. She usually just made most of this up but perhaps she did indeed have some remarkable gift for prophesying the future. She rubbed her face, removing some of the white foundation to reveal her florid cheeks and she appeared suddenly ancient.

"And these other cards?" said Rebecca, hardly daring to ask.

Madame Llyriad took a moment to compose herself.

"Well, we have a lot of swords, which is generally bad news, but look." She picked up a green card depicting a couple in medieval dress being attacked by a cherub with a bow and arrow. "It's the 'Lovers'. Look, and here we have the 'Knight of Cups', a young man who is pleasant and affable but generally superficial, languid and idle. Does this sound like anyone you know?"

Rebecca shook her head but Llyriad had been studying her and she could tell from a slight slackening of her lips and a certain look in her eye that she wasn't telling the truth.

"I think that's all I can tell you for the present," said Madame Llyriad quietly. She looked at her watch, feeling drained and thankful to bring the session to an end. "However, the overwhelming message that the cards have to say is that your job is obviously bringing you much unhappiness. Llyriad tried to pull herself together and focus upon the least controversial part of this unsettling reading. "May I ask, do you work in these parts?"

Rebecca shook her head again, also feeling drained.

"This is where you belong Rebecca. The cards are telling you to stay around these parts. There may be difficult times, very difficult times. If you leave you risk serious danger, not necessarily for you. You have..." With a great effort, Llyriad stopped and struggled again to compose herself. *What's happening? Where are these words coming from? What the hell's going on?*

Rebecca and Llyriad looked at each other in silence for several seconds. The words were still in the room, solid and piercing but slowly vaporizing.

Eventually Madame Llyriad spoke. Her voice cracking and unsteady. "We must talk again. In fact, I insist we do soon. I know these meetings can be unsettling. I feel there are many more matters that I can clarify for you but my powers are spent for now."

Rebecca took ten pounds from her purse and placed it on the table. She nodded at the clairvoyant, pulled back the curtain to let the welcome sunlight stream in and then left, feeling even more confused and unsure about her future.

Llyriad, on the other hand, was very sure, and as soon as Rebecca left, she picked up her phone...

***

Preston- October 2009

Cynthia looked at the clock on the mantelpiece wondering what her daughter Rebecca was doing at this precise moment. By now she ought to have the house on the market, at some realistic price. The quicker it was sold the sooner they could forget this whole unpleasant incident and get on with their lives. However, if Rebecca was bent upon having a place of her own then at least she could make sure that she was living somewhere close by.

In fact, strangely enough, she thought, there was a property down this very road that had gone up for sale while Rebecca had been away. Although it looked like it needed quite a bit of love and attention, it was bound to be in a far better state of repair than the pile of junk she would have been left by Sylvia. Actually, it wouldn't be so bad after all if Rebecca were to live in this very street. After all, her and Bill had always been very happy here. It wasn't too noisy and it was considered a respectable area.

If Rebecca was to buy the perfectly pleasant house in Sycamore Road then she would be able to pop in and see her daughter whenever she liked. Most likely Rebecca would still want all of her laundry done too. Cynthia nodded to herself thinking that she had never known Rebecca show any interest in ironing clothes and she would probably expect her father to do all her gardening. It was quite preposterous really, Rebecca ever imagining that she could possibly live independently from them. She placed the house details that she had gathered from the Estate Agents and stuck them behind the clock to show her daughter when she returned, which was likely to be very soon now.

Bill would be able to help with the decorating. She would be able to advise Rebecca where to buy all the curtains and carpets, in fact it might bring her and her daughter closer together. They would soon have the house looking decent, just like the one Rebecca had been brought up in. Cynthia looked around at her neat and tidy home, with its meaningful knick-knacks, souvenirs from happy, family holidays in Scarborough, Pwllheli, and once, further afield in Torquay (it had been a mistake to travel that far because throughout the entire vacation she had worried about the ability of Bill's ancient, spluttering Ford Cortina to cope with the journey back), and felt a sense of pride in her home-making accomplishments.

She knew that the awful, stone cladding would have to be removed from the front of the building but she was sure that could be easily sorted by her husband. Also, she had seen from the pictures in the Estate Agent's window, that one room for some bizarre reason contained mock, oak beams and a tasteless addition of a miniature bar but these things were cosmetic and could be removed without too much bother. Most importantly, the price was quite reasonable, so Rebecca would have more than enough money to make a decent down payment and providing she saw the sense in buying this particular property she was sure that she and Bill could help out.

She recognised it was inevitable that Rebecca would wish to move out at some point. Cynthia was just about married by her age and they had already been planning the wedding for a couple of years. Rebecca, as a dedicated career woman (maybe she would become a headteacher one day) would naturally wish for her own house. This inheritance must have added to these notions, so maybe it was down to Cynthia to make the acquisition of number 21 Sycamore Road actually happen.

Cynthia gave one of her rare tight- lipped smiles. Things needn't be all that much different after all.

Chapter 11
North Shields - October 2009

Flipping indifferently through some wallpaper samples, Caroline found she was unable to concentrate on the task in hand. A royal blur design with fleur-de-lyse like daggers seemed to be pointing directly at her throat and she felt a familiar buzzing in her head.

Later that afternoon she was supposed to be having a meeting with a tiresome client named Maureen Campbell, who would be expecting to see plans for the decoration of the large sitting room in her detached house in Whitley Bay. Caroline's mind however, was just sitting in a lotus position, amongst a muddle of booklets, dreary colour swatches and lifeless paint charts, spectacularly uninterested. Recognising the symptoms of one of her migraines she wanted to cancel and take refuge in a darkened room, but she knew that she couldn't.

This week was progressing too rapidly for her liking. She had left Rebecca alone for a couple of days and she wondered if her encounter with Susan Hope had been sufficiently negative to force her decision. Surely, she must see that that it would be preposterous to overlook this gift of a house? Ultimately, she knew that it would be down to her, to make the girl see sense, especially after Robert's revelations last night. It was now even more crucial that the house wasn't put on the market, as it was only a matter of time until *he* came sniffing round again like some venerable nemesis. She looked despairingly at the charts of lime greens and russet browns for some guidance. It seemed as if the web she had spun for the past thirty years was now beginning to unravel at an alarming speed.

Of course, he might have been mistaken. It had been such a long time since either of them had seen the man, how could he possibly be sure that it was him? So many years of running and hiding had taken their toll on them, but surely, they must have also taken their toll on him. He had been so much older than the rest of them. He could be dead. As long as Sylvia had been alive and living in the house, they had been relatively safe.

Robert had accused her of being selfish and she knew deep in her heart that he had a point, but it just wasn't fair. For such a long time she had planned and schemed for events to happen, and when her friend had been near the end, she had only been too grateful once more to accommodate whatever Caroline wished. Quiet, unassuming Sylvia had been a dear friend for many years, and she missed her trustworthy, sensible opinions on a daily basis. She had been able to go around to her house to let off steam and Sylvia had just listened to her histrionics without passing judgement. Perhaps *she* should have just gone and lived in the house? That would have been the obvious solution so as not to involve Rebecca in any of these ancient unsettled scores?

If Robert was indeed right though, it wouldn't take that man too long to find them both. There was nothing at all to link Rebecca with events from the past and Caroline did truly wish she could get to know the girl better. Also, surely Rebecca couldn't be anything but delighted to escape from the clutches of her judgmental mother with her puritanical ways. Procrastination was no longer an option. She needed to talk once more with Rebecca to see if she had reached any decisions. Caroline picked up the phone to speak with Mrs. Campbell. If she wished to choose someone else to do her interior designs, well, that was fair enough because she had more important matters to attend to.

***

Whitley Bay- October 2009

After the girl had left, Llyriad poured herself a much needed, large gin and tonic. She was amazed at what had just happened but the drink soon packed its punch, enabling her to get some perspective on recent events. Looking in disbelief at the cards strewn in front of her on the table, she realised that for the first time ever she felt in awe of their power. Usually, she blagged her way through readings. Most people had lost somebody dear to them or were experiencing some problems with their love life. Generally, she just looked at their approximate age, style of dress and the expression on their faces to be able to ascertain the type of twaddle they were wanting to hear. But today something had been different. It was as if the cards were actually speaking through her and interpreting themselves. Llyriad had the sensation that she was merely the vessel for some power to express its thoughts and concerns. But now she knew she was being ridiculous. The days of such fanciful illusions were something she had long ago consigned to her delusional past.

Yet there had been a disconcerting familiarity about the young woman. From the moment she walked into the room she had sensed that there was something of great significance about the encounter. Although the girl at first appeared guileless, with an attractive innocence, Llyriad knew from bitter experience that appearances are often misleading. She picked up the cards again, to study their esoteric images more carefully, as she had done many times before. Searching again for some mystical inspiration.

The 'Queen of Sword's, outwardly charming but inwardly scheming and cruel, sneered at her. She sat on her throne triumphantly with her stolen crown balanced on her long, tousled curls. However, she was a fake. These treasures were not rightfully hers and she was little better than a common thief. What was the significance of this scornful woman who had taken from others what was rightfully theirs? Llyriad of course knew the answer to this question.

Next, she scrutinized the strange 'Juggler' or 'Magician', the first card of the Major Arcana. On the card a novice trickster dressed in flamboyant clothes stood behind a wooden table mystified by a peculiar array of implements, like pieces of mismatched jigsaw puzzles that he is unable to piece together. He had weapons, knives and a whole range of dangerous tools at his disposal but he is ignorant of their significance. This will change however because he is clever and will soon learn the manipulative skills needed. These two characters would make a dangerous and formidable pair. But for whose benefit was she now interpreting these cards?

Most worrying or enlightening of all was the appearance of the' Moon' with its disturbing connotations of darkness, danger, fear and bewilderment. Two dogs were baying at a scornful moon which regarded them with indifference as a secretive scorpion observed the action, hidden beneath the waters. So, thought Llyriad, there are hidden enemies, a crisis to be dealt with but most importantly to her, a coming retribution which would soon be delivered for injustices that were committed long, long ago. As soon as Rebecca had left, Llyriad had made her urgent phone call and she could picture the smiling face on the other end of the line. Many years may have passed but scores still needed to be settled. She poured herself another drink, less tonic this time. It had been a remarkable piece of good fortune and she was now certain from where she remembered those eyes, that similar voice and those mannerisms. She nodded to herself and the waves of fat under her chin rippled luxuriantly.

***

Lancaster University- May 1979

It was one of those bright, May mornings, that was almost just a little too perfect. Spring was now in its full swing, with additional slides, seesaws and roundabouts. The blossoms were falling from branches like pink and white confetti.

"Isn't this wonderful Robert?" Sylvia breathed in deeply, savouring the fragrant air. "Did you ever think that the world could look quite so perfect?"

He watched her animated face, spellbound. "No, Sylvia," he couldn't think quite what to say, as he had never really given the trees, birds and flowers much consideration before. They were something that were just there during the different seasons.

"I knew you would understand Robert. You get it. It's because you and I are the same. I bet you can't wait to meet everyone soon?"

"Yes, yes, of course. It'll be great. They all sound fascinating," Robert lied. He was trying to push the forthcoming events of that evening, when Sylvia would be off to one of her strange meetings, to the back of his mind. He just wanted to concentrate on enjoying this moment, but he had a feeling he wouldn't be allowed to do that.

"You would probably recognize some people there. There's a boy called Neil from my history group … and you know Leo. He's often sitting by himself in the bar ... but they don't call themselves by these names you know."

"I'm not sure I understand why they use different names. Isn't that just confusing?" Robert tried to remain interested. He knew that would please her.

"No, of course not. When we're together we use our Requisite names. Leo is Loic and Neil's name is Cedonia. But the person I'm most grateful to is Llyriad, she found me and introduced me to everyone. She's wonderful. I know you're going to like her as much as I do."

Robert didn't feel quite so sure about that but thought he had better keep these opinions to himself.

"So, do you have one of these peculiar names then?"

"Of course. I do have a *peculiar* name. My name is Aradnia, Arr-ad-nee-ya." She pronounced proudly.

"I prefer Sylvia. It's a lovely name. I've never met anyone with that name before. It's unusual. Sylvan ... from the trees."

"Well, that's as maybe but I prefer Aradnia - far more regal." She sat up straight, adopting a stately pose. "Sylvia is a horrible name, I think my parents only chose it because it sounds similar to Cynthia, my sister's equally unattractive name. How many other people do you know with names like those? Cynthia and Sylvia. We both have middle-aged women's names. Not cool, definitely not cool." She twisted her face.

"Well, I like them both, they're both unusual names. Where did you get that name Aradnia from anyway?"

"There's some books Llyriad showed me. There was one about St. Cuthbert and Celtic Christianity, another full of Celtic names and one on Wicca and Wiccan names. We get the names from these books. Some people try to choose one similar to their given name. Llyriad's real name is Lydia. But I just chose mine because I liked the sound of it."

"Oh well then, maybe I should be called Rumplestilskin."

"Don't be ridiculous."

He knew he had made a mistake. "I know...you know, I was just messing about. But I still don't understand why people give themselves different names... I mean, surely that in itself is a little ... erm...."

Sylvia gave him a disapproving look.

"Anyway," continued Robert. "What's St. Cuthbert got to do with any of this? Surely the closest religion to the Requisite is paganism. You said some of those names themselves were from Wiccan sources. St. Cuthbert was an early Christian monk. I can't see any connection with him at all." Robert was actually studying Early Christianity and he was genuinely intrigued.

"Well, I mean, there are lots of things I don't understand fully but... I think it's something connected with Celtic Christianity." Sylvia stared into space, struggling to recall what she had read from Llyriad's book.

Robert waited a few seconds and then decided to help her out. "Okay, I know that when Christianity first came to Britain, some places, particularly those in the North, followed a type of Christianity that had come from Ireland not Rome. It was a different type of Christianity but nevertheless it was still Christian."

"Well, yes," said Sylvia. "But my understanding is ... that Celtic Christianity still retained many of the pre-Christian pagan features, you know, equality of women, harmony with nature, awareness of spiritual places, and St. Cuthbert, well, this is the type of Christianity he followed."

"He might have done initially... but not after the Synod of Whitby in, in, when was it again ... yes, 664 A.D."

"Well, wow," said Sylvia in mock surprise. "We really need to update your sticker chart by the end of the day. Okay, so when you join ...then you'll be able to ask somebody who knows more than I do. However ..." She looked at her watch and then punched him on the arm, "...come on Rumplestilskin - look at the time. We both have things we should to be doing."

Chapter 12

Durham - August 1104

In the seventh century, the area that was to become the kingdom of Northumbria was a wild, untamed land. Its pagan inhabitants worshipped gods as savage as themselves. Their religion was ruled by myth and magic, and cloaked in mysterious beliefs. The influence of the Romans had long since vanished. Although King Edwin, from his Royal Palace at Al Gefrin, enlisted the help of Paulinus, a Christian missionary, to baptize his subjects, his efforts became futile when King Cadwallon of Gwynedd invaded Northumbria, defeated and killed King Edwin at the battle of Hatfield Chase in 633 A.D. and seized the throne.

Edwin's son Oswald raised a small army and against all odds defeated the massed forces of Cadwallon at the Battle of Heavenfield in 634 A.D. According to legend on the night before the battle a worried Oswald was visited in a vision by St Columba and told he would be victorious. After a monumental struggle, the pagan forces were defeated, and Cadwallon was killed. At this very same time, a boy was born in the Border Hills who was destined to become one of the greatest religious icons of the North. His name was Cuthbert.

After the successful outcome of the Battle of Heavenfield, Oswald lost no time in sending for missionaries to reconvert the Northumbrians to Christianity. He developed a special bond with Aidan, an Irish monk from the island of Iona who set up a monastery and school at Lindisfarne. Aidan lived a frugal life and he persuaded the laity to do likewise. The monastery established by Aidan flourished and its monks helped found churches and other monasteries all over the North.

Seventeen years after arriving in Northumbria, Aidan died while at Bamburgh Castle where he had fallen ill.

On a deep, cloudless night, a shepherd named Cuthbert, was tending a flock in the Border Hills. While his companions slept Cuthbert watched and prayed. A shaft of bright light suddenly streamed from the sky and through it he saw a heavenly host descend to earth. He saw the host take up a shining bright soul and then returned to heaven. Cuthbert was deeply moved and the following morning discovered that Aidan, the much-loved Bishop of Lindisfarne had died that very night at Bamburgh. This so profoundly affected Cuthbert that he immediately returned the sheep he was tending to their owner and set off for the monastery at Melrose.

Although through his life Cuthbert had followed a path of simplicity and seclusion from the world, his cult was curiously marked by opulence and splendour. In death he was honoured like a great king. His shrine was magnificent. His body dressed in splendid garments as befitted his status. These included a fine white dalmatic (long sleeved vestment), a silk chasuble (outer garment) and a gold embroidered alb (white clothing similar to a surplice). He was wrapped in a beautiful Byzantine, embroidered silk cloth given by the Abbess Verca, with intricate stitching and fine ornamentations. The saint was laid to rest, but amazingly, eleven years later, when his tomb was exhumed, his body was found to be totally incorrupt. This was seen as a miracle, enhancing |Cuthbert's reputation and iconic status.

In 995 the 'community of Cuthbert' was founded and settled at Durham, guided by what they believed was the will of the saint. During the medieval period, Cuthbert became politically important, defining the identity of the people living in the semi-autonomous region known as the Liberty of Durham, which later became the Palatinate of Durham. Within this area, the Bishop of Durham came to have almost as much power as the king of England, and the saint became a powerful symbol of the autonomy the region enjoyed. The inhabitants of the Palatinate became known as the 'Haliwerfolc', ('The people of the saint'), and they believed that Cuthbert would protect them from outside threats. They believed that the saint would reward their devotion by using his saintly powers to defend his people and punish those who would harm them. A proliferation of miracles occurred, with pilgrims travelling vast distances to reach the glorious spectacle of the shrine, richly decorated with gold and jewels, to experience the magical healing powers of the saint.

A day of great significance occurred on the 29th of August 1104 for the followers of Cuthbert. As before, he was to be laid to rest in his newly built feretory shrine in Durham Cathedral. It was decided that the prior and nine brethren should open the coffin to examine the body. After deep prayer, mixed with fear and hesitation, they gathered enough resolution for the daunting task. Admittedly, they were afraid of God's displeasure but more worrying they might find that the miracle they had believed for the past 400 years may be no longer true.

Eventually encouraged by a particularly pious monk named Leofwin, they decided to go ahead and move the coffin from behind the high altar to the middle of the quire where there was more space. Upon removing the lid they found the venerated body lying on his side in perfect condition, as if he were merely sleeping. But this wasn't all that they found inside…

The other monks were overcome with joy and hysteria, weeping and prostrating themselves, but Leofwin was more concerned with the other objects that were inside the coffin. Nobody paid attention to him as he began re-arranging an ivory comb, a pair of scissors, a golden cross necklace and silver-worked chalice along with the most beautifully worked piece of tapestried silk he had ever seen in his life. As the other monks were preoccupied with chanting their penitential prayers, nobody noticed Leofwin slipping out of the cathedral with a bundle tucked inside his habit.

Once outside of the cathedral Leofwin began running fast. He wasn't a young man, yet, from somewhere he found a miraculous energy. He ran like never before in his life, through the streets, into the countryside and deep within Hamsterley Forest. Even then, he didn't stop because he daren't.

As Durham disappeared, so he began to wonder how he could have committed such a dreadful crime. He had not just stolen a religious artefact but had desecrated the grave of the adored saint. He, the holy brother Leofwin, had committed this appalling act. How could this have happened? This profanity was so totally out of keeping with his character, yet he hadn't been able help himself. Even though he hadn't had time yet to examine it properly, he knew he had never seen anything so exquisite before and now… it was his. His shame had been superseded by an inexplicable exhilarating force. Once he had seen the mesmerising fabric, he had no choice.

Hours later, he came upon a stream in a clearing in the woods. Dawn was breaking and he was exhausted so he knelt down and gulped from the water. He took the treasure from inside his robe and spread in out on the ground. As the images unfurled in front of him, he gasped.

In the centre of the shimmering, silvery fabric was the image of a Goddess with wild, raven-coloured hair, topped by a magnificent diadem, encrusted with scarlet, ruby and blue, sapphire gems. Her beautiful, powerful face and outstretched hand seemed ready to enslave the unwary. Around her lay grapes, figs and pomegranates. Beneath her, green and turquoise threads represented water, and the water was filled with sea creatures. He could see that the Goddess, the siren, had not one fishtail but two.

The silk was absolutely exquisite, even in the pale light, but what was it and what did the designs mean? Certainly, this woman had no place in Christianity. This was no Mary of that he was certain. With a strange beguiling smile the goddess on the cloth, with her beguiling, exotic beauty, seemed to compel him to worship her.

How, by all that is holy, he thought, had this marvellous, silk tapestry found its way into the coffin of St. Cuthbert? But most importantly for him at the moment were two questions. Where should he go now? What should he do with the cloth?

Running his hands across the fabric he felt a further surge of energy and a sense of total devotion to his mysterious Goddess. Leofwin was overwhelmed with a sense of tranquillity and well-being such as he had never encountered before.

***

St. Cuthbert's Cave, Northumberland – June 1979

Realising fully the horrific consequences of their actions, Robert and Sylvia ran back to their car. Negotiating the downward paths was difficult in their bulky cloaks. Scire lay at the foot of the cave with dark figures dashing to his lifeless body. Soon the others would realise what had happened. They would be after them and they would want revenge. In the darkness Sylvia stumbled on a rock. She held on a tree to steady herself.

"You alright?" Robert grabbed her arm.

"Yes, yes - just keep running."

The flames from the torches were becoming smaller. Robert's battered old mini was coming into view. Thank God they hadn't travelled with the others to this place, she thought. She darted a look over her shoulder. No sign of anybody following them yet.

She wrenched the car door open. "Robert, I'm sorry. It's all my fault. There was no need for you …."

"Just get in Sylvia," Robert snapped, "We just need to get away from here as fast as possible. There's some really scary people back there. They truly believe in all that craziness. They won't take kindly to what's just happened. We've just ruined their sacred ceremony and killed one of their leaders. God knows what they'll do if they catch us."

"Kill us, I should imagine," Sylvia said vacantly.

Robert gave her a quick, worried glance and then started the temperamental engine with immediate relief.

Sylvia suddenly remembered she was still naked under the cloak and despite the overriding terror, she was feeling slightly ridiculous and longed to be wearing her normal clothes. Robert was silent and concentrating on driving. The car hurtled dangerously through the dark, country lanes. He didn't want to use his headlights but he had to. He reasoned that they were travelling south but there had been no signposts as yet.

At least five minutes of silence was broken by Sylvia. "Robert, Robert, I am so, so sorry. There was no reason for you to be involved in all this nonsense."

"You already said that Sylvia. You didn't force me to become involved. It was my decision - even if it was a stupid one. Anyway, let's just concentrate on getting back to Lancaster. We can work out what to do when we're there."

Sylvia gave out a short, almost hysterical burst of nervous laughter.

"What's the matter with you?" said Robert.

"You seriously don't think we can go back to Lancaster, do you? You said it yourself, they're really scary people. We can't go back there. They'll be coming for us. That's exactly where they'll go first. We can't take that chance – that life has gone! If they find us, they'll do what we did to Scire. You can count on it."

"What d'you mean, what we did to Scire. It was an accident."

"They won't see it that way."

"Maybe – but that's what it was."

"It was still our fault – if the phial hadn't been empty – if I hadn't made you, y'know – if there wasn't a scuffle…"

Robert stared at the bushes flying by, stunned into silence.

"I did it," said Robert eventually. "It was nothing to do with you. I did it. They won't touch you." He almost believed this himself and it was worth a try.

"I don't think so Robert. I invited you in to the group. I made you late for the ceremony. I was up there with you. They probably didn't see exactly what happened anyway. We're in this together. You're stuck with me."

She gave him a curious look. She didn't take him for the heroic type.

The night was cold and there was no heating in the car. Sylvia shoved her hands into the deep pockets of the cloak. She could feel a smooth, crumpled material and suddenly shuddered with the horrible realisation of what it was.

Robert's eyes were fixed on the road ahead as Sylvia turned to the door and eased a section of cloth out of her large pocket. It was the sacred cloth. She'd forgotten she'd pushed it into her cloak. But now was not the time to tell Robert. Definitely not. Things were bad enough and he didn't need any more stress. She eased the cloth back into her pocket.

"That cloth, at the cave. It was Scire's cloth, wasn't it?" said Sylvia. "He was the keeper of the cloth. I always thought it was strange that he was its keeper rather than Dafo."

"Sylvia, will you just be quiet and let me concentrate on driving. We need to get as far away from here as possible. I don't know where we're going but wherever it is, we need to get there - fast."

She was definitely seeing a different side to Robert. What were they going to do? They couldn't go back to Lancaster. Obviously, they wouldn't be able to finish their degrees. They would have to leave all of their belongings where they were. These thoughts were whirling through Sylvia's head as she considered the magnitude of their actions. No, not *their* actions, because it was all her fault really wasn't it? She had been the one to persuade Robert to become involved in all this nonsense. It had been her who had become so fanciful and stupid, with Robert in the cave. Although ... he had gone along with it hadn't he? And he was the one who had actually pushed Scire. No, no, of course it had just been a ghastly accident. No, she couldn't shift the blame. It was all her fault.

"I think we should head for Durham." She said suddenly.

"Durham? Where did that come from? Why Durham? Do you know anybody in Durham?"

"Nobody- but isn't that the point?"

Robert was forced to agree. At least it was some sort of plan. They had to get somewhere safe and think things through. Because of their stupidity, in the blink of an eye, the whole course of their lives had altered. What the hell were they going to do? How would they live? What would their parent's think? He knew that Sylvia seemed scornful of the opinions of her parents, but he loved his and couldn't bear to disappoint them or hurt them.

***

Tynemouth - October 2009

Rebecca sat in her kitchen thinking about what the fortune teller had told her. It was probably complete nonsense ... but there had been some parts that seemed uncanny. The stresses and strains of work -well that was exactly right - but the fact that she had the power to do something about this seemed too good to be true. If she never had to go back to that wretched school, what a difference to her life that would make. Perhaps she wouldn't have to go through the next awful Ofsted. The very possibility of this thought made he [her] feel as if an enormous weight had been partially lifted from her shoulders. Maybe, just maybe, this could be the case.

Clearly Caroline was featured in the reading. *Charming and delightful* weren't words that she would use to describe her - but *childish and petulant*, absolutely. The woman however, had started to come out with some very weird ideas. Despite Caroline's annoying, rude ways, she hardly would have thought her capable of cruelty and malice. Then all that nonsense about hidden enemies and retribution. What was all that about? Supposedly, fortune tellers told clients what they wanted to hear or nobody would return to them. And as to all that drivel about the boorish reprobate next door - not in a million years.

However, the reading had further convinced her that she needed to see Caroline. Maybe she should try to be more open minded because she was beginning to realise that life-changing decisions needed to be made and knowing somebody like Caroline could prove to be useful. Rebecca went to find her phone just as the music started thudding from next door.

Chapter 13

Tynemouth - October 2009

After opening the rusted gate, Caroline trod carefully on the damp grass amongst the ancient graves. The writing on some was so eroded by centuries of extreme weather that the inscriptions could no longer be read. Just in front of her lay Harold Turner, who was *guaranteed with sureness and certainty the promise of resurrection to an eternal life*. To her left she noticed that a certain John Pilkington had *finished his course* on the 14th March 1844 at the age of 47 *having led an exemplary life*. Already, she had lasted three years longer than Mr Perfect Pilkington and his commendable life. Caroline had never been fond of graveyards

Generally, the churchyard wasn't in the best state of repair. Tombstones jutted out at awkward angles like decaying, uneven teeth. She arrived at a fresh burial site where the letters on the headstone stood out clearly, brightly gilded against the grey of the marble. Withered flowers flopped from a small metal pot as the funeral had been several weeks before.

Dearly Missed Friend
Sylvia Barton
Born 5th April 1959
Died 22th September 2009
Age 50
R.I.P.

Caroline shuddered as she always did when she saw the words. She really missed having her good friend to visit and share her problems with. The two of them had been friends for years, in fact as long as she had known Robert. Actually, all three of them had been close. She had helped them both out on so many occasions.

Caroline thought back to the first time their paths had crossed and how strange it was that she had no idea then what a significant part this quiet girl would have in their lives. Olwyn, as she was first introduced to her, sat quietly in the corner with her immaculate, dark bob and enormous, green eyes. Although she said very little, you could see she listened intently and was totally committed to the group's ideas. Caroline recalled that overcrowded room with them all squashed on the floor and bed. She remembered the image of a woman with wild, dark hair, Llyriad, with her jangling jewellery and flowing dresses. Her boyfriend Scire, lounging about on the floor, looking all mean and moody. Llyriad must have hated her so much in the light of what happened.

"So, Sylvia, what am I going to do? If you hadn't died then this problem would never have arisen. I just wish you were still here. I miss you so much. You know I do. I miss your kind words and sound advice. It's not bloody fair – you going and leaving me here to sort this out. How can I make Rebecca see sense? She can't sell the house, can she? Especially not now. And you know who Robert thought that he saw come into his shop the other day? Yes, *him*, alive – can you believe it? He must be some age now. I thought, no that's not true. I hoped that he might have died by now. Sounds awful, I know …but that's the way it is. The misery he's caused us over the years. Surely, he can't have tracked us down again, not after all of this time. And you're not here to help us now – it's not bloody fair. Anyway, anyway … I just hope that Robert was mistaken."

Caroline had no doubt that her friend was listening as she always had. She knelt down on the ground beside the new tombstone with her long red scarf trailing in the wet grass and gave out a loud, gulping sob. She would wait patiently for a reply from her friend, staring into the headstone, and beginning to get cold.

She had been motionless for more than ten minutes when her phone began to ring. She plucked it from her pocket and looked at the screen. When she realised the identity of the caller, she stood up awkwardly, stiff from kneeling and her cheeks folded into a deep smile.

***

Robert was serving a customer when Caroline burst into his shop.

"Robert, she's agreed, she's agreed…" Caroline's face was bright scarlet and he could see how excited she was.

"Just a moment Caroline." He turned his attention back to his middle-aged customer with a brown, leather jacket who was buying a rare book on the 1951 Alfa Romeo formula one racing car. "That will be nineteen pounds fifty please." The man produced a crumpled twenty-pound note from his pocket and Robert gave him his change.

As soon as the customer had left, Caroline turned to Robert again, who stood with his arms folded, his forehead corrugated.

"Robert, did you hear what I said? She's agreed. Rebecca's agreed to come round to my flat for dinner this evening. She's agreed. Isn't it wonderful? I knew she would. I just knew she would. I'm sure everything's going to be fine. We can sort everything out. It'll be fine. Don't you think?"

"Caroline, Caroline please, come and sit down. You're already making me feel tired. Sit down and tell me, slowly, everything that's happened." Robert pulled two, small wooden stools from under a table and they both sat down.

"Well, I went to see Sylvia … and …and … it's uncanny really," she shook her head in amazement.

"I don't follow you. Sylvia is dead. What are you talking about?" Robert's forehead creases became even deeper.

"No, I went to her grave and told her everything. I knew she would listen. I knew she would help." Caroline gave an expectant smile.

"Go on. What happened next. How could Sylvia help?"

"Well, I knelt down next to her grave and within minutes my phone started to ring. It was Rebecca and she said that she wanted to see me. She mentioned that there were certain things that didn't add up. That she had some questions that she wanted some answers to about her aunt. So, she's agreed to come round to my flat for dinner tonight." Robert could see that she was mentally deciding what she would cook as she spoke.

Robert turned in his seat. He didn't look at her but stayed in profile, gazing across the room, like a priest in a confessional giving penance "That *is* good Caroline but it hardly solves all our problems does it? D'you think that by cooking her an elaborate meal and plying her with a few glasses of wine, you'll actually persuade her to give up her teaching job and come and live in Tynemouth."

"No Robert, of course I don't. But it's a start in the right direction isn't it? I thought that you'd be more positive about it. I'm doing this for both of us you know. I'm going to be as charming and kindly towards her and…well, we shall see. Whatever else, she can't fail to be impressed by my flat and that will make her want me to help with the house won't it? You know what I mean?"

Robert gave an almost indiscernible shake of his head. He thought that Caroline was being characteristically over optimistic and was sure the events of the evening could not unfold the way she was planning, but he knew better than to say anything, just try and calm everything down. He was the string tethering her helium balloon.

***

Northumberland- October 2009

Derrick was thinking hard, having just received an interesting phone call relating to a something he had almost given up on years ago. When the full horror of the consequences of that night had become clear, nobody would have dreamed that after all this time, the matter would not have been resolved.

Although he had long retired from his job as professor, a lecturer in Theology, at Lancaster University, he still had links with a few people there. They were not so much his academic colleagues that he considered his friends, but those who shared common interests. You only needed to look at the contents of the books in his vast collection to know what those were. Age hadn't diminished his passion, but it had slowed him down and he still felt burdened by the consequences of one particular evening which ate away at him.

Admittedly, he'd had his part to play in the turn of events. But if he could just recover what had once been stolen, and was after all rightfully his, then he would be content. He was not a well man and time was not on his side.

He thought back to that night at St. Cuthbert's Cave when it seemed everything was going according to plan. Llyriad was by his side, angry, even before the disastrous turn of events. Wherever she had got the notion from that she and Scire would be the chosen ones he did not know. Scire had been standing on top of the cave ready to receive the phial and attach it to the arrow It had been Scire's crucially important job for many years to fire the ceremonial arrow and a whim of Llyriad's was hardly going to change that. After all, Scire was the keeper of the silk and the two jobs were intertwined. He remembered he had tried his best to ignore her but he could feel her presence, seething furiously next to him.

The two newcomers had disappeared into the cave and they had all waited. Time froze, standing still for what seemed an eternity to allow for the sacred ceremony behind the curtain to unfold. Suddenly, a sliver of light appeared in the sky. Dawn was approaching and would herald the beginning of the ceremony but still there was no sign of them. Scire, standing all alone, was beginning to look agitated. Next to him Derrick remembered he had felt a mood change, Llyriad sighed deeply, almost as if she was pleased that the pre-requisite details were not being properly adhered to and from the corner of his eye, he had thought he'd seen a slight smile play on her lips.

Eventually, after what had seemingly been an age, the two had appeared and climbed on top of the cave with Scire. Then everything happened so quickly. All three were out of sight WHEN screams and shouting could be heard. Where was Scire? He should have been holding the bow up in triumph but he wasn't. And where were the other two? They should have been there welcoming the solstice sun, but there was no sign of them.

For a brief, few seconds everyone had seemed be frozen, in a state of bewilderment. Then the crowd had surged forward. A mass of torches moving across the ground like giant fireflies. Llyriad was at the front, searching for her missing boyfriend. She found Scire's broken body lying motionless in a pool of blood on the other side of the cave. There was no sign of Verbius or Aradnia. As the sky filled with the brightness of the new morning light, it served only to highlight and magnify their miraculous disappearance and the horror of the occasion.

Derrick had gone into the cave suspecting the two of them might have been hiding, but there was nobody there. Even more importantly the sacred silk had vanished. Surely those two hadn't had the audacity to steal the cloth? But it seemed that they had. All that was left of the events were the burning candles and a small pool of liquid on the floor. Even after all this time, recounting the events only served to make his blood boil.

He remembered that he had realised much too late that urgency was required. How could he have been so stupid? Eventually, he had ordered everyone to leave quickly and as the angry mob ran down the hill to the car park, a small car could be seen disappearing into the distance. Too much time had been wasted and he cursed himself to this very day for not acting more swiftly.

Within the group things were never the same because of the murder of Scire and the missing silk. Attendance dwindled at meetings. When members crossed each other's paths they feigned non-recognition. Also, no matter how much he despised that treacherous pair, there was someone who hated them with much more ferocity. The incident had embittered her whole life.

And that person had just called him.

Chapter 14

Durham – June 1979

After carefully placing the cloth in her bag, Sylvia began to climb up the steep road to the Cathedral. Robert, realising that they needed to make some money fast, had gone ahead, asking around each of the many bookshops to see if he could find work. While studying for his A levels, he had a part time job in a bookstore in his hometown. Also, with his deep love of books, this seemed the obvious place to start.

While Robert visited the booksellers, Sylvia went off to see what Durham had to offer. Of what she had seen so far, Sylvia was impressed. It had similarities with Lancaster, but was much more impressive. In fact, it didn't really feel like a place in the North. It was as if someone had dug up an Oxford or Cambridge and repositioned it here. Interesting, old buildings with stone-carved frontages flanked the medieval main street. She noted each one with interest as she climbed upwards to approach the magnificent spectacle of the Cathedral. She would have liked to stop and explore but for some reason she couldn't, it seemed that she was being driven forward, urged relentlessly onwards.

As she approached, she studied the sanctuary knocker on the massive, ancient wooden door, a formidable Green Man with wild hair unfurling between grey, metal flames. She felt the magnetic pull even stronger. Inside, the building was as breathtaking as she imagined it would be. Everything seemed blanched ivory or white, and the golden light streamed through the richly decorated stained glass windows filling the building with God's presence and inspiring devout worship.

Huge, chevron patterned columns lined each side of the nave, and pairs met high above to marry and form beautiful, interlaced arches.

Walking down the pew-edged aisle she felt compelled to veer right to enter the feretory of St. Cuthbert. Her bag, slung over her right shoulder felt warm. She looked inside and saw that the cloth twinkled and sparkled with the light from the dozens of pillar candles around her. Sylvia felt a quiver of unease as she furtively fastened her bag.

St. Cuthbert's body lay under a simple stone slab with his name inscribed in the middle and a sturdy, tall candle at each corner. Above the slab was a colourful painting of the resurrected saint resplendent in royal blue, crimson and gold. On either side hung vivid banners depicting the Saint. Another banner depicted a warlike saint, King Oswald of Northumbria. His head also rested here, buried with St. Cuthbert.

Sylvia sat down next to an old man, bent over, his hands clasped together, praying, and found an overwhelming sense of calm. She felt that feeling of welcoming safety, as if she had come home. St. Cuthbert seemed to be sanctioning their journey as if this was where they were destined to be.

Somehow, she just knew that Robert would have found a job already and she felt sure that she would too. They would make their home here for some time and all would be well. They had found sanctuary.

***

North Shields- October 2009

Although where Caroline lived wasn't that far from Tynemouth, it was too far to walk as time was pressing, so Rebecca took a taxi to 'Dolphin House' which Caroline had said was near to a pub called the 'Magnesia Bank'. It was an impressive-looking development and of course Caroline lived in the top floor, penthouse apartment. There was a lift to take Rebecca four floors up. Caroline had the door open before she arrived.

"Hello, hello, lovely to see you Rebecca. Come in, come in and give me your coat,"

Caroline was wearing a blue, silk tunic embellished with sequins and beads. She quickly appraised Rebecca's choice of a plain, white shirt and jeans, before taking her sensible, blue coat. Rebecca could smell a delicious aroma coming from the kitchen and realised she was actually feeling very hungry.

"I hope you haven't gone to too much trouble for me," said Rebecca, trying her best to be civil.

"Now, sit down Rebecca. Let me get you a drink. Is white wine alright for you? I seem to recall you liked the wine I left for you on your first night here."

"Yes, that's fine," Rebecca waited three seconds before adding, "thanks."

Caroline went into the kitchen. Rebecca 's eyes went a portrait painting above the fireplace and immediately she had to put a hand over her mouth to stifle her laugher. It was supposed to be a depiction of Caroline painted twenty, if not thirty years earlier. She didn't seem to be wearing a dress, but was swathed in an extravagant midnight blue, silken wrap to and smiling provocatively to complete the image of a sumptuous courtesan.

Rebecca scanned the rest of the interior designer's enormous room with its garish carpet of swirling blue and red patterns. There were two, golden chaise lounges and two hand-crafted velvet chesterfield sofas, one deep blue and one a rich plum colour. Rebecca was sitting on a chaise longue that, she had to admit, was very comfortable. From the ceiling sparkled the most massive chandelier which wouldn't look out of place in the Versailles of Louis XIV. On every surface was a carefully placed object: a colourful Clarice Cliff vase; a blue Wedgewood plate; a Tiffany lampshade, a Faberge egg (Rebecca assumed that these weren't original but even in a counterfeit form they combined to convey a pretentious impression of wealth, elegance and taste). Tall bookcases were brimming with expensive-looking, leather-bound books and opulent, heavy, blue, velvet curtains draped from the two windows. Outside was a balcony, boasting a fine view, overlooking the river.

"Here you are Rebecca."

Rebecca's assessments of her host's taste were brought to a halt as Caroline handed her a large glass, and she thought she had better cut to the chase.

"Thank you ... and so, Caroline, about my Aunt..." Rebecca began.

"Oh, please dear, do forgive me ...please wait 'til we've eaten. There's plenty of time for that."

Caroline sashayed off back into the kitchen and returned moments later with two large plates of food which she placed on a long banqueting table.

Rebecca began eating and begrudgingly couldn't deny that it tasted gorgeous and was cooked to perfection.

"This is delicious Caroline, thank you."

Caroline smiled as she pushed the food around on her own plate. "There's plenty more in the kitchen." She took a long drink from her wine and after a short while of watching avidly as Rebecca ate, Caroline decided it was time for her to broach her all-important subject. "So, have you had any more thoughts about what you're going to do with your house?"

Rebecca stopped eating immediately, delicious as the food was, she was glad to be getting to the point of her visit. She wiped a small speck of sauce from the corner of her mouth.

"Well ...as you know, I'll have to return to work soon. I don't know if you realise ... but when I had the house valued, well I ... I was very disappointed."

"That's the property market for you," Caroline shook her head in sympathy, attempting to mirror Rebecca's disappointment. "I'm afraid Rebecca, house prices haven't risen around here for ages. And that house, unfortunately, is in great need of some loving care and attention."

"I know, I know, and that's just what I don't understand. You were my Aunt Sylvia's dearest friend - and you're an interior designer. So how come you never helped her sort the house out?" It was a question that had played over and over in Rebecca's mind. She knew the effect it would have on Caroline, but it had to be said and she couldn't think of any other way to say it. "I hate to think of her in those last months, living in that dingy, awful place. It must have been terrible for her. Why didn't you at least try to *make her* make the place more

["persuade her to"?]

comfortable? I mean, she must have been ill for quite some time." Rebecca' could feel her cheeks becoming quite flushed, uneasy at the, what she considered, necessary, brutality of her words. and she helped herself to the bottle of wine on the table.

Caroline flinched momentarily at the attack, even though she had been expecting it, but then instantly recovered her composure. She realised it was essential to remain composed and pragmatic. Aspirational rather than critical. Balance was essential.

"Rebecca ...oh, Rebecca dear...you didn't know your aunt. A lovely, lovely woman. She wasn't materialistic at all. She just liked to live quietly. A simple existence was all that she wanted. She was very, very stubborn ... and she didn't like change. I don't think she *ever* decorated the house. It remained the same as it was when she first moved in. That was just what she was like. She enjoyed working in the library, and reading of course, always reading. She organized a book group you know. Kept trying to get me to join but well ...that's not really my sort of thing. Sometimes we'd go to the cinema or theatre together, she particularly liked to see film versions of books she'd read. But having her house redecorated wasn't something that she thought important. And, although I didn't think that she'd been looking well for some time, it was only quite near the end that she actually admitted to me that she was ill at all."

"But what exactly was wrong with her? I mean I know she was quite old but nevertheless..."

"Your aunt was the same age as me," Caroline said abruptly, giving a scorching too-wide smile. "So, of course she wasn't *that* old." She quickly contracted the smile and gazed into the distance. "But my dear, she was unlucky. She got cancer. Pancreatic cancer. She probably had known that something was wrong for some time... but left it too late before doing anything about it. She never did like doctors and I can't say that I'm too fond of them myself. I don't expect they bother you? They didn't frighten me when I was your age. However, I think it's a cancer that isn't easily treated. It was a bad, bad time."

Rebecca could see from Caroline's face and tone of voice, her genuine distress at recalling this. She felt herself warm to her - a little.

"I see, so nothing could be done for her? That's so sad, so very sad. I can tell she meant a lot to you." Rebecca took a long drink from her glass. "Please, tell me some more about her. She sounds like a very nice person. I'd like to get to know more, after all she was very generous to me. I really need to understand. You see ... the way my mother describes her makes her seem like a completely different person to the one you're describing."

"Well, that comes as no surprise. Your mother – I'm sorry - but don't get me started on her." The balance had gone. "It always seemed to me that your mother was jealous of her sister."

Rebecca was very surprised to hear Caroline's voice become suddenly acerbic.

"But that doesn't seem to make any sense at all." Rebecca rubbed her head, trying to smooth the knots in her mind. "My mum has a doting husband, a much better house, and two daughters who have always been at her beck and call. What did Sylvia have by comparison?"

"Exactly," Caroline nodded. "But Cynthia never saw things as they were, because she was so eaten up by envy. Envy for what, I don't know, but there it is. She has always been a glass half-empty type of person."

Rebecca was starting to feel uncomfortable with this character assassination of her mother. Despite her being well aware of her mum's faults, it was a different matter to hear this negativity towards her coming from a woman who she barely knew. The warming towards Caroline had come to a sudden end.

"But how do you know this? By the way you describe her, it doesn't seem to be the things that my aunt would have said about her sister. Have you ever met my Mother? You seem to have some very strong opinions about her." Rebecca poured oil on the fire.

"No, of course not!" Caroline bristled and answered too quickly, with too much emphasis. "Your family live in Lancashire and I haven't been there for many years."

"So, you have been there then?" said Rebecca, fanning the flames.

"Well, as you implied earlier, I am quite old… in comparison with you. And by the time you get to my age you too will have visited lots of places. I pride myself that I enjoy travelling." Chiming from the ornate, antique clock on the far wall caught Caroline's attention. She saw that it was already 10 o'clock and she was no nearer to establishing what Rebecca intended to do with the house. She returned once more to the main purpose of the evening. "Anyway, I'm sure you must have come to the conclusion by now that it would make little sense to sell the house at the moment."

"No, I haven't decided yet," *Not that it's any of your business* thought Rebecca. "However, I do know that I need to be back home soon because half term is nearly over. I've got my class to think about and a lot of work to do to prepare for the next few weeks."

"But why? If you packed your job in you could get another one here."

"It doesn't work like that." *What planet was this woman on*? "Even if I were to *pack* my job in, I would have to work my notice which would be more than a month. Also, I would need to ask my headteacher for a reference ... I don't think she would be too happy about it all, coming halfway through the term ... and I can't believe we're having this conversation."

"Well, a month's not a long time in the grand scheme of things. The house is going nowhere."

"Yes, I understand that. I just need more time to work out what to do for the best. I need to make the right decision ... and not be rushed into it."

"So, you're not ruling out the possibility of living here."

"I don't know Caroline. There is a possibility ..." Rebecca could feel the effects of the wine clouding her judgement and didn't want Caroline to think that she had won, "... but only a very slight one. This isn't my home. I have no friends here. So actually, can't think of any reason to be here. Can you? Now please, if you wouldn't mind, could you call me a taxi, I don't know any numbers up here. It's getting late."

"But you aren't putting it on the market straight away..."

"I'm not sure, not sure. It seems unlikely but I need to think carefully. Thank you for the meal but I really need to go."

Caroline smiled and looked for her phone. All things considered, this hadn't been the worst possible outcome for the evening. After all, Rebecca hadn't dismissed her ideas completely.

Chapter 15
Gloucestershire- August 1952

Assuming from an early age, that a life in the Church would be his chosen career path, most of Derrick Stevens activities had been of an essentially ecclesiastical nature. His father had been the head of the local village church, a typical chocolate box variety of place, with charming residences and polite, God-fearing inhabitants. His mother dutifully filled the role of vicar's wife, flower arranging in the church, supervising the Mother's Union, chairing fete committees and bun sales. A flustered red-faced member of the congregation, the accommodating, sycophantic Mrs. Baxter, kept the Stevens' house in order. This suited his mother, perfectly.

Every Saturday, his mild-mannered father worked in his study, writing his cosy if repetitive Sunday sermons, which his curate Mr. Moon later edited. These, with weekly familiarity, largely encouraged people to be kind to one another. He was not a fire and brimstone man. Throughout the rest of the week, his time was spent visiting his deferential yet grateful parishioners, who were in spiritual or practical need. The Reverend Stevens wasn't ambitious and found great satisfaction from his job.

The vicarage was a delightful, white-painted thatched cottage, with candy-pink roses on a shabby chic trellis around the door. In the summer the garden displayed a myriad of purples, yellow and reds from the profusions of lupins, hollyhocks and delphiniums blooming in abundance, while the gardener, the Parish Verger, Mr Nicholson, tended to their every need. Inside the home, with its low-lying beams, chintzy patterned soft furnishings and tasteful rosewood furniture, the peaceful passage of time was marked reassuringly by an elderly, grandfather clock. Although an only child, Derrick's boyhood had been idyllically happy with doting parents, an aptitude for learning, and likeminded friends who joined with him in church-related activities of choirboy and boy scout.

Derrick had been born in 1928. His father owned a car and when he was old enough, each summer, the small family would go on holiday around Britain. Their educational holidays would always encompass visits to the Cathedral greats: Winchester, with its longest nave in Europe ; Salisbury, boasting Britain's tallest spire along with one of several Magna Cartas that are distributed around the country; Ely, the only building in the United Kingdom to be listed as 'one of the Seven Wonders of the Middle Ages'; Wells, proud of its second oldest mechanical clock in Europe and Exeter, featuring the longest uninterrupted vaulted ceiling in England. Derrick was spellbound by these breathtaking buildings built by mortals to glorify God and exemplify man's expectations of immortality. Even the words: cloisters, basilica, chancel, sanctuary and reredos had him in awe.

When he was in his early teens, the family travelled to the North. After first visiting the magnificent York Minster with its splendid rose window, they travelled further up the country to Durham. As he entered the Cathedral in Durham, almost stark in its simplicity compared to its more elaborate, southern siblings, but more breathtaking because of this - the young Derrick was transfixed. Even more entrancing were its inhabitants. Here he found the tomb of the father of history, Venerable Bede and then the final resting place and shrine of St. Cuthbert. Once, this place had been the most eminent destination for pilgrimage in England. thousands had flocked here for the magic of St. Cuthbert's healing properties and mystical cures. Most fascinating to Derrick was the fact that St. Cuthbert's body, when re-interred hundreds of years later, had been found completely uncorrupted. It seemed as if St. Cuthbert had found the key to immortality and the thought thrilled the young Derrick.

For the rest of the week the Reverend and Mrs. Stevens were more than delighted to spend their time indulging their young son's wishes. They visited the holy island of Lindisfarne, St. Cuthbert's Cave, the site of the Battle of Heavenfield and other places recommended in the book, 'Chronicles of Cuthbert', which Derrick had bought in the cathedral shop. Derrick's parents were extremely pleased by this newfound obsession and for their son to prefer a Northumbrian Saint as his hero.

Once they returned home the whim didn't fade. Derrick continued to be obsessed by all things concerning the ancient Northumbrian kingdom, but especially Durham Cathedral, and most fanatically, St. Cuthbert. It came as no surprise to anyone to anyone four years later when Derrick Stevens headed northwards to Durham University to read Theology.

***

Lancaster University - May 1979

Sylvia was making notes in the library for her essay, 'The Effects of Urbanisation and Growth of Theatres in Cities'. Although it was quite an interesting topic there were other matters she would much rather be researching. Unfortunately, if she didn't want to be kicked off the course, it was necessary that certain tasks were completed. She scribbled down some dates about the 'Hippodrome' in Birmingham before looking up to see a familiar person working at the table next to her. That dark brown bob and purple sweater definitely belonged to Olwyn, the girl from the Requisite.

Sylvia tried to get her attention several times. A boy with extremely bad acne and a brightly patterned sweater scowled at her from across the table. Olwyn eventually lifted her head, smiled at Sylvia and flicked up a hand in recognition.

"Olwyn," said Sylvia, ignoring the boy's stare. "Fancy a coffee?"

Olwyn looked at her watch, scrunched up her face but then replied, "Yes, okay, but just a quick one. I can't be too long. I've an essay on rock formation that needs to be finished today." She rolled her eyes and the boy with acne glared at them as they scraped their chairs under the table and headed for the door.

"This won't take long," said Sylvia. "I just wanted to ask you about…"

"Yes, I can guess," interrupted Olwyn. "Let's find somewhere quiet and I'll try and answer your questions as best I can." They both grabbed a coffee in the almost empty café bar on the ground floor of the library and Olwyn nodded towards a table in the corner.

"Well," said Olwyn, taking a quick sip from her cup, "I'll answer the ones I can anyway. I've only been involved with this a short while myself."

"It was Llyriad - she introduced me," said Sylvia. "I'm sure she thought I was stalking her … I kept following her about… I knew instinctively that she was involved in something interesting and I made it my business to find out what. Eventually she spoke to me and she could see I was genuinely interested. I was fascinated by the way she dressed … bit shallow I know… and I guess I kind of wanted to be like her. I think she picked up on this and it seemed to amuse her. So, finally, she told me of the next gathering and allowed me to attend ... I was so excited. But I didn't really know what it was all about"

Sylvia knew that there was something about Olwyn that she liked and she was instantly sure that they were about to become great friends. She smiled broadly, eyes wide with interest, inviting Olwyn to share her secrets.

"I remember you," said Olwyn. "I remember when you first came to that meeting in Llyriad's a couple of weeks ago. Her room's quite small isn't it - it was quite a squash. I haven't been part of the group long myself."

"How did *you* find out about it then?" Sylvia was surprised because she thought she was the only new member but then this was something else they would have in common.

A couple came across to sit at the next table sit at the next table. Olwyn's voice changed to a whisper.

"It was Leo, or should I say Loic to give him his 'Requisite' name. He was my boyfriend from home. I'm from Crewe and when I was in the Lower Sixth, he was in the Upper and that's when we got together. He was funny and made me laugh but more importantly I was fascinated by his ideas. He seemed to see things differently to everyone else I knew and this was very... well, attractive, I guess. Most of the other people at school were just interested in the same boring things. So, when he came here last year, I missed him ... I mean, I really missed him. I used to come and visit him at weekends. He told me all about the group and I was hooked. I mean ... not just because of what he thought ... the ideas genuinely made sense of things I'd always felt but hadn't been able to understand. I've always thought if myself as an environmentalist, but this is something even deeper, something special … to really believe, y'know what I mean? To really believe that there's a life force, an energy that runs through absolutely everything. And to be part of a group that follows those beliefs, that understands about the world as it was, before everything got crazy. That understands about mysticism and a spirit world through nature. Y'know?"

Sylvia nodded gravely, hanging on to every word of her new friend.

"So, … I knew lots of things about the 'Requisite' long before I came here," continued Olwyn. "That's the reason I worked really hard at my 'A' levels to get the necessary grades. Although why I decided to study geography I really don't know." She rolled her eyes thinking of the essay she needed to get handed in as quickly as possible.

From Olwyn's mouth everything seemed to be so matter of fact and normal but even more interestingly was the way she spoke about *always* having these ideas, and just not realizing it. This was almost exactly the same as her own thoughts.

"I've got a lot to learn then," said Sylvia, her chest tightened, fearing that the conversation might end. "But I already understand that it's not weird to believe in something ancient – something that's been lost, yeah? I suppose I just need to find out what to call it … how to deepen that knowledge … and how to hang on to it"

"We're all finding out. We're all, every one of us in the 'Requisite' - finding out and learning. We're fortunate that we've got good leaders in people like Llyriad, Scire and especially Dafo. He's great. Real name Stevens, Derrick Stevens. He's a lecturer here. Something to do with Theology. He's the driving force behind the group. He teaches us a lot. Like you said, he shows us that it's not weird to believe in something ancient. Following the ancient ways can give meaning to life. Pre-

Christian and pagan beliefs can help us. They had an obligation to the earth and so must we. Things they borrowed were sacred... and sacred things have to be returned. They were aware of spiritual places. The 'Thin' places where the veil between this world and the eternal world is thin."

"Yes, I've heard about those – amazing." Sylvia's eyes shone.

"Those people had a love of the environment and were at one with nature," continued Caroline, warming to the topic and her audience. "They were more democratic as well. The Celtic symbol of the Holy Spirit wasn't a dove, it was the V formation of wild geese, each one taking a turn to be leader. Cool or what? We're losing all that. Dafo has a quote he always uses. He says modern man is a 'specialist without spirit and a sensualist without heart'. And more importantly for us..." Olwyn grinned, wagging a finger back and forth between them. "He showed us how Pagan and Celtic Christian society believed in the equality of women and how they had great power in those times. Sooner we get back to those days the better, eh?"

Sylvia smiled back and leaned in to Olwyn, enjoying the complicity between them. "So, what's been the most exciting thing that's happened to you so far?"

Olwyn thought for a moment. "Exciting? That's an interesting word to use. It's more, erm ... stimulating and ... thought provoking. Dafo says we have to think differently, open up and expand our mind. But, if you want to use *exciting*, then ... oh well, that's easy, that's got to be the celebration of Litha. That was amazing."

"Litha?" Sylvia shook her head.

"Litha ... a midsummer festival – a fertility rite."

Sylvia leaned closer. "That's what happens at the solstice isn't it? I've read something about it."

"On the Summer Solstice, everybody from the group heads up to this cave in Northumbria, and there's a really cool, mystical ceremony," said Olwyn. "Two people are selected from the group each year to represent 'The Green Man' and 'Mother Earth'. Anyway, their union is enacted as a fertility rite, using all types of relics and sacred rituals. It's not a proper union of course – it's not *that* sort of group. Just symbolic. It ends with an arrow being shot at the sun, just when it's first rising at dawn. This was my first proper introduction to the group so I didn't really understand everything ... but I felt overwhelmed by the whole experience. 'Course we had a few things to smoke to get us going, in the mood, if you know what I mean. Dafo saw to that. Everything in the world just seemed to make sense and I'm sure it'll be even better this year."

"How do they choose?" said Sylvia, unaware now of anyone else in the room.

"Hush, keep your voice down. It's at a place called St. Cuthbert's Cave - for obvious reasons…up in Northumberland."

"No, no, how do they choose who'll be the 'Green Man' and 'Mother Earth?'".

"I'm not really sure. There's still lots of things that I need to find out?"

"Who was it last year? Was it Llyriad? I bet it was… I mean she seems pretty cool. I can see her doing it." Sylvia was already imagining herself and Robert filling the roles.

"D'you know," said Olwyn, just keeping a giggle under control. "I can't remember who it was - isn't that funny? I'm sure we can ask and find answers to your other questions at this week's meeting at Dafo's.

In fact, who will be the special couple this year might be discussed on Thursday. I wouldn't be at all surprised. By the way how you getting there?" Olwyn looked at her watch remembering that today's time was precious.

"I don't really know. I was thinking of asking a friend to give me a lift… but I'm not sure how to explain where I'm going and for what purpose. I'm not really sure *where* to go."

"Don't worry. Dafo lives at a place called Quernmore, its about 3 miles north east of here. Leo's got a car. A very old car. Meet me here at six thirty and you can come with us." Olwyn caught the time from the clock on the wall. "Anyway Sylvia…lovely to talk but really I need to get working. Those rocks are calling." Olwyn rolled her eyes again, pushed her chair back and quickly left the café, leaving Sylvia staring at her cup and reflecting deeply on their conversation.

She was plugged in and fired up.

***

Tynemouth - October 2009

"So, you say that Rebecca's having a meal round at Caroline's tonight?" Sebastian gave a small shake of his head and took another sip of his pint. He and his uncle were enjoying a drink after work at their local pub 'The Turk's Head' on Tynemouth front street. "But why," continued Sebastian, "should Caroline want to be friends with her? For that matter why would she want to spend *any* time at all with that bossy, old trout?"

Robert looked around at the empty seats, dark wood, perfectly fitting the dark paneled, walls. He looked up at the thick, ship's ropes hanging from the ceiling, ran his gaze along the pictures of sailing ships which he'd seen dozens of times and finally focused on a brightly-coloured sign advertising '10% off selected drinks'. He made a mental note that he should change his drink if they were having another one.

"Well," said Sebastian, not unpleasantly. "What d'you think? Think it's a good idea for Rebecca to …"

"I don't know…" Robert interrupted Sebastian before he could call Caroline any more names. He had wanted a quiet pint. "I don't know…it's up to her. She'll have her own reasons. I don't know."

"You must admit it's a bit strange."

Robert stared blank-faced at an antique, ten feet long map of the River Tyne on the wall, just to his right, buying time, collecting his thoughts, finding the right words. He didn't want an argument.

"Look, Sebastian," Robert continued looking at the map but his deeply, furrowed brow gave the lie to his casual glancing around, "Caroline is a good friend of mine y'know. Admittedly, she has her faults but nevertheless…"

"Oh, come on unc," Sebastian tutted. "I don't know why you bother with her. I've heard the way she bosses you about … I can't understand why you put up with it. I mean - who does she think she is? Whenever she's in a bad mood she always takes it out on you." He shook his head vigorously to emphasize the point.

"Like I said – she has her faults – don't we all?"

"Seems to me she's got more than her fair share."

Robert leaned back, letting the muted sound of 'The Righteous Brothers' from the juke box waft over them both. Buying more time.

Forced nonchalance. 'You've lost that loving feeling …now it's gone…gone…gone …woh oh woh oh woh'. He allowed himself a lopsided smile, hoping his nephew didn't notice. "There are … things … certain things … you don't understand about her," Robert measured his words. He was thinking about Caroline in her younger days and there was a slight glazing of his eyes at the memory. "We've been friends … for a lot of years and … she's got lots of good qualities."

"Such as?"

"Well," Robert looked quizzically at Sebastian. He knew his nephew didn't get on with Caroline but he had hoped it didn't amount to out and out hatred. "She gets things done. She doesn't mess about. She sorts things. She…"

"You mean she sorts everyone else." Sebastian almost spat the words out.

"No. I didn't say that. I didn't say that at all. What I'm saying is …. She helps …she…"

Sebastian blew out a long draught of air and laughed. "*Helps? Helps?* Helps who? Helps herself more like it."

"Like I say – she gets things done. She's dynamic if you like. She gets to the root of a situation quickly – no hesitation. She sees what has to be done – and she does it. She doesn't mess about. A lot of people owe a lot to Caroline. I'll admit, she takes no prisoners – but is that such a bad thing? If you're straight with her, she's straight with you." Robert gazed at the wooden paneled wall again. "She'll stand by you."

Sebastian gave him a puzzled look. "You seem very concerned about her. You're defending her? After the way she treats you? What's it to you? No…no…please, please don't tell me you've got feelings for Caroline. You can't have after the way she talks to you."

Robert took a long drink. He realised he *was* putting up a strong defence – too strong. Sebastian mustn't know about them. It was getting to the point where Sebastian would ask for specifics. It was time to change tack. "Well, if we're talking about feelings. What's it to you if Rebecca is having dinner with Caroline? D'you wish it was you having dinner with Rebecca?"

Sebastian gave a small, embarrassed chortle. "Whaaat?"

Robert raised his eyebrows purposefully and stared at Sebastian, pressing. "Oh, so you do wish it was you."

"Don't be daft." The answer was too sheepish to block Robert.

"I'm not being daft. I'm just seeing things as they are. Come on admit it."

"Admit what? There's nothing *to* admit."

"There's nothing to be ashamed of you know. If you like Rebecca – that's okay."

Now it was Sebastian's turn to gaze around the room. He settled his focus on the carved, wooden figure of a Turkish sailor jutting out from the corner of the bar and let it rest there for a few seconds.

"Yeah, well, I do think she's okay. She's a good-looking girl…"

"Not just that – good personality as well – and clever."

"Matchmaking, are we?"

"No. just trying to be helpful." *And throwing you off the scent*, Robert thought to himself

"Yeah, well, we'll see. I'm not in love or anything y'know. I like her that's all – want to look out for her. Make sure she doesn't waste her time on…" He stopped himself mentioning Caroline's name again.

Robert noted this. He was relieved that the trail was going cold, and recognised that he would have to try and avoid the subject of Caroline altogether.

They sat in silence, drinking and watching the Sky Sports presenter on the television directly opposite them. The sound was off. They were both glad to have avoided getting in to an argument.

Sebastian drained his glass. "Fancy another?"

"Well yes, I thought we were having just the one – but why not." Robert nodded at the advert. "Get two Kronenbergs eh?"

"Really? Okay, I'll get you that and I'll stick to my pale ale." Without waiting for an answer Sebastian slouched off to the bar. He had to go around to the next room as there was only one barman on and he was serving an older woman sitting on a bar stool. Sebastian glanced across as she was taking a long time to order. The woman had unruly, long, black hair. She was wearing a baggy, brown, hooded coat and had squeezed into bright, blue trousers. Sebastian noticed that the coat failed with its obvious intention of masking her plump frame.

The barman turned to Sebastian. He ordered the drinks and turned his attention to the conversation with his uncle. Maybe Caroline isn't that bad after all he thought to himself.

"Ah well, maybe Caroline isn't that bad after all," he said to Robert, handing him his lager.

"Well she *is* helping Rebecca with the house." Robert had obviously been thinking about the same subject while Sebastian was at the bar. "She's still quite young and probably doesn't know what to do. I mean it would be very foolish of her to sell at the moment with the housing market being the way it is."

"She doesn't look that young. She can't be much younger than me." Sebastian stroked his chin thoughtfully, "I mean... If you were to die and leave me the shop ... I would sell it as quick as possible and use the money to go travelling. Ooh, let me think ... Thailand, India, Bali. Maybe Rebecca wants to do that?"

"Thankfully, Rebecca is a little more responsible than you." Robert winced as he took a quick sip from his icy glass. "She's got a respectable job. She's a teacher, somewhere in Lancashire, and she *is* the same age as you. And another thing - remind me not to leave anything to you in my will." He hoped the last frivolous comment would bring some humour to the conversation, build bridges.

Sebastian didn't smile. "What good is a house to her in Tynemouth then? If she doesn't sell, she'll have to go to the bother of decorating it before she can rent it out? Anyway, why should it be of any concern to Caroline? Rebecca was her friend's niece - not hers?"

Reluctantly, Robert was being drawn into a discussion of Caroline again. "Well, I think, ... probably ... Caroline just regrets not having had children of her own. Sylvia was her very good friend, a very good friend to both of us. We were both devastated when she died. And ... I think that she's hoping that Rebecca will move up here and live in the house, not as a replacement for Sylvia but as someone, y'know, she can be friends with ... and she'll help her to decorate it."

How typically Caroline, Sebastian thought to himself, but decided not to share the thought with his uncle. "Clearly that's not going to happen is it?" He tapped the side of his glass petulantly. "Not, I mean if she has a job down there. She'd be crazy to give that up. Jobs aren't easy to come by." He stopped tapping and glanced slyly at Robert. "I'd love to be a fly on the wall listening to that conversation tonight though."

Neither of them noticed that the plump woman had moved along the bar, watching them both carefully and listening hard to their conversation. She was wishing she was a spider on that very same wall and my, what a web she would spin.

***

Chapter 16

Quernmore, near Lancaster - May 1979

Derrick always preferred the meetings of the Requisite when they happened at his home, because this was where he felt most in control of events. He sat on his leather chair in his study, amidst his fine collection of antique books and pulled contentedly on his pipe. It was a necessity that when major decisions were being made, that his home was to be the chosen venue. And rightly so, for with great satisfaction he noted that everything achieved had been largely due to his efforts. It was true to say, that if it wasn't for him there would be no Requisite. Derrick or Dafo as his brethren saw him, *was* the Requisite, but its actual, real purpose was rather different to that which the others imagined. Derrick smiled to himself, knowing that within a very short matter of time his plans would come to fruition and his ultimate goal would be accomplished.

Looking through the French windows of his fine home and across his large, well-kept garden, his gaze fell upon his excellent view of the stunning 'Trough of Bowland'. The stark branches of winter were once more cloaked in their vibrant green. This was his favourite time of year, with its promise of the Earth's rebirth, lengthening of the days and the gifts from nature of hyacinths, tulips and daffodils. His fondness for the blooms of the season had even influenced his own choice of Celtic name.

As his thoughts turned once more to that evening's gathering, he conceded that this event was long overdue. Many of the smaller meetings didn't really warrant his attendance. More importantly, it was hardly fitting for a senior lecturer to draw attention to himself and his extra-curricular activities, by sneaking round the campus of an evening. He was quite happy to let Llyriad chair the subsequent university events. She always gave him a detailed report on what had occurred at each meeting. A man of his age and eminence could hardly be expected to spend an evening crouching awkwardly on the floor of a hall of residence room. So, the more senior members of the group often had their own, far more comfortable gatherings in his library where members like Llyriad and Scire were invited to attend.

The most important matter on the agenda tonight was to begin the selection process to choose the couple for this year's Litha. Irritatingly, he knew that Llyriad would once more be disappointed and he would have to endure her barbed comments yet again. But, as he was forced to point out each year, her partner Scire had his own crucial role in the ceremony, especially so this year. So, really, it was quite out of the question. Surely, she must realise, as this was essentially a fertility ritual, that younger members of the group were much more fitting for the roles. For someone who considered herself so wise, albeit misguidedly so, her train of thought was unbelievably stupid and selfish.

Whoever was chosen for this role was really of little consequence. Once they had served their purpose, their role was largely obsolete, and they were regarded as being of little value. After they had had their moment of splendour, they resumed their usual place amongst the flock. Many quickly became disenchanted and left (with no doubt of the severe consequences which would befall them if they "leaked") which was why those who had been part of the group for some time had little interest in being selected. Disturbingly, Llyriad appeared not to have made this connection but then again, her lack of guile was perhaps an asset in itself. Anyway, in a short space of time all this would be of little consequence.

Derrick knew that there were some new recruits that he hadn't actually spoken to as yet. Llyriad had mentioned some names but he hadn't really been giving her full attention when she had been keeping him up to date on recent developments (often she found it difficult to separate the important from the mundane, the Requisite seemed to attract these types) but he did recall seeing some fresh new faces at the Esbat ceremony recently. Anyway, tonight's meeting would rectify that and allow him to assess the new members.

***

Lancaster University – April 1979

Sylvia dressed with care, wriggling into the new, white dress she had bought specially for the occasion. On this night the image she presented was to be of the utmost importance. Smiling admiringly at her reflection, she brushed her long chestnut curls till they shone like polished wood and applied her lipstick. She heard a knock on the door and looked in at her watch in irritation. It was nearly six and she needed to be going.

Robert's voice came through the door. "Sylvia, it's me. Open up Sylvia, I know you're there, I can see the light on."

He certainly could choose his moment.

"Robert, I'm busy. I haven't got time…"

"Sylvia just open up the door,"

Begrudgingly she let him in.

"Wow, you look amazing." His eyes widened as he looked at her until she felt like a cake about to be eaten.

"You must be going to some party. Is it connected with the ...?"

"Be quiet Robert. Yes, yes, you know it is... and I wish you could come too but you can't. You haven't been introduced yet and this party is a big deal. Do you understand?"

"No, Sylvia I don't – not really. I would like to go as well. You've explained to me what it's all about and I want to be part of it." *And I don't want you talking to other men, especially the way you look tonight.*

"You will, you will do... but not this time. Now go." Sylvia tossed a long black coat over her dress and pushed past him into the corridor. They began walking with Robert close on her heels. She was enjoying the feeling of power.

"Well what time will you be back? Can I see you later?"

"I don't know, do I?" Sylvia looked at her watch, feigning annoyance with him and quickened her pace.

"Can I come round to yours at twelve? I want to hear all about it." Robert matched each footfall, aware that he was sounding pathetic.

"Okay then, okay, but if I'm not back, I'm not back - see you later." She left Robert and hurried across the square where she spotted Olwyn.

Olwyn smiled at Sylvia and the two girls linked arms as they walked the short distance to the car park where Loic was waiting.

***

Tynemouth – October 2009

Rebecca sat in the dreary sitting room of her inherited house, number ten Huntington Place. She sat in silence, thinking that it would actually be preferable to hear some loud noise from Sebastian's music next door. It appeared that he mustn't be in because whenever he was his presence was obvious. She sat very still, thinking hard about her predicament. She wished with every fibre of her being that she didn't have to leave and go back to that school. She can't just leave her job like that - can she? There's nothing really, apart from that and her parents, keeping her there. Most of her friends went off to university and never returned. Why had she allowed her mother to cajole her into getting a job near them? She has no social life whatsoever. Even if she had friends, she was always so exhausted that she had neither the energy nor inclination to go out. This could be her life for the next thirty years.

Rebecca felt a warm tear begin to trickle down her cheek.

Perhaps she *could* apply for jobs up here. The Head would give her a decent reference just to get rid of her because it seemed she didn't rate her and there was certainly no love lost between the two of them. Her parents would obviously be upset but she needed to think of herself. It was her life after all.

It still left an important question though. One which still niggled away at her. Why was Caroline so bothered? Granted, it seems she had no children of her own and Sylvia was her friend, but nevertheless … There was something more personal in all of this. There had to be. Also why did she seem to hold her mother, Cynthia in such contempt? How could you despise someone you had never met? What could her aunt have possibly told Caroline. And what could have happened between the two sisters because her Mother's comments about Sylvia had been equally caustic.

It just didn't make to any sense to Rebecca. Her eyes fell once more on the photograph of the laughing couple. The smiling woman with the dress with the tassels. She looked like she would be such fun. She looked again.

What?

Yes!

Of course!

It had to be!

Why?

Why had she not seen it before?

Surely it was Caroline, not her aunt at all, and the kind looking boy - that was Robert – had to be. What a lovely couple they must have been in those days. No wonder her aunt had them as friends. Was this an omen about what she should do?

Were things becoming simpler or more complicated? It seemed that something about this place was developing a definite pull on her and that sometimes, maybe, just maybe, decisions didn't need to be made, as matters often resolved themselves.

***

Ledbury, Herefordshire – September 1623

Leofwin sat on a small, wooden stool next to the one window with small, thick pieces of glass in it. The other windows had oil-soaked, sacking covering them and gave a brown, gloomy tinge to the rest of his house. He pulled the green tunic and cloak further around is body to comfort him and thought back over the many years of his incredibly long life. He was weary now. Despite his appearance as a man in his mid- fifties, nobody could even hazard a guess at his actual age. He knew his days should have been up more years ago than seemed believable. Yet he was still here. Somehow, he felt like he had been stretched too thin. As if to keep the wrinkles at bay, he had been placed on a rack which had been turned tighter and tighter over the years. With each twist, so the pain had increased, especially over the latter years. Looking at his hands with their appearance of only half a century of living, he gave out a deep, moaning sound and rubbed his tired face. He thought again, as he had done many, many times, if he had made the right decision all those years ago.

 He shuffled across the one, large room of his house, barely lifting his feet, scattering rushes as he went. He took the heavy key from the bag at his belt, opened the large, iron-bound chest, and looked despairingly at the fragment, still splendid, if not in quite the same way. She would always hold him in her thrall… yet to others - what would they see? He had to admit the colours no longer shone and glittered so brightly, even under the glare of the tallow candle he was holding. Over time, the actual size of the material appeared to have shrunk. He placed the candle on his rough, wooden table, grimacing at the smell of the animal fat. Unfolding the cloth, he saw the beautiful face that had bewitched him all those centuries ago. How those eyes had sparkled and that double fishtail gleamed. He traced her outline with shaking fingers.

 Of course, after that day he could no longer be a man of the church. He had moved far south and had taken a wife. It had seemed the right thing to do. But he couldn't love her. How could he when his life was dedicated to his one true love and protectress. Nevertheless, there were children, many of them, and he watched them grow, marry and produce children of their own. Then they would die, leaving him alone again. And so, he remained unchanged. Year after year after year. When folk started whispering and pointing, with baffled expressions, he knew it was time to move on, to flee, abscond, get some peace. And then it would all start again. His body remained intact but he was weary, his mind indifferent and insensitive. Now was the time.

    Leofwin, heard the creaking from the door of his house. His grandson, Simon strode into the room and then stopped suddenly. Simon was instantly drawn to the strange cloth Leofwin was holding. To him it glittered and sparkled as if new. He didn't recognize the expression on his grandfather's face. He seemed hollow somehow ... and helpless. Simon was scared for him.

    "What is it? What ails you?" said Simon. He spoke in hushed tones and stared at the cloth, already overcome by wonder.

    "You must take it," said Leofwin quickly. Even with all his time he was impatient to do this. It was the right thing to do. "For I have had my fill. It is for you and you alone. I commend her to you. She will protect you now."

    "What? What is it you say?"

    "Please, please, take her. I cannot bear her any longer. She cannot bear me. She is uncommon wondrous but now needs another. It is time. She cannot be taken from you. You can only bestow her ...in your lifetime. She will bring great pleasure and great pain. It is something no other has had."

    "What does this mean? I do not know ..."

Leofwin's face veiled the disgust he felt for himself. The disgust at passing on this curse. But he knew he could not pass her on to anyone. She held him to that. He pitied Simon but he was helpless.

He handed the young man the silk without waiting for any response, eager to have it over with.

Simon felt an immense force of energy rush through his veins and as he held the material in his grasp. He was consumed by an overwhelming sensation of bliss. Something ethereal, mystical and sacred. He closed his eyes to keep out reality. He was completely engulfed by sensations so exquisite and wonderful they couldn't be described. He groaned with pain and ecstasy, exhilarated by serenity and blissful peace. He felt his whole being flow and pulse inside him and around him. Eventually, after many minutes he was released and he slumped to the floor.

He looked for his grandfather.

Leofwin was not there. Only a bundle of bones covered by a green tunic and cloak.

He was long dead, as if his passing had happened centuries ago.

The room became chilled and Simon staggered to his feet, staring at the remains, astonished and horrified at the sight. He finally realised he wasn't breathing and let out a loud gasp. But above all he knew, from somewhere deep inside him that he had to keep her safe and she would do the same for him.

Simon, or Scire as he came to be called, reached out, trembling, picked up the cloth, placed it gently in the chest and turned the key.

***

Quernmore, Near Lancaster- Lancashire – May, 1979

After a half an hour, Loic pulled into a long driveway and continued up a hill to where a large, red-bricked house was perched, surrounded by coniferous woodland. They could hear music, soft jazz with buzzing saxophones and a throbbing base. Sylvia was excited, all thoughts of Robert forgotten and she gave a beaming grin to Olwyn, as they walked towards the front door.

Scire appeared in the doorway with his pale blanket of shoulder length hair and deep-set, knowing eyes, beckoning them in. Sylvia found herself in a hallway with a floor of black and white tiles, a high ceiling and a spiral staircase.

"Good evening, I hope you are well, please let me take your coats." Scire forced a smile as they handed him their coats which he placed on hooks, keeping company with many others on the wall, before ushering them through a door on the left.

Sylvia looked around a handsome room, with fine bookcases and flickering candles. A room full of people, chatting, laughing and drinking from elegant wineglasses. She instantly recognised a few familiar faces from Lancaster. Loic helped himself to a drink. Llyriad, dressed in a snug, green dress was deep in conversation with some dark-suited men. Over by a marble fireplace in the centre of the room, she recognised the tall, charismatic man who had preceded over the events of the Esbat. There was a gentle hum of voices beneath the crackle of music from an antique gramophone player. The jazz had been replaced by the folk of 'Fairport Convention'. Sandy Denny's voice swirled rapturously around the room, evoking memories of a bucolic by-gone age. The air was thick with the scent from the candles-

sandalwood, jasmine and sweet-smelling vanilla, and the aroma of other, earthier products.

"That's Dafo over there," whispered Olwyn, digging Sylvia gently in the ribs. "D'you remember him?"

"Yes, well... hard to forget eh?" said Sylvia, examining the tall, slim middle-aged man, with the pronounced nose and distinguished appearance, deep in conversation with two other men of a similar age. She wondered if they were talking about the forthcoming Litha.

"Sylvia," Olwyn squeezed her hand. "that's a beautiful dress you're wearing," Sylvia was acutely but not awkwardly aware that she, in her white dress, looked very different to the others, in their dark colours and muted tones. Olwyn too looked lovely she thought, as the deep burgundy colour and simple tunic style complimented her dark glossy bob and high colouring.

"Your outfit is gorgeous too," said Sylvia. She noticed with satisfaction her pleasing reflection in the mirror over the fireplace as well as the admiring glances of some of the members.

"Aradnia," At first, Sylvia failed to recognise her new name. Then, as she felt a tap on the shoulder, she turned to face Llyriad.

"How wonderful to see you," continued Llyriad as her eyes swept Sylvia up and down. "And my goodness, don't you look the part tonight?" There was an edge to her voice. "There are some people that you really need to meet. Come with me."

Llyriad didn't wait for a reply so Sylvia followed her as she marched through the crowded room towards the fireplace which Dafo was nonchalantly leaning against.

"Dafo," said Llyriad, "this is Aradnia, the new recruit I was mentioning before."

Dafo turned and tilted his head. "Delighted to meet you Aradnia. However, I see you have no drink. How remiss. Llyriad bring this young lady some wine. Red or white?"

"White please." Sylvia noticed Llyriad's lips dropping very slightly.

"Now my dear, how are you finding being a member of our group?" said Dafo

His voice was clipped and precise and Sylvia felt a little intimidated.

"It's wonderful. Very wonderful. I feel honoured to be part of it." She rubbed her fingers nervously, clutching at her dress.

"Tell me, were you present at the Esbat? And what were your thoughts on that?"

Sylvia paused, feeling her cheeks burn, finding it hard how to articulate her feelings about the magical night.

"It was wonderful. Amazing. I haven't stopped thinking about it since. And … you … you were marvellous."

Dafo gave an approving nod before taking another sip from his goblet.

Llyriad arrived back, and pushed a wine glass into Sylvia's hand.

"Well Llyriad," said Dafo. "She has chosen the very best time of year to be initiated, hasn't she? The Solstice is our special time, isn't it?" There was a deep resonance to his tone reminding Sylvia again of the Esbat and his impressive performance.

"Yes, I believe so," Llyriad gave a strained, obligatory smile, as she cast dubious eyes once more over Sylvia's striking dress.

"Olwyn told me a little of last year's." said Sylvia. "She said it was incredible and…"

Dafo interrupted. "Olwyn? Olwyn? I can't quite recall …" He cast his eyes around the room. Llyriad gestured to where Olwyn was talking with Loic and two others. "Ah yes, of course. Loic's friend. "He turned away from the gathering dismissively. "Anyway, I expect you know that we shall have some important decisions to make soon."

Sylvia looked fixedly at Dafo and straightened. Llyriad noted the reaction.

"Yes, I am sure that Aradnia is aware that we'll be looking to select some special people for the Litha." Llyriad said with a tightness in her voice." What a pity she isn't part of a couple, because of course …"

"Those who represent the two sacred figures don't have to actually be part of a genuine couple," Dafo said quickly. "It is just the man and woman most suitable for the occasion. Dant omnia aliis Llyriad, dant omnia aliis – give everything for others." He delivered the coup de grace with ease and finesse.

"Yes, but that is what usually happens, after all …" Llyriad seethed but she was cut short again by Dafo.

"Anyway, my dear, let me introduce you to some others who would love to meet you." Dafo turned his back on Llyriad, leaving her in a dark place and gestured for an elated Aradnia to follow him.

***

Preston, Lancashire - October 2009

Cynthia was making Sunday dinner later than usual. Usually, they ate at lunchtime but as Rebecca would be coming back soon, she had been prepared, just on this occasion, to change the routine. She was definitely pleased that this week was over.

Once Rebecca was back, she thought, she would realise for definite where her bread was best buttered. No doubt, after having been all alone for the week Rebecca would be delighted to be home and looking forward to seeing her workmates and those delightful children. It was strange how Rebecca never seemed to say a great deal about her work these days but Cynthia took this to be a good sign. Possibly, her daughter would soon be looking for promotion. She would probably be waiting until the deputy head's job became free at her current school (the present incumbent, Mrs. Jones, must surely be retiring soon) which would save a lot of bother and upheaval.

And when she showed her daughter the details of the house down the road, Rebecca would be over the moon and admit that the sooner she got rid of that horrible house, with its unpleasant associations, the better.

It hadn't always been the case that Cynthia hated her sister. When they had been younger, they had in fact been quite fond of each other. But Sylvia just seemed to have had the privileges and opportunities that she had been denied. And what did she have to show for her life? Not much. People say absence makes the heart grow fonder but she didn't find this to be the case. For years Sylvia hadn't let her family know her whereabouts or what she'd been doing. In fact, to this day, Cynthia still wondered about the foul man and woman who had called on their parents. Nobody ever wanted to say anything about what had happened. That was definitely proof that Sylvia had been up to no good.

Cynthia thought back to that night-time visit all those years ago and her sister's extraordinary plea … no, demand for help. As it happened the arrangement had worked out rather well. And regarding it being revealed, well, maybe her sister's passing wasn't such a terrible occurrence. But why did she have to complicate matters with this damn house?

Chapter 17
North Shields- October 2009

Caroline didn't know whether she would be able to see Rebecca again before she went back to school but she wasn't as troubled by this as she might have been a couple of days earlier. There was something about the girl's manner that told her she wasn't completely happy in her current position. While she didn't wish unhappiness on the girl, the situation could definitely be used to her advantage. It was crucial that the house wasn't sold, at least not as long as she and Robert were alive. Presumably, they would outlive their enemies but then ... one never knew. Who would have thought that Sylvia would die? And even now Caroline couldn't understand how the death of her friend could have happened at all, especially given her unique circumstances. Perhaps once Rebecca had left, she ought to go and check that things in the attic were as they ought to be. But why wouldn't they be? Sylvia would have been bound to have mentioned it if anything amiss had happened. Nevertheless, it would do no harm to check.

Feeling restless, Caroline knew that she ought to be doing some work but after all Friday was nearly the weekend, so she reckoned she should give herself a little leeway. Maybe, if she went to visit Robert she would run into Rebecca and she would be able to gather more details of the girl's intentions. Although she was pretty sure that the girl had decided not to sell, a further affirmation would bring her some peace of mind.

As she pulled out of her car park, she noticed a white Clio behind her. She put on the radio and sang along to the tunes on Radio 2 as she headed to Robert's bookshop. She stopped at a red traffic light.

Looking once more in her mirror, she saw a blue Land Rover behind her but just beyond that the same white Clio. Caroline didn't know why, but there was something about this car that made her feel uneasy. Pulling away from the junction, Caroline decided to deviate from her usual route and pulled into a side street. She then continued zig-zagging through back lanes until she arrived at Tynemouth's main street. She had a good look in the rear-view mirror but there was no sign of the Clio. *My imagination's running riot* she thought to herself – *get a grip*. She smiled, noticing a parking space right outside 'The Turk's Head' and wondered if Robert had been in his local recently.

As she approached the bookshop, she could see Sebastian through the window, serving an elderly lady, but no sign of Robert.

"A very good morning to you Sebastian," she trilled ironically as soon as she opened the door, "Where's your Uncle?"

Sebastian grunted without looking up. "He's just gone out to the erm... Post Office. I think that's what he said but I might be wrong." The elderly lady tutted, annoyed by Caroline's interruption.

"I'll just wait for him here then."

Caroline sat in the café area, making sure she could see who was coming in. She swept the shop with grave eyes and gave a little shake of her head at the stacks of books piled high on the floor and then stared aimlessly out of the window at a ginger cat perched on the ledge. The cat looked back indignantly, threw up its tail and flounced off.

Caroline suddenly started and threw a hand to her face. A white Clio was coming along the street. The car parked close to hers and a bulky woman with black, dyed hair squirmed awkwardly from the car. An overcoat was draped over her and she had a general, saggy appearance. Caroline felt a sickly, nauseous feeling surge around her stomach. She pulled back from the window, slumped back in her seat and tried ineffectually to hide behind a menu as the woman walked towards the shop but then went straight past to go into the newsagent's next door. Caroline could feel the blood pulsing at her temple. It had to be her, it had to be. Couldn't possibly be anyone else.

Out of the corner of his eye Sebastian watched Caroline shoot out of her chair and scurry to the backroom which served as both office and storage space. Five minutes later Robert walked into the shop.

Sebastian waved an arm to rear of the shop. "She's in the back and behaving very strangely."

"Who is? What are you talking about?" said Robert, removing a hat and scarf with irritation.

"Caroline," Sebastian said in hushed tones. "I think she saw something outside. Seemed a bit put out by it. She had a very strange look on her face and then she ran through there."

"Caroline," called Robert, striding over to the back room and shoving the door open, Sebastian loping behind him. "Whatever is the matter? What's going on?"

They found Caroline pressed against the far wall, staring at the floor, visibly shaking. "What's wrong?" said Robert. "You look like you've seen a ghost."

"I have, I have, it's her, here - I'm sure it's her," A lump rattled in Caroline's throat and the words spilled out of her. "Has to be. Has to be. She's here. After all this time. She's here. It's her. I'm sure of it. Got to be her. After all this time. She's here."

"What's she talking about? Who's she seen?" said Sebastian.

Caroline jumped at the sound of the other voice, just noticing that Sebastian was in the room, and gave Robert a withering look.

"Funnily enough, when we were in the pub last night there was this old woman watching us and listening to what we were saying," said Sebastian pointedly, looking from Robert to Caroline "And... I've just seen that same woman out the window. Thought she was some sort of bag lady at first... but ... as she just got out of a car that seems unlikely."

Roberts shrugged, his face trying to veil the effect Sebastian's words were having, but he was more than a little alarmed at this sudden turn of events.

***

Lancaster University- May 1979

Robert walked around to Sylvia's room and was pleased to see that her light was on. *Good*, he thought to himself, that meant she was back and hopefully she would be glad to see him. Almost as soon as his hand touched the door it was flung open and Sylvia stood in front of him, dressed in blue pyjamas. To his delight she lunged forward, gave him a big hug and kissed him on the cheek,

"I gather you had a good time then?" he said.

"Robert, you wouldn't believe it." Sylvia's eyes were blazing, "I think I've got a real chance of being chosen."

"Chosen? Chosen for what?"

"The Litha. The biggest ceremony. The biggest ceremony of all, the most important one. Oh, don't worry, I'll tell you all about it later. You've got to come to the next meeting. Really, you've got to."

"Like anything's going to stop me Sylvia. You know I said that I would." Robert knew, at that very moment, he would jump through windows if Sylvia asked him to.

"The house was fabulous, very grand and tasteful."

"Hang on, hang on," laughed Robert, excited by Sylvia's excitement. "Whose was this house - and where was it? Tell me all about it." Robert realised it was very necessary to affect more than a little interest.

"A place called Quernmore, not far away from here." Sylvia sat on the bed hugging her knees. "Dafo's house. Dafo's the leader of the Requisite. I think he started the group. I've seen him around campus, I think he's a lecturer. Not sure which subject though. I think his name might be Derrick actually…"

"Derrick, Derrick Stevens? Theology – he's a Professor of Early Christianity- I go to his lectures."

"I think that might be him. What does he look like?" said Sylvia.

"Tall, white hair, receding. long nose. He's a brilliant lecturer- charismatic and passionate, very passionate about his stuff. He's written loads of book as well." Robert's eyes wandered off as he tried to remember the titles of some of the books.

"They'd be interesting to read. I spent quite a long time talking to him Robert. I think he liked me too. And I think he would like us both if we went as a couple."

He liked her too? Thought Robert. *What was she talking about? Surely, he must be at least the age of her father.*

Robert was beginning to feel a little jealous because he guessed that, despite being middle-aged, Derrick would be considered attractive by some. If, as he suspected, Derrick had taken a shine to Sylvia, where did he fit in? And without a doubt, if that were the case, Derrick certainly wouldn't be interested in meeting her boyfriend.

"For the Litha. They choose a couple." Sylvia thought, by the agitated look on his face, that Robert was not getting the point. "The couple best suited for the occasion."

"But it's hardly going to be you or me is it?" said Robert. "You've only just joined, and I'm not even a member yet."

"It doesn't work like that. They always choose a couple that are young …that look, y'know, good."

Robert wrinkled his brow, professing deep thought on the subject but he really couldn't be bothered to hear anything else about the Lith or whatever it was called. Once more, Sylvia was letting her fantasies run wild.

"Anyway, I'm glad you enjoyed yourself but I'm tired and need to get some sleep. I've got an early lecture tomorrow … with your *friend* actually." He said the words pointedly and picked up his coat. He was now confused over his opinion of Professor Stevens. Initially he had held the man in high regard but his seemingly inappropriate interest in Sylvia had somehow tainted him in Robert's eyes.

"Well, are you going? Or do you want to stay here?" Sylvia was not in the mood for being alone. She was much too excited.

"What do you think?"

Sleep, and lying next to Sylvia was all that was important now and he banished Derrick from his thoughts.

***

Quernmore, Lancaster – May 1979

After everyone else had gone Derrick was left talking with Simon. Although it was late, it was clear there were matters that Derrick was eager to discuss.

"I don't think Lydia was very pleased this evening." Simon sat across from Derrick in front of the fire, with the flames flickering, drinking whiskey.

"Well you know why don't you?" said Derrick, pulling hard on his expensive, Peterson gold, spigot briar pipe. "She thinks that you and her will be chosen. I was just trying to prepare her for another disappointment."

"She doesn't get it does she?" said Simon, shaking his head. "She thinks the role is of some importance, doesn't she? If she only knew…"

Derrick looked over at his friend and it seemed incredibly strange that more than thirty years had lapsed since they were both students together at Durham. He knew he looked fairly good for his age, but Simon looked amazing. He could pass quite easily for someone in their mid-twenties, with his elfin looks, wiry frame and shoulder length fair hair. Derrick knew full well the reasons for this and the fact that genetics, were not the cause of his practically wrinkle free face. As he watched his friend refill his glass, he understood that lifestyle could hardly be much of a contributory factor either. While Derrick carefully monitored what he ate and drank, Simon continued to behave as if he was still in his twenties - while he must be more than double this age.

"So, what did you think of Aradnia?" Derrick's opinion on this matter was evident, from the amount of time he had spent talking to the girl that evening.

"I don't really have any thoughts on her. I was never introduced to her properly," said Simon.

"Well, decisions need to be made soon, and I thought that she was perhaps a suitable candidate..." Derrick tried to meet his friend's eye but Simon looked away.

"Isn't there any way that it could be Lydia...I mean her heart's been set on it for quite a few years now. I know it's not that important ... but to her..., "

Lydia and Simon had been together for some time. What had seemed a good match several years ago, was beginning to appear odd. Lydia wasn't ageing well and Derrick was surprised that Simon hadn't found himself a replacement for her. Derrick never had time for such dalliances but he had never known Simon without an attractive female accessory. Over the years there had been plenty, but never for so long as Lydia. He was also surprised about his lack of interest in Aradnia as there was something about the girl that had reminded him of a younger more attractive version of Lydia.

"But you know that's impossible," said Derrick. Then his voice brightened and there was a curious gleam in his eye. There was an opportunity here. "That is, of course, unless ... unless you were to change your role in the event."

"I don't think so."

"Well, it could happen, could it not."

"I suppose you fancy doing it, do you?" Simon chewed the words and spat them out.

"It might be the best possible ...outcome. Take off some of the pressure."

"Take off some of the pressure – you're not kidding. My God – you know what would happen!"

"It has to happen sometime – even to you."

"You're really serious, aren't you?"

"Well ... why not?" Derrick chose his words carefully. "Surely, the responsibility must weigh so heavily on you Simon. Do you not feel ever so slightly tired? After all this time surely..."

"I can't believe that we're having this conversation," Simon glared at Derrick. "And if I'm tired... well, that's no wonder is it? It's my responsibility, my re-sp-ons-ib-il-ity." Simon gulped his drink and then slammed his glass down on the table. *Derrick didn't know everything. Although he knew far more than was good for him.* It was definitely time for Simon to be making plans for moving on.

"Now, Derrick I think it's time for me to go. Please don't speak of these matters again – ever."

Simon stood quickly and launched himself across the room.

"Well, just think over what I've said." called Derrick, but Simon was already halfway through the door, slamming it behind him. Nursing his glass, Derrick was furious. This had been going on for long enough. Scire had had his time and now it was his turn. He would see to it that he had his turn. It was only right and proper that the keeper of the cloth should be changed. After all this time it had to be the correct thing to do. *Had to be.*

***

Journey back to Lancashire– October 2009

Rebecca wasn't enjoying the train ride home, but she knew it was preferable to the actual arrival at her destination. Still, her dad would be there to meet her and she would be quite pleased to see him. No, she would be delighted to see him, as he wasn't the issue. As for her mother, well she was expecting a painful interrogation about the events of the past week. Was it really only a week? So much had happened in such a short space of time. However, could it be that she had been presented with a much welcome 'get out' card.

Looking at the neglected laptop in her bag, only made her feel worse. Tomorrow she would be expected to hand in this week's planning. She hadn't done it. Children would be assuming that corrections and improvements would have to be made from the work before half term. The books hadn't been marked. The other teachers would have spent much of their holidays catching up with their work. She had done nothing whatsoever. And those children...nobody had wanted that Year 5 class this year. Their previous teacher in Year 4 had gone off with stress just after Christmas last year and the subsequent string of supply teachers that had followed had simply exacerbated the problem. Rebecca chewed on her fingernails grimly.

"Cheer up. It's not the end of the world, love." The voice came from an elderly, well-dressed man sitting opposite. She gave him a reluctant half smile then looked away. It was only 5 o'clock and it was already nearly dark as the train pulled into Lancaster Station. She watched enviously, as the young students disembarked to have a Sunday night of frivolity before their lectures began the next day. They didn't know how lucky they were. A whistle blew and the soothing *chugeddychug* of the train began again.

Rebecca wondered what she should tell her mother of Caroline, if anything at all. Maybe at some point in the dim and distant past the two had actually met. She couldn't imagine the them hitting it off at all and she recalled Caroline's spiteful words about her mother. Right now, she didn't feel so inclined to defend her. She needed to be very careful how she handled the situation and the less she said about Caroline could only be for the best. Maybe if she painted a rosier picture of the actual house she had been left, then it might make her move there more palatable. Even Cynthia couldn't deny that Tynemouth itself was a lovely place to live. But no, that was doubtful. Cynthia would only ever say that where she lived now was the best place to be.

Possibly she should be more honest with her parents about how much she hated her job. They had no inkling whatsoever of what she had to face each day. But if she admitted the truth to them, she would feel an even bigger failure than she did now. Rebecca gave a long, low half-moan, half-wheeze as the train pulled into Preston station and then, remembering where she was, stared fixedly out of the window, not wanting to give the man another opportunity to comment on her mental health.

****

Lancaster – May 1979

Yes, thought Simon, the events of the evening at Derrick's house had merely confirmed what he had been feeling for some time It was necessary for him to make a move. Twenty years was too long for him to stay in one place. It was just too dangerous. To be perfectly honest he cared little for the Requisite now and he understood fully what Derrick's motives had always been. True, they may have been friends once, but that was a long time ago when their positions had both been very different. Now the esteemed professor outranked the lowly laboratory assistant massively ... except Simon had something that Derrick wanted - wanted more than anything in the world. No amount of money or influence, could give Derrick the precious object he desired unless it was bequeathed to him by Simon. His craving was becoming more obvious and increasingly more of an issue with the passing of time.

Back in his small, one bedroomed flat in Lancaster, he couldn't help but make negative comparisons between the affluence that poured out of the very bricks of Derrick's house and the basic state of his own home. Strange, how the cloth had certain powers but not others. Simon had been blessed and cursed, just like his grandfather before him. And there were times when he wished he could just destroy it. Despite having lived in this one place for the last twenty years, he had little of material value to show for it. This was the familiar recurring patter. No matter where he went, it was always the same. It was as if she didn't want him to succeed. His only achievement was to be to guard her well and so he would be rewarded in other ways. It had been Derrick who had persuaded him to move here in the first place. Yet as Derrick's career prospered, Simon's had floundered.

Simon now realised he had made a massive mistake, confiding in Derrick all those years ago. It had, for a short while, relieved some of the burden. At the time, Derrick had seemed dismissive of the cloth, but now that its power was self-evident, he had changed his tune and the yearning and craving for it had become glaringly apparent. Derrick had welcomed it initially as just another little gimmick to add spice to their ceremonies, especially the ridiculous Litha ceremony, where the 'Keeper of the Cloth' had the 'all so important job' of firing the arrow at the sun. Yes, definitely he wouldn't miss all of that nonsense when he had gone.

Although physically Simon retained his youth, inside he felt weary, as if somehow his very spirit was fading. When the Requisite had begun, firing the arrow was just one of the sect's little rituals that made the group seem mysterious and enticing. A return to the original Celtic Christian world and pagan nature worship. It had been a good cover for him. How alluring... but this was all just a perverted manipulation of that grasping megalomaniac. Only two people understood the cloth and its truly incredible gift. Each year at the Litha, it had been brought out and how Derrick's fingers increasingly must have been itching. Simon looked over with belligerence at the box on his shelf.

He shouldn't have driven home, but despite the amount of whiskey he had drunk, he certainly hadn't imagined the look of hunger in Derrick's eye or the thirst in his voice. Simon had suspected his intentions many times before, but never had his intentions been so transparent. However, it would have been foolish to refuse his hospitality. Derrick always kept a fine selection of whiskeys.

And Lydia, she was becoming much more of a problem. She was totally brainwashed by the group and her behaviour was just downright childish. Her desire to be the young 'Earth Mother' in this Litha was absurd. She was just too old. But even tonight, out of some misguided loyalty, he had tried arguing her case and Derrick, predictably, had merely attempted to manipulate the situation to serve his own ends.

It was clear that someone had been catching Derrick's eye that evening and what her role would become in the forthcoming events. It was all quite pitiful really, the way Derrick feigned the importance of these trivial events and ceremonies. Only he knew Derrick's true obsession and as this became an even greater consuming force, so it was inevitably time for him to be moving on. He thought back to the death of his grandfather all those centuries ago. If he were to allow Derrick what he wanted, the haunting memory of those ancient bones would become his immediate fate.

Although he still had some fondness for Lydia their relationship was not what it was. No longer did they have physical relations but she seemed oblivious to the significance of this. Seemingly her role in the Requisite was her whole world and their relationship was such an integral part of this to her, that she had failed to notice any cracks. Lydia had no idea that her days were indeed numbered- and quite a low number at that.

Chapter 18

Lancaster – May 1979

Robert was waiting in the lecture theatre for the 10 o'clock slot to begin. It was a large room, having plenty of flip up seats and an overhead projector with a white screen at the front. Around him, his fellow students were chattering and getting their papers and pens ready to take notes. Sitting on the next seat to him was a girl with a blue sweater and a swinging ponytail. She smiled at him, wanting to strike up a conversation but Robert's mind was on other matters.

Eventually a tall man with prematurely white hair and an aquiline nose wafted into the room. Assuming his place at the front with a confident air, he placed some notes on a stand and prepared to hold court. Robert imagined him talking to Sylvia last night and he felt a stab of jealousy that this arrogant man had been chatting up his girlfriend.

"The consequences of the Synod at Whitby in 664 were profound," began Derrick Stevens using his sonorous voice to great effect, "especially for followers of the Celtic form of Christianity which had been the pre-eminent form of the religion, especially in the most northerly parts, from Northumbria upwards. From this day onwards Christianity in the region was to follow Papal lead. The island was no longer to be viewed as an insignificant backwater with its peculiar branch of Christianity, but a crucial piece in the ecclesiastical chessboard of Europe. No longer a paltry pawn but a majestic bishop at the very least." Derrick raised his eyebrows, cleared his throat, paused for dramatic effect, and then looked down briefly at his notes.

"Fundamentally, the main bone of contention was regarding the time at which Easter was to be celebrated. The Celtic and Roman forms of Christianity had the most important fixture of the Church's year at different times. However, the Roman Easter was earlier. This meant a shorter time of Lent, when abstinence from pleasure in the form of rich food and conjugal rights was the norm, would need to be observed. King Oswald of Northumbria favoured the idea of closer links with both Europe and the Pope as he felt this would be advantageous to his political interests."

Robert was feverishly scribbling down notes. He was finding Derrick's lecture surprisingly interesting despite the misgivings he now had about the man.

"In addition, monks were now forced to wear a different tonsure. As part of the Celtic tradition, tonsures had been shaven from ear to ear," Derrick made a sweeping gesture with one hand making a rainbow-like arc across his head. "Whereas Roman monks shaved the crown, in recognition of the crown of thorns Jesus had been subjected to." Derrick used more elaborate hand movements to further illustrate this point.

"Nonetheless, many would have been greatly embittered by this decision. This wasn't the form of Christianity that had been brought by St Columba from Iona. The particular form of Christianity practised by the Saints Aidan, Colman and Cuthbert was more intrinsically suited to our island's inherent worship of nature. Ancient celebrations had never been abandoned, or beliefs forgotten. They had neatly been incorporated. Midwinter solstice merely merged into Christmas, Lammas into harvest and Ostera, festival of the fertility goddess, became Easter. Indeed, so angered was Colman by the outcome of events, that he resigned from his position as Bishop of Lindisfarne and one can only imagine the fury of the disenchanted St. Cuthbert as he journeyed back to that Holy Island." Derrick nodded his head and adopted a grave expression as if imagining himself as the disappointed saint. He then continued expounding his discourse for more than an hour before offering his final thoughts which he hoped would be considered controversial enough for his young, mainly female audience.

"However, one must also consider the significance of the role of women in the Church. Because their role in Celtic Christianity was of great importance, and certainly not seen in any way as inferior to that of men. Celtic women were able to function within their society on a much more equal footing with men. Indeed, the Irish Brehon law gave more rights to women than any other law code at the time. Women had political equality and could even lead the tribe. They had equal rights in divorce and to a share of property in such matters. They could hold any office open to men. The Celtic church afforded women positions of honour. Women like Brigid, Ebba and Hilda were leaders of mixed monasteries. St. Hilda, who was head of a joint monastery and convent at Whitby, was able to enjoy enormous power. Indeed, the great synod was held at her very abbey. When the decision was made, she must have been forced to relinquish all her authority, as the country became under control of the patriarchal Roman Church..." Derrick paused again to gaze at the audience, and gain the full effect for his final words, "... and its sexist, some might say, misogynist theology."

Robert noticed the girl next to him suddenly stop scribbling crosses and flowers onto her notepad and look up abruptly. He had to admit that Derrick knew his stuff and was indeed a charismatic speaker.

He was now looking forward very much to meeting this man when Sylvia introduced them to each other. And he had the feeling that this would be very soon.

***

Preston - October 2009

"Tell me you're joking Rebecca," Cynthia was furious and stabbed a roast potato aggressively. "So, not only are you considering giving up your teaching job but…you are actually thinking of going to live permanently in that… that …revolting hovel."

"It's not a hovel Mum and… Tynemouth itself is a lovely place." Rebecca, had decided to bite the bullet and not delay telling her parents of her intentions. She had decided on the train, the sooner she told her parents of her plans the better in the long run.

"You worked so hard to get that job. You love working in that school and teaching those children. Rebecca, this is nonsense… this where you belong… here with us. Your parents," said Cynthia, in a strange half-plea, half-growl.

"Now Cynthia, Cynthia, come on, calm down, love." Bill put both hands up. "Let the lass speak."

"You know, you've got no idea … no idea what it's like," said Rebecca. "I hate the job. Hate the job. It's too much stress with the planning, the marking, the lesson observations. That class that I teach…they're awful. Monsters. I can't teach them, can hardly control them….and we're due an Ofsted. I can't cope. I can't." The tears, which had threatened for the last few hours eventually came.

"Well, it's peculiar. Very peculiar if you ask me," said Cynthia, ignoring the sobs. "You have never, ever mentioned any of this before. Who's been putting these ridiculous ideas into your head?"

"Nobody," said Rebecca, taking deep breaths, recovering her composure. "It's just... while I was away ... I had time to think about things."

"Too much time." Cynthia rolled her eyes. "Well, you can just put these preposterous ideas straight out of your head. Jobs aren't easy to come by these days you know? Do you want to spend your life on benefits. That's what I can see happening you know. I mean... what will the neighbours think of you?"

Bill gave his wife an incredulous look.

"Well, mother, it's my life. I don't think it's a *preposterous* idea and ... I – couldn't – care- less – what- they – think." *So typical of her mother to bring up something so trivial* thought Rebecca. How many times over the years had she heard this?

"Your life! Your life! This talk of quitting your job," said Cynthia, now pacing the room," What will they think of you at school? What will they think of you? You'll be letting them down. You've got obligations my girl. Responsibilities. And even more importantly, what sort of a reference will your head teacher give you?"

"Cynthia," said Bill, as quietly as he could, "Rebecca must be tired after her long journey. Let's all just calm down and reason this out. Maybe we could talk about this tomorrow. The lass needs ..."

"Reason!" shouted Cynthia, making it sound like a criminal offence. "Young people just give up too easily these days. Work isn't supposed to be a barrel of laughs you know? In my day you just got on with it. I thought you had more backbone Rebecca."

Bill dug his hands deep into his pockets.

Rebecca worked her tongue around her mouth. It was the wrong time to bring up the fact that her mother hadn't actually held down a job for years. She hadn't worked since she'd had her children, and working as a secretary in a cosy office could hardly be compared with an horrendous teaching load.

"And another thing…" continued Cynthia, warming to her task. "Taking yourself off to some place in the north–east? The north–east for God's sake!" Cynthia wrung her hands conspicuously to add to her performance. "You never used to be like this Rebecca. What's come over you recently? A couple of years ago you wouldn't have been so feckless."

"Look - my aunt - who I never really knew," said Rebecca, as calmly as she could. "She was kind enough … and generous enough to leave me a house … and I just, just feel in some way, that she must want me to live there for some reason or other. Maybe it's just fate."

"*Fate! Fate!*" Cynthia inhaled the words and then blew them out so that they ricocheted from wall to wall. "Don't be so stupid! Sylvia did this to make mischief," Cynthia slumped back down at the table. "This is just pure spite. Spite from beyond the grave. If…if she had any compassion for her family whatsoever, she would have left the house to me. And don't get me wrong, I don't want … or need the money. But it would have stopped all this nonsense. I mean, the money would eventually go to you… and your sister, at the proper time. How do you think your poor sister Jessica feels about all of this?" Cynthia was playing as many cards as she could.

Bill kept his hands in his pockets and blew out a long draft of air.

"I knew you'd bring up Jessica," said Rebecca. "I knew you'd bring Jessica into this. But she's married and busy bringing up her kids. *She* – is - happy. She's not stuck in a job she hates or in danger of becoming an old spinster – I can't even have a night out – there's so much work to do. I wish you cared, cared just a tiny bit about my happiness. And less about what the bloody, neighbours think." The room seemed to float as Rebecca pushed back another tear.

Bill took his hands out of his pockets and took a half-step towards Rebecca, feeling dreadful for failing to recognise how miserable his daughter had been.

"Now, now, love, we do. Course we care about your happiness," said Bill. "There's nothing we want more - don't we Cynthia? We had no idea you were so unhappy in your job. P'raps you could get one in a different school. Your mother just wants what's best for you. We both do. And *we are* pleased about your windfall but it's just, y'know, if you lived far away ...then we wouldn't get to see you that often."

"But Dad, it's not in another country. It only takes a couple of hours to get to Tyneside by car. You could both come and visit me. And I can come back at weekends. You could stay and help me decorate. It's not worth selling at the moment but once it's done up ... and the market might improve ..." Rebecca had no axe to grind with her dad.

"I just don't understand why you don't sell it and be done with it," said Cynthia slowly. "If you'd only let me come up there with you in the first place ... well, the problem would have been sorted by now." She defused and shot a glance across at her husband, focusing on the 'improving market' comment and feeling that there was still a glimmer of hope.

Bill put his hands back in his pockets, gave what he hoped was a conciliatory smile to his daughter and wife and pulled back, miles back. He looked around the room hoping that someone would come in to repair the situation and put everything back to normal. But no-one did.

***

Tynemouth – October 2009

Sebastian was sitting in The Turk's Head, waiting for his uncle. Robert had just had gone to the bank after closing the shop. Looking round the pub Sebastian was wondering if there would be any more sightings of the strange woman, but at the moment he and the barman had the place to themselves. Now he thought about it, the woman had definitely been listening to their conversation. But why? And Caroline had been completely freaked out when she saw her outside the shop, which in itself was strange. It was as if Caroline had recognised her from the past, in which case his uncle would probably know her too, as their lives seemed to be inexplicably linked in so many ways. In the pub his uncle hadn't seemed perturbed, but maybe he just hadn't seen her, he wasn't the most observant of people anyway.

Just then the door opened and Robert walked in.

Sebastian waved an arm. "Over here unc, I've got you a pint."

"Thanks, I just needed to get that money to the bank. You know I don't like leaving too much in the shop,"

"I wouldn't have thought we would have taken too much money today but I guess it's best to be on the safe side. Especially at the moment."

"Especially at the moment?"

"Yes."

"Why – especially at the moment?"

Sebastian gave his uncle a mock, grave look. "I mean, there seems to be some peculiar people hanging round, doesn't there?"

"I'm not sure I know what you mean," said Robert, taking a quick drink. On the alert already, understanding where this was going.

"Well, Caroline was going berserk about that woman she saw through the window. I recognised that woman from the other night. She was in here. She was sitting over there." Sebastian pointed with his glass to a place on the other side of the bar. "Didn't you see her?"

"I can't say that I did," Robert shrugged. "But then you went to the bar and I can't see around corners. Anyway, I wonder how Rebecca is getting on, she'll be back at school now I expect."

Sebastian wasn't going to be put off by his uncle trying to change the conversation.

"But you must know who she is… you and Caroline must have spoken. I've never seen her in such a flap. She looked positively frightened. And then," Sebastian remembered an earlier visitor. "You remember that old guy who came into the shop. *You* looked really frightened then. Are the two connected? What's going on? Are you two in some kind of trouble?"

"Frightened? Sebastian, calm down. You're letting your imagination run away with you."

"I don't think I was imagining it."

"They *might* be people we know. But then… perhaps not. I don't know. It's possible that they were people we knew years ago, when we were students. It could all be coincidental though…and they could just look a bit similar."

Neither Robert nor Sebastian looked convinced.

"Since you were students...you mean you've known Caroline that long? I didn't realise. So, if these are the people you think they might be, why are you scared of them? And ... has this got anything to do with that girl Rebecca?"

Robert had never seen his laidback nephew agitated like this before. Usually he was indifferent to, well, almost everything. He twisted round and gave him an exaggerated, puzzled look.

"Why on earth should this have anything to do with her? Sebastian, I'm tired and you're not helping matters. Can we not just sit quietly and enjoy our drinks. Don't worry - we're not in MI5 or anything like that." *If only we were*, thought Robert, *it would make things a lot easier*.

"Ah well, that's good to know then. At least I'm not part of some secret service, intelligence gathering operation."

"No, you never were. Not for the last twenty-odd years anyway," Robert beamed a smile at his nephew, sank back into his seat and took a long drink, waiting for the next question.

Sebastian knew he was on to something by the reaction of his uncle. He was genuinely concerned about him. He didn't like the look of the man who had visited the bookshop, or the woman he had seen outside, but he supposed he had better let things drop, for now.

"So, what do you think Rebecca will do with the house? D'you think she'll sell it?" Sebastian reverted to safer territory and Robert gave him a grateful look, acknowledging the change of tack.

"Well according to Caroline, she seems to think she is going to keep it and come and live in it herself," said Robert. "Well, that's what she hopes anyway."

"Eh? How can she do that? You'd need loads of cash to do up that place. What about her job?"

"Sebastian, Sebastian. More questions I can't answer. Let's just talk about something else, eh? Fancy some crisps?"

Robert stood up quickly and went to the bar.

***

Northumberland – October 2009

As the white Clio sped across the panorama of the Northumbrian moors, the driver felt a surge of positivity that eventually she was on the right track and some progress was finally being made. The purple heather carpeted the hills with such beauty that even Lydia couldn't fail to be moved by it.

The purpose of her journey was to talk to Derrick, who she hadn't seen for years. Although they had kept in regular contact, this was largely via telephone and more recently by e-mails. Actually, she wondered how she would find him and indeed what he would think of her. Lydia was under no illusions. The years had not been kind to her. Hardly surprising really, as the horrific effects of that particular evening years ago had eaten away at her like a canker and she'd taken solace in food and alcohol.

However, recent events had led her to feel that retribution wasn't too far away. At last, they had discovered their current location and the prize was in sight. This was of more concern to Derrick than herself. Her driving force was suitable revenge which could be leisurely if necessary, but from what she could gather from him, time was increasingly important.

Since his retirement, Derrick had lived in Northumberland, very close to Holy Island. This would seem the obvious place for him to live out his later years, but incredibly, after all this time of searching, his raison d'etre was so close by. Lydia wondered how long they had been in Tynemouth and how they had been able to remain so elusive for all those years since Lancaster and Durham and probably numerous other places. She had until recently almost given up hope. But how strange and fortunate, that Robert's bookshop had been mentioned online.

In the distance Lydia could see Bamburgh Castle rising majestically on the skyline. Only a few miles to go.

The arrival of the internet should have made their detection much easier especially if you wanted to advertise your business. However, until very recently little trace online could be found of a certain interior design company or a particular bookshop. In fact, thought Lydia, it was amazing that anyone could run profitable companies in such an old-fashioned manner. She was well aware of why *they* did this. However, no one is completely undetectable. People leave reviews even if they're not requested by the owner. And Lydia was pretty sure Robert was ignorant of their existence.

A lot had been achieved in a few short weeks.

If a certain young woman hadn't come to have her fortune told, then possibly she would be none the wiser. Whitley Bay was a good a place as any for a clairvoyant to have as a base, but who would have believed in such good fortune and it hadn't been too difficult to narrow the search down after that.

Interesting conversations had been eavesdropped in the 'Turk's Head' too but Robert had been oblivious, as usual. Generally, leopards don't change their spots. However, the young man seemed to have his wits about him.

Although she had been stalking them relentlessly since then, it wasn't until last week that they had been alerted to any suspicions. It was pointless trying to drive down side streets, Lydia knew exactly to which bookshop Robert's girlfriend was going. She needed them to see her. It was time to put on a bit of pressure.

She knew that Derrick had also paid them a visit and even Robert couldn't have failed to recognize his distinctive looks. She couldn't imagine Derrick would have changed much over the years but now he must be looking older and frailer due to his condition. Still, she would see for herself in a matter of moments as she spotted the turning for Holy Island.

***

North Shields- October 2009

Whilst she looked through her kitchen window at the buildings on the other side of the river in South Shields, Caroline chewed her fingernails and worried. Now down to the quick, the skin was raw and close to bleeding. How, after all these years? How had she been able to trace them, especially at this time when everything seemed so precarious? It was essential that she of all people, kept well away from Huntington Place, so as not to draw unwanted attention to the place. From that point of view maybe it was a good thing that Rebecca wasn't there at present, but then again, the house and its special contents were left vulnerable and unguarded.

Sebastian lived next door she remembered and perhaps he could keep an eye on the place. Not that she held any great opinion of him, with his slothful and neglectful ways, but needs must. Of course, he wouldn't need to actually know anything because all he would need to do was to move the post and perform other simple tasks. Even he could manage that. It would be considered quite normal for a person to ask a neighbour, albeit one as incompetent as Sebastian, to keep a watchful eye on an empty property. This thought settled Caroline's mind for a short while as she opened the fridge to pour herself a glass of wine.

All that day, Caroline hadn't left the apartment for fear of being followed and she now paced her floor like a caged tiger. Who knew for how long she had been being watched? Not only her but Robert and Rebecca too. They had been so careful, for obvious reasons, not to draw unnecessary attention to themselves or their businesses.

Caroline sank back onto her sofa, curled her feet under herself and began looking through swatches of fabrics and wallpaper patterns. It was useless though, she was unable to concentrate and, as she took a glug from her glass, her mind began to drift back. In particular, she remembered a time in Durham when a worried Sylvia had come to visit her. Sylvia had taken the train from Lancaster for the day and they met in the cathedral coffee shop.

Both the girls had been delighted to see each other, but Sylvia's news hadn't been good. It seemed that Derrick was taking a sabbatical in Durham University for the year and Sylvia had thought it was imperative that they knew. She could have told her this by letter but she had wanted to see her friend. Although they had only been in Durham a few months, they had been forced to move.

Her train of though was disturbed by her phone. She saw Robert's name register and breathed a sigh of relief as she picked up.

"Robert, I'm going crazy here but I daren't go out." She spoke quickly but unusually quietly, as if fearful of being overheard.

"Well there's been no sign of her here today, not that I've seen anyway. Sebastian hasn't noticed anything either," Robert used an overly calm tone, sensing Caroline's unease. "Although he's taking a very keen interest in matters of late. Too keen for my liking."

"Sebastian, yes, I'm glad you've mentioned him." Caroline's mind returned once more to Huntington Place.

"Actually, I've just been for a drink with him and I'm getting tired of fending questions. I've got a headache just thinking about it."

"The old internet nonsense?"

"No, not this time. He's sensed something's bothering us both and he's determined to get to the bottom of it."

"You haven't told him anything, have you?" The edge crept back into Caroline's voice.

"Of course not ... but I can tell he isn't going to let it go."

"Come over Robert… I'm going out of my mind here."

"I can't drive, I've just been for a few pints with Sebastian."

"Oh, come on Robert. I haven't seen anyone all day and I want to talk face to face." She knew Robert would come.

"Very well, but I'll have to walk. I should be there in about half an hour"

"Get a taxi."

She knew he wouldn't.

"See you in half an hour or so," he said.

***

Lancaster- May 1979

As the sunlight streamed through the gap in her curtains, Sylvia woke, overwhelmed with such a feeling of happiness and anticipation. Robert had long gone to his lecture and after last night's events things were certainly going according to plan. It couldn't have been more perfect if she'd scripted it herself.

It was definitely the best, most sophisticated party she had ever been invited to. Certainly, it had been a sharp contrast to the teenage cider-swilling affairs of her pre-student days. Everything had seemed so civilized with the fine wine, choice of music, elegant décor, intelligent conversation and the way everyone had been dressed and conducted themselves. However, as she recalled her own appearance, when she had caught a glimpse of herself in a mirror, she smiled, holding close that precious memory. A moment she would treasure forever. That dress had been worth every penny and the huge dent it had made in her grant for that term, was completely justifiable. It was now on a hanger on the handle of her wardrobe. Once again, the sequins and trimmings on the white dress glinted and sparkled at her in triumph.

Dafo, had been so charming and seemed to be genuinely interested in her, much to the annoyance of Llyriad. Sylvia couldn't help but take a certain pleasure from this. The next step was to get Robert on board. Once they were both established members of the Requisite… well, this

Litha ceremony was going to be an unbelievable experience for both of them. She almost wished she had gone along with Robert to his lecture that morning but no, it was very pleasant lying in bed, reliving the events of last night.

Sylvia closed her eyes and imagined her and Robert as the central characters in the forthcoming ceremony. Everybody watching in awe, as they headlined in the sacred ancient ritual, becoming god and goddess themselves. This would be an occasion they would always remember and Robert would be eternally grateful to her for their exquisite moment of divinity.

However, she knew she needed to be wary of Llyriad. It was obvious that she wanted the part for herself, but she was way too old. Sylvia pictured herself and Llyriad standing next to each other and Dafo making comparisons in her favour. Llyriad was no doubt furious by the outcome of last night and Sylvia knew that she had made an enemy.

Llyriad's displeasure was the only fly in the ointment today. After all, the woman had introduced her to the Requisite in the first place and she ought to be grateful to her. Perhaps Sylvia should try to think of a way to make amends but in the meantime, she wanted to re-run last night's events through her mind once more.

Chapter 19

Alnwick, Northumberland – October 2009

The black and white flag on the sat. nav. came into view and Lydia knew she wasn't far from her destination. Her Clio swung into a driveway and up a slight hill to a detached, Edwardian house with turrets, well-tended grounds and stained glass on the impressive front door. Lydia smiled, thinking to herself, 'same old Derrick'.

She rang the doorbell and was surprised to find it opened by a stern-looking, middle-aged, Asian woman who eyed her carefully.

"This is Derrick Steven's house isn't it?" said Lydia

"Oh yes, well, I understand you must be the person called Lydia – is that right?" Giving her a further up and down look, she gestured for Lydia to enter. "I'm Mrs. Singh by the way. Mr. Stevens' carer."

Lydia stared at Mrs. Singh for a couple of seconds too long, processing this information and preparing herself for what to expect. *He must be in a really bad way*, she thought to herself.

Mrs. Singh took Lydia's oversized, threadbare coat with just a hint of disdain while Lydia stared at the ornate staircase dominating the hallway.

"Come this way please," said Mrs. Singh, "He's been expecting you."

Lydia was ushered along the corridor and into a darkened room with closed curtains and a dank smell. Hearing heavy breathing she looked over in the corner of the room where a shrunken figure sat on an armchair.

"Llyriad is that you?" A voice rasped uncertainly, but nevertheless it still held traces of the enunciation that was once so characteristic of Dafo's speech. "Please take a seat. It was good of you to come all this way to see me."

Lydia sat down on the nearest chair she could recognize in the gloom. Eventually her eyes became more accustomed to the light. She saw Derrick and couldn't help but allow the shock she felt to register on her face. Although seated, Derrick was shrunken in all senses. A diminished version of his former self. Only his nose seemed recognisable, flanked by sunken, rheumy eyes, surrounded by jaundiced wrinkled skin. A dead man sitting.

"As you can see Llyriad ... forgive me for using the old name ...old habits .... As you can see, I am not well," said Derrick. "That is why I needed to see you urgently. If you'll excuse me, I'll get straight to the point. I believe your recent findings are the only thoughts that provide me with any hope."

Lydia stared, blank-faced.

"What is wrong with you Derrick?"

Derrick grabbed onto the stick resting by his chair and awkwardly hoisted himself to his full height. She could now see the full extent of how painfully thin his limbs had become, like easily-broken twigs.

"It's cancer... late stage ... so nothing more can be done." He waved a dismissive hand. "But what you have discovered has given me some much-needed hope." The effort of standing had been too much for him and with obvious annoyance, he fell back into his seat.

"Well," Lydia composed herself, "I've found their whereabouts in Tynemouth. And I'm glad to see that it gives you some hope. It's given me hope too."

There was a knock on the door and Derrick's carer came in.

"Would you like me to bring some tea?" She asked.

"Yes, if it's not too much trouble Mrs. Singh, that would be delightful. So very kind." said Derrick.

Mrs. Singh disappeared

Lydia had never known Derrick to be so polite, in fact, almost deferential.

"So, as I say, to get to the point," said Derrick. "Have you found out where exactly they're living? I know that Robert has that bookshop. I visited him there last week."

How the hell did you manage that? Thought Lydia.

Derrick noticed Lydia baffled expression. "Yes, I have good and bad days," he said. "Unfortunately, today isn't one of my better days. But ... that's by the by. I was able to trace his whereabouts from a review online for his bookshop and Mrs. Singh drove me there. However, I was unable to trace where they are actually living.

"Well, Robert lives in a flat over his bookshop and she ..." She couldn't bring herself to use the woman's name. "*She* lives in another flat quite close by.... in North Shields. Do you know the place? It's overlooking a marina and from there she runs some type of 'interior design' business. She used 'interior' and 'design' as if they were hideous diseases.

"So, they don't live together then."

"No, they don't. Well, I think that's all about keeping us off their scent. And that's why they avoid using the internet. But they aren't as clever as they think, are they? Yes, I found some reviews about Robert Fairfax's bookshop as well, which is why I moved to the area. *She* was a little more difficult but eventually I found her."

"I see." Derrick rubbed his bony fingers together, thinking hard.

"Well, I thought we could start off by ruining their businesses. A few unkind reviews would be a beginning. Before moving on to more severe measures, something drastic but slow. I want to see the look in their eyes as they suffer. Then I don't want to see them ever again. I just want them to know that it's us, finishing them off."

Lydia looked hopefully at Derrick, she had thought they could do this today, as Derrick with his eloquent turn of phrase could produce writing more waspishly cutting than she would be capable of doing.

"So, do you have the precise address of where she lives?"

"Yes, of course. I've been following her"

"And do you think you would be able to get inside to find a particular object and bring this to me?"

He was becoming suddenly more alert. A weird light gleaming from his haunted eyes.

The conversation was abruptly curtailed before Lydia could fully register her surprise. The door banged open as Mrs. Singh came into the room wheeling an ancient, hostess trolley with a pot of tea and biscuits.

"Could you pour the tea?" Mrs. Singh nodded at Lydia as she left the room.

Lydia gave Derrick a long, hard look. "So, you want me to break into her flat?"

"There are matters which need to be attended to … immediately."

"I didn't know you wanted me to break into her flat."

"Well, why did you think I wanted to see you? I'm in no state to do it am I?" Derrick tried to throw his arms out wide but couldn't extend them as much as he wanted so he collapsed them onto his lap.

"I just want vengeance ... retribution," said Lydia. "There has to be a reckoning."

"Of course, you can have your revenge – after you have brought to me a particular object."

"What d'you mean, I can have *my* revenge, what about you? Don't you want revenge for what happened that night? To punish them. They ruined the Requisite. You know that."

"Yes, yes they did. But not in the way you imagine."

"Not in the way I imagine! What the hell does that mean? Wasn't murder enough to ruin it? What d'you mean?"

"There are certain other aspects which need to be addressed first. After, you can do what you like with them."

"I have kept in touch with you for all these years because I want revenge," said Lydia. "That day when my love, my only love, was killed…it ruined my life. All these years I've been searching. Tracking them down. And I thought we were singing from the same bloody hymn sheet. They need to be punished. They can't get away with it. They- need – to - suffer. Blood for blood."

Derrick let out a long wheeze, exasperated, as if trying to explain an obvious problem to a child.

"Listen Lydia. That night something was stolen. Something that didn't belong to them. Something that I need and deserve." Some of the old steeliness crept back into Derrick's voice.

"What are you talking about?" Lydia became suddenly taller, louder and wider, puffing herself up in indignation. "Is that what you were searching for when we went to … "

"Keep your voice down woman."

"What I lost was infinitely more precious than some inanimate object," She hissed. "What about Scire? He was stolen from me and every day since then I've been waiting for this moment. Don't you understand?"

"Yes, yes, of course. It was a terrible tragedy. Distressing for everyone, especially you." Derrick lowered his voice to a whisper. "But this object, this cloth … is invaluable."

"What d'you mean – invaluable? What kind of cloth? What is it?"

"This is connected with Scire you know? The cloth belonged to him."

Lydia's face clouded over.

"The ceremonial cloth? The silk, from the cave at the Litha," she said. "I thought you removed it after the … the…. after what happened. You said you'd cleared everything away. Obviously, you hadn't, as our little trip years ago proved, but nevertheless…" She paused and stared at him for a long few seconds, crinkling up her eyes, thinking hard. "And anyway, what's so special about it?"

"I will come to that presently. You didn't know everything about him you know."

"If he hadn't been taken from me so cruelly then I might have…"

"But listen. This is important." His eyes were burning into her. He had thought this through carefully and realised he had no option. The next words would determine the outcome. He could get the cloth and maybe save his own life. It all depended on Lydia now. "You knew Scire for maybe eight or nine years, I guess. Did you never notice anything strange about him? Particularly about the way he looked."

"I adored the way he looked."

"You misunderstand me. When you met him you must have been, what - in your twenties? Then, when he died you were obviously thirty-something. Did *you* look the same?"

"No, of course not." While the deterioration in Derrick was shockingly apparent, she knew herself that she herself wasn't exactly wearing well.

"Scire hardly changed all the time I knew him, and I was acquainted with him for a lot longer than you. Hardly changed at all – no lines, wrinkles, creases. Now don't you think that's strange? It is indeed very strange. Extremely, extremely unusual." He let the words settle between them. "When I met him, I thought he was the same age as me - but he wasn't."

"What are you saying?" Lydia sat stock-still, searching his face. It seemed as if a curtain was being drawn around them, trapping the words, distilling and purifying them so that there was no mistake.

"Scire was my senior," Derrick nodded his head slowly. "By a good many years. A very good many years."

***

Lancaster –May 1979

Sylvia was on her way to visit Llyriad. She had a favour to ask but she wasn't too sure how well received this was going to be after the events of the party. She strode across the main square of the campus, busy with the hubbub of students. As she walked, she tried to banish from her mind an essay which was pressing to be finished. She was well aware that she had been neglecting her studies lately.

When Robert had come back from his lecture fired with enthusiasm, she couldn't have been more delighted. Obviously, Derrick's lecture had done the trick and now he too wanted to be in on the Requisite. Animated about the Synod at Whitby and various Northumbrian Saints, his enthusiasm was beguiling and Sylvia had just had to give him a big hug. She promised to cook him a splendid meal that night. It would have to be spaghetti bolognaise because that was the only meal she knew how to make, but she was sure he would love it.

In fact, all in all, the whole day had been so thoroughly perfect so far, that even her meeting with Llyriad couldn't tarnish it. The sky was a warm, cornflower blue, the perfect weather for a wearing a lovely summer dress. She acknowledged that it probably wasn't suitable for this particular visit, as her choice of party outfit had obviously annoyed Llyriad. She made a snap decision and went into the campus 'Spar' shop. *Surely a bottle of wine and some flowers would make amends,* she thought.

As Sylvia arrived outside Llyriad's room, she could hear orchestral music playing. She knocked gently on the door. Llyriad appeared wearing a large, pink, dressing gown and looked at her as if she were inspecting an unfortunate cockroach about to be squashed. It was obvious she hadn't been out of bed long. Her hair was matted and her face still bore traces of last night's make-up. She looked like the kind of person who gets up in the morning and wonders why.

"Sylvia. What do you want?" she growled, and Sylvia noticed her choice of name with unease.

"Erm... I just wanted to speak to you."

She offered the flowers and wine.

"And what are these for? Guilt presents eh?" Llyriad took the gifts and threw them onto her bed. "Well, at least you know that your behaviour was out of order last night," Llyriad spoke to her from the doorway, blocking her entry. "But don't think for one moment that some flowers and a cheap bottle of wine lets you off the hook."

"I'm, I'm sorry. I didn't mean to upset you."

Sylvia hung her head, hoping the act of penitence was convincing.

"No, no, don't do that. It won't work. Now, if I were you, I would just clear off and leave me alone. I've got a splitting headache."

"But Llyriad," she began, "There was something I wanted to ask you."

"Sylvia, just go away. I really can't be bothered with you today."

Llyriad really wasn't looking her best and Sylvia wondered just how old she actually was.

"It's important, please, please listen," said Sylvia, moving closer, and lowering her voice. "I know someone else who wants to join."

She looked expectantly at Llyriad hoping for some affirmation of approval.

"Oh, for goodness sake!" glared Llyriad, "Who've you been prattling to now? You were told to keep this information to yourself and now…it seems you've been telling all and sundry."

"No, no, it's not like that. Robert my boyfriend, he's really keen to be part of this and I wondered if…"

"*You have got to be joking!* You do know that everyone is going to rue the day you came along? I can see right through you. I-know-what-you-are -doing. And don't, for one minute, think that it's going to happen. Your boyfriend - how convenient - just get lost!"

Sylvia just managed to take a step back and avoid the door slamming into her face.

***

Tynemouth – October 2009

Sebastian was sitting in the 'Turks Head'. He pushed his half empty pint to one side and pulled a laptop from his bag.

He knew his Uncle would be angry, but really, he was just a fool to himself, he thought. Realistically, his business should be making a much better profit than it was and it was only Robert's pig-headedness that prevented it. The same must be said of Caroline. She was just as bad but he wasn't bothered about her business. She could go bankrupt for all he cared. The two useless Luddites just wanted their heads banging together and he needed to be the one to oblige.

Opening up his computer he googled 'Local Bookshop reviews', clicked onto 'add a new review' and began typing.

'I found 'Tynemouth Books' to be an excellent establishment with a wide selection of books and some very rare additions. All subjects are catered for here - both new and second hand. Also, the proprietor, Mr. Robert Fairfax and his assistant, Sebastian, are very pleasant, friendly and willing to help you find any book you require. There is also a fabulous café selling a range of delicious snacks and drinks. Also, very competitive prices.

It is placed only a short distance away from the Tynemouth Metro on the Front Street, so is very easy to find and reach. Why not combine it with a trip to the seaside? I would certainly recommend a visit.'

5/5 stars. *****

A satisfied customer.

Smiling, Sebastian hit the send bar and the review was posted. After all, what harm could it possibly do? It could only bring the business much needed custom. Robert would thank him eventually.

He took a sip from his pint as he waited for his uncle to join him. This was the fourth time, over the last few months, that he had posted an excellent review and he was sure that already there had been an increase in sales.

There had definitely been more customers through the door, even if some of them had had a most peculiar effect upon both his Uncle and Caroline. There was certainly some mystery going on there between those two. It was as if they were both frightened and this fear was binding them together in a far tighter knot than he could understand. This had to be why they spent so much time in each other's company. Also, he had the feeling that, Rebecca was in some way involved, and that was why Caroline was so hell-bent on keeping her here. Sebastian needed to find out because, although he didn't like to admit it to anyone, he was worried about Rebecca. Actually, he was becoming fond of the girl with her reprimanding, schoolmarm manner and wouldn't like to see her in any trouble.

By comparison, the solution to improving Robert's finances was simple. If only his Uncle would see sense, he knew he wasn't very computer savvy but Sebastian would be more than capable of handling the selling of books online. It was a challenge he would actually enjoy. Also, as Robert had no children of his own, perhaps they would one day become partners and after…well who knew? Meanwhile, he would keep posting his reviews and see what effect this had.

Sebastian closed the lid of his laptop and slipped it into his bag, just as his uncle walked through the door.

North Shields – October 2009

After leaving her Clio well hidden in the supermarket car park, Llyriad walked through the streets of North Shields past the 'Magnesia Bank' pub and arrived at Dolphin House in a few minutes. As she reached her destination, she saw that *the woman's* VW Beetle was parked outside. Unfortunately, these modern developments had good security, particularly those on the top floor. Access was not impossible but it would be difficult. She would have to wait and think this through carefully.

She spotted a café across the road which overlooked the block of flats and was soon sitting at a window seat with a pot of tea and slab of chocolate cake.

She kept a careful watch on the apartment block and reflected on her conversation with Derrick at his Alnwick home. She had been angry at first, thinking that Derrick didn't want revenge but had his own selfish agenda and had lured her to his house under false pretenses. However, the conversation that unfolded had been extraordinary, incredible.

Thinking back to her relationship with Scire, it was strange that she had never noticed what Derrick had pointed out yesterday. Perhaps she had just chosen not to see. When she had first met Scire she had been young, fresh faced and working at a bar in Durham. She had fallen so completely head over the heels in love with him. Their relationship was so entwined by their involvement with the Requisite that it was inevitable that they should both move to Lancaster where Scire's best friend Derrick lived.

When she had been younger Lydia had never really placed much importance on learning and qualifications, but she soon realised if she was to be seriously involved in the cult and earn the respect of Derrick she needed to be studying. Most importantly, to keep Scire happy, she needed to mend her ways.

So, after much hard work and unbelievably passing two A levels at night classes, she was able to gain a place as a mature student at the University to study sociology. Scire had thought it better that she had her own room on the campus, which she had thought nothing of at the time, as she still continued to spend plenty of nights at Scire's flat. However, Derrick had been brutally honest with her when she'd met with him at his house in Alnwick. He told her that Scire had been losing interest in her for some time. Scire had confided in Derrick the night after the hideous party.

At the time she wouldn't have accepted this but in hindsight maybe there were indications. When she had been studying, she had found comfort eating a necessity and her weight had started creeping up. No longer was she the attractive young barmaid that Scire had met. But he looked exactly the same. She had tried to dress flamboyantly to disguise her figure, with swirling skirts, baggy tops and scarves but honestly - who had she been fooling?

She hadn't slept all night thinking about what Derrick had said. Scire's, flawless face kept coming to her over and over again. A man called Leofwin handing it to Scire centuries ago! It was astonishing, nothing more than the stuff of fantasy…but was it? Many people believed in a metaphysical, supernatural world. Who was to say mysteries like this didn't exist? Weren't religions themselves founded on mystery and mysticism with transcendental, paranormal explanations. And wasn't this the whole basis of the 'Requisite' and the nature worship of pagans and Celtic Christians? Were their lives a lie? Finding this supposed, miraculous cloth had clearly become an obsession with Derrick, one of the most intelligent and sober of men. But surely it couldn't help him now. He was far too weak and ill. Even this fantastical fabric would be of no use to him. He had left it too late and they had taken too long to find it. If Lydia got the cloth for him, and it was what he said it was, Derrick may be its keeper temporarily but very soon it could fall into her hands. So, if this cloth could have preserved Scire and made him remain unblemished, what could it do for Lydia?

She would still take great pleasure in ruining two businesses ... and two lives, but maybe her priorities should be altered. Perhaps she needed to concentrate on finding this cloth. Last night she had consulted the cards and the combination of High Priestess, Moon and Star had also pointed her in this direction. She needed to get this magical material and it surely couldn't be too difficult to find knowing what she already did. With that woman living here and Robert over his bookshop it must be in one of these places. However, it was extremely doubtful that she would have trusted Robert to keep it at his place, so it must be in her flat. But if this was the case, why had the woman changed so much over the years? Admittedly she didn't look too bad for someone in her fifties, which was quite clearly her age, but surely that shouldn't be the case if what Derrick said was true.

Lydia glanced through the window, saw a familiar figure walking towards her VW Beetle and then driving off.

Chapter 20

Newcastle- October 2009

In the smart coffee shop with the tasteful black and white decorations, the tall woman was writing up a report about a property that she has just been valuing. She tutted then frowned as she glanced at her watch. Today, she was wearing a pin-striped trouser suit teamed with a neat cream blouse. Although not a particularly attractive woman, Susan Hope always prided herself on being smart. She felt it was important to cut a professional image, especially in her line of business. Running an estate agency was a cut-throat business after all and she's been in the game for a very long time now.

Caroline breezed in, quickly spotted her friend and pulled up a chair next to her.

"Punctual as ever Caroline," said Susan sarcastically. "So, how's tricks?"

"Not too bad," beamed Caroline.

"Well you certainly seem a lot happier than last time I saw you. What's happened?"

"The house. Rebecca's not going to sell it after all... and she's coming back up here in a couple of weeks." Caroline had applied her brightest, reddest lipstick liberally to reflect her mood.

"How's she managing to do that? What about her job?"

"Well, I think she's taking sick leave at the moment... but I think she's planning on resigning."

Caroline's glee was misplaced in expecting Susan to congratulate her.

"Caroline, I don't know what you think you're playing at but I think you're being very selfish. It's that girl's career you know. I certainly wouldn't appreciate anybody interfering with my life like that. It's very difficult to get another job. These days, if you've got a job, you don't give it up until you've got another one in the bag. Certainly, I would advise her not to quit her current job until she's got another lined up here."

This was not the reaction that she had been expecting from Susan but then she knew she could be such a negative person. Caroline decided not to listen.

"Anyway Susan, I just wanted to thank you for your role in all of this. If you hadn't helped me with your under valuation…then who knows what the outcome of all of this could have been."

"To be honest Caroline, I think any part I played in this was against my better judgment. And I don't really get what the big deal is anyway. Why are you so concerned that Rebecca doesn't sell the house? And why are you so concerned that she leaves her job and comes to live up here. What's in all of this for you?"

"Well… you know that Sylvia was such a good friend. Well … Rebecca is her niece…and I know this is what she would have wanted."

"Mmm, no Caroline. That's too neat and tidy. There's something you're not telling me. I know you too well. There's something in all of this that benefits you - but I don't know what."

Bloody woman, thought Caroline

"Well, Susan, all I know is … Sylvia hated Rebecca's mother. Apparently, she's an awful woman and she wants to ruin her daughter's life so…" Caroline knew her words sounded lame.

"Yes, I get that. I get you were good friends. I hear what you're saying about the mother. But how is it any of your business to *force* the girl to do what she doesn't want to do? If Rebecca still wants to sell this house, well, she would have the money in her pocket to do with as she likes …"

"No Susan." Caroline said quickly. "That isn't going to happen.".

"Okay, okay, okay." Susan held up both hands. "I know you don't want her to sell it but I just don't get why. I'm curious that's all. There's more to all of this than you're letting on. I'm sure of that. I'm allowed to be curious aren't I?"

Caroline smiled sweetly. "Anyway," she said, "another coffee?"

***

Preston, Lancashire- October 2009

Sitting upstairs in her bedroom, Rebecca had felt like a teenager again. She could feel her Mother huffing and puffing downstairs. Although the posters of pop stars had been replaced by prints of favourite pieces of artwork, the decorations and furniture had remained unchanged since she had been a child. In another ten years' time possibly everything would be just the same - except she would be almost forty and an old spinster. Actually, she thought, she would rather have a life like Caroline's than her own. In fact, if she compared the lives of her mother and Caroline, she knew which one she would prefer. She pictured the unfastened, voluminous red coat, swirling down the street and Caroline off on some crazy mission. The image of the insufferable woman made her smile.

The words raced through her, '*You will regret this decision. There's nothing for you in the North- East. This is just another example of my sister's spitefulness. Only a matter of time, then you could be a head teacher'*. How could she make her mother understand that she hated the job? And it was a job. The career and vocation idea had gone years ago. The stress of the never-ending and often needless workload had seen to that. And while calling in sick was a temporary solution it didn't resolve the problem of uncompleted plans and unmarked books. The very fact she wasn't there gave someone the opportunity to poke about in her classroom looking for further failings.

Being in the house with her mother all day was nearly as bad to being in school. To be honest, she almost wished she was in the company of interfering Caroline, annoying Sebastian, kindly Robert or even that crazy fortune teller, Llyriad. Another meeting with that woman might clarify the thoughts in her head. Although, the more she thought, she realised that there was actually nothing that needed to be deliberated. The decision had already been made You only get one life and she didn't much like the way hers was going. She had been offered a get out clause and despite her mother's misgivings, she knew had to take it.

Feeling positive for once, Rebecca opened her laptop and stared at the blank screen. A letter of resignation had to considered carefully.

***

Durham – June 1979

Robert, burst through the door of their small room in the bed and breakfast to find Sylvia lying on the bed, reading a magazine.

"Somebody looks pleased with themselves." Sylvia propped herself up on one arm, guessing immediately the reason for his good mood. "You've got a job, haven't you?"

"Too right. It's at a bookshop called Heron's." Robert rubbed his hands together. "And guess what? I start tomorrow."

"Well I think that this calls for a celebration." Sylvia jumped off the bed, put on her coat and grabbed her bag. They set off to the centre of town, along a rough, cobbled street.

"Robert, I like this place. Don't you? It has a good feel to it don't you think? I think we've made the right decision. Don't you think?"

"Well, yes but … we didn't really have a lot of choice, did we? We could hardly stay in Lancaster. God knows what I'm going to tell my parents…" The enormity of what had just happened was still sinking in for Robert.

"No, I mean about coming here to live. It feels a good place to be." Sylvia looked appreciatively at the magnificent Cathedral towering above them." I went in there before. It's fantastic – you'll love it."

Robert nodded. He needed to try and keep positive about this bizarre situation he now found himself in. Each morning he woke not knowing if he were living in a dream or a nightmare.

They soon arrived in what appeared to be a market square, dominated by an ill- proportioned statue of Charles William Vane

Stuart, a Lord Lieutenant of Durham, sitting astride a horse with disturbingly short legs and a very large head.

As they turned the corner, Sylvia noticed that the street was laced with the smell of toasted teacakes and then they came across 'The Shakespeare' pub. The front was festooned with hanging baskets, brim full of pink, orange and yellow begonias. "I like the look of this place. Come on. Let's go in." Robert obediently followed Sylvia through the door.

While Robert went to the bar, Sylvia sat down on a hard, wooden seat by a circular table, carefully placing the bag on her lap. She looked at the frothy sea of white-haired men, as they sipped their pale ales, deep in lively conversation and debate. On the olive-green walls were pictures of old Durham, the Sanctuary Knocker on the door of the Cathedral and predictably, considering the name of the pub, the bard himself. As she looked at the impressively shiny glasses sparkling over the bar, Robert arrived back with their drinks.

"So, as I was saying before…don't you think we have made a good choice coming here?" She looked at him expectantly.

"I suppose it's as good a place as any. But what are we going to tell our parents?"

"Let's not worry about that now. After all, we haven't been here long and you've already found yourself a job. Now that's pretty good isn't it? Don't you think?"

He thought Sylvia's optimism seemed somewhat premature.

"I doubt my parents will see being a shop assistant as the ideal career move Sylvia. Do you? I think they were expecting something a little more ambitious."

Robert hated to disappoint people, particularly his parents.

"But it's a bookshop you'll be working in. You like books, don't you? There could be lots of worse jobs you could be doing. Especially round here where most people work down the coal mines. How would you like that?"

Robert swallowed a large mouthful of lager and didn't bother to reply to her.

"Anyway, so you liked the Cathedral, did you?" said Robert, thinking he'd better change the subject. "You know that it was built for Saint Cuthbert, don't you?"

"Yep. Read about him inside, and that other one…Venerable Bede."

"Body exhumed, but still intact? Incorrupt. Apparently, it hadn't rotted even after hundreds of years."

"Yes, yes, I do know about Saint Cuthbert you know." She played with the zip fastening on her bag. "After all we were both members of the Requisite, weren't we?"

"Didn't someone say if was because of that cloth. Supposed to be from his coffin. The reason that his body was preserved? You know that special cloth that was in the cave – difficult to see it by candlelight. Supposed to be his cloth. Do you remember all those fancy patterns and symbols? The one that Scire looked after." Robert thought back to their ridiculous folly and the reason they were now in this horrible predicament.

"I remember the cloth – of course. More silk though I think." Sylvia finished her drink.

"Well I guess he won't be the guardian of the cloth now." Robert said absentmindedly. "Wasn't it supposed to have special magical properties? Honestly, the stuff we swallowed. Didn't do him much good did it?" Robert gazed at the ceiling and shuddered, remembering the events of only three days ago. "Do you think he's dead?

"I don't know." She didn't want to think about it. "He could be. It was a bad fall."

"Why haven't we heard from the police?"

"I don't think the Requisite will want the police involved. Dafo'll cover it up. Bound to. It's not the kind of thing you want to go public with. Not going to do his career any good."

"They're not going to let us get away with it though?" He looked hopefully at her.

"I wouldn't think so. A lot of them really liked Scire. They looked up to him. They'll be wanting revenge for him that's for sure. And they'll not want any of this getting out. They'll not want an investigation into the group. They'll want to make sure we say nothing."

"Thanks for that. Don't sugarcoat it will you? I'm feeling bad enough."

"Just saying. We have to face facts. If they find us, they'll kill us – probably."

"Bloody hell. Can you just stop. I've got the message."

"We have to stay one step ahead. Keep our wits about us."

Robert turned in his seat to give her a long, cool look. "Are you enjoying this?"

"'Course not. But we have to be practical that's all. We have to try and think clearly. No good getting all emotional. What's done is done. We have to look after ourselves."

"Okay, you look after the practical side. I'll be emotional for both of us."

"Robert, will you get me another drink now please?" She put her empty glass on the table.

"I wonder who'll be the keeper now? Dafo, I expect. I'm surprised that he wasn't already. I mean wasn't it him who started the group?" Robert, not for the first time, was wondering about the true purpose behind the Requisite group.

"Robert, I've finished my drink." Raising her voice, she began to attract the attention of the white-haired men.

"Don't you think Dafo will probably take care of the cloth now?"

"No, actually I don't."

"Well, I doubt the job will be given to Llyriad…"

"No, it won't."

"Well who do you think it will be?" Robert had eventually started listening to what she was saying.

"It can't be any of them 'cos we've got it. It's here." She placed the bag on the table and opened it. She had been waiting for the right moment to tell him. This wasn't it but she had to tell him.

"What? Don't be ridiculous. You're not telling me that…" Robert stared inside the bag.

"Yes… that's it. That's the cloth."

"Sylvia," he hissed, and drew disapproving glances from two men on the bar stools. "D'you realise what you've done? They'll go crazy. They really believe in all that nonsense. They really believe in the bloody cloth. We'll never be safe now. Why did you do such a stupid thing?"

"I didn't do it on purpose," said Sylvia evenly. "It was an accident. I didn't realise I'd come away with it, you know…"

"No, no, no, no, this is stupid," he grimaced and rubbed his head with both hands. "If they didn't have enough reasons to get us …"

"We just have to keep calm."

"*Keep calm? Keep calm*? We'll need more than keeping calm. We'll need to …"

"Listen. Listen Robert. Don't raise your voice. People are looking. We have to act normally. It'll be alright."

"How d'you know?" said Robert. "How d'you know it'll be alright?"

Sylvia gave a slight shrug of one shoulder. "Well, they can only kill us once."

"Not very funny," said Robert, blank-faced. "I'm having a heart attack here."

"Okay, but before you have your heart attack can you please get me another drink … quietly. I think I need a large whiskey this time."

Sylvia put the bag on her lap. Inside she could see some skeins sparkling and threads glistening.

Robert put the two double whiskeys on the table and downed his in one.

***

Chapter 21

Preston, Lancashire- June 1979

Sylvia's parents had just enjoyed eating their evening meal. It was past eight o'clock and already dark outside.

"Lovely," said Cyril, giving his wife a big smile. "You always make a great steak and kidney pie. It's your signature dish.

"You're not wrong," said Maureen, settling back into her chair. "That was delicious. Even if I do say so myself. The bad news is that it's your turn to sort the dishes and..."

She was interrupted by a short, sharp rap on the front door. Maureen frowned and tipped her head slightly. "Whoever could that be at this time of night? Strange time to come calling?"

"Well, we won't find out by sitting here." Cyril gave a loud sigh in mock irritation. "I'll go and have a look." He hauled his overweight body out of his chair, slipped on discarded slippers and lumbered along the passage to the front door. Through the glass he could make out two figures, one tall and the other shorter, stockier. His wife leaned forward as far as she dared and peered along the corridor behind him. She also observed the two outlines and there was just the beginning of a slight fluttery feeling in her stomach.

Cyril opened the door to a towering, distinguished-looking man with keen, interested eyes, long swept back hair and a prominent nose. Next to him was a woman with unruly, dark hair and, he already noted, a distinctive domineering expression.

"Yes. Can I help you?" said Cyril

"Ah, hello, good evening," said the tall man. "So sorry to bother you at this late hour. We were looking for Sylvia – your daughter?"

"That's correct, Sylvia is my daughter but she's not here at the moment," said Cyril.

"Oh, such a shame," replied the tall man. "We've come quite a long way to find her and it would be…"

"Look, I'm sorry, she's not here…but what's this all about? said Cyril, "And who's asking for her. It's very late."

The tall man nodded sympathetically. "Yes, of course, again, I do apologise for interrupting your evening but it is rather important that we find your daughter …may we come in, this will only take a moment."

"Well … I don't know, as I say…" began Cyril, but he was interrupted by the dark-haired woman barging past him and placing herself in the middle of the corridor with an aggressive stance, arms folded like a suit of armour. The tall man smiled at Cyril and then he too pushed past into the corridor.

Maureen got up and stood by the lounge door, the fluttery feeling in her stomach was now a full - blown swarm of butterflies. "What's going on? Who are you? What do you want with our Sylvia? What's she done now? Are you the police? She's always getting herself into trouble with her daft antics." She blinked watery eyes, unnerved by the intrusion of the two strangers.

"Sylvia's at university," said Cyril, finally letting go of the door but leaving it slightly ajar, just in case.

"I'm so sorry," said the tall man. "Please let me explain. We're not the police. We're friends of Sylvia. Same amateur dramatic group. We have a very important production coming up and unfortunately, we've mislaid a crucial prop – indispensable really – and we think that Sylvia may have accidentally taken it … a day or so ago. We desperately need it back."

"Well, I'm sorry but we can't help you," said Maureen, preening to regain her composure. "I didn't even know that our Sylvia was part of a drama group. She's certainly not here."

"Any idea where she could be?" asked the tall man.

"No – no idea," Maureen shook her head.

"And what about Robert?"

"Robert, Robert who? I don't know of any Robert."

"Her boyfriend."

"I didn't know she had a boyfriend. We don't know any Roberts do we Cyril?"

"Oh, she most certainly has," said the tall man. "We think that he may have aided her – accidentally of course."

"Well, she's not here. Her or any Robert," said Maureen. "As far as we know she's at university…in Lancaster,"

There was a long pause. Maureen glanced across at her husband, unsure.

Cyril took his cue. "Look it's pretty late. You can see she's not here so I think you should leave now. If you give us your names, we'll tell her you came the next time she calls."

"Well, if we could just have a quick look round. Just to make sure," said the tall man, smiling.

"A look round? Listen, we've told she's not here." Cyril straightened, looking to assert himself. A lump rattled around his throat. "That should be good enough for you. You can't just come inviting yourself into our home. She's not here. It's time for you to leave. You're upsetting my wife."

Cyril made to walk towards the front door and pull it further open but the tall man shot him a glance which froze him in his tracks, a look full of menace which promised easy violence. Maureen caught the glance, her face crumpled like a paper bag and she began to wring her hands with alarm. She twisted her mouth as if trying to say something but the words remained hidden, too scared to break free.

"I think that would be terribly rude," said the tall man. "After all we have come a long way and we really need to make sure that Sylvia is not here." He smiled, but not with his eyes.

The woman brushed aside a long lock of dark hair, walked along the hallway and closed the door quietly. She came back, fixed a long, hard look onto Cyril, a special look – difficult to interpret. Cyril stared back, uncertain as to what to say or do. There was a small clicking noise. He looked down at the woman's right hand held by her side and could make out the glint of a short, steel blade. He looked again, yes, he was right, he *could* make out the glint of a short steel blade. He was doubly uncertain of what to do, having never faced an obviously formidable woman menacing him with a short, steel blade - certainly not in his own hallway anyway.

"Get in there."

The woman gave the order softly and nodded in the direction of the lounge. She didn't need to shout or snarl. The three syllables triggered an involuntary action from Cyril and Maureen. There was no option. Fight or flight? They could see they stood little chance in a fight and there was nowhere to take flight to. Cyril and Maureen went in and stood by the fireplace.

"Sit."

They were now on automatic pilot. They sat down beside each other on the sofa. Obedient and submissive, hoping this would all go away soon. The woman walked across to the telephone and yanked the cord from the wall.

"Stay in here," said the woman. "We won't be long. If you move it could get messy."

The door was firmly shut and at last Maureen, cradling her husband's arm, allowed the tears to come. They held on to each other and listened to the sounds above them for several minutes. Sounds of drawers being pulled open and emptied, contents strewn about. The ripping of mattresses being slashed apart, wardrobes gutted. Eventually there was no more banging, only the sound of muffled voices and then the heavy tread of disgruntled feet on the stairs.

The lounge door was pushed open. The dark-haired woman burst in and careered around the room, kicking over side tables, emptying bookshelves, turning over a cabinet bursting with crystal glasses and china ornaments, smashing as much as possible. She had given up hope of finding what had been stolen and instead was bent on wanton destruction as compensation for her disappointment.

"No, no, not the... not the..." Maureen made to remonstrate with the woman but *television* was too long a word for her tongue to contend with at the moment and so she concentrated on trying to keep breathing.

The tall man had searched the kitchen but had found nothing. He came into the shambles of the lounge and stood beside the woman.

"Oh dear," said the tall man. "It seems you were telling the truth. But still, we really, really need to find what was taken – sorry, stolen."

"We need to find the thieves," said the woman, pointing the knife at them. "And we will."

Cyril and Maureen held hands and stared at them. Cyril felt a soothing warmth in his trousers beginning to spread down his legs and tried to stop his lips trembling. Maureen could feel the bile backing up, ready to burst out, but she was too paralysed with fear to be sick at the moment

"If ... and when you hear from them," said the tall man quietly, rolling the words around in his mouth. "Tell them that Dafo and Llyriad came to see you. They'll know who we are." He gave a scorching, disturbing grin.

Llyriad walked casually across the room to an intricately inlaid, highly polished, mahogany table. "Just in case you forget our names," she said, and proceeded to carve D-A- F-O and L-Y-R-I-A-D into the top of the table with her flick knife. Scratching each letter carefully and as deep as possible, gouging long grooves.

"Just let them know what to expect when you hear from them," said Dafo. "I'm sure you can imagine what will happen to them if they don't hand over what they have stolen. And, of course, please don't involve the police in this. We don't know where Sylvia and Robert are ...yet ... but we do know where you are ... and we may need to carve our names somewhere else, just so you don't forget us. Cheerio, enjoy the rest of your evening."

Cyril and Maureen sat perfectly still and heard the front door quietly close, ice running through their veins.

Cyril squeezed Maureen's hand and stared at the smashed dinner plates on the floor, the remains of the steak and kidney pie seeping into the carpet. "Least I won't have to do the dishes, love," he said quietly.

***

Tynemouth- February 1999

When Sylvia met Caroline off the train at Tynemouth she was shocked. Although she hadn't seen her friend for a good few years the change was horrifying. Always slim, Caroline now looked positively skeletal. Her skin was a murky yellow and her eyes sank deep into her head encircled by dark skin. Her wrinkles had deepened and white strands didn't so much thread through as engulf her thinning, bobbed hair.

"Caroline," said Sylvia. "you must be so tired after your long journey, let's get you home." She placed an arm reassuringly around her friend's bone-thin shoulders and took her suitcase. "It's only round the corner. I'm afraid it's not much of a place. I'm doing it up at the moment. I bought it with some inheritance money from mother."

Caroline didn't speak at first, conserving all her energies for putting one foot in front of another. She nodded however, remembering that after a long stay in a care home Sylvia's mother had eventually died and she was amazed there was any money left at all.

"You're sure it isn't far?" said Caroline, holding on to her friend.

"No almost there. See that shop over there," she pointed to a small bookshop across the street. "That's Robert's. He just bought it and he's *very* excited about it. Well, as excited about things as Robert gets." Sylvia forced a laugh, hoping to jolly her friend along a little. Eventually they turned a corner and stopped outside a small, unprepossessing terraced house.

"Here we are," said Sylvia, as she put the key in the lock before ushering her friend indoors. "You make yourself comfy and I'll go and put the kettle on." Sylvia turned the gas fire full on, plumped up some well-worn cushions and gave Caroline a beaming smile.

Minutes later the two sat side by side on the well-worn sofa, two mugs if tea in front of them on a small wooden table.

"Thank you. Thank you ever so much for letting me stay here," said Caroline. "I was at my wit's end, really. No one to turn to."

"Listen, the pleasure's all mine, really. You're welcome anytime. I just wished I'd finished working on this place," said Sylvia, looking around the shabby room.

"Sylvia, there are things I must tell you." Caroline's eyes had taken on a haunted look.

"There's no hurry. I can see you're tired. Just take your time." She held her friend's hand and patted it gently.

"I'm not just tired Sylvia. I'm not well." She clasped Sylvia's hand more tightly, as tightly as she was capable of. "Seriously not well. I'm dying."

"What? What's wrong with you?" Sylvia gasped.

"It's cancer. Stomach cancer." Caroline's eyes filled with tears. "I know I haven't got long to live."

"How long have you known? And why ... why haven't you told me before now?"

"I don't know. I don't know. I suppose I thought the chemotherapy would work. I had hoped not to tell you. But now ... I've got nowhere else to turn."

"You've had chemo? Caroline, you must have known for ages. Why didn't you tell me? I might have been able to help. Sorry, I know what that sounds like. But I could have helped in some way."

"The thing is Sylvia, I had to give up my job and sell my flat. I have nowhere to live." She ran her hands through her hair and Sylvia was alarmed at how sparse it was.

"Shush now. That's one thing you certainly don't need to worry about. Consider this your home. For as long as you need it. You can have a great time here. It'll just be just like university. You were always such a great friend to me at Lancaster," said Sylvia, hoping to make her voice sound as positive as possible without sounding forced. "I don't think I've told you that before - but it's true – you were a great friend then, and still are. Best mates eh? Anyway, there I go, getting all sentimental. We don't need that do we? We need a plan. Don't you think?"

***

Preston to Tynemouth – November 2009

Rebecca was once again sitting on the train to Newcastle but this time with much more luggage. As she looked out of the window she thought about how easily matters had just slotted into place. Once she had made up her mind, she had discovered a fortitude within herself she had not considered possible, despite the angry protest from her mother.

A little smile came to her lips as she thought of her mother's ranting. Eventually, her dad had somehow placated his wife as well as pointing out that it wasn't really that far away. They would easily be able to visit and he was sure that Rebecca would often come back to their home. In response to this Rebecca had nodded and tried her best to make the right noises.

However, it was the ease by which she had been able to extract herself from her teaching position that had been the most surprising. Mrs. Elliot, the headteacher, had been more reasonable than she could have possibly imagined. Not only had she not needed to work out any notice but she had been given the assurance that should she need a reference, then Mrs. Elliot would be happy to provide her with an excellent one. Also, if she left immediately, then she would be provided with three months' pay. Although she had only spoken to her headteacher briefly on the phone, the tone of the woman's voice had been the most pleasant she had ever known her use. Strangely enough, Rebecca had not even needed to go into school, as all of her personal belongings had been brought round to her parent's house by the caretaker of all people. He had looked uncomfortable when he had arrived on the doorstep, with an assortment of boxes and bags, but all Rebecca could feel was relief. She refused to think anything untoward about the speed of this severance and put such thoughts to the back of her mind.

So, a new chapter of her life was about to begin and she couldn't help but feel a little excited. Even if Caroline would delight in the fact that she had got her own way, did this really matter? Obviously, the woman seemed to have taken a shine to her, for whatever reason, and she ought to consider that as a positive. She imagined Caroline in her big red coat, jumping up and down and doing a victory dance and she smiled again.

Despite their initial introduction, Sebastian didn't seem to be so bad, she thought. If you overlooked his untidy appearance and inability to use a comb, there was actually something quite likeable about him, particularly his lop-sided smile. Also, it would be good to know someone of a similar age to herself. Maybe, when he had played his awful loud music on that particular day, he had actually done her a favour. After all, if that Mrs. Hope hadn't offered to set such a paltry amount for the house, events would be playing out very differently.

There seemed to be a good relationship between Sebastian and his Uncle Robert. On more than one occasion, she had seen them both going to the pub across the road, after work. The pub looked a cozy place, somewhere she would like to go. Perhaps she could engineer to be invited herself. Who was to know what the future held in store?

Robert was definitely someone she would like to get to know better. When her parents came up to visit, she could see him and her dad getting along. Her mother, of course was something else and she could definitely see sparks flying between her and Caroline.

As the view from the window was becoming less rural, she knew that she soon would be arriving, and her new adventure would be about to begin. She had her own house, three months' pay, and she wondered what would happen next. Maybe, she ought to go and visit the clairvoyant again. Her words had been quite prophetic last time and it certainly couldn't do any harm could it? Rebecca gathered her cases together as the train pulled into Newcastle Central Station.

***

Durham- June 1979

Back at their room, the fragile cloth was lifted carefully out of Sylvia's bag and spread out on the bed.

In the centre of the shimmering silvery fabric was a large, goddess figure with jet black hair, topped by a crown covered in jewels. Although undoubtedly beautiful, Robert thought her face stern and her outstretched hands seem to want to take him into her possession. There was a cruelty in her manner. In her white arms she held what seemed to be a selection of fruits: grapes, figs and pomegranates. Beneath her, the green and turquoise skeins were woven into waves amongst which he could see an array of fishes. It was absolutely exquisite. With her strange mesmerising smile, it seemed this goddess on the cloth demanded to be worshipped. But Robert felt more than a little apprehensive about her.

"It's the Mother goddess," whispered Sylvia. "That first night we went to the Esbat ceremony, when you were curious as where I had been. She was who the ceremony was…"

"Sylvia, what the hell ...what the hell have you done?" Robert couldn't take his eyes off the tapestry on the bed. "As if it wasn't enough, us killing Scire. Why the hell did you take this? There's no way they aren't going to come to get this back. There's no way ..." Robert's voice, harsh at first, became suddenly subdued.

"I just couldn't help myself. It was there and ...it was as if it was asking to be taken, I didn't mean to... and you know what it is. It's cloth that Scire kept. The one brought out each year for the Midsummer Litha." Sylvia traced the outline of the goddess reverently with her fingers.

"Yes, I know, I know that but I think I might know why it's so special. And, why there's no way Derrick will let us get away with having it. In fact, I've had big doubts about the very purpose of that bloody Requisite." Robert stared at the face on the cloth, so dangerously beautiful.

"Now you've lost me Robert. You know what its purpose is. It's about living our lives similar pre-Christian times, when nature was what was important, not Popes or a judgemental God administering retribution and punishment, don't you think?" Sylvia offered the explanation she had been fed dozens of times.

"Yes, yes, I know that, but when Christianity first came to Britain, it wasn't like that" said Robert, using both hands to stab out the words. "The avenging God of the Old Testament came much later. At first the old ways could be accommodated within the Christian faith. The two beliefs went hand in hand. Pagan and Christian. But after the Synod of Whitby everything changed. Celtic Christianity, was replaced by the Christianity followed by Rome. People must have been devastated. Being forced to be apostate overnight. At the Synod of Whitby, King

Oswald declared that his kingdom would follow the customs of Rome and not those practised by the Irish monks at Iona and... St. Cuthbert in Northumbria."

"You know," said Sylvia, "Today, when I visited the shrine of St. Cuthbert in Durham Cathedral, the cloth was in my bag and I had the weirdest feeling that something, y'know, made us come here. And when I was next to his tomb... It was as if...I can't explain this but I felt such a sense of belonging . As if I was where I should be. It was as if I had come home...but I've never been here before. Ever. What's going on?"

"I don't know, but when St. Cuthbert died, his body was wrapped in a special silk." He stared again at the siren's lovely sadistic face and lowered his voice further.. "It was supposed to have magical properties and when his body was exhumed years later it remained intact. This was repeated lots of times, in front of witnesses, and his body was always exactly the same as the very day he died. It was supposed to be evidence of his beatitude. But the last time this happened...the cloth was stolen and nobody knows what became of it. After that, whenever the coffin was opened, St. Cuthbert's body had decayed as normal. Maybe it wasn't you that was coming home."

"You don't think that this is...?"

"I don't know," said Robert. "But you know who's the leading expert in this field?"

"I think I might be able to guess."

Chapter 22

Tynemouth - November 2009

It was a bright day in late Autumn as Rebecca retraced her steps from Tynemouth station to her new home in Huntington Place. This time she wouldn't be disappointed by its state of disrepair, because this time it would be her project to make the property her own.

As she passed Robert's bookshop, she could see Sebastian sitting on the floor, sorting out books but Robert was nowhere to be seen. Soon she arrived at her front door, which didn't look nearly as neglected as the first time she came there. Once inside she realised that the heating was already on and the place smelt as if had been freshly cleaned.

She opened the curtains, the light flooded into the room and she felt a genuine pleasure to be there. There could be only one person who was responsible for the improvement, and since all of her worries had recently disappeared, she felt it would be inappropriate to be angry with her. She went to put her cases in the bedroom but soon as she got to the top step, there was a hesitant knock on the front door.

Knowing who this would be, Rebecca went promptly downstairs. Dressed in jeans and a smart, navy reefer jacket Caroline stood on the doorstep, smiling nervously.

"Rebecca it's so lovely to have you back. I've missed you." From behind her back she produced a bunch of cream roses and surprisingly waited on the step to be asked in.

"Come in, please, Caroline... but how did you know I was back right now?"

Caroline looked a little sheepish.

"I was in Robert's bookshop and I saw you."

Rebecca realised that she must have spent an awful lot of time there today, watching through the window.

"Do you mind if I take off my jacket," She looked around uncomfortably." It's rather warm in here. I hope you don't mind as... I still have a key ... I thought I would make the place more presentable for when ... I mean *if* you came back. I hope that wasn't presumptuous of me... I know it's not my friend's house any more. However, I did put the gas, electricity and phone into my name ... change them into yours of course, whenever you like...but I thought it would be nice for you to have the place warm and the internet available..."

"No, it's fine Caroline, honestly, fine." *Who is this person?* thought Caroline. This humility wasn't a trait she had associated at all with Caroline. "I'm pleased. Really. The place seems ten times better than what I remembered."

Caroline removed her jacket to reveal an unexpectedly plain, navy shirt. The outfit actually quite suited her.

"I was worried... you see, I know that I can be a little overbearing and some people find me hard work...but Rebecca, I'm just so pleased that you've come back." Caroline glanced at the roses left on the hallway table.

"Mind, you'll need to put those flowers in some water or they'll die." The pair looked at each other for a split second and then burst out laughing.

"Right away ma'am." Rebecca stood up straight and saluted. "Now, would you like tea or coffee? I'm assuming you've put milk in the fridge." Caroline laughed again.

My God, I'm enjoying myself, Rebecca thought.

"But of course. Coffee for me please, milk with no sugar." Caroline visibly relaxed, strolled into the sitting room to claim the comfiest chair.

Rebecca came into the room with two mugs.

"But I must admit I was very glad to get your text saying you'd be coming up today." Caroline gushed. "Are you staying for long? What did your mother say? And what have you told them at school?"

"Well," Rebecca was pleased with what Caroline had done, in fact she'd been very kind and helpful and she would be glad to reward her with good news. "I-have-quit-my-job. And my mother isn't happy ... but I'm a grown woman and its time I made my own decisions."

Caroline's eyes swivelled and then swivelled again and it seemed that her face became one, huge, red grin, almost filling the room. She bobbed from side to side and then front and back, unsure about rushing forward and engulfing Rebecca in the biggest hug she would ever get in her life. Her arms waved up and down as she tried to make a decision but then settled for a rapid, open-handed clap in front of her face like giving a very fast, excited version of a Hindu *'namaste'* greeting, accompanied by a strange, squeaking noise. "Bravo. Oh, bravo. You've made the right decision. Definitely the right decision. And you don't need to worry about money. I know your Aunt didn't leave you any money but she left a good few thousand to me and... I think she would really want you to have it... especially under the circumstances"

"No, really," Rebecca shook her head emphatically. Uncertain herself now as to how to address this wobbling, fizzing, vision. She'd heard of people levitating, in a state of excited hysteria, but never thought she would see it. "It's not necessary," she said eventually. "I have some money."

"Well, I imagine you will want to get started renovating this place as quickly as possible. I suggest you get the rewiring and plastering sorted first. So, please, let me at least pay for those. And I was thinking... as it won't be very nice here while those are being done ..." Caroline took a deep breath, and then another one and then remembered to stop clapping. "Please, please come and stay with me. It won't be for long and I promise I won't boss you about or interfere with what you're doing."

Caroline bit her tongue, worried she might have overstepped the mark, especially when things were going so well.

"That's very generous of you Caroline, very generous, but let me think about that please, and I'll get back to you."

"Of course, that's fair enough, and now I think I had perhaps better leave you in peace." She gave another short squeal accompanied by a deep, contented, aaaooommm sound and looked at her watch. "Well, it's half past four now. I just wondered, if you weren't doing anything special... I'm meeting Robert and Sebastian for drinks in the 'Turk's Head' at six and I... I wondered if you'd like to join us".

***

Journey back to Lancaster- June 1979

"Perditio tempus. Perditio tempus indeed. A waste of time," said Derrick. "Still at least that's one place we know that it definitely *isn't*."

Derrick and Llyriad were now heading back North, in Derrick's black Jaguar.

"Not completely though," said Llyriad. "The parents have been left with something to think about, haven't they? And they know that their precious daughter isn't doing what she's supposed to be doing. Now her and her boyfriend can both kiss goodbye to their degrees and careers. Still not enough though."

"To be honest Llyriad," said Derrick as he indicated to turn onto the M6. "I think we made a massive mistake there. It was obvious from their reaction to our news that Sylvia hadn't been there recently."

"We needed to make sure. If we'd found that piece of fabric … then we would have known they were lying and we could have made them tell us where they were."

"We needed to get information. We should have concentrated on them more. Also, I'm not sure I agree with your interrogation techniques. A little more personal, yet incisive injury was needed, I think. More forensic less demolition."

"Well, I'm pleased with what I did there. After what she did to me… any upset we can cause to her or her family …it's no less than she deserves. If I had this knife next to her throat," she produced it once more from her pocket, "I would have no qualms about what I would do with it."

"The point of the exercise was to retrieve the cloth and that hasn't been done." Derrick glared at the road ahead.

"No, no, no, Derrick, the point was and still is…to get those two. To be honest, I couldn't really care less about an old piece of cloth. I just want to get my hands on them."

"What's done is done. Now we just have to…" Derrick stopped mid-sentence. He knew that he needed to be careful not to say too much about the significance of the ancient relic. "But you *are* right… it can't remain unpunished. The question is however, where to look? I genuinely believed that her parents have no idea as to their whereabouts."

"Okay, but I bet they aren't too delighted to learn their dear little girl has a lover," said Llyriad, continuing to play with the knife.

"Llyriad, we know nothing of the details of their relationship." Derrick wondered how he could have thought today's preposterous mission with this dim-witted woman was a good idea. However, it was crucial that the cloth was somehow recovered and her help in this matter was essential. "Do we know where Robert is from? Perhaps they've gone to stay with his parents?"

"Not sure," said Llyriad shaking her head. "Somewhere down south though, I think."

"Well, we'll need to get the address from the university admissions office. We may have to pay a visit there too. A bit more subtly this time. We don't have to leave a mess. Just do what we have to do to extricate information. Whatever's necessary." He gave her a sideways glance. "And can you please put your flick knife away."

***

Durham- June 1979

Sylvia was taking a shower. Robert couldn't stop looking at the cloth resting on the bed. This woman was bad news.

If this cloth was what he thought it was, he knew that Derrick would soon be on their trail. Also, their location was probably the most predictable place they could possibly have chosen. As Durham had been home to the Nature Goddess Silk for many years, it would be the most logical place for them to begin their search. Robert knew that this was quite possibly what they had in their possession from the details of a particular article, written by his lecturer on the significance of this cloth. If this was indeed the case, then pieces of the jigsaw puzzled were beginning to slot into place.

He racked his brains trying to think of the specifics of the article he had read which he believed had been simply entitled, 'The Nature Goddess at Durham'. 'This beautiful cloth,' he pictured the words, 'made by Byzantine weavers had originally been placed in St. Cuthbert's coffin and was held responsible for the preservation of his body. However, it had mysteriously disappeared some hundreds of years ago and after that event, the Saint's flesh was no longer immune to decay.' Since then, no trace of the silk had been recorded, but those precisely written details showed that Derrick must certainly have seen it at some point. Also, Scire, as keeper of the cloth and close friend of his, must have permitted him to view the material. And he must have done so many times because Derrick was not the sort of man who took no for an answer.

The man's passion for St. Cuthbert it would seem, was to be strangely overshadowed by his complete obsession with this very silk.

If this indeed was the magical shroud held responsible for the preservation of the saint's body, then it was priceless, and the man would more than likely kill to possess it. It was amazing he hadn't insisted that Scire give it to him or he hadn't stolen it. Robert wondered how on earth Scire had come into possession of it in the first place. Maybe Derrick believed that if you obtained it by a dishonest method then it would somehow harm you. So, when Scire fell to his death, that would have suited Derrick's purpose ideally. Robert's mind was racing.

He studied more closely the figure on the cloth. It no longer seemed an object of beauty. The colours seemed gaudy and the woman evil, with her raven, black hair and mesmerising, feline eyes. He wished he could remember the particulars of the article. 'Ataragatis' was the name that sprung suddenly to mind. This was who Derrick had suggested was the figure embroidered on to the cloth. Robert thought from what he could recall, that she was some Middle Eastern fertility goddess. If he could just read a copy of this article again then he might have some verification to the identity of the cloth.

He looked at the pale outstretched arms, offering up temptingly an abundance of fruit to ensnare her victims. The enigmatic smile, beguiling and promising unspeakable delights. And then, strangely, something he hadn't noticed before. He saw that she was in possession of not just one fishtail, but two. How on earth had an image of a doubled-tailed mermaid, fertility goddess come to be placed in the tomb of the devoutly Christian Saint Cuthbert?

"Sylvia," he called down the corridor to the bathroom, "Are you finished yet? We need to go out."

Sylvia emerged from the shower wrapped in a towel.

As soon as she entered the room, her eyes were drawn immediately to the bed. Before she made any attempt to dry herself, she tenderly touched, folded and then carefully placed the cloth in her bag. Robert thought back uneasily to how Sylvia had sat in the pub, cradling the bag on her knee and how her eyes had lit up when she touched it. They needed to find out quickly with what they were dealing with.

"We need to go to Durham University Library," said Robert.

"Why?" Sylvia stepped into the jeans she had bought only that morning from a charity shop.

"Because I've remembered reading something written by Derrick…and I think it's about the contents of your bag. There's bound to be a copy in the University library."

"Really, what did it say?"

"Well, if that's the cloth from St. Cuthbert's coffin, we might be able to confirm it by reading Derrick's description."

Sylvia nodded, processing this information, as she put on her coat.

"Was there any clue as to who the woman is supposed to be?"

She put the bag over her shoulder and clasped it tightly.

"It's not just a woman…it's a mermaid and guess what else?" He knew Sylvia would love this.

"A mermaid? Really?" Sylvia's eyes grew round.

"And, amazingly, how we hadn't noticed it before - she has two tails."

Sylvia, placed the bag on the bed and removed the cloth again, needing to see for herself.

"How have we not spotted this before?" said Sylvia,

Robert shrugged. "No idea. Dazzled by the colours? Dazzled by her face? I don't know. But I know one thing – I do not like this cloth."

Sylvia frowned, then folded the cloth again, reverently, protectively.

***

Tynemouth – February 1999

Caroline caught a glimpse of her own sorry appearance in the mirror, and turned her attention to watching her friend. It was now twenty years since they had been at Lancaster University and Sylvia's appearance had barely changed. The dowdiness of the faded furniture only seemed by contrast to emphasise her radiance. Maybe she had gained some weight, but her skin showed little trace of lines and her hair was still lustrous and dark. Sylvia's appearance, as always epitomised a picture of youthfulness and vitality. Sylvia noticed her friend's gaze smiled her lovely, infectious smile, almost as if she were still only twenty.

"Sylvia," Caroline sighed wearily. "I must say how well you're looking."

"Thank you," said Sylvia, slightly embarrassed at her friend saying this, considering her own appearance. "I would like to say that this was due to my healthy lifestyle… but I think we both know not that's not the case. Look, don't give up…I think there may be a solution to all of this." said Sylvia, tentatively at first but then her face brightening.

"It's very kind of you to say I can live here. It's greatly appreciated. At least that is one less thing I have to deal with…"

"No, more than that…your cancer. I think I've got a way that we can beat it…" A peculiar look appeared on Sylvia's face.

"No, no, don't go there, it's impossible. I'm resigned to it. The doctors have told me I have only months or even weeks to live." *So, Sylvia thought of herself as a doctor now, did she?* If she wasn't so tired Caroline would make her anger more obvious. "They can't offer me any treatment you know. Palliative care, when the time comes - that's all."

"Doctor's don't know everything do they?" said Sylvia.

"I'm not being funny but...it doesn't help y'know, building hopes."

"No listen, listen, please. Do you remember when Robert and I fled from St. Cuthbert's cave we ...or should I say, I, took a souvenir."

"I *had* forgotten but I think it was a cloth of some sort."

"Yes, but listen, it was a very important silk... I never told you the full story. It was used to wrap the body of St. Cuthbert in and it was said to, no, *has* magical qualities. You know his body was preserved until... well, until the cloth was taken. Then his body started to rot. And somehow... yes, I know it sounds crazy but... this very same piece of material came to be in the possession of Scire. You know, Scire who died on that night. Well, anyway to get back to the point, my appearance hasn't changed very much over the years has it? Well that's no coincidence...you see... I have been keeper of the cloth. That cloth. That's why I look this way. My skin's hardly changed. I believe it. Seriously, I think it's true."

Caroline's eye's glazed over not knowing what to make of the mad notions of her fanciful friend.

"Don't you see?" Sylvia continued. "The cloth is upstairs, here. It's in the attic. It can help you. I know it. If I leave it and you live here then you become the keeper - don't you see? I believe it will keep the cancer at bay. Truly, I do. Come on, it's at least worth a try isn't it?"

"Sylvia that's just not very likely. Mad in fact. I've had accepted my fate and really could do without any false hopes."

"No, you must become me. You have to. The cloth doesn't like swapping keepers. We can swap names, swap everything. We can sort out details later. We can do it. And…you know … I'm still frightened Derrick will find us. That's why we've moved so many times. He's still looking for his revenge and the cloth. He knows what it can do That's why Robert and I don't live together. Even after all this time. If you become me it'll make it harder again for him to track us down. We can help each other. Don't you think?"

"This is crazy."

"I know. I know, but what've you to got to lose? If it doesn't work you've lost nothing at all. But if it does work?"

"It's madness. Like expecting a miracle. It'll never …"

"You were in the Requisite. You were at the ceremonies. You saw …"

"We were young, impressionable. We wanted to belong to something strange and exciting. Looking back – it was all so ridiculous. Just playing at otherworldly stuff. It was all just nonsense. Surely you see that."

"Was it though?"

"Sylvia this is just…"

"Okay okay, but just think, just think. You've got nothing to lose. And if you won't do it for yourself, do it for me and Robert. Be the keeper of the cloth and change places."

"This is just insanity, Sylvia."

"No *Sylvia*…call me Caroline."

***

Tynemouth- November 2009

Llyriad was sitting in the small corner room, hidden behind the bar and out of sight of the rest of the pub. She had been distracted by a large, stuffed sheepdog, in a glass case at the end of the bar. This was 'Wandering Willie', who died in 1880 after searching for his lost master for many months and was sent to the taxidermist by the then owners of the 'Turk's Head'.

She had been nursing a large gin and tonic for some time. She finished it with a deep gulp and returned to the bar for another. As she paid for her drink, she heard the creak of the door and scuttled back to her hiding hole, trying to stop the ice cubes clinking in her glass. She was pleased to note that her objective was soon to be achieved.

"So, the usual unc?" Sebastian strolled across the floor and was leaned against the bar. "I'm glad today's over. The shop seemed even more quiet than usual."

"Sebastian, that was quite normal for a Monday. You know business always picks up as the week goes on."

Robert rolled his eyes knowing exactly where this conversation was heading and sat down resignedly at his favourite place by the back window. Two minutes later his nephew came across with the drinks.

"Well," said Sebastian. "You know that online you can…"

"Enough, enough please. I know what you're going to say. I don't like the internet, so let's just leave it at that. Anyway, we should have company shortly. Caroline's going to be joining us this evening. "

It was now Sebastian's turn to roll his eyes, and around the corner, on other side of the bar, hidden by a partition, a pair of ears pricked up with delight.

"And she's bringing Rebecca with her," said Robert watching his nephew for a reaction.

"Rebecca? How can she be here…it's term time surely?" Sebastian couldn't conceal his interest at this news and he took a large mouthful from his pint.

"Well, apparently, according to Caroline, she's persuaded her to give up her teaching job and come and live here."

"But that's mad." Sebastian slammed his glass down on the table. "Rebecca surely had a promising career as a teacher and because of that selfish, egocentric woman's whim… it's madness."

"Shush, they're here. Let's just leave it."

Caroline came marching into the room, triumphant, like a Roman commander at the forum, ready to receive the public accolade for her victorious campaign. Rebecca following closely behind. Caroline was beaming, as she pulled out a chair, removed her red coat with a flourish and sat down, motioning for Rebecca to sit next to her.

"Lovely, to see you again, Rebecca," said Sebastian.

"Isn't it marvellous Robert?" Interrupted Caroline, speaking directly to Robert, and completely ignoring Sebastian. "Not only is Rebecca back, but she's agreed to stay with me while we get to work on rewiring the house… and doing the boring bits of the renovation. After all there's no point in wasting any time."

She smiled first at Rebecca, then Robert.

"Oh, I didn't realise you were an electrician Caroline," said Sebastian.

Caroline didn't even bother to look at Sebastian, let alone reply.

"Now ladies what can I get you to drink?" Robert took his wallet out of his pocket as he stood up.

"White wine for me... a large one," said Caroline. "I think Rebecca will have the same."

As Robert walked over to the bar, Llyriad, who had been craning her neck, retreated back into her corner room shell like a tortoise. The information she was gleaning from this particular conversation was much more interesting than she could possibly have hoped for.

"So, Rebecca," Sebastian moved his chair, facing Rebecca, his back to Caroline. "Is it true that you've left your job and you're now living here? Have you got another job at a school here?"

"Yes and no." said Rebecca, slightly taken aback. "I resigned from my job... and no, I don't have another one her - yet. I'm going to take a break and spend some time on the house I've inherited." She could have added, *not that it's any of your business*, but decided against.

"Ah, okay," said Sebastian. "It's just that I always thought it was much better to get a job when you already had..."

"Oh, is that right?" said Caroline, her eyes slamming into him. "There speaks the high-flying Sebastian. You're hardly in any position to be handing out career advice."

"So, Rebecca," asked Robert, arriving back with the drinks. "How are you settling in? I expect you'll be glad when you can get properly sorted out in your own house."

"Actually Robert," Caroline gave him an indignant look. The forum plebeians were spoiling her 'Triumph'. "Rebecca is happy enough staying with me for the present."

"Now, don't you be getting all huffy with me," said Robert, coating it with a smile. "Yes, no doubt she is, but I'm sure she would rather be living by herself and not with some middle-aged woman she hardly knows."

"Well, anyway," Caroline realised she needed to remain calm and keep her new-found poise. "This wine isn't too bad, don't you think Rebecca? It isn't the best as this isn't one of my favourite places. There are lots of much nicer bars and restaurants around here and we'll have to go into Newcastle soon ... there are some wonderful places ..."

Caroline's voice boomed, asserting herself and she managed to irritate the barman who could hear every single word.

Llyriad was enjoying listening to this conversation very much. Sylvia, or Caroline as she now preferred to call herself for some peculiar reason, seemed to have become even more pompous and overbearing than she could possibly have predicted. She was clearly making a spectacle of herself. She deserved to be ruined, totally ruined ... and more. Llyriad would bankrupt her pathetic business, and Robert's for good measure. Also, judging by what she had just heard, Robert no longer seemed to worship her as he once did and she needed to sour that relationship further.

However, one step at a time...first she needed to recover the cloth which had to be kept in Caroline's apartment where Rebecca was now conveniently staying. It was definitely time for Rebecca to have another tarot card reading but this time a home visit would perhaps be more appropriate. All she had to do was catch Rebecca alone and coincidentally bump into her. Llyriad finished off her drink, gave herself a satisfied smile and made a discreet exit by the back door.

She had hoped to go undetected but Sebastian noticed her. He didn't say anything to the others who were too engrossed in their conversation. He wanted to think this through for himself. That was definitely the same woman he'd seen before. The one who'd scared Caroline.

Chapter 23

Tynemouth – March 1999

Caroline studied her forty-year old face in the mirror, she noticed changes which she was sure hadn't been there a few days ago. Fine lines were etched around her eyes, there was slackness about her jaw that she hadn't noticed before and the waistband on her skirt was feeling uncomfortably tight. No doubt she needed to pay more attention to what she ate and think horrible thoughts about doing some exercise.

Tracing her fingers from her parting, she could see strands of white, alarmingly threading paths through her chestnut hair. Most of her friends had been dyeing their hair for a good few years. It was, she sighed, to be expected at her age. In fact, she needed to go immediately and get some dye as soon as possible, before anybody noticed her inexplicably rapid ageing. She certainly hadn't expected it to happen as quickly as this. She had flattered herself that her youthful appearance had been partly down to her natural good fortune rather than the total invocation of the silk.

However, it had been essential that she gave up the cloth. It was amazing that they hadn't been found so far, especially considering the number of moves they had forced to make in the early years until now. First Durham, then Edinburgh, Shrewsbury, Swindon, Gloucester… the list seemed endless. They had been living in the Tynemouth area for a couple of years now. Robert had his bookshop and her interior design business was beginning at last to attract some clients. Now that the real Caroline was living in her house, she had needed to move out and distance herself. Her new apartment, in the marine development in

North Shields would be hers soon and in the meanwhile she would just have to suffer the run-down flat she was renting.

Robert had insisted that she stayed there at his flat, but that was impossible. It was much too dangerous and she didn't think she could cope with his untidiness. She was no longer in her twenties. After all these years, the relationship they had actually suited them both just fine. If they'd been married and living together, they would probably have fallen out. This way they both had their own space.

The new Caroline had bumped into the new Sylvia the day before and the transformation of her friend had been remarkable. Their paths had crossed when they met on the Tynemouth high street and from the heavy bags she was carrying it was obvious that new Sylvia now had the energy for shopping. Days earlier, she would have been far too weak to attempt this. But now...Sylvia had a spring in her step and a smile on her face. She was wearing jeans that showed off her trim figure and a flattering, blue sweater. Her greying bob had been restored to its original darkness by artificial means obviously, but nevertheless... and she was wearing subtle make-up. She was almost unrecognizable.

"Wow, "Caroline gave her friend a hug. "You look amazing."

"Sylvia...I mean Caroline," she laughed sounding like the girl she had known twenty years ago. "I feel amazing too. I haven't felt like this in years."

"I'm so pleased." Caroline gave a curious smile. "Tell me have you looked at the cloth at all?"

"Oh yes." She replied, "Oh yes. It's so beautiful with all those lovely patterns and colours. And that magnificent mermaid - who is she?"

"It's some nature goddess." Caroline looked uneasy. "Tell me where is it? Is it still in that box in the attic?" Her voice took on a peculiar edge.

"Oh no. It was much too gorgeous to leave up there. I have it on my bed and look..." she whispered glancing down at her body. "It's working. It must be. I haven't been to the doctor yet but I just know."

"No, *you must not keep it there*. It needs to be in a box in the attic. You have to put it back there *immediately*." Caroline's tone was unpleasant. "Don't go to the doctors. You mustn't draw attention to yourself. Don't decorate the house or get workmen in. You have to remain as anonymous as you can. It's a prerequisite. You will be well, I know that, but by being the keeper there is a price to pay. Now you have to go home. Go home and put the silk in the box. Keep it in the attic and leave it there. It has to be secret. *It has to be secret*."

Caroline didn't know where the words came from and felt shocked but compelled to say what she needed to.

The new Sylvia was confused and seemed to visibly shrink. She stared at Caroline with a crumpled, stunned face.

"Yes, of course, of course, I'll do as you say," said Sylvia, concentrating on recording in her mind every word and syllable from her friend ready to play back later when she had time to try and figure out what had just happened. She wondered if perhaps her health battle wasn't going to be the easy victory she had begun to assume.

***

Tynemouth – November 2009

Sebastian was furious. As soon as he got back to his untidy flat, he opened a can of beer and lit a cigarette. How dare she? He was allegedly *'hardly in any position to be handing out career advice'* and the scathing way in which she had referred to him as *'high flying Sebastian'* had stung him bitterly. He knew his parents saw him as a disappointment, merely working in a bookshop, but he certainly didn't need a reminder of this from her of all people.

All he had been trying to do, he thought to himself, was look out for Rebecca, who seemed a decent enough sort of person. Well, if she was taken in by that evil witch - then more fool her. He had actually been thinking of striking up a friendship with her, but not now. Rebecca had become contaminated by association. In fact, in the pub it was almost as if she was trying to copy Caroline's mannerisms. What was all that about? Didn't she see that the woman had effectively ruined her career? Nobody gave up a permanent job unless they had another lined up. Even he knew that. What could she have been thinking of? Just to satisfy Caroline's whims… it was incredible. But why was Caroline so obsessed with her? She had no children of her own so she must see Rebecca as some daughter substitute toy.

Sebastian stubbed out his cigarette and quickly finished his can before opening another. It wasn't as if Caroline had a proper career. Interior designer for God's sake. He had heard about the mess of her own place - utterly tasteless it sounded. And any clients she managed to bamboozle needed their heads sorting. In fact, how she was able to maintain her lavish lifestyle was a great mystery because he couldn't see how anybody so lacking in good taste could carve out a lucrative career in her field.

His uncle's friendship with her was unfathomable. What terrible hold did the despicable woman have over him? He was convinced that Robert's inability to grasp modern technology was fuelled by *her* primitive attitude. If he could somehow get his uncle to see sense and sever all links with the woman then the two of them could reap the benefits of a half decent business. He lit another cigarette.

He thought about the mysterious woman in the pub. If this was who he thought it had been, then this was somebody Caroline was frightened of. How could that be? What did the woman know about Caroline? He had seen Caroline's reaction when she noticed the woman in the street outside Robert's shop. Caroline definitely had skeletons in her cupboard. What could they be? Sebastian's anger was shifting to curiosity. Maybe, he needed to track this woman down because possibly, she could provide him with a useful ally. Caroline had belittled him once too often and she would live to regret it.

***

Durham- June 1979

Nature Goddess Silk at Durham by Derrick Stevens

'In the many discussions of the various problems relating to the development of early medieval silks, it is surprising that the magnificent seventh century silk found in the coffin of St. Cuthbert has received so little notice. It is surely one of the greatest achievements of early Byzantine weavers. As to the whereabouts of this cloth now, it remains almost as great a mystery as the identity of the figure on the cloth.'

'A connected roundel surrounds a half - length figure whose arms are raised but not necessarily with a worshipful implication. The hands hold batons or vegetable forms from which hangs a scarf that passes over the chest of the figure. On the scarf are many images of fruits. The lower half of the figure is submerged in water which fills the lower part of the roundel. Ducks and fishes float on the water'.

'The beautiful figure wears a tunic with tightly fitting sleeves and is covered with intricate patterns. The yoke is ornamental with pearls and drop beads. Drop beads are placed on the ends of her long dark hair and a jewel encrusted tiara adorns her head. The figure is clearly that of a nature goddess and the double fishtail suggests Atargatis.'

"It has to be surely?" Sylvia was certain that it was the cloth in her bag after reading Derrick's description.

"Got to be, this has to be describing our silk," agreed Robert. "And to describe it in such detail, it's clear he's studied it very closely."

They had located a copy of Derrick's article at the university library in Durham.

"Scire must have shown it to him. "Sylvia felt a pang of guilt as she remembered watching him fall from the top of the cave.

"Honestly Sylvia," Robert guessed what she was thinking from the look on her face. "There was nothing we could have done to save him. We did the only thing we could."

"I know... but I shouldn't have taken the cloth, should I? Who is Atargatis anyway?"

Robert began searching in the relevant section.

"Ah this looks promising." He went to the index in a hefty volume, 'Female Deities in Ancient Times''.

"Got her," he said. He turned to the page and began reading. "Atargatis was a goddess of Syrian origin whose worship spread to Greece and Rome. She was a great mother and fertility goddess of the earth and water. Doves and fishes were sacred to her: doves as an emblem of the love goddess and fish symbolic of the fertility and life of water. As she was so closely associated with fish she is often represented with a single or even double fishtail. Atargatis may have been the inspiration for the Greek love goddess Aphrodite whose worship is said to have come from the East." Robert pictured their cloth once more as Sylvia took over the reading.

"There was a temple in honour of her at Cyprus," she said. "that was richly decorated and had a big golden statue inside of both her and her consort Hadad... Just think that's who we represented... only a few days ago – wow. Next to this temple was a sacred lake filled with fantastic fish. Listen to this Robert, these fish were actually encrusted with jewels on their skins. Imagine that..." Her voice was becoming increasingly excited.

"That's just like the fish on the silk. This is really mind blowing, isn't it?" whispered Robert, aware of one or two students raising their heads.

"In ancient times, Atargatis had been a beautiful and powerful priestess who fell in love with a humble shepherd boy," continued Sylvia. "He, being merely mortal, did not survive her divine love making and unfortunately died. She however, became pregnant, but was so distraught that she threw herself into the ocean to drown. As her beauty was so great, the gods changed her into a mermaid and she became Atargatis, the divine goddess of the sea."

"It just doesn't make sense though does it?" Robert stared at the pages. "The thing I just can't fathom. Why did this cloth with the mermaid goddess come to be in St. Cuthbert's coffin? I mean, what on earth would it be doing there?"

"But is it really that odd?"

"Well, yes. I don't remember any reference to mermaid goddesses in the Bible. It doesn't really have a place in Christianity does it?"

"Maybe it does though. Not in the Christianity of today perhaps… but the Pagan influences in the early days. This is proof of Pagan influences on Celtic Christianity. Mysticism and nature worship. And that's how it links with the Requisite. Worship of nature and the mother goddess. That's what Atargatis is, don't you think? It's from the coffin of St. Cuthbert and the figure on our silk is a nature goddess."

Robert looked up sharply at the word 'our'.

"And that's why Derrick isn't going to rest… until he's got this silk," said Sylvia, imagining how furious Derrick must have been when he discovered the cloth was missing.

"I wonder how long Scire had been keeper of the cloth?" A picture of the fresh-faced Scire came to Robert's mind. "He looked to be in his early thirties so… it couldn't have been that long… and how on earth did *he* get it?"

"He looked to be in his thirties - but was he?" Sylvia was talking quickly, her eyes shining. "What did the cloth do to St. Cuthbert's body? I mean, according to the legend…his body was incorrupt wasn't it? What will it do to us? Is that why it's so important to Derrick?"

Robert and Sylvia looked at each other, realising the implications of what they had just learned, and why the silk was so desirable.

Chapter 24

North Shields – November 2009

Rebecca checked the coffee table one more time. She was sure that was where she had left her keys but they were nowhere to be seen. She had searched the benches in the kitchen and all the surfaces in the bedroom. Caroline would be back soon. She'd used the last of the milk for her visitor's coffee and she needed to go to the shop to get some more. Despite Caroline being so accommodating, she doubted very much that she would be impressed with Rebecca losing her keys after only being here for a couple of days. They had to be somewhere in the flat because there was nowhere else they could be, unless …

She thought back to her strange meeting with Madame Llyriad only a couple of hours earlier. Rebecca had just been putting some rubbish outside when that familiar figure with her large bag had just happened to be walking by.

"Well, my dear," Llyriad put her bag on the ground and turned to face her. "Fancy seeing you again. I have often thought about the last time we met. What a remarkable coincidence."

"Oh yes," Rebecca felt a little embarrassed remembering her last encounter with the woman. Visiting fortune tellers wasn't something she was in the habit of doing and she looked about to see if anyone was watching.

"I think there's a lot more that needs to be said. Perhaps if you invited me in… as it happens, I have my cards with me."

"Oh, I see. Well, I 'm not sure that's such a good idea. It's a bit inconvenient. You see this isn't my home. I'm just staying with a friend at the moment." Rebecca wasn't sure how Caroline would react if she came home to find a clairvoyant in her flat.

"As you please. But there are things that I can tell you…" Llyriad undid a button on her coat, assuming she would be asked to go inside.

"Well, okay then," Rebecca relented. She knew she was desperate to hear what the woman had to say for herself. "But I can't let you stay for long."

Llyriad needed no further invitation. She moved quickly, surprisingly light on her feet for a woman of her size and was soon up the steps into the hall. Rebecca joined her and they took the lift to the penthouse apartment.

"Looks a very nice place you have here," said Llyriad. Her eyes landed on Caroline's voluptuous portrait and she suppressed a snigger as she greedily drank in the flat and its contents. "A white coffee with three sugars, that would be splendid."

Rebecca went to make the drinks in the kitchen. When she came back, she was surprised to find that, not only was Llyriad still wearing her coat but she was standing in the open doorway.

"I am so, so, sorry my dear. My watch has stopped. I just noticed your clock and I have an appointment in twenty minutes. Look, you know where to find me. I'm afraid I will have to dash. I'll let myself out. Again, so sorry."

Llyriad darted along the hall and Rebecca gave a thankful sigh, relieved to hear the lift door close.

She wasn't sure when Caroline would be back. And curious as she was as to what Llyriad had to tell her, she didn't think Caroline would be very pleased to see the woman sitting in her home. However, her initial thankfulness, was soon to be replaced by concern when she realised that her keys were missing ...

***

Whitley Bay – November 2009

Llyriad was amazed at how easily her mission had been accomplished. Now all she had to do was get the key copied and place the original somewhere on the ground near the flat. 'Caroline' as she was calling herself, would think her guest careless and untrustworthy ... and she would have replica keys. She laughed softly to herself and the laugh turned into a sort of gurgling sound like an ancient, faulty radiator rattling.

The apartment was just as awful as she imagined it would be. Expensive furnishings undoubtedly, but in poor taste, especially the outlandish portrait of 'Caroline' hanging on the wall. Her high opinion of herself was unbelievable and deluded. How the woman managed to find clients willing to part with their cash for her to ruin their houses was totally beyond Llyriad's comprehension.

Llyriad wondered if Rebecca had discovered the keys were missing yet. Once, she had the keys cut, she needed to get them back promptly because even someone as irresponsible as Rebecca would soon be able to put two and two together.

Then all she would have to do was bide her time until the place was empty and the cloth would be hers. She was sure that this had to be its location. The question was, should she tell Derrick? Surely, even the cloth could do little to help him now. It was a wonder he was still alive, thought Llyriad. At least, he had been yesterday because of the number of calls from him which she had ignored.

He hadn't really been straight with her all this time, had he? Revenge for what had happened had never been his main agenda. He just wanted that cloth for himself. In fact, when Scire had been murdered by those two, matters could have ended very well for him if only he had managed to get to the cave a little faster. No doubt Scire's death would have suited his purposes very well. If only they hadn't taken the cloth. That must have been eating away at him all these years. For him the silk had been all that was of importance. Soon, not only would it be hers but she would also be able to enjoy herself in the flat with a sharp knife … starting with that hideous portrait. She nodded heartily, appreciating the thought.

***

Alnwick, Northumberland – November 2009

Derrick couldn't understand why Llyriad wasn't returning his calls and he was aware that time was fast running out. The cloth should have been his all those years ago. He thought back to when he had first visited Durham Cathedral as a young boy- a moment that had shaped his whole life. His fascination with St. Cuthbert wasn't so much pre-occupied with his piety and devotion, but more about how his body could have been preserved. Research into the Nature Goddess Silk had resulted in him carving out a career for himself in studying, writing about and lecturing in Early Christianity. Of course, he was interested, even passionate about these things, but the greater driving force had always been his need to possess that cloth.

Surely, it had to be more of a coincidence that his path has crossed with that of Scire's. Scire, who should just happen to be the guardian of the cloth. But how? There was nothing particularly special about him was there? That such a mediocre person should have this exceptional privilege was beyond his understanding. Derrick deserved the cloth and Derrick would have the cloth, no matter what price had to be paid.

So many people were just contemptible. The Requisite - those gullible fools. It was just perfect for his purposes. Celtic Christianity, with its appeal of belonging to a bygone age and worship of the Mother Goddess had been so much in keeping with the zeitgeist of the time. The existence of the silk had added extra credibility. However, only he and Scire were aware of its power. The rest of the Requisite had been unaware of its true significance and some even ignorant of its existence.

So, whatever had compelled those two to steal it? To this day he found it unfathomable. True, Robert had been a student of his. However, the silk was not a topic he ever mentioned in his lectures and Robert hadn't seemed the most enquiring-minded student that he had come across.

He had to admit that he had enjoyed the power and he had been genuinely moved by the theatricality of the ceremonies. Celtic Christianity? Nobody really knew how those ancient people had worshipped and little really was known of the ceremonies of the Druids. The whole existence of the Requisite had been down to the fabrications of him - Derrick Stevens, all created to keep close company with Scire and the cloth. And, when he had been forced to conduct the ceremony to scatter Scire's ashes, he was really making it up, as most evidence suggested that Pre-Christian Celtic peoples buried their dead. Burial of course, was not an option he had.

That Llyriad had remained true to the cause, even long after its disbandment, was a reflection of her stupidity and misplaced loyalty towards her lover. After the final Scire ceremony, there had been no more meetings of the Requisite. The events at St. Cuthbert's Cave had left a bitter taste. Members became scared. Nobody wanted to face the consequences of having had any involvement in Scire's death. That is, apart from Llyriad, who certainly didn't want to forget.

Still, it had suited his purposes. The cloth was so close to being his. Now, when he needed it so badly, was not the time for her to doubt him. If she wanted her misguided revenge for the unfortunate events of thirty years ago, then that's what needed to happen. If he was going to get his prize then she must have the assurance that his motives were the same as hers. The fate of the two thieves really didn't matter to him.

Derrick tried her number again, but again there was no reply.

***

North Shields- November 2009

Caroline had been to what was now Rebecca's house, to supposedly check on the progress being made by the electrician and plumber. She was pleased to note the state of disarray. It would be a long while before it would be finished and Rebecca would be staying with her for at least the foreseeable future. Earlier that morning she had woken up in a panic, imagining that the workmen had taken it upon themselves to go into the attic and come across the silk. She realised that she hadn't checked on the safety of the box and its contents for some time. As she struggled with the loft ladder and pulled herself up, in what she conceded was a rather ungainly manner, she was annoyed to hear sniggers from the men working below.

Once she had verified the position of the wooden chest, closed and still in its usual place she climbed back down the ladder. She remembered there was a key kept in a tin under the sink and she would be able to use to lock the door to the attic.

Strangely, as she was thinking of keys, she arrived back at her apartment and noticed a bunch of keys lying on the pavement that looked remarkably similar to those she had given to Rebecca. She picked them up and tried the one for the apartment block front door. The door opened. This was very careless of Rebecca, and while she was eager to keep on the right side of her, such neglect needed at least to be mentioned.

"Rebecca," she called as she walked into the lounge, jangling the missing keys as if they were the vital missing pieces in a detective story. "I think you've lost something. I found these lying on the ground outside."

"Oh, thank goodness for that." Rebecca appeared visibly relieved. "I've been looking for them everywhere."

"Well it might have been a good idea if you thought back as to what you were doing earlier. I presume you must have just put some rubbish out and not needed them to get back in."

"Err…yes I did get rid of a bin bag earlier." Rebecca knew for a fact that she hadn't taken the keys outside with her. "I guess I must have dropped them then."

"Well, I know it was only an accident dear and no damage was done but nevertheless … please will you take a little more care in future."

Caroline just managed to stop herself from tutting before taking off her coat and marching into the kitchen. Here she was surprised to see two full mugs of her good coffee which had been left to go cold. She was finding out traits of Rebecca's character which she didn't particularly admire.

Rebecca followed Caroline into the kitchen to find her rinsing the cups. She waited for the question. Should she say Robert or Sebastian had been round for coffee?

"Rebecca, I know I said for you to treat the place as your own and have anything you like to eat and drink." Caroline looked at her with a forced smile. "However, making yourself not one but two cups of coffee and completely forgetting about drinking them…well, it just seems a little wasteful don't you think?"

"Oh, yes, of course, sorry about that. It was with looking for the keys… I got myself in a bit of a flap and forgot." Rebecca was relieved that Caroline had leapt to the wrong decision. She hoped that this would be the end of the Llyriad incident, and she definitely wouldn't be searching her out for another reading. But she had an ominous feeling this event would have some unpleasant repercussions.

"It doesn't really matter," Caroline remembered that she was trying to keep Rebecca on board. "Now what shall we do with the rest of the day? I've just been round to your place and those workmen are looking very busy. Still, it should be some time before it's habitable for you? Why don't we go into Newcastle? Yes, I think it might be quite good fun to do some shopping. We could look at furniture and some things for your house."

Rebecca's initial reaction to this was that it should have been her going round to check on the progress being made on her house, however in light of what had just happened with the keys she thought she had better keep this to herself.

"Okay, sounds good," Rebecca wanted to put all thoughts of her unwelcome visitor to the back of her mind.

"However, sorry, sorry," said Caroline, flapping her hands. "I've just remembered. We might be better off going tomorrow. I have a few things that I need to get done today."

"That's a shame I would really like to have gone…"

"No, no. If we go tomorrow, we can make an early start," said Caroline abruptly, still a little annoyed by the girl's carelessness. The tone of her voice was so sour that it made Rebecca shift her body weight from left to right and she felt her cheeks burning, not quite sure if it was with anger or embarrassment.

Chapter 25

Tynemouth- November 2009

Robert was pretending to tidy a bookshelf to as he was watched the large woman ambling along. Llyriad went into the tea shop on the opposite side of the road and both Sebastian and his uncle couldn't take their eyes off her. Sebastian wondered once more what on earth the mystery could be. He knew for certain there was one. He still hadn't forgotten those hurtful jibes that Caroline had made. This woman definitely had something on Caroline and he was determined to find out what.

A customer came in and as Robert was dealing with her Sebastian saw his chance.

"I'm just popping out unc."

Robert looked up and nodded. "Don't be too long".

Looking through the window, Sebastian made sure that his uncle was busy with the customer and then hurried across the road. He walked into the tea shop, saw Llyriad sitting on a table next to a bay window and made himself comfortable close by. After ordering a cup of tea from the waitress, he played with the teaspoon and tried to catch Llyriad's eye. He cleared his throat loudly. She looked in his direction and he smiled at her.

"Are you here on holiday?" Sebastian asked. "Visiting relatives?"

"No," Llyriad, instantly recognised Sebastian from the visits to the 'Turk's Head' and couldn't believe her luck. "I live here actually."

Sebastian hadn't been expecting such a pleasant voice and tried to place the accent.

"Oh right. I work in the shop across the road - the bookshop. It's my uncle's."

"Good for you."

"You work in Tynemouth?"

"Not quite. Though not far away. I'm a clairvoyant. Madame Llyriad," she said with a flourish and produced a yellow and black card from her pocket. 'Madame Llyriad, Clairvoyant Extraordinaire. Find out what your future holds.' "Are you interested in having your fortune told?"

"Possibly... I just wondered ... do you know my uncle or his friend Caroline?" He knew he hadn't time for any lengthy preamble.

"Why do you ask that?" She weighed him up formally with a judgemental stare which she knew would be expected of her. It wouldn't do to make this too easy for him.

"It's just ... I've seen you around in a few places recently and..." Sebastian knew this would sound really odd. "I thought Caroline was looking at you strangely. I mean, like... like as if she recognised you."

"No, I don't think that's possible. I haven't been living in these parts for very long."

She poured herself another cup of tea.

"Where were you living before? My uncle and Caroline haven't always lived round here either."

"Oh, I've lived all over the country, all over. That's the nature of gypsies you know. So, is this Caroline your aunty then?"

"No, no, God, no. Thankfully, he's got more sense than to marry that old bag."

Sebastian shook his head too much and then stopped, alarmed that he was shaking his head too much, that it made him look childish and also hurt his neck.

"You aren't a great fan of hers then?" said Llyriad.

"Too right, I can't stand the woman."

"So …. what has this Caroline woman done to you then?"

"Well, where shall I begin? She's the most rude, bossy and conceited person I've ever met. What my uncle sees in her is beyond my comprehension."

He'd already decided to make a leap of faith. See if she bit

"Really," Llyriad tilted her head encouragingly.

"She's so spiteful and … she's made her friend's niece give up her career. I mean, just to satisfy her own selfish ideas."

Sebastian was hoping his deliberate imprudence would catch her off guard.

"That seems a *very* peculiar thing to do… it makes no sense whatsoever. I wonder what the *ideas* could be? Your uncle and her must be devoted to each other …somehow."

Every word and syllable artfully booby-trapped. Llyriad wasn't going to waste this opportunity to find out more. She was also puzzled as to the connection between Caroline and Rebecca.

"Well she's never bothered to have children herself. So now, she fancies pretending she's got a daughter I reckon."

"And what do you think of the girl?" Llyriad still couldn't believe her luck, getting all of this inside information from such an unlikely source.

"Well, I thought she was all right at first. But now ...that woman's got her claws in her and she's been, I dunno, corrupted somehow. I would say that Rebecca has been well and truly *Carolined*."

Now was the moment, thought Llyriad. This young man would make a perfect accomplice. He hated her too. She had to take a chance. This would be the breakthrough she'd been waiting for.

"Very well then. As you're being very honest with me, I'll be honest with you," said Llyriad. "I did know them both - a long time ago. And they did me a great wrong. In fact, that is the main reason that I'm here now."

Result, thought Sebastian.

"What did they do?" he said, using his open-faced, innocent expression.

"Well," Llyriad was pleased to share her grievances but knew she needed to tread carefully. "For one thing, they stole something that didn't belong to them. But that's only part of it."

"What? What did they steal? Was it money? Caroline always seems to have lots of spare cash?"

"This was something massive. Irreplaceable. But look, I don't know if I can trust you. I don't even know your name and … you are Robert's nephew after all." Llyriad narrowed her eyes into slits.

"I'm Sebastian, and yes, you can trust me. I don't like the woman one bit. She's a nasty piece of work… so if I can help you in any way, count me in."

"Good. I think we can help each other a great deal. We need to swap phone numbers."

Llyriad offered a hand, Sebastian shook it and left to return to the bookshop. They were each equally happy to have exchanged secrets for valuable information.

***

Robert caught sight of Sebastian and as he left the tea room. He was sure he had been up to no good. Why would Sebastian go and spend money in there, when they had a perfectly good café on the premises and he could make himself a free coffee anytime he wanted.? It was the same place he had seen Llyriad disappearing into earlier. Surely the boy couldn't have been meeting her. No, that was just ridiculous, how could the two of them possibly know each other? More than likely there was some innocent explanation. There were some young waitresses who worked in that café. That was the most likely the cause of Sebastian's interest.

The door jangled as Sebastian walked into the shop.

"Go anywhere nice?" Robert immediately asked his nephew.

"What? I just went to the bank."

"What did you go to the bank for?"

"Same as most people. I needed to get some money out." This wasn't at all like his uncle, to question his whereabouts and it felt awkward.

"It took you rather a long time just to go to the cash point, didn't it?"

"I had some other things to buy too." Sebastian crossed his arms defensively and stood squarely facing his uncle.

"Really? What was so urgent that you needed to buy them immediately?"

"What's the matter with you?" Sebastian snapped." You're never usually so interested in what I'm doing."   "Just making conversation. Making sure you're keeping out of trouble," Robert laughed, attempting unsuccessfully to make light of matters, but he couldn't stop himself. "Anyway, what've you bought? I don't see any bags.

"I bought a card actually…for a friend's birthday. D'you want to check my pockets?" He'd never been cross examined by his uncle like this before. He knew he must have been watching him.

"No, of course not. I'm sorry, sorry Sebastian I'm just a little on edge at the moment."

There was really no point going on like this, thought Robert. Sebastian was obviously lying to him but it was probably due to some reason of little consequence and the poor lad most likely felt embarrassed, as did he for his cross examination.

"That's okay. Don't worry about it."

Sebastian was just relieved that his uncle has stopped his questions. He knew how furious his uncle would be if he had heard any of the conversation in the tea room. But he hadn't and there was absolutely no reason for him to do so. However, Sebastian realised that he needed to be much more careful. Now that he and Llyriad had each other's phone numbers they could organize more discreet liaisons. Anyway, although Llyriad hated Caroline, she didn't seem to think too badly of his uncle. She probably just felt sorry for him being entangled with Caroline. Thankfully, any revenge plans seemed to be directed towards Caroline … and Sebastian didn't have a problem with that at all

Robert began pricing some books and began thinking about their situation. All these years he and Caroline had avoided being caught. They had always been one step ahead. They knew that Derrick would have been employing people to track them down. A stranger asking difficult questions had been their cue to up and leave. Friends and family had been shunned. It was too dangerous to visit or be visited. Phone calls were kept to an absolute minimum and just to say they were okay. Every two or three years they were on the move, never leaving forwarding addresses. He understood how reckless they had been in going to Durham in the early days. It was an obvious mistake and they had so nearly been caught. A chance sighting of Derrick in the town Square giving them just enough time to run, leaving everything behind. Now, however they were older, no less vigilant but tired of the constant running.

They had stayed in Tynemouth much longer than most places. But it seemed they had been found at last. Llyriad and Derrick were here. It was too complicated to run now. Other people, close to them, were involved.

Also, the house was empty, the silk left unattended. Soon it would be occupied by Rebecca. She would be the keeper of the cloth. She would be implicated. She would be in as much danger as them. She would be accursed and confounded as much as them. He was appalled and ashamed that they had done this to Rebecca. And what would be the effect on her? As far as he was concerned, he wished they could just give the silk to Llyriad and be done with it. But he knew that couldn't happen. Even if it did, it wouldn't really change matters. She would still want blood for Scire. They would just have to be extra vigilant …and be ready for anything. They knew what Llyriad and Derrick were capable of.

Robert looked at the clock and was thankful when he saw what the time was.

"Fancy a pint Sebastian?" said Robert, building bridges. Sebastian never turned this down.

"Actually unc, I'm sorry, I can't tonight … but if you're locking up, I'll get going - if that's alright."

"Of course," said Robert, surprised at Sebastian turning down the chance of a pint. "See you tomorrow …and have a good night."

Sebastian waved and disappeared into the street. As soon as he was outside, he reached for his phone where he noticed three missed calls from the same sender. He rang the number back.

***

How fortunate that Caroline's behaviour had annoyed him so much, thought Llyriad. Sebastian's words were etched in her memory: rude, bossy, conceited, selfish, spiteful. Music to her ears. Who would have thought that she would find such an unlikely ally?

He was quite a good-looking lad as well. He reminded her a lot of his uncle when he was younger but there was a malicious streak in Sebastian that his pathetic uncle had never possessed. She recognised in him a common yearning for revenge and soon this little puppy would be doing her bidding. Of that she felt sure.

The payback plan would have to be mostly targeted at Caroline. Sebastian did seem to have some fondness for his uncle and without question Caroline was the real villain of the piece. Obviously, she wouldn't tell Sebastian the actual details of the silk, only that it was an expensive antique. She had told him that they had taken something that didn't belong to her. Well, she had also taken Scire's life. That would be the version of events she could tell Sebastian. On that Litha,

Caroline had deliberately pushed Scire off the cliff which, more than likely, had been the case.

She heard her phone. Sebastian's name flashed up on the screen.

"Llyriad, are you free tonight? Can we meet?""

"Absolutely, of course."

Chapter 26

North Shields - November 2009

As they left Caroline's new flat and headed down the street towards the Metro station, Caroline and Rebecca had no idea that they were being watched. Caroline, as usual, was waving her arms about theatrically, and Rebecca was clearly hanging on to her every word. Both were oblivious to anything other than their largely one-sided conversation.

Llyriad and Sebastian were sitting in Llyriad's car.

"Have you been in her flat before?" said Llyriad. "D'you know if she has any trunks or boxes or cupboards where the cloth might be kept?"

"No, I've never been in her flat," said Sebastian impatiently. "I told you that last night. Why do you think she'd invite me? The woman hates me for God's sake."

"All right, okay," said Llyriad as she felt for the replica keys in her bag. "Let's just concentrate on the job in hand."

"Come on then let's get on with it," said Sebastian.

As soon as the two women were out of sight Llyriad and Sebastian headed towards the entrance to the building. Llyriad located the correct main door key. Once inside they took the lift and then a second key allowed them to enter the penthouse.

Sebastian walked into the lounge, stopped abruptly and scanned the room. Then he scanned the room again, marvelling at the sight. He threw his head back over heaving shoulders. Suddenly, large wet eyes reappeared and at last he could make a sound. His breathy giggle bounced around the room and then he collapsed into an enormous explosion of laughter.

"Good God," he pointed at the portrait of Caroline. "Just look at it, look at it. If nothing else, just the sight of that has made the break-in worthwhile for me."

"I know, I know. It's unbelievable, but that's how the cow sees herself. She was nothing to write home about when she was young. Pathetic. In her dreams…" Llyriad took a black marker from her pocket and added a sweeping, Salvador Dali moustache above the pouting, red-lipped mouth on the portrait.

"Oh, yes, yes, please. Give it here." Sebastian took the pen, to add two horns growing out of Caroline's shiny, auburn hair.

"So, I wonder where this cloth is then?" Sebastian shook himself and glanced around the room. He pulled out a large drawer filled with heavy, silver cutlery and knocked over a fine, porcelain vase. The knives, forks, spoons and broken pottery, he noted with pleasure, made an interesting mess on the floor.

"Well not there, that's for sure," said Llyriad, as she pulled out the two further drawers of the sideboard and turned them upside down, scattering the contents across the plush carpet to add to the pile. "Come on, let's try the bedroom."

Caroline's bedroom was decorated in shades of rose gold, with a large, luxurious bed in the middle of the room, carefully strewn with an assortment of expensive cushions. At the bottom of the bed, was a large ottoman which Llyriad flung open and began pulling out sweaters, skirts, blouses. All the clothes she noted, with designer labels, and presumably no longer worn, as Caroline appeared to have two further massive wardrobes in the room. Llyriad thought of her own meagre collection of clothes and her cheap, rented flat.

Meanwhile, Sebastian was busy pulling out bedding from drawers and cupboards. He flung open the wardrobe doors and dragged the jackets and dresses out.

"What exactly does it look like?" said Sebastian. "I'm not sure what I'm looking for."

"I don't know exactly what it looks like but it's made out of silk...and it's very old. I imagine it has fine embroidery and such like... no, it wouldn't be shoved in a drawer...it would be in a special place."

Ten minutes later, Llyriad cast her eyes around the room in exasperation.

"I was sure that this was where we would find it, but I can't see where it could be. Where could it be? Where is it?" she thundered about the room, her face so scarlet with fury that it looked like she was melting. "It's not here - dammit! Where the hell is it then?"

"Llyriad, we need to be quiet. You can't run about shouting. We're making too much noise and one of the neighbours'll hear."

"But this can't be a wasted journey...we must find that cloth." Llyriad growled.

"Never mind. It's not a wasted journey. Look at the state of her flat? How d'you think she's going to feel when she sees this."

Sebastian went to the kitchen and came back with a large pair of scissors and a sharp knife. "Even if we haven't found this silk ... I can think of other places to look, and well... I think we have time to do a little more damage here."

Sebastian slashed the portrait of Caroline from top to bottom. He gave the scissors to Llyriad and they turned their attention to the sumptuous sofas and curtains.

***

Tynemouth- November 2009

Robert was surprised when Sebastian had phoned him that morning to say he wasn't feeling very well and he wouldn't be at work. It was a particularly grim, grey day and Robert wasn't feeling too good himself. Maybe they both had the same virus. But this was very unlike Sebastian. Although he was often late, he was rarely ill and even if he had a cold, he would usually just put up with it. He had told his uncle that he had an upset stomach but something just didn't seem right. Also, yesterday, his nephew's behaviour had been very odd. Firstly, there had been his inexplicable visit to the tea shop and then he hadn't wanted to go for a pint.

Robert understood Sebastian's frustration over his refusal to use the internet in their business but he couldn't begin to explain to the boy why. He knew his nephew had been writing reviews for the shop. He was sure that had alerted Derrick and Llyriad but Sebastian couldn't have known this ... or could he? Robert wondered if there wasn't something more sinister going on. He hadn't seen this deceitful side to Sebastian before - and he didn't like it.

Robert thought back to the many discussions he'd had with Sebastian about Caroline. Sebastian had been asking a lot of questions. He seemed to have become obsessed with her. He had to admit that Caroline herself hadn't been helping matters. Her barbed jibes at

Sebastian certainly hadn't calmed relations between the two of them. Sometimes he wished she would just bite her tongue. Knowing her as he did however, he knew she was incapable of ignoring Sebastian's sarcastic comments. Of course, much as he kept these anxieties to himself, he was aware that Sebastian couldn't help but feel he was a failure in his parent's eyes. Knowing this, Caroline couldn't resist going for his Achilles Heel. There was no love lost between those two and it couldn't benefit his and Caroline's particular situation.

But even more distressing was Sebastian's possible relationship with Llyriad. He was now sure that some meeting had occurred between the two of them the day before. A friendship of any sort between Sebastian and Llyriad could certainly result in no good whatsoever. There was only one thing that Robert could do. He needed to go round to Sebastian's flat to check on his sick nephew, but he had a feeling that the lad wasn't going to be in, and if that was the case, who knows what mischief was being made?

***

Newcastle – November 2009

Already, Christmas was well and truly in the air in Newcastle. and as soon as they reached Monument Metro station, Caroline and Rebecca went to see the display in Fenwick's department store window. This year it was based on the book of 'The Snowman' and Rebecca was most impressed, just as Caroline hoped she would be. Rebecca hadn't seen a shop window quite like this before. Certainly, she hoped she would be well and truly settled in her new home before

Christmas day and became excited by thoughts of decorating a tree just as she liked it. Perhaps she might even invite her Mum and Dad up for a few days, maybe for New Year.

After looking at sofas, chairs and soft furnishings, Rebecca bought some pale, yellow curtains (not to Caroline's taste) and some bed linen (equally neutral). Although these were nothing like her own preferences, Caroline was pleased with herself for keeping her thoughts hidden and she offered to pay for them. Rebecca flatly refused and Caroline felt a great deal of satisfaction knowing that it was down to her, that Rebecca was able to do so.

Whilst the two of them lunched on pasta in one of Caroline's favourite Italian restaurants. Rebecca took in the surroundings of white washed walls, candles, paintings of the Coliseum, Leaning Tower of Pisa and gondolas in Venice. The place, to Rebecca's surprise, didn't seem to be anything out of the ordinary, but Caroline seemed to be on friendly terms with both the waiters and owner. The very fact that she was quite quiet was an indication to Rebecca that Caroline obviously felt comfortable there.

Caroline, however had a different reason to be quiet. She was thinking of the conversation she had had with Rebecca's ex-Headteacher, Mrs. Elliot. At first the woman had been hostile and it was clear she didn't hold Rebecca in high regard at all. However, when she realised that Caroline was offering her money, some to be given to Rebecca as a severance payment but most as a donation to the school, then she soon changed her tune. She had definitely done Rebecca a massive favour there, thought Caroline. She was far better off where she was now, but of course Rebecca must never know this. In fact, it said a great deal about the girl's naivety that she had never asked any questions about the odd situation and she looked fondly at Rebecca, quietly enjoying her food.

"Would you like some more wine?" Caroline asked, filling her own glass generously. "That's the good thing about coming here on the Metro - you can have a few drinks."

"Thanks," Rebecca wound some spaghetti round her fork. "And thank you, Caroline, for everything that you've done for me. You've been a big help."

The two of them clinked glasses.

"It's my pleasure my dear," said Caroline.

The genuine smile on Caroline's face, combined with the wine and food made Rebecca feel truly happy.

"You know that I don't have any children ... and since your Aunt passed away... well, I feel like I have a link through her with you. We were very close you know?"

Rebecca looked pretty in the candle light and reminded Caroline so much of herself at that age, although she knew she had been an entirely different personality, far more calculating and worldly wise than Rebecca.

"You know I wasn't really happy in my job," said Rebecca. "It was making me miserable, work, work, work. Pressure and stress. And my parents...I just couldn't explain. They couldn't understand. How could they? I was safe in a secure job. A safe pension. A safe life. They will have seen my resignation as being a failure. Giving it up. Throwing it all away. You know, I was becoming more and more ...despairing, despairing that I'd ever be happy again, able to lead a *normal* life, able to have time, oh God, just to have time, that's everything, time. I didn't ever think that I would find a way out...but then all of this happened so quickly.

"Fate works in strange ways sometimes, don't you think?" Caroline raised her glass to Rebecca. "Life isn't about what happens to you but how you react to it. You've shown great courage. You should be proud of yourself. Once those workmen have finished, then you can get your place organised. Just as you like it. You have as much time as you want"

Caroline smiled, not one of her booming, grandstanding smiles which were well rehearsed, almost robotic and executed purposefully, but a sincere, warm, comforting smile. She was hardly able to contain her delight at Rebecca's words, savouring and relishing them. She felt as if someone had danced into her chest and was skipping around doing somersaults, thrilled that Rebecca had opened up to her for the first time and also that she was being able to help, no, shape this young woman. A master craftsman to her apprentice.

***

St. Cuthbert's Cave – June 1979

Once it became clear what had happened to Scire and that they wouldn't be able to catch Robert and Sylvia, the Requisite group had quickly dispersed from the scene of the crime. Even Llyriad, with her keening and wailing had accepted a lift from Olwyn and her boyfriend after being assured by Derrick that Scire's body would be taken care of.

When Derrick was certain that everyone had left, he returned to the cave to recover the cloth. He found it wasn't there. Wasn't there? *Wasn't there?* His thoughts immediately began to run amok. His mind went blank and a momentary madness came over him. He found he was drowning, going deep, deep down, down, thrashing about, fighting for some escape to breathe again, desperately trying to swim, to surface and gulp in air. But then his years of rigid, methodical self-discipline took over and he breathed and breathed again, sucking hard, listening to the blood flow through his body concentrating on it, bringing him back to sanity. He knew instantly who had taken it. Had to be them. "Verbius, Aradnia." He clamped his jaw around the words. It couldn't possibly be anyone else, but he couldn't race after them because Scire's body needed to be dealt with quickly. This, after all, had been a death, which would be seen to have happened in extremely mysterious circumstances and once the police and press started their digging who knew what would happen? Irrespective of whether he was in possession of the cloth or not, the matter of Scire's body needed to be attended to immediately.

Derrick ran to the exact spot where Scire had fallen, but there was no trace of the body. He quickly scoured the area guided only by moonlight. Was he still alive? Could he have crawled away? Could someone else have moved it?

He returned to the spot and noticed a green cloak and some fragments of what could possibly have been bones on the ground. Derrick stared at them and shuddered, incredulous and amazed. He could hardly believe what he was seeing. But there was no confusion. He understood perfectly. He remembered what Scire had told him a long time ago. As soon as ownership of the cloth was relinquished then natural ageing would take place. Derrick had believed him because of the evidence of his own eyes. He had witnessed Scire remain the same over decades, but this…this was astonishing, unimaginable. This was evidence, real evidence. The unthinkable had happened, actually happened This was positive proof of something he had craved for all his life, something miraculous, something supernatural. As soon as ownership of the cloth had been relinquished this is what would naturally happen. Scire's body had degenerated immediately. Gone to dust. Scire had never told his exact age but from what he had divulged to Derrick he could quite possibly have been five hundred years old!

Derrick felt the rising tide of panic in his chest and he stumbled, like a drunk staggering sideways home. He knelt on the ground, unable to stand steadily any longer. He slapped his cheek hard to stop the crashing waves in his head and forced himself to think. In one way this solved a problem because no corpse meant no police involvement. But what would he tell the others? Llyriad, in particular, would be wanting the release and closure that a funeral would bring. But what if? What if? The thoughts were crashing about in Derrick's mind, colliding into each other. He just needed one rational one and clutched at them frantically as they spun around. No time to sort through them, he just needed one, lucid idea. Trying to keep calm, he ran back to the now abandoned car park to retrieve an empty box from his car. Returning to the spot he hurriedly scooped up the fragile remains of Scire. He carefully placed the box into the boot and set off to drive back to Lancaster, distressed and angry.

The night had been only partially successful.

Chapter 27

Alnwick- November 2009

Derrick was lying in his bed feeling awful. His books lay about him, unopened. From downstairs he could hear his carer, Mrs. Singh, blustering about, irritating him even more. His mobile phone started to ring and as he lifted it from his bedside table, he saw Llyriad's name register. At last...

"Llyriad, is that you?" He said feebly. "Have you got it?"

"No Derrick, I'm afraid not. I am not the bearer of good news. I haven't found it and it's definitely not in her flat."

"You mean you have actually looked...and looked carefully."

Derrick wondered, not for the first time if he could trust Llyriad. If she had searched the flat where it surely had to be, then the treacherous woman could more than likely have decided to keep it for herself.

"Yes, yes, I *have* looked everywhere inside her flat it's definitely not there."

"But it must be" Some life force was returning to him, seeping angrily through his aching bones like venom. "I need it badly and you promised me you would find it. And why haven't you been in touch for ages either? I've been sitting waiting to hear from you ... and now this dreadful news... is this news all you have for me?"

"Actually, Derrick what I really wanted was revenge. You always knew that and at least to some extent it's begun."

"What do you mean? What have you done? Nothing to jeopardise the cloth, I hope. It must be there. What about the bookshop? Have you tried there?

Sebastian, listening to the conversation through Llyriad's speaker phone, flashed her a wary look. There was no way that his Uncle's bookshop was going to be getting the same treatment.

"No, I can't say I have looked there...but her flat was the most likely place. And believe me, it wasn't easy getting in there either. So, I think you should be showing some gratitude for my efforts. I'm the one who's been doing all the hard work while you do... whatever it is you do these days."

"You press me too hard Llyriad. That's the whole point isn't it?" said Derrick. He clenched his fist so that the already taught skin was bloodless. "What do you think I do? Not much, as I'm no longer capable and that is why I need the cloth *now*." His voice took on an unpleasant edge, making a hissing, gasping sound.

"Well, perhaps if you got yourself down here then we could both go and speak to that Robert. Maybe when he sees the state of you then he might see some reason. At the very least we can squeeze them a bit more, turn the screw. See what happens."

Llyriad knew this was unlikely to happen. And she also knew, that once Caroline reported back on the state of her flat, it wouldn't be too long before she and the bookseller put two and two together. Then there certainly wouldn't be any reasonable negotiations with Derrick.

"So," Derrick eased out of bed and walked shakily towards the window. "If that's what needs to be done, then so be it. Semper fortis, Llyriad, semper fortis – forever strong. I'll come down and meet you and we shall go together."

"Well if you think you're capable," Llyriad looked at Sebastian and frowned. "But look, I have to go now."

After the phone call had ended Derrick crumpled back onto his bed and considered the feasibility of his proposal. Forty miles away, Sebastian and Llyriad thought about the possible consequences of their actions and what could be done next.

***

Preston, Lancashire   November 2009

Cynthia had been staring at the same page, same article, for the past fifteen minutes. Next to her sat a cold cup of tea, and a half-eaten custard cream biscuit. She wondered what her daughter was doing. It was now two days since she had left and she had heard nothing. She still could not grasp any motivation that would cause her daughter to give up her career, leave her parents and home. She couldn't understand it at all.

She had just been to visit her Rebecca's sister Jessica, but their relationship wasn't the same, and Jessica was just so preoccupied with her babies. She certainly hadn't raised her girls like that. All that cuddling. Goodness knows how her spoilt grandchildren would grow up. She certainly wasn't going to lavish any more affection on them, they had plenty already.

There was a key at the back door and her husband came in.

"Ready for another brew love?" Bill wandered through from the kitchen. "I've got the sugar."

"Have you heard anything from her?" She checked her own phone again, something she rarely did usually.

"No love, but she's only been gone a couple of days. Give her a chance to settle in."

"I miss her though, Bill." She put a hand to her face and there was a slight catch in her voice.

The words slammed into him and then settled like thick, cloying porridge. This was new. His wife certainly wasn't the sentimental sort. She was taking this really hard and his heart ached for her.

"Now, love. Come on. She'll be alright. I miss her too."

"What do you think she's doing? I mean she must be lonely. She doesn't know anybody up there. It makes no sense does it? She had a lovely home and a good job here."

"Cynthia, there's no point keep going over the same things." He remembered how badly she had behaved when Rebecca had first gone away to university. "She's your daughter and she just needs to spread her wings, so to speak. And, didn't she mention someone called Caroline she'd become friendly with. I mean, it's not like she had a lot of friends here is it? Didn't have time for them with all that work she did at home."

Cynthia shot him a glance, her cheeks hollowed as she sucked hard.

"Well she *used* to have plenty of friends didn't she? What happened to Claire and Helen? They were always playing together weren't they?"

"That was when they were little girls love, wasn't it? Come on Cynthia, that was years ago… I think Claire got married, moved down south somewhere…possibly Bristol, I think. And Helen…I don't remember but I'm sure she doesn't live round here anymore." Bill shook his head thinking of how much easier it was then.

"But that Caroline, she must be our age." Cynthia's brow furrowed. "She was a friend of Sylvia's, wasn't she? Why would a young girl want to hang around with a middle-aged woman? Especially, someone who'd been a so-called friend of my sister. It's hardly an example of good character judgement on her part, now is it Bill?"

"Look Cynthia, she's gone and there's nothing we can do about it. And she's hardly a young girl anymore. She's twenty-nine years old for heaven's sake. Newcastle, Tynemouth – they're not really that far away are they?"

"Well if it's not that far away why don't we go and visit her - now." Cynthia's eyes brightened. "I mean, it would be a lovely surprise for her wouldn't it?"

"Cynthia, its four o' clock. It'll be dark soon. It's too late to go today... and she's hardly had time to settle in. I don't think she'd appreciate us just turning up."

"But I just think of her, sitting all alone and cold in that horrible house."

"Come on Cynthia, it's the North-East, not the North Pole. Please love, let's just wait until she contacts us, then we can suggest that we visit. It'll be alright."

***

North Shields- November 2009

Caroline and Rebecca, laden with shopping bags, walked up to the apartment block. Caroline nursed a peculiar feeling. Something felt wrong, although she couldn't quite work out what. Rebecca could see the tightness in Caroline's face. Everywhere around seemed eerily silent, apart from the sound of the quickening pace of Caroline's heels, clicking on the pavement as she looked up anxiously at her windows.

They stepped out of the lift, tick, tick, tick, tick, and Caroline opened her front door, tick, tick, tick, tick.

At first the noise sounded like deep gulp of air, like the tide being sucked out before returning as a foaming, smashing, brutal tsunami. It changed and the air hissed like spit on hot coals. Finally, Caroline's whole body shook as the hideous wail erupted through the depths of her stomach and crashed around the shattered room. Caroline's hands bounced in front of her as if she were playing an invisible piano.

"Oh, my God!" she shrieked when eventually she could form words. "Oh my God! OhmyGod! OhmyGod! OhmyGod!"

"What the hell? What the hell happened? What the…," Rebecca joined in as best she could, although no match for Caroline.

On the floor was a ready to be lit bonfire of clothes: coats, scarves, blouses, dresses, handbags, skirts and trousers. Piled high, all ripped, split and torn.

Caroline stumbled across to the pile, crunching on pieces of blue and white porcelain, and Waterford crystal vases. She pulled out a dress reverently from the pile.

"Shit. Shit. Shit. Shit," she said, in a high, pitiful voice.

Her eyes gulped in the room and she saw her beautiful, chenille, handmade curtains, shredded and ripped, hanging like tattered ribbons, sunlight streaming through the gaps.

Rebecca stood apart, aghast, unable to comprehend the scene.

Caroline stared at the far wall and gaped. "Of course," said Caroline, shaking her head slowly, her mouth twisted into a kind of lop-sided smile. "You had to do that didn't you? You had to do *that*. Bastards. You bastards," she said quietly. The words fell unnervingly lightly, like soft snowflakes.

Rebecca followed her gaze and saw Caroline's portrait, hanging at an awkward angle. The canvas had been slashed several times but the horns on Caroline's head and the curving moustache on her face could still be seen. Rebecca threw up a hand to her mouth. She couldn't help herself. She coughed and shook her head, stifling the laugh. She coughed again, concentrated hard and looked across at Caroline. "Bastards," she said discreetly.

Caroline staggered one step backwards as if shot by a tranquillizer dart and slumped on to the sofa, her frame folding like a wreck, cracked and broken. She sat very still and then brought up a hand and stared at it. She twisted her mouth and gave out a sound like a chair being scraped across a wooden floor. The hand was covered in damp soil where her pink begonias had been newly planted between the gaping, deep slits in the blue, velvet Chesterfield.

Rebecca crunched unsteadily over to the bedroom and edged closer to the open door. She held on to the doorpost to steady herself amid the debris and ruin of Caroline's life, trying to avoid tripping over the shattered remains of deluxe glassware. She gazed into the bedroom, like Howard Carter looking for the first time on wonderful things, but the room wasn't intact, and the wonderful things had been gouged out and defaced. It had been thoroughly and barbarically excavated.

"I can't bear to look in the other rooms. It's everywhere isn't it?" said Caroline, now giving herself over to trembling shoulders and quivering hands.

Rebecca nodded.

"Caroline," said Rebecca. *Soft voice and slow movements, that's what's needed now*, she thought to herself. "What's happened? I don't understand. It's just been methodically trashed."

"I think I understand." Caroline managed to get the words out. They sounded mechanical. Her stomach churned and she felt as if she could be sick

"But nothing seems to have been taken," said Rebecca. "I don't understand this. They haven't taken anything. This is just pointless… just …."

"Oh Yes, they were looking to steal. But they wanted to take more than these things. And when they couldn't find what they wanted …" Caroline stopped herself, even amidst all her grief she, knew couldn't say anything about the cloth. "Anyway, they wanted destruction. Just destruction. They wanted to take everything…yes everything from me."

"What do you mean? It sounds like you know who's responsible for this."

"I think I do," she said quietly. She dusted down her skirt and blouse slowly, resigned to her nightmare. "But I don't understand how. I don't understand. I mean … the security on this place is pretty tight. How would anyone get access?"

Now it was Rebecca's turn to feel nauseous as she recalled the visit of Llyriad and the missing key. This was all her fault. But she didn't understand how there could possibly be any connection between Caroline and the clairvoyant.

"I'll call the police," said Rebecca. "We'd better not touch anything."

"No, we don't need the police."

"What?"

"We don't need the police."

"But you have to call the police. Your place has been wrecked. Thousands of pounds worth of damage. It's carnage"

"This wasn't about the damage. That was just an aside. An added bonus for them."

"What? What d'you mean?"

***

Tynemouth – November 2009

From inside his flat, Sebastian watched the workmen at Rebecca's new house getting into their van at the end of their working day. They were laughing and joking, which only served to make Sebastian feel even worse about his actions of that day. He imagined that Caroline and Rebecca must have returned home by now and how devastated Caroline in particular must be feeling. Understandably, he had felt anger towards her but this punishment was in no way justifiable. What had he been thinking of?

This was all Llyriad's fault, he thought. Why had he listened to the words of the wretched woman? Such behaviour was little short of insane. No doubt at this very moment, the devastated woman would be ringing the police and his and Llyriad's fingerprints would be everywhere. There was probably even CCTV camera footage of them entering and leaving the building. This had all happened because of the shame of his lack of ambition.

They had succeeded in getting some petty revenge but to what purpose. There had been no sign of the silk anywhere and they had certainly searched thoroughly enough. Now Sebastian even doubted its very existence. Llyriad had just attempted to glorify the reasons for her feeble hate campaign and unwittingly he had been dragged in. All because of an accident that had happened to her lover years ago and her need to blame someone. It was probably nothing to do with either Caroline or Robert. The hatred and bitterness had just festered in Llyriad over the years.

And it had all happened so quickly. Yesterday, when he had first spoken to the woman in the tea shop, seemed like weeks ago and this morning waiting outside Caroline's flat was another lifetime. She was obviously planning a similar vendetta on his uncle and he couldn't allow this to happen. This morning when he had spoken to Robert on the phone, it was clear that his uncle didn't believe his lame excuse for not coming to work. He realised that Robert must have been watching as he went on his Judas mission to the tea shop. He had only wanted to discover the details of the mystery surrounding Caroline and his uncle. The senseless destruction had not been his intention at all.

Llyriad was not just a clairvoyant, she was a witch and she had cast her wicked spell on him. Well that was the end of it. He would have nothing more to do with her and her evil. There had to be some way that he could make amends for his wrong doing. Only a few days ago, he had been entertaining the idea of becoming friends and maybe more with Rebecca. If he had not allowed himself to be annoyed by Caroline's stupid quips, then none of this would have happened.

Chapter 28

Tynemouth – November 2009

Caroline flew into Robert's shop, bursting through the door just as he was putting up the 'closed' sign. She was distraught. Her hair was tangled, her face ashen and she had panda eyes where her mascara had run.

"Caroline," called Robert as she as she roared into his office. He really, really, wanted to keep out of her way, in the manner that perceptive people would avoid a tornado. He feared the worst and followed her in. "What's the matter? Whatever is wrong? What's happened?"

"It's the-them Robert…they've been in my flat. The mess…you would, wouldn't believe it. They've ruined the whole place. I mean, the whole place."

"Calm down, please. Have this seat. What are you talking about? And who?" Although he already knew the answer.

"No, I don't want to sit down," Caroline glared at the chair as if it had betrayed her. "They must have been looking for the silk. When they couldn't find it, they decided to trash my place. My beautiful portrait…It's ruined. Everything's ruined."

"Caroline, it's only a picture. You can get another one painted. And I'm sure once you have tidied up…"

"No Robert, you don't understand." She glared at him. "They - have - completely – completely – and – utterly - trashed the place. All my clothes, shoes, vases, furniture. The lot. They've been very thorough. All spoilt. All in all, they must have caused thousands of pounds of damage."

Robert began to realise the scale of what had happened. He shuddered at the impact this would have on Caroline, and by association - him.

"You haven't called the police, have you?

She rounded on him with clipped, stabbing words. "Don't be stupid Robert. I'm upset but I haven't lost my mind."

He stood his ground, waiting for someone to tell him what to do, but nobody did, so he sat down heavily in the chair.

"I'm getting sick of all this Caroline," he said. "That damn cloth. It's ruined our lives. Our lives could have been so different."

Caroline stood for a long time, gazing at the floor, composing herself. So long that Robert wondered if she were in some kind of trance.

"I know it's been hard," she said eventually in a cool, rational voice, as if she were giving a weather report. "But just think of the good it's done, don't you think?"

It wasn't a question just a short, confirming statement.

Robert gave a short, incredulous snort. "*Good*?" he said. "And what good exactly has it done? Living in fear. Living on our nerves. All it's *done* is forced us to look over our shoulders for the past thirty years."

"What about Sylvia? If it wasn't for the cloth, she would have died years ago wouldn't she?"

"But she's dead now. The cloth stopped working its magic didn't it? For some mysterious reason. I mean... how can you just keep on, not getting old? Impossible. Sylvia survived because of mind over matter. She believed the cloth was curing her so it did - but only for so long. Which is just as strange I suppose. I wonder why she stopped believing."

"No Robert...I don't doubt it. There's a power to it. From the moment I gave up being the keeper of the cloth and moved out of the old flat my body started to age. Look, look at the lines around my eyes. They weren't there a few years ago ... and my neck ... it takes a lot more make-up to hide things now."

Robert did as he was told. He studied her face. She was right. Caroline had succumbed. And he saw for the first time that she, the ever-youthful Caroline, had indeed changed. The lines about the eyes and forehead weren't deep but they were there nevertheless, and he hadn't noticed them so much before. He gave her a strange, half-pitying, half-shocked look.

"You'll have to come and stay with me for a few days," said Robert. "Until you get things sorted out and the place put right."

"Rebecca won't mind me moving in with her," said Caroline, forcing a nervous laugh. "I could certainly do with a little youthful rejuvenation."

"Do you really think that Rebecca will really want you living with her. After what's just happened. Don't you think she'll realise someone's out to get you?"

"Well, actually, I don't think she will have a lot of choice in the matter."

"And how do you work that one out?"

"Don't you think it's rather odd that someone managed to get into the flat?" Caroline said flatly. "I mean, there was no sign of any break in."

"Rebecca hardly let them in now did she? I mean you two had gone shopping in Newcastle this afternoon...that's when it happened didn't it?"

"Yes, and yesterday I found a bunch of my keys on the street outside my flat...where Rebecca had supposedly dropped them." The familiar glint in her eye had returned.

"What are you saying?"

"It's too much of a coincidence. What I'm saying is ... someone took them, had them copied and put them back where they knew they'd be found, without Rebecca knowing about it. Careless girl. But she might have realised this herself by now. She must be very embarrassed."

Robert thought about Sebastian going into the coffee shop across the road and who he must have met there. 'Yes', he said to himself, it *was* too much of a coincidence.

They both sat very quietly and wallowed in a bout of synchronized head shaking.

***

Heysham, near Morecambe, Lancashire - October 1979

Llyriad, Olwyn and Loic walked close behind Dafo, as they made their way to the cliff's edge at Heysham. Here, by the ruins of St Patrick's Chapel, where the graves were cut out of the sandstone with a space above each one for offerings to the gods, was deemed a suitable place to scatter the ashes of Scire.

It was considered a thin place, and had often been used by members of the Requisite when wanting some solitude or reassurance. At the Autumn equinox, when the sun was a red globe sinking into the waters of the Irish Sea. That was the moment which had been chosen. The crowd was small, a much less significant number to that which had assembled a mere three months earlier. After the events at the Litha, most members had severed all links with the Requisite.

The crowd stood silently, dressed in suitable dark colours and watched Dafo as he stood on the rocks. He and Llyriad were the only members wearing in the long, green cloak of the Requisite. He had a casket in one hand and a white stick in the other. The ceremony began and he held up both to the sky. It seemed as if the cloth should be there, wrapped around the remains of its former keeper. Llyriad began to cry but quickly stifled the sobs. Dafo turned and gave her a formal, emotionless look. Such a vulgar display of emotion was unseemly, but for once Llyriad just didn't care.

The crowd offered up outstretched arms, palms facing upwards, staring out to sea and there followed four minutes of silent prayer.

Going through the motions, Dafo's usual passion for theatricality seemed wanting, but he managed to pour the required gravitas into his oratory.

"Mother goddess, Atargatis, we give back to the waters your son Scire." He poured a handful of ashes from the casket, and a gust of wind blew them out to sea. "As the spirit of St Aidan was seen by Cuthbert as he went to join his heavenly parents, so we watch your dear soul fly upwards." Dafo threw a further handful out to the west.

"Deep peace of the running wave to you. Deep peace of the flowing air to you. Deep peace of the quiet earth to you. Deep…" Derrick stopped momentarily and stared at the casket, long enough for the crowd to glance at him. "...peace of the shining stars to you."

He then pointed the stick to the north, east, south and finally the west before emptying the remainder of the casket into the sea. Olwyn squeezed Llyriad's hand as the sun disappeared into the sea and the sky turned a deep ecclesiastical violet.

Dafo turned to the gathering.

"We give our brother to fire, air, earth and water. May his going be sheltered and his welcome assured. Scire, may you smile in the face of your soul friend. May you..."

Llyriad looked up sharply. "I am your 'am cara'," she shrieked. "I am your soul friend. Wait for me Scire- my one love – my soul friend. Wait for me beyond the portal. I must stay here. I must stay here and avenge you. You will be avenged. You will not die in vain."

The crowd turned to Llyriad with sympathetic and uncomfortable eyes. They felt her pain but they wouldn't be joining her to avenge Scire. They were all, to a man and woman, relieved and not a little astounded that the police hadn't been involved in the murder of Scire. This gathering was their tribute to Scire but it would be the last gathering for them.

Dafo held his arms outstretched and turned three times in a circle, slowly and deliberately, concentrating all eyes on him and giving himself time to think. Llyriad, for all her unpredictability and mindless loyalty, had a passion which could be put to good use.

"My brothers, my sisters," he said in a low, intense voice. "There is a gateway that each of us must step through. The sadness and pain we feel is our knowledge of the fact that we cannot yet cross that thin place. But we will be united again. We will be with our loved ones. We are left behind for a reason." Dafo paused and looked directly at Llyriad. "We remain here to bring order and absolve our pain. To reason and release our pain though the ending of any injustices."

Llyriad narrowed her eyes and returned his stare.

"Let us leave this sacred place and go in peace," said Dafo

This was the last of the rituals that would take place. It was the final act of the Requisite. Although it would leave a massive gap in their lives, this gap would soon be filled. Olwyn had already joined an amateur dramatics group and Loic was playing rugby tomorrow.

***

Whitley Bay- November 2009

Llyriad sat in her cramped, one- bedroom flat in Whitley Bay and compared it unfavourably with the sumptuous luxury that had been evident at Caroline's place. Why should that thief and murderer have so much when she, the greatly wronged Llyriad, had so little? She thought, with some satisfaction, about the havoc she and Sebastian had caused. Especially pleasing, was the defacement of the portrait and the spoiling of the clothes. Perhaps she should have taken some of the items and sold them.

Nevertheless, it was strange that Sebastian should be the one to have taken the knife to the canvas. It was decidedly strange that he had been so easily enticed into her campaign. Especially, as his grievances against Caroline seemed quite inconsequential by comparison with those of her own. Still, Caroline's loss had been her gain. And she thought with some glee of Caroline's rose gold walls with ketchup seeping into the slashes.

The illusive silk however, was still to be found. The only other possible place it could be was the bookshop or Robert's flat above it. It was unlikely that Sebastian would assist with any damage to these places. He seemed to have some misguided loyalty to his uncle. But maybe, if she could just persuade Sebastian to jump back on board, then he could do a little digging there of his own.

Derrick said that he was going to come and help. From the sound of him on the phone, it was extremely unlikely that he was capable of even leaving his house, let alone making a relatively short journey south. Another one to whom life, albeit until recently, had been also been kind. She thought about how different her life might had been were it not for Scire's tragic death. Even now that terrible night was etched in her mind. She remembered seeing Scire's body tumble. Everyone had ran to see if he was still alive but Derrick had somehow managed to get there first and stood over the broken body. Then he had gone up to the cave and started yelling about murderers and thieves. At the time she hadn't thought it odd, but the disappearance of the cloth appeared to distress him more than the death of his friend.

Suddenly, all thoughts of poor Scire had been forgotten as everyone scattered. But what had happened to his body? She had never seen it again. The next time she encountered the remains of her love was at the scattering ceremony organized by Derrick. At the time she had been too overwhelmed with grief to think clearly but something was clearly amiss. She had never seen a death certificate. Derrick had dealt with everything which she was very grateful for at the time. It should have been Llyriad, as Scire's partner, to sort out matters but she could see now that her strategy for dealing with her grief had been to direct her feelings into hatred. Hatred of Scire's killers but most particularly Sylvia or Caroline as she now called herself.

Llyriad for the first time was beginning to doubt her own judgement. Something just wasn't sitting quite right and Derrick's involvement in the whole business was suspicious to say the least.

Scire had possessed so few belongings that these had soon been dealt with. She had kept some of his clothes as they still held his smell. The rest had been collected by Derrick. What was really weird was that, in no time at all, it was almost as if he had never lived. It seemed to her now, looking back, that Derrick had purposefully obliterated all evidence of Scire's existence. Now why would he do that? Of course, she realised that if the events of that particular night had become public knowledge then quite a few questions would need answers. She understood Derrick's haste to clear things up. But Derrick's behaviour at that time, and since, suggested something else.

So, now she desperately hoped Derrick did manage to come down to Tynemouth. If he didn't, then another visit to him was certainly needed. It was as if a light had been turned on after all this time. Derrick hadn't really cared at all about Scire's death, he had just wanted that cloth and this was what everything was about. He must have been delighted when Scire fell, in fact until that point, events couldn't have orchestrated themselves better…that was until the actions of Robert and Sylvia.

Now she knew that time was definitely of the essence. Derrick's involvement was not clear cut at all. Derrick hadn't wanted police involvement in case suspicion fell upon himself. The Requisite had been fabricated by him and its entire purpose was merely an elaborate way by to gain possession of the silk. Was Scire's fall actually caused by Robert and Sylvia? Llyriad was starting to question whether her quest for revenge for the past thirty years had been misguided.

Perhaps her hatred of Sylvia was more personal than she liked to admit. She had introduced Sylvia to the Requisite and instead of showing gratitude she had sought to outshine her. It should always have been her and Scire as the chosen ones. There was still so much that didn't make sense. There was the whole business of Rebecca that she couldn't quite understand. From listening to snippets of conversation in the 'Turk's Head', she had gathered that Rebecca was the niece of some friend who had recently died. Was this friend of any significance to events?

Why was this mysterious girl living with Caroline? It was unbelievable how simple it had been to get into the flat and borrow the keys. She didn't imagine the girl for one moment would have been so naive. She thought back to the day when the Rebecca had come to her for a tarot card consultation and tried to remember the details. She recalled that she had surpassed herself with her reading and she tried to remember what had actually been said.

She remembered that the 'Juggler' had featured, indicating that big changes were going to happen. That, no doubt, had been the move up here, and she remembered that the Moon had told that Rebecca seemed to be having problems at work. The 'Temperance' card disclosed that her parents had been a controlling force, which was probably another of the reasons she had relocated up here. And, ah yes, the 'Queen of Swords', that was the most interesting one - undoubtedly 'Queen' Caroline - who wouldn't be feeling nearly so monarch-like now, stripped of her regalia.

But the reading had also indicated that Rebecca ought to be fearful of this woman. There was definitely more to the relationship between these two than was apparent at first. This was something Llyriad felt she needed to investigate, as something told her it held a link to the cloth and maybe more answers. How that was possible she wasn't sure but she was going to make it her business to find out.

***

North Shields – November 2009

Rebecca was feeling wretched and was trying, as best she could, to restore some order to Caroline's flat but the task seemed impossible. When Caroline left she had gone to a nearby shop to get some cardboard boxes. She was putting the broken crystal and porcelain into the boxes including the remains of a valuable Tiffany lamp.

There was no doubt in her eyes that this was all her fault. If only she hadn't seen that dreadful fortune teller in the first place. Rebecca thought back to her first meeting with the woman and the manic expression she had on her face as she gave her reading. Obviously, there was history between Caroline and this woman, but for the life of her she couldn't think what this might be.

If she hadn't allowed Llyriad into the flat yesterday, then this would never have happened. If only she hadn't left the keys lying on the coffee table… but how was she supposed to know what was on the woman's agenda?   If Caroline had known the real sequence of events, she would think that Rebecca was not just neglectful but stupid and possibly even treacherous. Llyriad must have been stalking them and she wondered if Caroline had been aware of this too.

Despite her interfering and overbearing manner Caroline had shown nothing but kindness to her. How could she ever repay her? Her efforts to tidy up had made only the slightest dint in the mess. How could she ever make amends? She looked around the room once more, remembering how only a few hours earlier everything had been so different. She heard a key in the door.

"Rebecca," called a familiar voice. "Are you there?" Caroline came in, clearly putting on a brave face and trying not to look at the carnage

"Yes...Oh, but how are you Caroline? This is all just so ... horrible."

"I know...but at the end of the day these are just objects. The main thing is that no one's hurt. You and I are both safe. I mean, imagine if they had broken in when we were here."

Who is this stoic? thought Rebecca *This woman has so many sides to her.*

Caroline went into the kitchen and came back with a large glass of wine in her hand, thankful that the vandals hadn't focused their attention on the fridge. Rebecca noticed that she hadn't offered her a drink but Caroline had clearly other more pressing matters on her mind.

"But all of your lovely things..." Rebecca felt the need to say something but wasn't sure quite what.

"Shush dear, yes things, that's all that they were but nothing is irreplaceable. Anyway, Rebecca, I'm glad to see you've made a start in putting the place back together. But don't worry, I'm going to hire some of those industrial cleaners and just totally gut the place. Actually, I've been meaning to redecorate for some time now. To be honest the place was beginning to look a little tired."

Rebecca nodded. She was glad that her aunt had been fortunate enough to have such a surprisingly philosophical friend.

"I've often heard people say that when their house has been burgled, it feels contaminated," said Caroline. "Like it's not theirs anymore. Well, I refuse to dwell on that. I'm going to look for the positives. So, what do you think Rebecca? I'm afraid that the decoration of your place needs to be put on hold. The plumbing and electricals are almost finished and we both urgently need a place to live. You don't have a problem with having a lodger do you?"

"No, of course not. Of course, you can stay." Rebecca knew she could hardly say anything else. But why, she thought, couldn't Caroline go and stay with Robert

Chapter 29

Whitley Bay –November 2009

"So, is that the end of it now? I'm sure Caroline and Rebecca must have discovered our handiwork by now." said Sebastian still feeling ashamed of their actions.

"Yes, I would guess they have… but we still haven't found the cloth," said Llyriad.

"Well Llyriad, there's no way I'm doing the same thing to my Uncle's shop."

"Sebastian, it's got to be somewhere hasn't it?" Her eyes drilled into him. "You do realise it's very important, don't you?"

She needed to keep him onside.

"Well, you and this Derrick seem to think so but come on is it really worth all this effort…" Sebastian thought it was time he should be going. He didn't know why he had gone back to Llyriad's dingy flat.

"No honestly, Derrick is seriously ill but he thinks the silk will cure him. You know Scire. my Scire. Well, I was with him for over ten years." She knew she had to go out on a limb. "When I met him, I was in my twenties and assumed him to be the same. But when he died, I was in my late thirties…and I looked it, but he looked exactly the same."

"Llyriad, some people are just lucky like that." *And you are obviously not one of these*, Sebastian thought to himself.

"But Derrick met him when *he* was young and he says he looked the same then."

"So, what are you saying – that the silk has some sort of magic powers – come on."

"That's exactly what I'm saying."

"I know you're saying it but you don't expect me to believe it do you? It's science fiction. Impossible. Absolutely ridiculous."

Llyriad grunted in the manner of someone feeling both totally superior and deeply insulted.

She took a deep breath. "What do you believe in. Anything? Religion? Ghosts?"

"What's your point?"

"That just because we don't understand something, it doesn't mean it can't be, or exist. A few hundred years ago everyone thought the earth was flat. Scientists still don't know how memory works. Why do you think so many people follow a religion – there's no actual evidence. But there's been sightings of ghosts. Do you think you'll go to another place – or is this the end? Just because *you* can't understand. Some people choose to have faith. Belief can carry you to many places."

"Well how come Scire died. If the silk made him immortal."

Llyriad pulled back, mulling over the words.

"You know I've been thinking about that recently…a lot. He fell, but not from a great height."

"So, where was the silk? Why did it not save him?"

"Did he die from the fall?" Llyriad said, lost in thought. "Was the fall really high enough to kill him?

"You saw his dead body, didn't you?"

"Yes, but Derrick was there first and there was blood everywhere…. but what if the fall didn't kill him. As soon as he fell those two took the cloth. And once it had gone, well, it could no longer protect him could it? I mean... he was no longer the keeper of the cloth was he?"

"Maybe not," said Sebastian. "But look at Robert and Caroline. They're both in their fifties and they look their age. Now don't you think that Caroline, if she had discovered the secret of eternal youth, well, she would use it to her full advantage, wouldn't she?"

"Yes, I agree. I guess so," said Llyriad in a spiky kind of voice. "But it must be somewhere."

"And this Scire. He could, if what you say is true, be ... well, possibly really old, I mean, really, really old. And once he died wouldn't his body revert to its real age. That seems logical – if I can use such a word in this conversation."

"I don't know. I never saw him again. The body I mean."

"Really? I thought people went to see bodies before funerals."

"I didn't go to his funeral. I don't know when it was. I went to the scattering of his ashes."

"I thought you loved this guy?"

"I did love him."

"But you didn't go to his funeral."

"I was a mess. It was a weird time. I couldn't face it."

"Who did go to his funeral then?"

"I ...I don't know. Derrick never actually told me when it was."

Sebastian gave her a disbelieving look, which she totally understood. They were lifting up a rock and all kinds of things were crawling out.

***

Tynemouth - November 2009

There had been a hostile atmosphere in the bookshop, as Robert and Sebastian busied themselves and tried wherever possible to keep out of each other's way. They were like two, large goldfish, eyeing each other nervously and frantically flapping about, trying to remain at opposite ends of a small bowl. Sebastian had given Robert no explanation for his strange behaviour or mysterious illness which quickly seemed to have disappeared. Nevertheless, Robert couldn't help the niggling feeling that it was no coincidence that his absence had coincided with the break-in at Caroline's, and that he was somehow involved. There was an unpleasant shiftiness about the lad that he hadn't noticed before. Neither of them had suggested a drink after work for a good few days and Robert wondered for how much longer the two of them would be able to work together.

Sebastian, for his part, felt only shame. In fact, he had left his phone in the flat as he didn't want to be troubled further by unwanted calls from Llyriad. No doubt at this very moment, he thought, she would be skulking about somewhere, concocting her spells. Purposely, Sebastian kept well away from the window, as he wanted neither to catch a glimpse of the noxious woman, or be seen himself. Likewise, Robert was also so engrossed with the task in hand, that he also failed to notice the large car that had pulled up outside the shop.

From inside the black Mercedes a frail, old man was being bundled out and helped into a wheelchair by a solid, middle-aged, Asian woman. Once the chair was secure on the pavement, the woman disappeared back into the car and sped off to park it. Derrick waited for her to return as he wasn't capable of moving the chair very far on his own.

When the shop door swung open, Robert turned to stare at the fragile figure of Derrick. His skin was a crinkled, ancient manuscript yellow, his eyes dark-rimmed and sunk deep into his skull. Mrs. Singh pushed the chair into the centre of the room and then returned to the car as Derrick had asked her to do. Sebastian kept well back, behind a bookshelf, unobserved by Derrick but able to see his uncle and hear what was happening.

"Long time Robert. Hasn't it been?" Derrick's voice rattled. "I shan't beat about the bush… as I am sure you know why I am here."

Robert was confused. Surely Derrick, in this state hadn't been capable of trashing Caroline's place. He glanced round to gauge Sebastian's reaction and was clear that the two were unknown to each other. Perhaps he had misjudged the lad and he had played no part in the crime after all."

"Has the cat got your tongue Robert? You know exactly what I have come for don't you?"

"Yes, I know what you want, but it isn't here."

"Well…if it isn't here and I know it wasn't at your girlfriend's place - where is it?"

"I don't know." Robert's was trying to think fast. Derrick had just seemed to admit that he was responsible for the carnage in Caroline's flat but how was that possible? The man was clearly incapable of walking, let alone slashing fabrics.

"Robert, I am appealing to your better nature. Look at me. You can see I have little time left. I'm getting worse by the day. I need that cloth and quickly. You know why." There was an unattractive, deferential pleading look in his eye.

"Derrick, I'll admit that you don't look well… I can understand why you broke into Caroline's flat … but I can't understand why you trashed it – mindless destruction – that's not your style."

"Believe me, that was nothing to do with me. Do I really look capable of such an act?"

"Very well, it might not have actually been you but you clearly know about it. So, it was probably down to you. You must have had something to do with it."

"I knew that Llyriad was going to break in but as far as I was told, she was just looking for the silk. There was no mention of any damage being done. According to her, the silk wasn't there… but there's part of me doesn't quite believe her. In fact, I am not sure I can trust her at all."

The old man looked overwhelmingly weary and sad. Robert was surprised with himself. This confrontation was one he had been dreading for years, and pity for the man was the last thing he imagined he would have been feeling at this very moment.

"I know the silk wasn't and still isn't there." said Robert. He didn't know what information he could share with Derrick because it wasn't his decision alone, and he couldn't imagine that Caroline would currently be at her most magnanimous. "I mean, couldn't Llyriad have just left when she found it wasn't there. All that vandalism was just spiteful. Moronic."

Sebastian winced.

"Actually, I don't know what she did there but I do know that Llyriad has a bigger axe to grind than me. Look Robert you know that silk is rightfully mine. Just tell me where it is and I can get out of your life."

**

Preston, Lancashire- May 1980

Cynthia had just finished putting her young daughter Jessica to bed. Her husband Bill was reading Jessica a bedtime story when there was persistent banging on the door. It was a terrible November night. The rain was lashing down and the wind howling. Opening the door tentatively, to her surprise, Cynthia saw her sister Sylvia with a tragically pale face standing on the doorstep, along with a young man, both of them dripping wet. In Sylvia's arms was a white bundle.

"You had better come in." Cynthia opened the door wider and then turned to shout. "Bill come down here - straight away."

"Sorry, sorry Cynthia. We're sorry to disturb you," Sylvia said, in an uncharacteristically meek voice, "but it's such awful weather."

Cynthia ignored any pleasantries.

"And who does that baby belong to?" Cynthia pointed at the child as a bewildered Bill came down the stairs.

"It's ours." Sylvia looked at the young man. "This is Robert, my boyfriend ... and this, this is Heaven, she looked down at the baby in her arms who began a loud wail.

"*You are joking*," said Cynthia. "I hope you're joking. And since when did you become a responsible enough person to have a child.

"Now come on Cynthia," said Bill. "Sylvia, bring the child and your friend into the lounge. Get yourselves out of those wet coats, before we do anything else. You'll catch your death in those soaking things. Sit yourselves down by the fire. Let's put the kettle on."

Bill took their coats to hang up before disappearing into the kitchen, while Cynthia sank into a chair, lips forced tightly together.

Sylvia tried to settle the wailing baby while Robert sat nervously beside her, stroking the child's fingers, and staring helplessly into the open fire. Only the crackling of coal embers broke the silence.

Bill came back into the room with a mismatched tray of cups, saucers, a teapot and custard cream biscuits. His wife remained speechless and watched on suspiciously.

"So, Sylvia," Bill smiled, trying to ease the tension. "Introduce me properly. I didn't catch their names before."

"You heard her before Bill," said Cynthia, now perched on the edge of her chair. "This apparently is Robert, and that is their unfortunate child, Heaven – for heaven's sake."

"I'm pleased to meet you, thanks for taking us in," Robert smiled apologetically and rose to shake Bill's hand. He looked across at Cynthia's seething face and realised it would be imprudent to attempt another handshake.

"The thing is Cynthia," Sylvia began as she cuddled her daughter protectively. "We were wanting to ask you a favour…"

"Oh, here we go…" said Cynthia. "Yes, you only call on your family when you want something." She gave her sister a familiar look of contempt. "Remember the trouble you and your reprobate acquaintances caused our parents not that long ago. And look what that did to them. Not surprising you've come to me. With your disgrace is it?"

Robert shifted in his seat uncomfortably. Cynthia scowled at the distressed baby her sister was failing to placate and Bill sipped awkwardly from his cup.

"Cynthia ...I'm your ... sister. Flesh and blood," Sylvia chewed her lip, determined not to cry. "This is your niece and we need your help. Her life is in danger and we ..." She paused to carefully consider words as Cynthia held her head inclined to one side at a confrontational angle.

"Go on then," Sylvia challenged.

"We love our child desperately," said Robert's shifting his gaze from Cynthia to Bill and back again. "But we aren't in a position to keep her safe and we wondered if ...."

"Just for a short while," Sylvia broke in. "Could you please, please take care of her. It wouldn't be for long just until we get everything sorted out."

"And why should I not be surprised by any of this from my sister?" said Cynthia slowly. "I mean...really, people shouldn't have children if they are incapable of looking after them. I believe it's called responsible parenting. I mean...you can't even get the child to be quiet, can you? The baby's in distress ... obviously wanting to be fed. I take it that you aren't even married. No... this one at least looks as if he's got more sense to marry the likes of you. In fact, I bet as soon as you have dumped your unfortunate accident ... and don't think it's going to be here... I reckon he'll be off as quick as a flash, just like all of the others."

Robert glared at Sylvia, incredulous. "Now, I don't know you," he said. "But likewise, you know nothing of me, and you just can't go making assumptions about people like that. I happen to love your sister very much. Come on Sylvia, we don't need this."

"But Robert, we do, we have to," said Sylvia. "You know we can't keep her safe. We can't go on like this. We need help ... and Heaven needs food." She bent down awkwardly and took a bottle of milk from her bag.

"Would you like me to heat that up?" said Bill, glad to have a job to do.

Then, to everyone's great surprise, Sylvia thrust the red-faced wailing baby into to her brother-in-law's arms. Once she was settled, to everyone's astonishment, she immediately stopped her crying. Bill rocked the baby, who began softly chortling and gazing up at him. He was both amazed and delighted. He had never had the same rapport with his own daughter and had always felt a little awkward with small children.

"Once she's been fed," said Robert, watching the almost immediate bonding between his daughter and Bill. "We need to get going Sylvia. Obviously, we're going to get no help from your sister."

His eyes narrowed as he looked across at her but Cynthia ignored him. For once she was enjoying watching her husband's pleasure. She thought about how many years it had taken them to be blessed with Jessica ....

"You do realise you can't trouble our parents with this don't you?" Cynthia's brief smile disappeared.

"Well yes of course, I know that they would see..." Sylvia cast her eyes downwards to the floor.

"Having a child out of wedlock - the ultimate sin," Cynthia's watched her sister squirm uncomfortably. "And you would bring the most terrible shame on them. You would break their hearts ... as if you haven't already caused them so much pain. Our mother - it could kill her. I doubt it would trouble old dad so much..."

"What do you mean, he would just back up mum like he always does." Sylvia knew how terribly her parents would react.

"Well, little sister," said Cynthia. "It shows what a long time it is since you've been home to visit, doesn't it? Alzheimer's." She announced with a flourish. "In fact, he doesn't know one day of the week from another. I don't know how much longer before he will need to go into a home but you know what mum's like. Forever the martyr. She'll keep him at home for longer than she should. And she's hardly in the best of health."

"But when did this happen?" Sylvia was thinking about the last time she saw her parents. She hadn't noticed any marked deterioration in either of them.

"About six months ago..." said Cynthia.

"But that was when I last saw them," said Sylvia.

"Exactly. A strange coincidence isn't it? And they say these things can be brought on by shocks or disturbing events."

"That's absolute rubbish. Don't listen to a word she's saying." Robert put an arm around his distraught girlfriend. "Cynthia, you can't know this."

"And you're the expert, are you?" said Cynthia.

"My father's a GP, so yes, I think I do know a lot more about these matters than most. I remember him talking about many of his elderly patients suffering first from memory loss, forgetting names ... then increasingly worse symptoms, walking unsteadily, not recognizing people, getting lost outside, not turning off appliances, generally not being safe. He knew all about Alzheimers."

"Well, obviously, an excellent doctor – breaking the Hippocratic Oath like that…" Cynthia jumped in with glee.

Robert stood up quickly, glaring at Cynthia and then moved across to Bill.

"I'm sorry Bill. Give me back our baby please. Come on Sylvia. Get your things. We need to leave. We won't get any help here."

Bill put up a restraining hand. "Now, hang on. Just hang on a minute Robert. It's pouring down outside. This baby'll be freezing out there. Let's all just settle down and try and talk thinks through."

***

Tynemouth- November 2009

Despite Huntington Place having none of the luxurious trappings of her North Shields apartment, Caroline was enjoying the simplicity of her lifestyle with Rebecca. The two of them had most meals together in the kitchen or occasionally they went out to a local restaurant. Quite often Robert came round and it was almost as if they were a little family, watching the television together. A couple of times they had even been to the 'Turk's Head' after Robert had closed up his shop for the day. She thought it was strange that Sebastian hadn't joined them. Most likely, he was just sulking because of her presence there. It was odd to think of him living next door and the dreadful music from the other side of the wall was a constant reminder.

The knowledge that the silk was close by gave her a feeling of wellbeing and she was sure that her skin was looking much better. However, she couldn't go up into the attic and look at the material. It was crucial that Rebecca knew nothing of its existence. Maybe the break-in had actually been no bad thing after all.

Caroline also realised that it was essential she gave Rebecca some space, especially as this was only a small house. So, at the moment, she was sitting in the main bedroom, reading the books that had once been her friend's. Some would say it was a curious collection for a middle-aged woman, but she understood exactly why they were there. Some of the books on Celtic Christianity transported her back through the years. She picked up 'Thin Places Where You Wouldn't Expect' and was instantly whisked back to her days with the Requisite. Even now when she thought of the events leading up to Litha celebration, those old feelings of excitement were easily awakened. She still accepted that thin places existed, where the dead could be reached, where loved ones could communicate. She still held on to the belief. It seemed wonderful to her that such things could happen, even though she hadn't experienced anything herself.

It was strange to think that this was the very bed that her friend had died in. She had thought it best that she took this room as Rebecca might find it a little creepy. She was glad to feel close once more to her dear friend, who she still missed so badly. The grave, which she often visited, had felt like a thin place to her but if she really wanted to try to speak with her properly, she knew there was only one place to go.

Caroline still didn't understand how her friend could possibly have become ill again especially as she was the keeper of the cloth. There were definitely questions that needed answering.

Engrossed in her thoughts she glanced aimlessly out of the window.

Boom!

What she saw hit her like a backhanded slap. She let out a short yelp and pulled back quickly, appalled. Her whole body erupting with small electric shocks, like hundreds of tiny spiders scuttling about.

A couple, in late middle age were getting out of a blue, Ford Cortina right outside number ten Huntington Place.

She needed to get out. She needed to get out right now.

***

Journey to Tynemouth- November 2009

They had begun their journey from Preston as soon as the rush hour traffic had cleared, Surprisingly, Cynthia had enjoyed the run up the M6 to Carlisle especially through the mountains on the edge of the Lake District and across the A69 to Tyneside. It was a clear, bright November day with a strong wind, that made the white clouds scud across the sky like illusive will-o-the-wisps. Her and Bill should go on more outings she decided. When the girls had been young, they had always been off somewhere or the other. They stayed in caravans and rented cottages by the seaside. Now there had seemed little point when it was just the two of them.

However, now it seemed they had a reason for travelling north-east and Cynthia had enjoyed making ham sandwiches and boiled eggs along with a thermos of milky coffee. They had sat in a parking area just outside Penrith to have their packed lunch. Certainly, thought Cynthia, there was no need to waste money at one of those motorway service stations.

"Oh, look Bill," She pointed at the road sign as they drove on. "It says Newcastle is ten miles away. We're nearly there."

"I told you it didn't take very long didn't I?" Bill was sucking on a peppermint. "I just hope she's pleased to see us."

"Of course she will be. Why wouldn't she be?" Cynthia was feeling the happiest she had been since Rebecca had left.

"You know love, it might not be a bad idea if we gave her a ring. Then she would know we're coming. I mean…she might not even be in." Bill tried to reason with his wife as he was well aware that the day might not go according to plan.

"Don't be silly Bill, of course she'll be in. I mean…it's not like she's got a job is it? Don't forget she's unemployed." Irritation crept back into Cynthia's voice, as she remembered the promising career her daughter had just thrown away.

"I'm sure Rebecca has been making good use of her time, unemployed or not. By all accounts, that house needs a lot of work doing to it? She's probably up to her ears in wallpaper and paint. Yet another reason why she might not be pleased to see us." Bill shook his head.

"Stop being so negative. The house has two bedrooms doesn't it… we'll be able to stay overnight."

"Cynthia, the whole reason we set off early was so we could drive back again." This was the only reason that Bill had agreed to come.

"But it'll be dark by then Bill. You said you preferred to drive in the light."

Bill wasn't really bothered. It was Cynthia who didn't like travelling in the dark. He didn't care one way or the other and Cynthia never drove.

"Let's just take one step at a time, love" said Bill. "If needs be, we can always book into a Bed and Breakfast."

****

Tynemouth – November 2009

Rebecca had quite a shock when she opened the door. And she had mixed feelings about what she found there. On the one hand her parents hadn't told her they were coming and the place was still a mess. On the other hand, they were her parents after all and she had genuinely missed them.

"Well, are you not going to invite us in?" Cynthia said, eyeing the cracked paintwork around the windows and on the door.

"Yes of course, of course, sorry, just got a bit of a surprise that's all. Come in." Rebecca gave her dad a hug, and attempted to do the same to her mother. Cynthia however was proficient in avoiding such bodily contact and easily body-swerved past her daughter into the house.

"Here's the front room. Have a seat and I'll go and make us a brew. I've got lots to tell you but I'll bet you need a drink first."

As Rebecca busied herself in the kitchen, Cynthia assessed the room with disapproving eyes. Really, she thought, her daughter had been here a couple of weeks now, surely, she ought to have made more progress than this. It was strange though, because this room just didn't feel like a place her sister would have lived. It was dour and it obviously hadn't been decorated for years. She looked at the mantelpiece and spotted a picture of a young man and woman. They were both laughing. Her sister may have changed over the years but that picture was definitely her.

"I know it doesn't look like it." Said Rebecca placing a tray on the table. "But I *have* made a start. Plumbers and electricians have been in. I've got a plasterer coming in next week and then it's time to begin the fun part - decorating." She looked apologetically at her dismal surroundings.

"I'm sorry love...we should have left it a little longer before coming," said Bill.

"Well, you'll just have to take things here as you find them," said Rebecca. She hoped they hadn't assumed they could stay over as there was no room for them. "Also, it's a little tricky at the moment because I have company staying with me."

"Company? Who on earth have you got staying with you?" said Cynthia, her already granite eye taking on an extra coldness. "I mean, you don't know anyone here, do you?"

"It's Caroline, Aunt Sylvia's friend." Rebecca used her matter-of-fact voice, knowing this would come as a great surprise.

"Why hasn't she got her own home?" said Cynthia. "I mean, I suppose I could understand it if you were renting out a room to a girl of your own age for extra money and company. But surely you would wait until you'd decorated. Anyway, how old is this Caroline for goodness sake?" She gave her husband a despairing look. "Not much younger than me I'll bet."

"I'm not sure how old she is but she's been so kind to me. When the workmen were here, she let me stay at her place which was lovely. With all the dust and the mess...it would have been really horrible here."

Cynthia was now hanging on her daughter's every word, intrigued to learn everything about this peculiar situation.

"So, Rebecca," said Bill. "That seems generous of her, but why is she now living here?"

"Oh, it was shocking. Something terrible happened. Some people broke into her flat and totally ruined the place. But look, why don't I introduce her to you."

"Oh, that's awful. The poor woman," said Cynthia, imagining how devastated she would be if the same thing happened to her house, but then they had excellent security and an expensive burglar alarm, so that was an unlikely scenario for her to have to deal with.

"Caroline," Rebecca called up the stairs. "My parents are here. Why don't you come down and meet them?"

There was no reply. Rebecca ran upstairs and knocked on her bedroom door. As there was still no answer she tentatively opened the door. There room was empty and she certainly hadn't heard Caroline leave.

Chapter 30

Tynemouth November – 2009

From the back room at the 'Turk's Head' Llyriad had been watching events unfurling across the street with great interest. It seemed that Caroline had been forced to move down a few notches in the world. This little backstreet house in Tynemouth was certainly greatly inferior to her last place, and this pleased Llyriad enormously.

For the past few days she had been stalking Sebastian. He was refusing to answer his phone so she had little option. There were still more jobs that she wanted him to do for her. Following him from work one night, she had been delighted to discover that his flat was in clear view from the pub. All she had to do was wait here, have a few little drinks and it would be only a matter of time before she would bump into him and his uncle one night after work. However, it seemed that recently neither of them had been in the mood for a pint. Llyriad didn't need to use massive powers of deduction to work out why this might be. So, when she discovered that Rebecca and Caroline were staying in no less than the house next door, Llyriad was pleased to be making good use of her time.

This afternoon was particularly interesting. A couple who were no doubt of a similar age to herself and who could only have been Rebecca's parents had come to visit. She could see from the look on the woman's face that she disapproved of the situation. Llyriad just couldn't understand the friendship between Rebecca and Caroline. To her it just didn't make any sense whatsoever. But then a few minutes after they had entered the building, a furtive-looking Caroline had come sneaking out of the house and gone flying down the street.

Llyriad moved to the front of the Turk's Head. The barman gave her a strange look but Llyriad was far too preoccupied to notice. This pub really did have the most excellent location she thought, from this window she had also just witnessed what she thought impossible. Somehow, Derrick had managed a car journey from his house to here and was just leaving. Granted, he looked dreadful and that awful woman had clearly driven him but she had to admit she was impressed with his sheer determination. No doubt he had come to beg Robert for the silk which had to be somewhere in that shop, but surely Robert wasn't just going to hand it over?

Then, almost as soon as he left, Caroline arrived. She appeared to be in a state of anxiety before she even entered the bookshop. Why would the arrival of Rebecca's parents be of such a concern and how would she react to Robert's news? This day was just becoming more fascinating as it progressed. And from her front row seat, Llyriad felt as if she were about to watch a spectacular firework display.

***

"Robert, you won't believe what's just happened," gasped an out of breath Caroline. "They've come to see Rebecca. What are we going to do?"

An ashen-faced Robert stood facing the door, still mulling over the conversation he had just had with Derrick.

"What are you talking about?" said Robert eventually. "Listen Caroline…let me speak for once."

"But Robert…Rebecca's…" She couldn't think what Robert could have to say was anywhere near as important as her revelation.

"No Caroline, I've just had Derrick here," Robert was adamant that he would be heard first. "And you know what he wants, don't you? Don't say anything just listen. He looks close to death. I'm sick of these games. Let's just give it to him. I don't see how it can do him any good though. He's coming back in an hour. I was going to come over and speak to you but…"

"Robert!" said Caroline quickly. "We can't go round there. Not now. Rebecca's parents - my sister and her husband Bill – d'you remember? They're there now. They can't see us. Don't you understand?"

"Yes, yes, I follow- but they must be here on a flying visit. We can just wait until they've gone. Surely you must have realised they'd show up eventually.

"But once they've been here, they're bound to return. It's only a matter of time before I'm seen. All my efforts at forging a bond with Rebecca are going to be lost."

"But don't you see? If Derrick has the silk …then it's no longer our problem is it? Just imagine …"

"Robert, looking after that cloth has been our life. Don't *you* see? If we just hand it over to Derrick…well, I don't know … look what he did to my flat. This isn't only about the cloth. It's about what happened to Scire. There was always more to this than just the cloth *and you know that*, Robert Fairfax."

"But it wasn't our fault? Scire's death was nothing to do with you was it? And I certainly didn't push him - it was just a tragic accident."

"That may be so but if I hadn't made you do… what we did in the cave, then it would never have happened."

"Fair enough. But let's take back control. We've never been in control. Always running. Let's get rid of the damn thing. Give it to him. Let's try and lead a normal life."

"I still think it's been all my fault."

"And was I really that difficult to persuade? No, I think we were equally responsible for that. If Derrick gets to have the silk …well that could well just finish him off, and we'll be rid of him." Robert glanced at the clock. Derrick would be back soon and wanting some answers.

"But what about Llyriad?" Caroline knew how much the woman hated her and for her, that was what this was all about.

"We'll just have to see what happens?" said Robert. "But we need to keep our wits about us. See how far she wants to go."

"Yes," said Caroline. "I wonder".

***

Llyriad put her phone down and watched the front door of the 'Turk's Head'. Two minutes later Derrick was pushed in.

"Well, have you found out where it is?" said Llyriad.

"I'm going back over to Robert's shop in an hour. He *will* tell me then. I'm certain he'll see sense." Derrick turned to Mrs. Singh and nodded. Mrs. Singh gave a very slight roll of her eyes and left the pub.

"I can't see Caroline, as she calls herself, letting it go. Especially, after what I did to her flat, but I think I know where it is."

Llyriad sounded very pleased with herself but Derrick found himself disgusted with the malicious gleam in her eye.

"If you've searched her place and it isn't there. It obviously has to be Robert's bookshop doesn't it?" said Derrick.

"Well, no. That's not where it is - but it is close by," Llyriad pointed out of the window. "See that house over there, number 10. Well that used to belong to Sylvia or Caroline as she now calls herself. Do you remember Olwyn?" Derrick remembered the name and racked his brain trying to place her. "Well she died a short while ago and her niece Rebecca, who Caroline seems to have befriended, is living there now. In fact, they both are. Anyway, I didn't get it at first, but that's why."

"That's why what? You're not making any sense." said Derrick.

"Olwyn's real name was Caroline. She and Sylvia swapped places to keep us off the scent. So, I reckon Olwyn lived in that house and kept the silk safe. Now her niece has inherited the property and the new Caroline wants her to stay there. To look after the silk. Though I doubt she's even told her where it is or what it is."

"Yes, I see. I see. I understand. Quite a bit of deception going on. They've gone to extraordinary lengths."

"They had to," said Llyriad, the venomous glint returning to her eye.

"So, this girl is her real niece. "Derrick was concentrating hard, pleased to have something other than his illness to think about.

"Actually, I have a sneaking suspicion that there might be an even closer relationship between the two."

"I'm astounded that you've found out all of this information. So, any suggestions as to what to do next?"

"Well we can't go there at the moment because it looks like the place is full of visitors. In fact, it looks like the girl's parents have arrived. And it seems like there's no love lost there between them and Sylvia. I've just watched her sneaking out and going to the bookseller."

"I can see why you are sitting in this public house Llyriad. From this one room it's possible to see everything you need."

"Exactly. It's been an excellent place for gathering information, but nowhere near as useful as Sebastian."

"Sebastian? I don't recall anyone with that name. Was he another member of the Requisite?"

"You know how we came across those reviews for Robert's bookshop? You remember… that's how we came across their location. That was all down to dear Sebastian. He's Robert's nephew and just happens to work in the shop with his uncle. Funnily enough, he thinks his uncle is a dinosaur not using the internet in his business. While we however know the real reason. Sebastian hates the new Caroline and played right into our hands by writing those little reviews."

"Why does he hate the new Caroline?" Derrick remembered how lovely Sylvia had looked all those years ago at his party.

"Her attitude, the way she talks, the way she bloody moves. That's what he says. She belittles him at every opportunity. Just for being the rude, arrogant woman that she is. But he's been extremely useful to me and…he lives in the flat next door to Rebecca."

***

Sebastian had forgotten until very recently that the old lady, as he thought of Sylvia, had given him a spare key to her house in case she ever locked herself out. She never had done, but when Sebastian came across the key, he couldn't believe his luck. If that cloth was going to be anywhere, it had to be in the attic of her house. If he could find it, he could give it to Llyriad and she would be gone and leave them to get on with their lives. Yesterday, when he was sure that Rebecca and Caroline were out, he had let himself in. It was certainly quite a come down from Caroline's last place. He had been able to have a good search, but annoyingly, there was a lock on the attic door. He didn't want to force it. He didn't want them to know someone had been searching. Still, he thought, keys aren't usually that difficult to find.

It didn't seem like he would be able to get in today, as Rebecca had visitors, obviously her mum and dad. But then, he watched the three of them stroll down the street to the seafront. With them out of the way he could continue his search. He made an excuse to his uncle to go home for a short while. Robert was too distracted to care. He collected the keys and as he left his house he glanced across the road to the 'Turk's Head' and saw Llyriad through the window. She never stops, he thought to himself. She spotted him so he ran across.

Once inside the pub he saw that Llyriad had company. Well, company of a sort, because the old man in a wheelchair had the most ghastly, wrinkled skin he had ever seen. He seemed to be far more suited to be in the land of the dead than that of the living and was giving a good impression of an unwrapped mummy. Sebastian recognised him from the bookshop.

"Sebastian, how lovely to see you." Llyriad gushed. "Can I introduce Derrick to you."

The old man's face creased and the wrinkles formed into a half-smile. He offered a hand and Sebastian decided at the last moment to accept it although he didn't shake it, thinking that it didn't seem that secure.

"So, Llyriad," said Sebastian. "I think I can guess why you're here. You might be in luck. I've just seen Rebecca and her parents leave the house. We need to be quick though. I don't know how long they'll be but they were well wrapped up for a walk along the front."

"Excellent," said Llyriad. "Now we just have to work out how to get in."

Sebastian noticed Derrick's wheezing, and thought of the sheer amount of effort it must have taken for him to make this journey and how important it must be for him to get the silk.

"I think I can provide a solution to that problem," said Sebastian as he placed a bunch of keys on the table.

"What are those for?" asked Llyriad.

"Oh, they're just the spare keys to number ten." Sebastian replied nonchalantly. Derrick and Llyriad looked at each other and Derrick managed another half-smile.

"The silk's in the attic I reckon, and there's a lock on it. I found a key in the cutlery drawer that looked about the right size. Didn't have time to use it yesterday because I thought they'd be coming back soon, but I guess that's a good a place as any to start…"

***

Caroline and Robert both watched the clock on the wall, realizing that the hour was long past and there was no sign of Derrick.

"Where do you think he can have got to? I was sure he would be back by now," said Robert. "I always thought he was the punctual type."

"We can't tell him Robert. We can't let him have the silk." Caroline grabbed Robert's arm.

"To be perfectly honest I don't think we will need to." Robert stared blankly at the window.

"What do you mean?" She asked.

"Well if he's teamed up with Llyriad, which we know he is, there's only this shop or number ten where it could possibly be. It's quite obvious from my appearance that I'm not in possession of an immortality cloth don't you agree? And… since you have been stopping there recently…well, don't you think she'll have been watching you? I wouldn't be at all surprised if the two of them are together right now."

"I didn't think I would see it in this light' but it's a blessing of sorts that Cynthia and Bill are here. At least that means they won't be able to attempt to get inside today. I can't see Rebecca just letting them in. They would have to break in and I can't imagine Derrick being very capable of that sort of thing. Not with the state he's in. And Llyriad's not the nimblest of people either is she?"

"Maybe she isn't, but that didn't stop her getting into your flat now did it?"

Caroline gave twisted her mouth and started chewing a fingernail.

***

Sebastian took a chair upstairs to stand on while he tried the key in the lock attached to the loft door.

Derrick and Llyriad waited in the drab sitting room. Llyriad knew that there were certain matters that needed to be discussed.

"You know that I know, don't you?" Llyriad began.

"Know what? What are you talking about?" Derrick gave her a puzzled look. *The woman was always guaranteed to display doltish behaviour*, he thought to himself. *Vacuous as ever.*

"You've always wanted that cloth, haven't you?"

"That's true. But never so badly as I do now." He gave a feeble laugh and his lips uncurled into a nearly, kindly smile. "I will be eternally grateful to you Llyriad, for helping me…"

"All these years I've been after 'those two', particularly her. Wanting revenge. But it seems I've been a fool, haven't I?"

Derrick spotted the unpleasant note creeping into her voice and shuffled uncomfortably in his wheelchair.

"Llyriad, I don't know what you are talking about. We nearly have that cloth. Why don't you go and help Sebastian. They could be back at any moment."

"You meant it to happen, didn't you?"

"What are you talking about woman?"

"That night at St. Cuthbert's cave. You meant it to happen."

"Don't be ridiculous."

"It was always your plan for Scire to die wasn't it? What did you do…loosen the rocks? Tripwire? How convenient that it seemed that those two had caused it. Most useful for you. And the fall, the rock wasn't that high, was it? The fall might not have proved fatal. Do you know what I think? I think you finished him off."

Llyriad's eyes were blazing and Derrick had become an even more ghastly shade of yellow. The air around them stopped and an eerie silence enveloped them.

"Don't be ridiculous," said Derrick eventually. "Scire was my oldest friend. Why would I…"

"Oldest being the operative word Derrick. And all because you wanted that cloth. You fooled and tricked everyone, didn't you? 'The Requisite of St. Cuthbert'," she spat out the words. "More like, 'The Requisite of Derrick Stevens'."

There was a little twitch at her temple. Derrick saw it and wondered how near she was. It was like sitting opposite a time bomb.

"Llyriad this is nonsense." Derrick gave what he thought was a tolerable imitation of a deeply concerned look and fixed her with sad eyes, like a drowning man seeking a lifeline. He knew she could be erratic, disturbed. She needed to be deactivated. "You know we have searched for many years to get revenge on those two. You know the cloth is important to me but not as important as avenging Scire's death. It was always uppermost in my mind, avenging my friend's death. My dear friend. I loved him as did you."

"No, Derrick. I wanted revenge. You just wanted the cloth," she looked at him, interested as to what he would do next, like watching a caged animal. "That was the only part of the ceremony that didn't go according to plan. Wasn't it? They weren't supposed to take the silk, were they? And to be honest I really don't know why they did. How could they possibly have known of its powers? You must have been *so, so* bloody annoyed."

"Llyriad…you've got it all wrong. I would never harm Scire. I loved him. 'Amor enim mirabilis', 'love is a wonderful thing'."

"No Derrick, 'vos nunquam dilexit', 'you never loved'."

Derrick gaped at her, amazed. Caught off balance and helpless.

"And what happened to his body?" said Llyriad, not waiting for any reply, pressing home her advantage,

"His body? Why you were there when we scattered his ashes at Heysham. Don't you remember?"

"No, his actual body, his corpse. There was never any funeral. What happened to his body?"

"I think I'm in," an excited Sebastian called from upstairs.

Llyriad gave Derrick a last withering glare and then started up the stairs. Derrick struggled to get out of the chair.

Within seconds Sebastian had pulled down the loft ladder and was in the attic. Llyriad was soon up after him, heaving herself through the loft opening. Derrick was using all the effort he could muster to get up the staircase. Although it was pitch black in the attic Sebastian could make out a few shapes of suitcases and boxes of Christmas decorations. Llyriad used her cigarette lighter so that Sebastian could see better. Considering the state of many attics, this was quite empty and over in the corner was an interesting looking box. Sebastian took a screwdriver from his back pocket and crawled over.

"It's got to be in there." whispered Llyriad.

"Have you found it yet?" A voice rasped from below.

"I think so…" said Sebastian. "I'm just prising the box open."

***

Durham – September 2009

Sylvia wasn't feeling well but she had just done what needed to be done to keep everyone safe. This had just gone on for too long but almost immediately she felt terrible. She ached everywhere, she felt dizzy and so, so tired. This piece of cloth had wrecked their lives, and perhaps once it was back where it belonged, all would come good.

She began thinking back over her life. For so long now she had lived in that miserable house. Well half- lived actually. Who could call that constant fear of being found a proper life? She had never married or had a family. Since Loic there had been no-one. Once she had felt so alive and full of hope for the future. If only she could turn back the pages of time and she would never have had anything to do with the Requisite with its awful repercussions. But she had loved Caroline and Robert. They had been her only true friends really. After the fiasco at St. Cuthbert's cave they had disappeared and nobody knew where they had vanished to. But Sylvia had secretly kept in touch with her. And now, she never thought of herself as Caroline and certainly not as Olwyn. She had become Sylvia - completely.

She had visited them in Durham. Having nowhere else to go herself, she settled on Tyneside as a place to live. Firstly, in Newcastle where she did a further degree in Librarianship and worked many years for a library at the University there. Then when she had become sick, Caroline had inherited some money and she had suggested that her good friend should live in a house she had bought in Tynemouth. She had been delighted. However, the move had not been as altruistic as it first seemed, but she had gone along with it through necessity and had become Sylvia, 'The Keeper of the Secret'.

Robert and Caroline had always had the companionship of each other, even if they hadn't been able to live together, but that hadn't been the case for Sylvia. She never found anyone else to love in that way since Loic all those years ago. Caroline had told her everything. Not being able to tell him what was happening was so very hard. In part it was to protect him as well. She had lied about where she'd gone so he couldn't find her. It had to be done. That had been the end of them but if it hadn't been for him then she never would have had anything to do with the ridiculous cult in the first place.

The Requisite had all been delusional rubbish anyway. Hindsight is a fine thing and it was now so crystal clear that it was all about Derrick and his fantasies. There was only one thing he had been obsessed with. It was only recently it had dawned on her. Scire's accident was in fact no such thing at all. Derrick had orchestrated the event himself, just to get his hands on the cloth. Even after all of these years he still searched. Now pointlessly. Her actions today had seen to that. She had the feeling of having done something worthy because she had ended it. But she could never tell Caroline what she had just done. Not in this life anyway.

During the past few weeks she had noticed a growing feeling of being watched. This was nothing new but never with such intensity or as frequently. If she left her house, crossed the street, went to the shops, she was haunted by a sensation of eyes following her. This wasn't her imagination and she knew she could tell no one. In fact, the whole convoluted business should have been ended years ago. Sylvia knew she had made little of her life but here was something meaningful she could do at last.

It was in the attic. The closely guarded secret she had been protector of for so many years. She had climbed up the ladder and opened the box. A piece of material lay inside. She had never actually dared to look at it for a long time, not since she had been berated by her friend all those years ago. In fact, she was scared of it and its power. She owed her life to it but at what cost? Even in the dim torchlight the skeins of thread glistened and sparkled but she knew she shouldn't look. Trembling, she folded the silk and placed it inside an old, leather bag.

Despite her tiredness and aching Sylvia now felt a great relief. She no longer feared death. The cloth was back where it belonged with St. Cuthbert in Durham Cathedral. She had left the bag in a little niche close to his tomb. She had gone very early in the morning and waited for a long time next to the Saint's shrine until nobody was around. She had made pilgrimages to the resting place of St. Cuthbert many times before and knew the exact place where the silk would be placed when the time came. Although she understood that she was signing her own death warrant, the time was right. She had no way of knowing when it would be discovered and if it would be recognised for what it was. Still, that wasn't her problem and she could rest in peace, knowing she had done what needed to be done. She hoped Caroline and Robert wouldn't be too angry with her.

She sat back in her easy armchair, comfortable and worn out. Bit like her, she thought to herself. She closed her eyes, thinking over the day. She was utterly exhausted and started drifting off gently, her body relaxing, becoming lighter.

A voice swirled around her. An awareness of a voice. A breath. Words unintelligible at first. She tried hard to open her eyes to see who was there. No-one. She sank back in her darkness and the words came into her, flowing through her, helping her. *From the tangle of our lives, you can wear the perfect tapestry.* she recognised the words, *of our joys and failures and achievements, and unfulfilled dreams,* she knew it from her days in the Requisite. *Death comes silent for some, with sudden swiftness for others,* a prayer from long ago, centuries ago, *yet unavoidable, certain. Teach us to number our days and apply or hearts to wisdom.*

The words kept repeating, over and over.

She fell further back, further, deeper. She was being acknowledged. There was an ancient gratitude. She knew it. She was glad. It had been the right thing to do. She was happy, comforted. She went deeper, deep inside herself. To the very heart. To her being. She could feel her life, her essence. And a sweet, sweet, blissful numbness came ...

Chapter 31

Tynemouth – November 2009

"What's that smoke in the sky?" said Robert. "Looks like there's a fire."

Feeling uneasy, he walked out into the street closely followed by Caroline.

"Oh my God," said Caroline. "It looks like it's number ten."

They both started running.

***

Fifteen minutes earlier Sebastian had emerged from the loft.

"What do you mean it's not there," rasped Derrick. "It has to be there. It's got to be there."

"Well, it's not," said Sebastian.

"Well, where can it be?" said Derrick, breathing rapturously from his exertions in climbing the stairs. "Where can it be?"

"Obviously somewhere else," said Llyriad.

"I was certain it was here," said Derrick. "Time is running out. I need that cloth."

"Yes, I know you do Derrick," smiled Llyriad coolly. "But we'll just have to continue the search elsewhere."

"Where else though?" Sebastian threw up his arms. "I can't think of where to look."

"The bookshop. It has to be," said Derrick.

Sebastian glared at him.

"Listen, we need to get out of here," said Llyriad. "We don't want to get caught for nothing. Sebastian, why don't you go back your house and hide those keys in case we need them another time. I'll help Derrick down the stairs."

Sebastian nodded, glad to be going, and quickly left the house.

"Where do you think it is?" said Derrick. "You know where it is, don't you? You just didn't want him to know. Sensible."

"As a matter of fact, I don't know where it is. And I don't care now."

"What do you mean – you don't care. You want revenge, don't you?"

"Correct Derrick. I do want revenge. I haven't forgiven Caroline. This house means a lot to her."

"You can't be … no, that would be insane."

"Not insane *Dafo*. Just a suitable ending. An ending to my pain … and yours."

"What are you talking about woman? Listen…"

"You killed my love. You ruined my life like you ruined so many other lives. And now you've broken into this house for revenge on Caroline. You'll destroy this house just like you destroyed the flat. There's no stopping you when you put your mind to something. Unfortunately, you tripped and fell, before you could get out of the burning building."

"Llyriad, this is madness. We can work together. We can…"

It was hardly a shove. More like a nudge. Derrick was in no condition to counter it. He tumbled down the stairs, boney limbs cracking, and crashed into the wall at the bottom, motionless.

Llyriad walked slowly down the stairs and stepped over Derricks prone body. "It wasn't that high *Dafo*," she said. "The fall might not have proved fatal."

She went into the living room and took out her cigarette lighter.

***

"Oh my God! Oh my God!" Caroline couldn't believe her eyes. Ten Huntington Place was engulfed in flames and smoke was pouring from the roof. "The cloth!"

"Never mind the damn cloth. Is anyone inside?" shouted Robert. "Phone the fire brigade – quick!"

Rebecca and her parents walked around the corner.

They heard the fire before they saw it, loud cracking noises as the windows exploded, sending shards of glass onto the street. They ran to the house just in time to stop Robert trying to get into the building.

Caroline was shouting something which couldn't be heard above the fire.

"What on earth…" Cynthia waved her arms about in shock. She had immediately recognised her sister. She gave a short shriek, almost a yelp. Bill held on to her as if she were about to take off. Eventually she found some words bouncing among the concrete and the bricks and the fire and used them. "Sylvia… what's going on? I thought…I thought you were dead… what's happening? What's going on for God's sake? What are you doing? Why are you here?"

Caroline waved a high palm to her, stopping her, like a traffic cop controlling motorists. She paced back and forth on the pavement, chewing her fingernails, occasionally slamming her feet down as if trying to stamp out the fire. She had more important things to consider than her sister's bafflement. Even Cynthia realised now wasn't the time for her questions.

The Fire Brigade arrived and ushered everyone across to safety. More shouting. More arm waving. Hosepipes were on full blast and the flames started subsiding. Firefighters rushed in and out of the house. Smoke was everywhere, churning and choking the air. A siren announced the arrival of an ambulance. Different shouting. The lifeless body of a badly burned, elderly man was brought out, placed on a stretcher and covered with a cloth. A distinctive nose pushed up the folds of the cloth further than normal. Robert and Caroline both instantly knew who this was. This was not the cloth he was hoping for. There seemed little doubt who was responsible for the fire.

***

Although, the house in Huntington Place had been badly damaged, it was covered by insurance and was able to slowly be repaired. After the initial shock, Cynthia was actually quite pleased that her sister was still alive. Rebecca was delighted to have Caroline as an aunt and Robert as an uncle, as there was now no reason why they couldn't get married. Also, while the house was being repaired Caroline could stay in Robert's rather cramped flat. Most importantly to Cynthia though, was that Caroline insisted that Rebecca would never know her true parentage and this sealed the truce between the two sisters. Although they would never be close friends there developed a mutual tolerance as they both wanted the company of Rebecca.

Nothing was heard of from Llyriad. Sebastian continued working in the bookshop. He was much quieter. He and Robert didn't go to the pub much after work. After a few weeks he left to try and find a job in London.

Caroline found the box in the attic which had suffered little damage from the fire. But there was no trace of any silk inside. It seemed that Sylvia had taken the mystery with her to her grave. However, if she had no longer been keeper of the cloth, maybe that was the reason she had become ill again. Perhaps Sylvia had given the cloth to someone or taken it somewhere. In a few weeks it would be winter solstice and if she wanted to try for a definitive answer then there was one last journey that she and Robert needed to make. To a place which knew a time when the world was softer.

***

St. Cuthbert's Cave – December 2009

We walked quietly along the fern fringed track which eventually became a steep, uphill slope. Only the sound of their footsteps crunching the dry bracken, disturbed the stillness of the Winter Solstice. The night was freezing, a bat circled above, marking its territory. A bitter chill cut through the trees, like shiny, sharp scissors.

This time, no torches lit our way and we struggled with our footing on the muddy path, having only the dim light from Robert's torch to help us. Robert had agreed to make this last journey with me. I needed some kind of release and he was by my side, as ever. He reached for my hand and I knew he was thinking of the last time we made this journey. Despite all that had happened, or maybe all the more because of it, I knew he still loved me, and I him.

Our breathing became shallower, as the path grew steeper and we approached the entrance to the cave. This time there was no Scire balanced precariously on the rocks above or anyone gathered beneath. There was no Dafo, mastering the ceremonies. Only the stark, pine trees remained to witness events. We could see our breath in small clouds leading us on. As the midnight hour approached, darkness would be reaching its very peak. I prepared myself. I had to have faith. To believe and give myself up. Soon, the goddess Atargatis would give birth once more to her sun. This would begin to wax and thrive, basking in its mother's adoration. The days would grow longer. From the darkness, light would be born. If I was to discover the whereabouts of the goddess silk, this would undoubtedly be the time.

We knelt on floor of the cave, at the very spot where the cloth had once been laid out in all its splendour, exquisitely embroidered in silver and gold threads. From this exact place Robert had first glimpsed the enthralling gaze of the goddess as she had taken possession of Aradnia and Verbius.

Now, the two of us held our breath, as if half expecting the cloth to miraculously materialise in front of our eyes. I checked my watch. It was midnight and still nothing had happened.

I looked around the cave for a sign. I was almost sure I could hear the faintest of drumbeats. Looking at Robert, I remembered how amazing that night had been, and how that moment of madness had resulted in our daughter.

Robert played his torch on the graffiti plastered all over the cave walls. Dates, drawings, symbols, messages, names were etched into the rock. More names, scrawled in bright colours, going back decades. Like cave paintings, marking existence and time. Tributes, memorials.

Then, something turned my head, Not a distraction but something tangible. Something took control of me. Pushing my head firmly to the side. Pulling my head backwards. Forcing me to look up to the ceiling of the cave. I tried to pull back but it was impossible. I tried to put my hands up to my head but they wouldn't obey.

I felt something rolling down my face, something warm and wet. A tear. I knew it was a tear but I also knew that it wasn't mine. My body was being used, being used to convey some meaning, some definition of meaning. I didn't understand and I realised I wasn't meant to understand, just to be there, just to sense awareness of time and place, to feel ancient, remembered things. A kind of belonging in that place, a belonging of souls, not of time. My breathing was involuntarily suspended for a few seconds by something inside me, subduing me, enchanting, compelling me to fully feel what was happening. My body flowed, wave after wave after wave. I could smell blood and skin and decay. I could feel hope and longing and bliss.

Something was coming. Coming from the other side. From beyond. Through a greyness. Unable to open my eyelids, I sensed a figure but could not see it. Floating, swaying, arms outstretched. It was all around me, all encompassing, shielding me, giving safety, sanctity, shelter.

The meaning came in wafts of breath, brushing my forehead, my hair, my eyelids, streaming through me.

Thy,

Protection,

And in protection strength,

And in strength understanding

I was trying to breathe

And in understanding knowledge,

And in knowledge the knowledge of justice,

Forcing myself to stay

And in the knowledge of justice the love of it

And in that love the love of all existence,

Trying to breathe

And in the love of all existence the love of the goddess,

And in the love of the goddess all goodness,

Cast your vision,

In her sights.

The words echoed and drifted in my body for several minutes. And then I was released at last, ecstatic and full and enraptured. I inhaled deeply, amazed not only at the energy pulsating and surging through me but also at what had been given to me and what I thought I understood.

"Robert, Robert, help, help me."

Robert moved to my side quickly. "What is it? What is it? What's the matter?"

I blew hard, choking, fighting for breath. "Help. Help ... me."

He threw an arm around me and instantly I gasped again, trying to breathe.

"Up there. Up there. The torch." I panted, gulping in air. "Can, you, see ...see, that up - up - there? The long crack, at the top, a slit ... in the stone."

In the torchlight we both clearly saw a thin, flaking crack in the stone. Robert gave the torch to me, pulled himself on to a huge rock at the side of the cave and stretched as far as he could, straining, aching with the effort. In the torchlight I could see his breath, billowing out in short, quick bursts.

"The crack's deep," he said. "I can just get my fingers in. There's something inside. Hidden. Deep down."

He teased out a small, clear plastic bag and flicked it down to me.

I could see there was paper inside and pulled it open. I saw a note, a letter. It was from our friend, our dear friend. I couldn't help myself, I just kept repeating, "Thank you, thank you, thank you."

Dear friends,

    Firstly, if you are reading this, by now I will be long dead and I just want to thank you for your great friendship and also for giving me the luxury of being able to choose when to die for myself. Nobody is, or should be immortal, that isn't the way of things or the way they are supposed to be. If Derrick was responsible for the death of Scire, he did in fact do him a kind of favour.

    When I first came into possession of the silk, it felt wonderful. I was rejuvenated and free from disease. However, it comes with a price. Being the keeper of the cloth is both a blessing and a curse. You see, I felt like I was being eaten. As my cancer had subsided, so my soul had been stolen. If Scire had been in possession of it for many years, I don't know how he could have lived with himself. It wasn't easy though, for the goddess didn't want to part company.

    But I will get to the point. Where is the cloth now you are probably wondering? Well I took it back to the place it really belongs, Durham Cathedral, of course. I put it as near to St. Cuthbert's body as I possibly could. By now, someone had discovered it, realised what it is and has given it the reverence it deserves – or does it?

    So dear, dear Caroline and Robert please don't be angry with me. Leave the cloth be and forget about it. Life is precious and to be enjoyed but its true value lies in the fact it isn't infinite and neither should it be. When I returned the cloth, I felt such a great sense of peace. It was as if I had fulfilled a prerequisite- the Prerequisite of St.

Cuthbert.

Your loving friend, always.

Olwyn, Caroline and Sylvia.

XXX

(I will look forward to seeing you both once again, when it's your time)

Printed in Poland
by Amazon Fulfillment
Poland Sp. z o.o., Wrocław